The Wicked Wedding of Miss Ellie Vyne

JAYNE FRESINA

sourcebooks
casablanca

Copyright © 2013 by Jayne Fresina
Cover and internal design © 2013 by Sourcebooks, Inc.
Cover design by Alan Ayers
Cover image © Aleksandra Smirnova/Fotolia

Published by Sourcebooks Casablanca, an imprint of Sourcebooks, Inc.
P.O. Box 4410, Naperville, Illinois 60567-4410
(630) 961-3900
Fax: (630) 961-2168
www.sourcebooks.com

Printed and bound in Canada.
WC 10 9 8 7 6 5 4 3 2 1

To Jan-Jan

Chapter 1

Brighton, June 1822

HE DIDN'T SEE HER AT FIRST. STAGGERING THROUGH AN arch in the tall privet hedge, confident he'd finally located an exit, James Hartley found himself trapped instead at the very center of a moonlit maze—a vexatious piece of trickery through which he'd stumbled haplessly for the past half hour. At this rate he'd never find his way out. Cursing loudly, he reclaimed his hat from the prickly hedge, struggled to reorganize his brandy-soaked brain, and focused his fuzzy gaze.

Thus, the ice queen appeared.

On a stone bench, flanked by neatly trimmed topiaries, sat a woman clad from head to toe in white and silver. She was so ghostlike and luminous under the bright summer moon that he toppled sideways in surprise, once again ensnared on the hedge by buttonholes, cuffs, and any other part of him with a convenient notch.

While he fought the grasping tendrils of the privet for a second time, the woman turned her head to

calmly observe all the fuss, and he saw she wore a black
eye mask. Her smile was begrudging, her head bent in
slight acknowledgment of his presence. Anyone would
think she was the real Marie Antoinette, not just a
woman costumed as the ill-fated French queen.

James had left the masquerade ball for fresh air and
escape—particularly from women—but he couldn't
very well turn away without a polite word. Not now
she'd seen him. Besides, there was something about
the way she sat, very calm and still, that suggested
she wouldn't trap him in conversation. In fact, she'd
turned her back again now, dismissing James as
someone of no interest.

Well, good. Most people expected him to be
full of charm twenty-four hours a day, and it was
a terrible burden. As Grieves, his valet, had dryly
observed, this was the dark side to being an Infamous
Rake—the valet's description, not his. But James was
not in the mood tonight to chat and flirt with her.
Whoever she was.

He straightened up, brushed himself down with his
hat, and looked at her again.

She still paid him no attention.

Was there something wrong with her? Perhaps she
was ill. Women, generally, did not ignore James Hartley.

With one hand to his mouth, he cleared his throat
loudly. Still nothing.

Perfect, because the last thing he wanted was to
entertain a strange woman and cheer her out of a bad
mood or tears or a headache. He'd tolerated enough
sobbing females exclaiming over the great love they had
for some other man, while smearing their tears, their

confessions, and their runny noses all over his shoulder. Lately, for some reason, James had gone from being the problem itself to being the one with whom they shared their problems. Then, once they'd had reassurance from him, they ran off with another fellow. When James recently complained to Grieves about becoming a combination confessional and advising father to these young women, the valet had remarked, "This is what happens, sir, to aging rakes. Women begin to view them as harmless and one of their own."

It was a thought so distressing he didn't leave his house for two days.

The woman on the bench kept her rigid pose, back turned to him. If she was ill, she may need his assistance.

On the other hand, perhaps she'd left the over-crowded ball for reasons similar to his, in which case she was probably annoyed to have uninvited company. Yet whatever she felt about his clumsy arrival, she stayed. No doubt she was hoping *he'd* leave. Ignore him, and he'd go away. Was that her plan?

Hmm. Rather discourteous of her.

Had she been expecting another man to appear under that arch? Glancing back at the darkness through which he'd stumbled, James thought he saw a shape withdraw, slowly absorbed by the denser shadow. A subtle movement rustled the leaves of the privet, no more than a passing rabbit might. Someone up to no good. So the ice queen had a secret assignation planned. Ha! She'd simply have to forget about it, because he was not going back through that maze to be lost again, solely for her convenience. He had as much right to be there as she did, and James needed that bench. He'd drunk a great deal of brandy, and fresh air multiplied the less pleasant effects. All he wanted was to sit, before his legs crumpled.

He approached to introduce himself and abruptly reconsidered. Dressed as a highwayman from the previous century and wearing a leather eye mask, he could be anyone. As could she. There was much to be said for anonymity.

He swayed forward in a teetering bow. "May I join you, madam?"

Her lips parted, exhaling a small, weary sigh. "I don't own the maze. Or the bench."

The voice sounded faintly familiar, as did the tone of delivery, but he could not ponder it for long. If he didn't sit down immediately, he'd fall down.

"I'll take that as a *yes* then," he muttered.

She tipped her head back to look up at him, and moonlight gleamed on her tall, white-blonde wig. Tiny jet beads around her mask shimmered like the stars overhead. "I can't stop you, can I?"

"No." He tripped forward, knocking his knee on the edge of the stone bench and almost falling into the prim little topiary at one end of it. The sullen creature did not shift over to make room and instead claimed the center of the bench, her ridiculous panniers spread out on either side. To sit, he had to push her frills and the rigid underframe aside with his thigh. Blinking hard, he dizzily examined the side of her semimasked face. "Marie Antoinette," he growled.

"Indeed." Her gaze was fixed on a point of some distance. "And you must be Dick Turpin."

"Honored." He put out his hand, but she ignored it, and eventually he used it to scratch his chin. Damn. He hadn't shaved today. Just his luck to meet a pretty woman, alone, under the moon, and look like an unshaven ass. Unfortunately, Grieves had gone off visiting relatives for a few weeks, and James was in Brighton alone for an impromptu visit. Things had a tendency to go awry without his capable valet to keep them in order. He should never have given his man an entire fortnight holiday, but Grieves could be the most enormous sulk if he didn't get his own way.

"Must you breathe all over me?" the woman exclaimed.

He hiccuped. "You could leave, madam."

"I was here first."

True. In his pickled state, he was actually glad of her closeness to keep him upright. If she suddenly left the bench, he suspected he might, in fact, tumble over. He tried folding his arms but abandoned the idea after a few attempts.

She gave another sigh. "Isn't the sky beautiful tonight?"

Aware that looking upward could send him to the grass, flat on his back, he merely agreed with her, his gaze pinned to her cheek.

"I wonder how many stars there are," she added.

"Millions. Even more we can't see with the human eye." He wondered again why she hadn't got up and left. Most women would, considering his improper proximity. "Were you waiting for someone, madam?"

"Yes, as a matter of fact." She finally turned her head and looked at him. "I'd promised myself that the next man who came through that arch would be the man I married. Whoever and whatever he was. I'm being hounded into it, you see, and I'm afraid I'm rather tired of men in general, so I decided to take my chances. Why not? Marriage is all about taking a gamble, isn't it? I've done plenty of that."

He frowned hard, trying to focus. She didn't blink. Her eyes, half in shadow, peered at him through the holes in her mask.

Before he could reply, she added, "And then *you* stumbled into view." An odd, halting laugh interrupted her last word. She shook her head, the pearls dangling from her ears, spinning and dancing. That laughter sounded familiar too, but he just couldn't get his thoughts to behave in any sensible pattern. They were all over the place, weaving about like his body on that small bench.

"*Me?*" Did she know him?

If she did, she covered the slip. "A soused highwayman. How terribly appropriate." Once more she turned her face up to the glistening, star-dimpled sky. "All those little lights up there, and the one that falls to earth for me is you. Oh, the absurdity!"

Bracing his shoulders, he made a concerted effort to sit upright without leaning on her. "I could be quite a catch, madam. I could be a most eligible bachelor."

"Could you?"

"A great many people are mistaken about me." He watched her lips bend in a little smile. "They make aslumptions."

"Aslumptions?"

Wait a minute. That didn't sound right, but he had to explain it to her somehow. It was most important that he get his point across and make her look beyond what folk usually saw. Why it was so necessary for a stranger to know the truth, he really couldn't say. Perhaps it was her smug face and those softly pouting—rather lovely—lips.

"Yes. Yes." He waved his hand impatiently then grabbed her ruffled lace sleeve for balance. "They get it all wrong."

"Do they?" She sounded amused as she watched his fingers abuse her dainty lace.

James drew his stomach in, chest pushed out. "One day they'll eat their words."

"Will they?"

She wasn't listening. Women did that superior thing with their mouths when they were certain of being right, and nothing could convince them otherwise. "Yes, they damn well will. You'll see. I'll find my way, my purpose."

She shot him a bemused look through the holes in her black silk mask. "Aren't you a little old to still be seeking a purpose?"

"Aren't you a little old to still be looking for a husband?" Not that he knew her age. He was guessing, of course. From her confident attitude, he'd say late twenties at least. Definitely no blushing, giggling debutante. And there was her own confession of being "tired" of men, which suggested she'd been around the social circuit long enough to acquire a weary distaste for it. Much as he had.

Who the devil was she?

Her lips were pursed very tight now, as if she thought he'd insulted her by alluding to her age, but he'd meant only to shoot her own arrow back at her.

It was rather unsporting of her to take offense. Like most women, she didn't play fair.

"I don't really want a husband," she said. "If I wanted one, I could have had one by now."

She had a heart-shaped face with a very determined chin. Her lips reminded him of sweet, fancy little sugar cakes served on fine china and handed around by silent butlers at very exclusive hotel teas. Delicate confections he would get a slap 'round the cheek for swallowing three at a time when his grandmother caught him in the act.

The ice queen's neck was slender and long, accentuated by that ridiculously tall wig. She most definitely had all her parts in their place, he thought, slowly admiring every inch of her swanlike neck and the jutting swell of bosom below it. Hoisted inward and upward by a tight corset, her shapely flesh was almost bursting out of its lace.

A moment ago he'd been running away from women *and* conversation. In just a few short minutes he'd changed his mind about both. Could be the drink, he reasoned. Things often seemed most awe inspiring when under the influence of brandy.

So, if she didn't really want a husband…

"Then what do you want?"

"Isn't it strange no one has ever asked me that before?" She looked down at her lap. "You'll laugh."

"I most certainly will not." He slammed a hand to his heart, hiccupping again. Inwardly he cursed himself for prompting her to tell. Now he'd hear all about a man who wouldn't or couldn't marry her. Or some such nonsense. And he'd listen patiently

then reassure her that the fool didn't know what a
mistake he'd made. Finally, after spilling a few tears
and borrowing his kerchief, or his sleeve, she'd run off
back to the ball.

Why couldn't he have told her he didn't care about
her problems? No. He had to open his stupid mouth
and ask, didn't he?

Softly she said, "I want a little room filled with
books. There should be a fireplace and an old dog
sleeping in a basket beside it. A few comfortable chairs
with lots of pillows. All of it overlooking a pretty
garden. A little place of my own, where no one ever
bothers me. That's all."

The pearls hanging from her ears were still now,
her words forced out as if shy to be heard. Moonlight
touched the smooth orbs of her bosom above the
bodice of that elaborate ball gown, and James wistfully
followed the rapid lift and fall with his woozy gaze.

"Is that too much to ask?" she added.

He hastily quelled another hiccup. "No. Not at
all. Not at all." That was all she wanted? He'd give
her a house full of such rooms, he mused. Anything
she wanted. "It seems you'd be a vast deal more
economical to keep than most women I know."

"Do you mock me, sir?"

"No!" he replied, wounded.

"Kindly stop staring at my bosom."

He felt his face heat up. It was unusual for James
Hartley to be flustered by a woman, and he didn't like
the sensation. "You chose to wear that style gown, I
assumed you wanted them to be looked at."

Expecting a slapped face, he was surprised when she

laughed. It was a delightful, smoky sound, deep and more than a trifle lusty. He didn't know any women who laughed like that, unguarded and naughty. Or did he? He squinted hard at her lips, trying again to think coherently.

"I suppose you're right," she conceded eventually, her eyes two warm beacons of reflected starlight through her mask. "I wouldn't have dressed this way if I didn't want to be noticed." Again he sensed she would never normally admit this. Because they were both hiding behind masks, it was permissible to speak with honesty.

"And you wanted to be admired," he pressed.

"And...yes"—she inclined her head—"I wanted to be admired."

Leaning closer, he crushed her silk skirt with his thigh. "What's your dog's name?"

"My dog?"

"Old fellow. In the basket. By the fire."

"Oh." She flushed prettily under the edges of her mask, and he got the sense she was surprised he'd paid attention. It ruffled her proud feathers to be proven wrong about him. "I haven't got one yet."

"Why not?"

"I haven't got a home to keep him in."

He frowned, grasping her lacy sleeve tighter in his fist. "Where do you live then?"

"Nowhere," she said. "I wander."

A light breeze blew the sounds of the crowded ballroom toward them through the hedges of the maze—violins, laughter, the chink of glasses, and a sudden swelling blast of chatter, as if doors had swung open.

How much longer did they have before someone from that world intruded? Suddenly he couldn't bear to think of going back into the fray alone, without her.

"I'll make a confession too," he said. "I drank too much brandy tonight." He sincerely wished he hadn't, for what he needed now were his wits about him and breath that tasted of mint leaves. Then he could have kissed her the way she needed to be kissed. As he knew, instinctively, she never had been. There was too much sadness in this strange wayfarer, and the husky laughter that spilled out of her made it all the more poignant. Because he saw through it.

Amazing how brandy always made him deeply perceptive. Sober, he could be a complete numbskull, so he'd been told.

"Evidently. You won't be holding any carriages up tonight, Mr. Turpin."

"Hmmm?" *Turpin?* Who the devil—?

"Your costume, sir," she reminded him, smiling.

"Aha, yes! I could take you as my prisoner. I'm known for my charming, seductive ways. You won't be disappointed."

She chuckled playfully and raised one hand to his chin, fingertips lightly stroking stubble. "You flirt with the Queen of France, sir. I can only suppose the drink has made you too bold. Beware what you do."

He gazed again at the soft pink pillows that formed her lips. Sweet confectionary, made to be admired and then devoured. Dear Lord, he wanted to sink into them, kiss her hard, ruthlessly. "Let's escape the maze together." He meant it. This one could not get away. He wouldn't lose this one to another man. He grabbed her wrist, bringing it to his lips. "Run away with me."

"I am tempted, sir. You have no idea how tempted. But I know that one of us, if not both, will regret it by light of day."

He pressed his lips to her knuckles. Her skin tasted the way it looked—warm, tender, and as mouth-watering as a sugary marzipan novelty. Very subtly perfumed. He advanced his kisses along her slender arm and under the lace ruffles that tumbled from her elbows.

"Mr. Turpin," she chided, "you take advantage of the moonlight."

Blood pumped faster through his veins, hot and dangerous. He skipped the rest of her arm, advancing directly to the décolletage, where he planted a damply impassioned peck to the gently heaving mounds. First one, then the other. She made no move to prevent this brazen caress. James shifted even closer, slipping just the tip of his wayward tongue into the scented valley between her breasts. He felt her shiver, heard her quickening breath. But again she didn't stop him. Slowly his tongue wound a path upward to the side of her neck, where he kissed her excitable pulse and inhaled more of that delicious, alluring scent. His sweet tooth unable to resist, he tasted her skin, gently sucking it between his teeth.

"Mr. Turpin! I can allow this to proceed no further."

She stood quickly, one hand to the patch of skin he'd made wet with his mouth. He almost toppled over.

"Don't go. Stay." He clutched for her hand and somehow caught three of her fingers. "Please."

At the word "please" she faltered. She glanced over

at the hedge. "I hear someone approach. I fear this pleasant interlude is over, sir."

Still he gripped her fingers. He was ravenous, his need mounting. He wanted to feast on her here and now, in the grass. "How can it be over, madam? 'Tis only just begun between us."

"Tomorrow you will wake with a sore head. You will have forgotten me."

"No." He envisioned his body over hers, covering her, caressing her, and teasing her clothes away. Under the moon and stars he would cast all gentlemanly constraints aside and mate with her. It was dangerously close to primal, brute need taking over.

Her free hand cupped his rough chin and lifted it, until he felt the warm moonlight bathe his face. "Then come find me again when you're sober. Catch me if you can."

Despite his brandy-soaked breath, she kissed him on the lips, and it was no tentative, maidenly touch. It overflowed with yearning, tore through his hazy reality, left his world reeling. And he returned the kiss with equal measure. From the first touch of her tender mouth to his, he was a lost man, the flame ignited deep within and consuming his rapt soul.

As their lips parted, she whispered softly, "You're fortunate, sir, that although I can seldom afford it, I'm partial to the taste of fine brandy."

The extraordinary woman fled, disappearing through the shadowy hedge in a blur of silk. James made one lunge after her but caught his foot on a tuft of grass and fell forward onto his face, where he stayed, finding it too much effort to move again.

✦

Lucky for him, his pockets were empty this evening, or she could have relieved him of more than his kiss, just for a lark. Drunken fool.

Ellie Vyne ran through that maze as if Lucifer's minions were at her heels. Reckless, she chose turns without the slightest idea which direction she traveled. A fragile laugh bubbled out of her, snagged and shattered on each jolting breath. Of all the men in the world, why did it have to be James Hartley who kissed her that way? Why was he—her long-sworn enemy—the one man who kissed her just the way she wanted? Now he'd got her in a most irritating and irrational state of confusion.

He was a Hartley, she was a Vyne, and as such, they were heirs to a feud that began years before. In addition, he was the most infuriating, hypocritical rakehell she'd ever met, and the man who never thought of her as anything but a nuisance.

The man who was hopelessly in love with her best friend.

Now she'd gone and kissed him, like a complete and utter lackwit. Good thing he wouldn't remember it by morning.

Perhaps James Hartley's worst sin was that he once, within her hearing, referred to her as "a girl with neither beauty, grace, nor sense." And then he took it a step further. "Ellie Vyne?" he'd remarked loudly to a roomful of guffaws, "or Ellie *Phant*?"

She was just sixteen at the time and had never forgotten it. How could she? Well aware of her shortcomings as a rather plump girl who always seemed to be where she was least wanted and never around when she was required, the last thing she needed back then was James Hartley pointing her faults out to the world at large. She'd always sworn she'd get her vengeance one day. Perhaps, she mused darkly, that was why she kissed him. What other reason could there be? In truth, his spiteful comment all those years ago had done her a favor. It made her determined not to be crushed, never to let another word wound her. After that, she made certain to dance every dance, no matter who asked her, never to seem as if she cared about anything beyond a jolly good time. Most often it worked. She had only the occasional lapses in confidence.

Her skirt brushed against the privet, making the crisp leaves rattle with a ghostly shiver. There was a break in the hedge. She ducked through it, still running, and saw the house ahead of her. Aglow with candlelight, crystal, and mirrors, it was a treasure box overflowing, held in the curved sleeve of dark blue velvet sky.

A woman swathed in ruby tassels and amber silk, reminiscent of a gypsy fortune-teller's tent, flew across the lawn. Tripping over curly toed slippers, she called anxiously, "Oh, James! James darling, where have you gone?" Once in sight of Ellie, she cupped a hand to her mouth and shouted, "Have you seen a gentleman in the guise of a highwayman?"

The poor woman looked quite desperate—and foolish, in what might only be described as a harem girl's costume. Apparently dignity had gone out the window this evening. James Hartley had that effect on women.

Ellie jerked a backward nod over one shoulder. "He's in there. Lost." Someone was going to have to rescue him, and it couldn't be her.

The slave girl waved her thanks and scurried onward. Before Ellie had taken another step, a second woman appeared, this one dressed as a nun but with a little too much paint on her cheeks and a brassy, unnatural shade of red hair peeping out from her wimple. She trotted giddily down the terrace steps. "James? James, I wish you did not hide from me like this." The unlikely nun let out a sharp curse as she stubbed her toe on a stone planter. Then she noticed Ellie. "I say, have you seen a tall, handsome fellow in a tricorn hat and a leather mask? Did he come this way?"

Ellie struggled to quell the mischievous smile that pulled on her lips. "Oh yes. Dick Turpin's in the maze, Mother Superior."

The second woman ran on, lifting her habit to show a pair of ankles in fine silk stockings.

Again Ellie moved forward, only to be stopped by yet another searching young lady, this one dressed as a shepherdess, plainly in want of a sheep. Before the third woman even spoke, Ellie pointed over her shoulder. Frowning fiercely, beribboned crook clasped in both hands, the angry shepherdess marched off in the same direction as the other two women.

Ellie watched the figures retreat and suddenly caught a shadow, a flutter in the corner of her eye. Someone, hovering behind her, had retreated hastily from the moonlight and merged with the tall hedge. She waited, but whoever it was, they did not approach to get her attention.

Curious. Perhaps she'd imagined it.

She quickened her steps toward the brightly lit house and gave in to another burst of laughter, thinking again of her enemy, stranded and hapless in the maze. For just a few moments she'd made him want her. Sweet victory for the girl he'd once dismissed. It was a powerfully good feeling. But such rare sensations were best in moderation. Wouldn't want it to go to her head.

Chapter 2

London, six months later

ELLIE VYNE NEVER HAD MUCH SYMPATHY FOR MEN, until she temporarily became one. Disguised as the "count de Bonneville," donning satin breeches and an old-fashioned powdered wig to gamble among Society's decadent rich, she discovered a surprising fact. Contrary to previous conjecture, the male animal did not necessarily have all the fun. True, they could burp as they chose without reprimand, and sit with their legs in any pose comfortable. But they too had pitfalls to dodge, because the female sex could be just as single-minded in pursuit of sport and just as reticent to take no for an answer.

For instance, the "count" was lucky to get away with his true identity intact—likewise his trousers—since Lady Ophelia Southwold proved herself such an overeager strumpet that evening. While pressing a lavish diamond necklace into the count's gloved hand in payment for her IOU, the lady also extended a startling offer, whispered so hotly in his ear that the steam nearly wilted his wig. An offer he was obliged to refuse for reasons obvious only to himself.

It was fortunate Lady Southwold's fingers never ventured any higher along the count's breeches, or she would have shared his secret and suffered a nasty shock.

Followed by disappointment of severe magnitude.

Ellie could laugh over the incident now she had safely retreated to a rowdy inn on the outskirts of London. Kneeling on the bed, in the count's lace-trimmed shirt, she counted out the guineas won after another night of fleecing unsuspecting aristocrats and rich young bucks about Town. She carefully lifted Lady Southwold's necklace and studied the five enormous diamonds hanging on little clips. Ellie never wore much jewelry, other than the pearls left behind by her mother—and those were elegant and understated. But this necklace was nothing like that. She'd never seen diamonds so large. And heavy. They would surely drag a woman's shoulders down by the end of an evening. It really was possible to have too much of a good thing.

While this had been a fruitful outing for the charming, elusive "count," when Ellie looked at those ugly diamonds, a shimmer of foreboding lapped at her senses. It ruffled her nerve endings like the tongue of a sly, cooling zephyr. Perhaps tonight had been *too* fruitful. It could be time to hang up the count's breeches before the ruse was discovered. Truthfully, she was surprised she got away with her masquerade as long as she did. It didn't say much for her looks, Ellie mused, that she was so easily disguised as a man. Or else it said little for the masculine appearance of today's aristocratic gentlemen.

Her winnings packed safely away, she peeled the itching theatrical eyebrows carefully off her face, finished a glass of brandy, blew out her candle, and tumbled back across the bed. Sprawled in the moonlight, she yawned heavily, listened to the general ruckus from below, and pondered the strange direction her life had strayed. As the main caretaker of her family since the age of eight, she'd always known something different waited in her future, but she never imagined the road she traveled would be quite like this.

Tomorrow morning she must become plain Ellie Vyne again, in muslin, petticoat, and bonnet, expected at the very proper, well-ordered house of her half sister and brother-in-law. They took her in reluctantly, hoping—according to her sister's last letter— that she would not mortify them too much while she was in London. No one reading her sister's sharply penned missive could realize the truth: that it was Ellie who single-handedly funded both her younger sisters' debuts and provided their wedding dowries. Had they left all that to their father, they would have been gray and rheumatic before their first foray into Society. But in the minds of her sisters, Ellie was an embarrassment, a woman who refused to live within the constraints of propriety and instead made her own rules. Frequently her sisters lectured her about the importance of fitting in, but although Ellie made it her life's work to do the very opposite, she did so in such a good-natured, merry way that no one really knew how to stop her.

Her mysterious beginnings did not help matters. Her mother was a shipwrecked, pregnant widow when she married Admiral Vyne, and nothing much was known about Ellie's deceased father. Her mother, Catherine, had been too brokenhearted to talk about him, and Ellie never dared raise the matter in case it disturbed the fragile disposition of Catherine's marriage to the admiral—a much older man, who, although vain and proud himself, must frequently hear how lucky he was to have a wife so much younger and fair of face. As if no one could understand how he managed it. Then along came Charlotte and Amelia, her mother's children by the admiral, and Ellie had a new family. After her mother died, they were all reliant on Ellie to look after them, but lately her half sisters took it into their heads to reverse the roles. They had the joint idea of getting her married to the first dull fellow willing, and shuffled off into obscurity before she caused them any further worry.

Ellie's future schemes, however, involved only a well-earned rest with no meddling man sticking his nose in. The money she won tonight as the count would pay off the last bills incurred by her sisters' wedding trousseaus, and if she found somewhere discreet to pawn that diamond necklace, she could even begin repairs on her stepfather's roof at Lark Hollow. Then, at last, she might enjoy some peace. She planned a visit to her aunt Lizzie in the tranquil village of Sydney Dovedale, where she could fill her lungs with some good, honest air.

For some time now, Ellie had felt herself rushing along a bumpy road, her horses very nearly out of control, the reins slipping through her fingers. If she could only slow down a while, sit where it was quiet, do nothing but breathe! In the country, one might ponder the beauty of nature without actually having to do anything in it, just feel. She would soon be rejuvenated. Wandering the pleasant lanes of Sydney Dovedale, she could let the count disappear for a while, if not forever. She might even write her exploits one day in an anonymous book and put him to rest officially.

She was twenty-seven—the same age her mother was when she died—and really too old to wreak any more havoc. It had been fun while it lasted, but now it was time to settle into spinsterhood. The only thing she could possibly regret about her life was missing out on children. She liked the idea of a child very much, but one could not be had without a husband. Well, strictly speaking, a babe could be had out of wedlock, but she had enough problems without causing more scandal for herself.

Resolved to retirement and the end of mischief, she'd just let her eyelids drift shut when a sudden commotion rattled down the hall, and her chamber door was almost ripped from its hinges. Ellie bounced up, wide awake again, clutching the shabby coverlet to her shoulders.

"Where is he? Where is the villain?" Lantern swinging from one fist, riding quirt brandished in the other, a tall figure climbed over the ruins of the door and peered angrily at her through a trembling swathe of bronze light. A fine, ethereal mist rolled off his wide shoulders where the frigid night air met the heat of his body. He might have been a monstrous dragon from some dark fable coming to feast on a sacrificial maiden—had he not been a very real human being, identifiable by the coarse mutterings of complaint about his bruised knuckles. Only a man could complain at something of his own doing.

Besides, she was no virginal maiden.

And in the next breath, they both exhaled the same startled word: "*You?*"

Ghostly strands of mist formed around his lips, and his face was flushed. He'd come out without a hat, and his hair, faintly gilded by a summer that now felt so long ago, sprung up from his head in all directions. He must have dressed in great haste, for his shirt was more off than on. She wondered whose bed he'd just rolled out of to embark upon this madcap chase. Adding to his undone appearance, he sported a bloodied lip and a blossoming bruise on the upper ridge of his right cheekbone. Apparently he'd put himself through the gauntlet to get here.

Ellie's heart was thrusting like the paws of a fox with hounds hard on his tail. For the past six months she'd stayed out of his way, and since the social Season had yet to begin, she didn't expect to see him in London so soon.

"James Hartley! What are you doing here?"

❧

He might have known he'd find *her* there, in the thick of it.

Mariella Vyne, brazen strumpet and notorious menace, had the audacity to sit up in that bed and question *him*. Somehow he bit down on a large slice of his anger, although not all of it could be swallowed at once. "The count," he demanded, striding up to the bed, floorboards groaning indignantly under the weight of his feet. He almost hit his brow on the low beams but ducked in the nick of time. "Where is he, Vyne? I know he's here somewhere. I tracked him to this inn."

She shook off what appeared to be a sleepy haze and pointed at the window. "You missed him. He's gone."

He raised his lantern higher, and the arc of light swung over a pair of riding boots by her bed. "Barefoot?"

"He heard you coming and fled in haste."

He looked at the brandy bottle and empty glass, then quickly assessed the rumpled sheets before returning to the woman wearing the count's lacy, extravagantly ruffled shirt. "What the blazes are *you* doing here with him?" Stupid question. It was quite clear what she was doing there with that villain.

"How dare you break into our room, Hartley? Get out!"

Instead, he set his lantern down, held his quirt in his teeth, and proceeded to check beneath the bed before searching under the coverlet, his gloved hands clutching at her bare legs. She scrambled up the mattress, away from his reach.

"You won't find him *there*, will you, for pity's sake?"

Abruptly he felt the sharp pain of something shattered against his back, accompanied by a loud "crack." A shower of broken pottery rained across the bed. When he retreated, he saw the handle of the broken ewer still in her hand, her eyes gleaming with victory.

As he opened his mouth to curse, the quirt fell to the bed, and he slid backward, shaking pieces of clay from his coat and hair.

"I'll bring that crook to justice, Vyne." His hot temper slithered farther out of reach—just as she did. "I give you fair warning."

She snorted. "What has he done to get your drawers in such a knot?"

"Stolen something of great value to me."

"Your mirror?"

James glared at the vixen in the rumpled bed. "Very droll. I see no civilized man has yet taken you in hand, Vyne."

"Oh, they wouldn't dare try."

Angry breath oozed out of him in a cold laugh. "I'd advise you to steer clear of the count—if I ever thought you'd listen to good sense."

Faint amusement twinkled from beneath hastily lowered, long, dark lashes. But her haughty lips were set in their usual stubborn moue, poised to argue. "As if *you* have any right to lecture me, Hartley! Your own history of mistakes with the opposite sex would require more bound volumes than the *Encyclopedia Britannica*. Tend to your own affairs before you meddle in mine."

They both sprang across the bed for his fallen quirt at the same time, but he got there first. She leapt to her feet on the mattress, clutched the coverlet to her seminaked body, and primly ordered him, once again, out of her room.

He stood firm, holding the quirt across his thighs. "Where has he gone, Vyne?"

She raised her chin, tossed her dark, tangled hair

over her shoulder and, in a grand flourish that put the actress Sarah Siddons to shame, exclaimed, "You'll never find him, Hartley. Torture me all you like, I'll never betray him." He rather got the impression the wench was enjoying herself now. Well, he'd soon nip that smug expression in the bud.

"It might interest you to know, Vyne, the lover you so gallantly protect was witnessed this evening flirting excessively with Lady Ophelia Southwold. Not so loyal to *you*, eh?"

To his surprise, she merely laughed. "Encroaching on your property, Hartley? Wasn't she your latest hussy? One of them at least."

He ignored that. "I came here to retrieve the diamonds he stole from that lady. They belong to me."

"To you?"

Aha. That got her. Unless he was very much mistaken, a half pint of impertinent, rosy bloom had just drained from the dratted woman's cheeks. "The Hartley Diamonds," he explained. "Priceless antiquities that French villain stole from Lady Southwold."

"He *stole* them? Is that what she told you? I don't suppose she mentioned what else she offered him? It seems your fair lady is not so faithful either."

He gave his quirt a practice swing, letting his gaze wander upward over her disheveled form. The ruffled collar of the count's shirt framed her long, slender neck and drew attention to a bosom undeserving of his notice or his admiration. Although it received both, in some very dark, disobedient part of his being.

It was a very good thing she clutched that coverlet around her waist, for she was evidently not wearing anything but the shirt. Not another stitch. Naked as the day she was born under that bit of lace and silk.

James cleared his throat. Back to business. "Get your clothes on, Vyne. I'm taking you with me. Someone should save you from your own stupidity."

"Don't fool yourself, Hartley. I do not need rescuing."

"Have it your way then, shameless hussy."

"Thank you. I shall. Pompous, hypocritical twit."

Half-turned away, he regained a breath and then looked back at her. "You are, quite possibly, the most irritating, truculent creature I've ever known. In the fifteen years of our acquaintance, you haven't changed."

"Seventeen," she corrected. "And your existence is equally trying on my nerves."

"You're an ill-mannered, brazen—"

"And you're a vain, mean-tempered—"

"Lying, scheming—"

"Arrogant wretch."

The lacy shirt slipped down over one shoulder, leaving her flesh bared.

"Put your clothes on," he muttered, gloved fingers tightening around his quirt. "You're coming with me."

"I most certainly am not."

"Indeed you are. Before I take my whip to your behind." He moved around the bed and eyed her warily, amused to see the supposedly fearless Ellie Vyne back up against the wall and hold that coverlet like a shield around her body.

"Touch me," she warned, "and I'll scream."

He tried to relax his jaw and save the wear on his teeth. She stood very straight on the bed, like a woman defending herself in the dock—as he was certain she would one day. He was only surprised it hadn't happened yet.

"Aren't you supposed to be chasing after the count to get your diamonds back? He must be miles away by now, and here you are quarrelling with me, Hartley."

James tapped his quirt lightly against the palm of his left hand. Why *was* he still there? Had that lacy sleeve just fallen another half inch from her shoulder? Good Lord, he could see the swell of her breast now above the ruffles. And her darker nipple through that fine silk. His throat went dry; a harsh breath stalled there as he felt the instantaneous quickening of his manhood.

Don't look. Not at that.

She was an annoying little chit who did nothing but make mischief at every turn and constantly mocked him as a fool. Mariella Vyne was out of control. Tempting as it might be to consider reining her in, he'd long since decided some other man could have that strife. They were welcome to it.

Look at anything else. Anything—

Suddenly, he caught her sliding an anxious glance at the copper bed warmer. He hadn't noticed it until now.

Curious, he moved toward it.

With nothing else at hand to use as a distraction, Ellie opened her grip on the coverlet and let it fall away from her body.

He stilled. Thick silence descended over the strange, lantern-lit scene. His sternly questing gaze abandoned all other subjects of interest and swept her slowly from head to toe, taking particular note of her naked legs.

She knew the "count's" shirt barely skimmed the top of her thighs.

The slight movement he'd taken away from her was now reversed. Unconsciously done, no doubt. Even men who had access to any number of willing women every night of the week could become dullards in the presence of a half-naked female. It was a primeval neediness, she supposed, some void in the male animal that kept them constantly on the hunt. Each slow, deliberate beat of his eyelashes fanned the tiny bumps now sprouting liberally across her skin. The silence became oppressive as he stared at her legs.

"I hope you mean to pay the good innkeeper for his door, Hartley." Despite the tone of bravado, every pore on her body tingled with anticipation.

His regard hardened and cooled from August sky blue to a wintry steel gray. He shot her knees one last, lingering scowl—probably meant to shrivel her bones to dust, spun around, and stalked out, trampling the broken, jagged planks where once there stood a door.

"Give my regards to Lady Southwold!" she shouted.

But he was not leaving yet. She heard him arguing now with the innkeeper in the passage.

Thank goodness she'd distracted him from prying inside the bed warmer. Had he looked there, he would have found tonight's winnings, his precious diamond necklace, and the count's wig. But for now, the count de Bonneville had won a narrow escape. And so had the notorious Ellie Vyne.

Almost.

He reappeared in the broken doorway. "Get dressed, Vyne. I'm not leaving without you."

"I told you, I don't need rescuing. Go away."

He looked at her steadily, his height and the breadth of his shoulders filling the doorway. "Who else will save you, if I do not?" She thought she caught a subtle lightening of his stormy eyes, but from that distance it was hard to tell. "No one but me is fool enough."

Damn and blast. Stubborn, pig-headed brute.

She supposed she might as well let the villain escort her to her sister's house as long as he told no one where he found her.

❧

"Not tell where I found you?" he exclaimed, prodding her up into the hackney carriage with his quirt. "Why the devil should I keep your assignation with that crook a secret? Your family ought to know what you get up to. Again."

"Do shut up, Hartley. Shall I write to your grand-mama and tell her you gave the Hartley Diamonds to your latest harlot?"

He slammed the carriage door shut, his face white and pinched in the moonlight.

"Your family ought to know what you get up to," she chirped, throwing his words back at him. *"Again."*

He had no answer to that, just a frustrated curse. Naturally, it was all well and good for him to enjoy love affairs before marriage. She, being a woman, was supposed to have no wicked urges and keep herself encased in iron drawers until she found a husband.

"Ever hear of uneven standards?" she shouted through the carriage window.

"No," he quipped. "Is it a race horse?"

Quietly seething, she watched him mount his hunter to ride alongside, and then the carriage wheels rumbled forward.

In common with most of the world, which was always so eager to think ill of her, James must have assumed she was recently the Duke of Ardleigh's mistress. She knew that rumor had flourished for a year or so, but her duties had actually been little more than those of a nurse. She'd traveled with the duke, made certain he took his tonic as prescribed by the physician, and amused him in the evenings with card tricks and ribald tales. Naturally, the duke enjoyed everyone thinking he still had the energy to misbehave, so he never bothered to correct the mistaken ideas about their relationship. For Ellie, it had been a very convenient way to keep any marriage-minded suitors at bay and travel with a degree of freedom most women never enjoyed.

It was the duke who first came up with the idea of disguising Ellie at a party and introducing her as the "count de Bonneville" for a jest at the expense of his peers. He was a fun-loving, larger-than-life fellow, and it was a great shock to many when the duke died suddenly in his bed. Most people assumed it was her fault, naturally.

That's what happens, she'd heard people say, *when an elderly fool takes up with a wayward slip of a girl half his age.*

Ellie settled back into the seat, her shabby, much-traveled trunk at her feet and the hatbox of concealed valuables beside her on the leather cushion. For a moment, she weighed the idea of giving his diamonds back with no further ado. Stealing another glance through the window, she observed him trotting beside the carriage, his noble profile cast in pewter moonlight. It was tempting to imagine he'd come to rescue her from the count's lecherous clutches, and if she squinted hard, she could picture him in armor, a handsome, gallant knight ready to defend her from brigands on the road. She'd never been rescued from anything before; she was usually rescuing other folk.

Suddenly something plucked at her nerves with ice-cold fingers—the sense of being followed again. She twisted around, squinting into the dark through the tiny back window of the carriage. The lights of the inn had already faded, and the carriage was surrounded on all sides by the rattling shadow of naked trees. There was no sign of any other traveler, but the feeling of being stalked remained. It was a sensation she'd felt several times over the past six months, but for want of any proof, she always put it down to her unfettered imagination.

She turned again on her seat and lowered the sash window.

"By the by, Hartley, what *have* you been up to this evening? Your eye is swollen with a nasty bruise. You ought to—"

Before she could finish, he began another lecture he somehow felt entitled to give her. Ellie swiftly closed the window again and slid back in her seat.

Well, he can whistle in the wind for his damned diamonds then. He should never have loaned his treasures to a faithless woman like Ophelia Southwold to wear, so she'd let him sweat a while. He needed a lesson.

So much for a quiet retirement and the end of

mischief. But it was hardly her fault that this man came and poked his nose into her business. James Hartley really ought to be more careful with his family jewels, or any notorious woman might get her hands on them.

As indeed, she just had.

Chapter 3

"THAT VYNE WOMAN IS A DANGER TO HERSELF AND TO anyone who has the misfortune of crossing her path!" He rustled the newspaper angrily as he turned another page, not having focused on a single word of print that morning. "Truly, she is a menace, Grieves."

"Goodness gracious, sir," his valet replied with polite concern. "Women knew their place in my day. Alas, they've become quite unruly."

"If one knew where she might leap out, some form of defense against the assault could be prepared, but her unpredictability is part of the horror. One never knows where she'll turn up." James shook his head. "To be sure, she will be under my feet again sooner or later." Allowing the corner of his paper to bend inward, he peered crossly over it. "Do you know what she had the unmitigated gall to ask me?"

Grieves stopped pouring coffee and put on his attentive face, which was only two-and-a-half creases removed from blankly disinterested. "I shudder to imagine, sir."

"She asked me if I'd heard of such a thing as uneven

standards. *Uneven standards!* As if men and women should be held to the same measure." He returned his gaze to the newspaper and flicked the wilted corner to attention again with a sharp jerk of his wrist. "I begin to think she is unhinged."

The valet finished pouring his coffee. "Was that before or after she hit you with the bellows from the fireplace, sir?"

"It wasn't a set of bellows. It was a jug." James ducked his head to show the small cut on his forehead, along the hairline, where a stray shard of pottery had wounded him.

"It is a good thing, sir, that you have a large, hard head, accustomed to having objects broken over it."

James crumpled the newspaper in his fists before tossing it to the carpet. "Good thing for her, you mean, that I'm a tolerant fellow and did not have her arrested on the spot." He couldn't think about Ellie Vyne for too long, or he might start picturing her bare legs again. That could lead only to trouble.

"'Tis a pity, sir, that the scold's bridle has fallen out of use."

"Indeed it is." Sighing, he leaned back in his chair. "My patience with women in general is not what it was, Grieves. Sometimes I feel as if I've become a mere plaything in their hands. An object of fun, to be used and then tossed aside with no regard for my feelings."

"How dreadful to be thus powerless in the hands of females. And that reminds me, sir, you received another billet-doux this morning from the diminutive Lady Mercy Danforthe."

"Good Lord! Does no one have charge of that creature?"

"It seems not, sir. If they have charge of her, they don't appear to want it. This is the tenth letter she has sent in the space of one month, ever since you saved her life in the park."

James stirred his coffee with an unnecessary degree of violence. "I did not save her life. I wish you would stop referring to it as such. It just so happened, I was the only one with the wits to ride after her pony when it took fright." He now wished he'd looked the other way, because he was quite certain the girl was more than capable of controlling that pony herself. She brought back memories of his old bulldog. But not knowing any of that at the time, he'd acted purely on instinct to stop the runaway pony and save the little mite clinging to it.

"In the young lady's mind, you are her savior, sir. She will brook no argument. I understand Lady Mercy is not often argued with successfully by anyone, even her brother, the earl. She knows her own mind, I am told, and is given rather more of her own rein than is good for her. Or for the world."

"Disgraceful." He shook his head at the horrid idea of young girls knowing their own mind. "What is she—twelve or thirteen?"

"Approaching the age of ten, I believe, sir. A very trying age to be sure. I daresay the worst is yet to come."

James huffed into his coffee. Lady Mercy Danforthe was an endearingly freckled moppet with flame-red hair and a peculiarly stubborn nature. And also, apparently, a lurid imagination. Her love letters, penned to James almost every day, were as shocking in language as they were colorful—always decorated lavishly with painted hearts and arrows. "It is a sad state of affairs, Grieves," he muttered, leaning farther back, resting all his weight on the groaning rear legs of his chair, "when no one has control over a chit of ten. It can lead only to tragedy."

"I quite agree, sir. I've always maintained that young females should be locked away, out of sight and hearing, until they have survived their formative years."

After swaying dangerously for a moment, James thumped the front legs of his chair back to the carpet. "Too many stray wenches running about the place, doing as they please, and somehow always underfoot. 'Tis a dangerous world out there, Grieves. How can a man turn a new leaf, amend his ways, with everything set against him? Not even my own grandmother has any faith in me that I'll one day find the right woman."

"The *right* woman, sir? Meaning one sanctioned by her?"

"Naturally."

"That explains why she is holding a New Year's Eve ball for you at Hartley House, sir. And inviting all her eligible acquaintances."

"She's *what*?"

"I'm sorry, sir." Grieves bowed his graying head. "I thought you knew. Lady Hartley mentioned it to me when she was last in Town."

Dabbing hard at his lips with a napkin, James snapped, "Wonderful! A cattle market."

"It seems as if Lady Hartley has given up waiting for you to choose. She kept referring to your *Great Mistake*, sir. How you cannot be trusted not to make another similar."

James cooled his coffee with a hearty sigh. His grandmother was a meddling old woman, but he knew exactly what she referred to as his "Great Mistake." Two years ago, he'd made a mortal fool of himself by proposing marriage, for the second time, to Miss Sophia Valentine, who finally rejected him in favor of another man. A humble farmer. The humiliation had wounded him to the core. But there were other mistakes he'd made, far more serious ones, of which his grandmother remained unaware.

A decade ago, he'd lost an illegitimate son. A housemaid with whom he'd enjoyed a brief affair became pregnant, but having been dismissed from her post, she didn't tell James until she was ready to deliver. At that time he was away from London. He returned as quickly as he could, but the woman had disappeared from her lodgings by then, and no one knew where she had gone. He'd searched for her family, but found none. Ten years later, when Sophia Valentine threw him over forever, she accused him of having deserted the pregnant housemaid, of deliberately leaving her and her newborn son to die alone. James had been shocked, horrified. If he'd known about the baby before it was too late, of course he would have helped in any way possible. But the fact remained that a woman and child had died. James must be accountable.

He supposed, with hindsight, he should have known the truth when the maid was dismissed from her post—that there was more to it than the vague excuse he was given for her leaving. However, he was younger then, foolish and thoughtless, finding his pleasure where he could, turning a blind eye to the darker facts of life. And to the consequences of his sins. He'd never known the woman and her child had died until Sophia threw it in his face when she made her choice and left him forever. He'd opened his eyes that night and did not like what he saw in himself.

Forced to look inward and question, where previously he'd always assumed he knew best about everything, James had made the tumultuous decision to turn a new leaf.

Now, whenever he thought of that housemaid and her child—which was often—the cold heaviness of grief and regret settled in his stomach. A grievous mistake that he might have prevented, but it was too late to save them now. All he could do was make recompense in his own life.

He groaned, and his coffee cup fell to the saucer with a rattle that set his teeth on edge. "I must find my Marie-Antoinette."

A low sigh slipped out between the valet's lips. "The one from Brighton, sir?"

"Yes." He'd been searching for months, looking for her in every pretty face, every sad smile.

"I thought we'd given up on that idea, sir."

"Certainly not."

"But we are not even sure she exists, are we, sir?"

He scowled hard at his cup. She existed. Somewhere. Yes, he'd fallen flat on his face and woken with a nightmarish headache, but he hadn't conjured her out of thin air. His imagination was not that creative. She was real. Six months later, her kiss still lingered on his lips. If he was truly going to turn his life around, he needed her beside him, just as he'd needed her on that little stone bench to keep him upright.

It was positively infuriating that she refused to be found when he needed her so very badly, and while other saucy vixens, like Ellie Vyne, popped up all over the place, trying to distract him from his new course.

Grieves gestured at the egg before him and said somberly, "Shall I crack it for you, sir? Or do you feel up to it yourself this morning?"

James snatched the butter knife from the valet's hand, muttering under his breath, "Up to it? *Up to it?* Here!" With one swing of the polished blade the eggshell was cracked in two, and a satisfying blob of bright golden egg yolk oozed out onto the tablecloth. James grinned, feeling slightly better.

Grieves set the silver toast rack beside James's coffee cup. "And now, sir, to the business of the day. Shall you be dining in this evening?"

"I don't think so—no—I have a party I must attend."

"Ah, very good, sir. As it is Tuesday, I shall be out, of course."

James glanced slyly at the valet. Grieves always had Tuesday nights off, and what he did with them was something he never discussed in detail. "Your club, is it?"

The valet hesitated. "Yes, sir. The Gentlemen's Gentleman's Club. We look out for one another."

That was it—never any more explanation than that. "Grieves, I confess myself fascinated by your Tuesday evening excursions across town. What happens at your club?"

"Sir, as I told you before, I am not at liberty

to discuss the matter. All members are sworn to secrecy."

"I suppose you all sit around complaining about your masters, eh? Planning rebellion."

"Yes, sir," Grieves replied, his expression unchanging. "You have guessed our purpose exactly." He moved around the table, hands at his sides. "And now I must remind you, sir—as much as it pains us both—that Mr. Dillworthy will be arriving soon after breakfast."

There, alas, went his improved mood. "What the devil does he want?"

"He wishes to discuss the matter of escalating costs at the Morton Street—"

"Damn it all, Grieves!" James looked at the toast. "How many years have you been with me now?"

The valet sighed. "Almost five, sir. And it doesn't feel a day over ten."

There was a pause. Master and valet both perused the breakfast table, then each other. Finally the table again. Eventually, Grieves realized his mistake and hastily began cutting the toast slices into the preferred "soldier" shapes more suitable for dipping in runny yolk.

James gave a small grunt of approval. One must have toast soldiers with one's egg or else the entire day was off on the wrong foot. There weren't many reliable things in his life, but a few habits devotedly maintained kept his world from spinning too rapidly. He would feel dreadfully alone if not for those small, comforting reassurances. His valet had suggested it was a sign of old age advancing. James refused to believe it.

"Now that we have taken care of that pressing

matter, sir, once again to the unavoidable and immi-
nent arrival of Mr. Dillworthy regarding the Morton
Street home."

"Hmmm?" He was busy dipping a toast soldier into
his egg yolk, anticipating the first comforting mouthful.

"He is, I understand, distressed at the rising costs
associated with the renovations and—"

"Dillworthy's been grumbling into your ear, has he?"

"It seems he cannot make you sit still long enough
to grumble likewise into yours, sir."

"No." James smirked. "You ought to practice
evasion a little more yourself." He knew poor Grieves
was frequently the target at which people—failing
to capture *him* in conversation—aimed their arrows,
settling for a circuitous route in hopes of eventually
reaching his ear with their concerns.

"Mr. Dillworthy is concerned, he tells me, with the
number of charities to which you've donated considerable sums in the past year. Lady Hartley disapproves
your choices, sir, and as the Hartley family accountant
for some years, he has—"

"Grieves, I am thir…over one and twenty, as you
know."

The valet raised a sharp eyebrow. "Quite well over, sir."

"As a consequence, and disturbing as it might be
to my grandmother's loyal slave Mr. Dillworthy, I am
capable of making my own financial decisions. For too
long I paid no attention to my money and how it's
spent. Now I know where every penny goes. And it
goes where I decide."

"To a home for unwed mothers?"

"Precisely. I want those renovations in Morton

Street finished as soon as possible, and cost is no object. I've told Dillworthy this many times. Then my grandmother corners him when she comes to Town, and he quivers like a spineless jelly."

"Lady Hartley objects to the idea of young ladies giving birth out of wedlock, and she is of the opinion that charities like that one merely encourage sinful behavior. Such women, she says, should be punished and chastity promoted."

"Grandmama does her bit to promote chastity, without a doubt," he replied wryly. "I happen to disagree with her. Now I have control of all my money, I daresay I'll disagree with her more often. I'm beginning to like the sensation."

Grieves collected the scattered pages of newspaper, folding them neatly. "It is a great pity, sir," he quietly observed, "that too many people are unaware of the good that you do."

James shrugged. He didn't take on these commitments for Society's approval.

"I suppose most folk care to hear only about your failures, so they can feel better about their own lives," the valet added. "Success makes for less interesting gossip."

"Yes, Grieves, people are generally horrid, selfish buggers. Except you and I, of course."

Grieves swept crumbs from the tablecloth with a tiny silver pan and brush. "Might I inquire, sir, if you were able to retrieve the Hartley Diamonds the other night? You left the boxing club in such haste when you heard that Lady Southwold had given them to—"

"No. I was not able to get them back. But I shall. That French crook will not get away with this."

"And Lady Southwold, sir?"

James winced at the topic, but at least Grieves was distracted from further talk of the accounts. "Lady Southwold is quite evidently not my mystery woman from Brighton. Her knuckles are bordering on manly, and she breathes too hard."

"Gracious, sir, how frightful. Audible breathing is such a terrible habit. One of many you cannot abide in women these days."

He looked up, eyes narrowed. "Hmmm."

"One wonders, sir, if your list of unacceptable traits might outweigh the acceptable ones to such a degree that the right woman will never be found."

"Nonsense. I met her in Brighton." Now if he could only find her again, his entire world would be put to rights. "She is my future wife and the mother of my many children. We must find that woman, Grieves. We simply must. She is the one for me, and none other will suffice."

Grieves made a small sound that might have passed for gentle agreement, but was very nearly a skeptical sigh and could almost be an "oh no." It was one of many similar noises in the valet's repertoire, muted exclamations that could serve several purposes. "Although it pains me to bring the fact to your notice, sir, we have depleted the possibilities. All those ladies you once thought she might be have each subsequently proven unsatisfactory."

"Then we must search further. Evidently, I've overlooked someone, although it seems impossible. I'm always most observant."

"Yes, sir. I'm sure nothing gets past you." The valet moved to the window, his smooth stride barely a whisper across the carpet. After a moment, he spoke again, his tone jauntier. "Now that we know Lady Southwold is most definitely not your mystery lady, it is perhaps a good thing, sir—if I might venture—that the count de Bonneville has taken her off your hands."

"*Count!* Ha! He's a rotten confidence trickster. My grandmother's lapdog has more noble blood in its veins." James grabbed another toast soldier and rammed it headfirst into his egg yolk.

"And you say you found the redoubtable Miss Vyne in the villain's bed, sir? One imagines that she's quite enough trouble for one man to handle without poaching Lady Southwold away."

He grunted, not looking up from his breakfast.

The valet began fussing with the drapes, chuckling under his breath.

"What strikes you as so humorous this morning, Grieves?"

"I was just observing to myself, sir, how you always said you would not wish Miss Vyne on your worst enemy." Grieves coughed into his gloved hand, discreetly palming a smile, but not before James had seen it. "An odd coincidence, is it not, that she should now be in the company of your worst enemy?"

James frowned at his egg. His swollen eye was hurting. So was the cut on his brow. "Another female given too much rein," he grumbled.

He wouldn't be at all surprised if the Vyne woman knew exactly where the count might be found, and the Hartley Diamonds too. She could almost certainly get them back for him with little effort. James doubted many men were strong enough to refuse her anything she wanted.

There! Damn. Now he'd gone and thought of her legs again. Letting that woman into his mind was like setting a kitten loose in a basket of wool.

⤶

"It is impolite to read at the table, Ellie," her sister Charlotte exclaimed in a frigid whisper.

Hastily closing the book, she slid it away out of sight on her lap.

"It seems you have forgotten all about manners these days," Charlotte added.

Ellie really hadn't thought that reading at the table would matter, since her brother-in-law ate his breakfast with the speed and elegance of an ill-tempered boar, not saying a word to anyone and with eyes fixed fiercely upon his plate. But pointing this out would upset Charlotte. Upsetting Charlotte was never a good idea, for she had ways of punishing the miscreant. Ingenious, dastardly ways.

"I managed to secure an invite for you to Lady Clegg-Foster's party this evening. I hope you will be on your best behavior, Ellie. You do have an appropriate gown? If not, I suppose I can lend you one of mine, if you promise not to get it stained or torn. My maid will have to let out the"—she lowered her voice, glancing timidly at her distracted husband— "*bosom*, for yours is quite…but Simpkins is splendidly efficient, and I'm sure no one will notice you had to be squeezed into it, like stuffing into a goose. Sadly, I have nothing in a stripe, and my white muslin is a little too youthful for you."

Very dastardly. Just like that, for instance.

"Why do I need a stripe?" Ellie inquired sweetly.

"Why, because it has the effect of lessening a fuller figure. A downward stripe is most beneficial for a woman of middle age."

"I'm twenty-seven."

"Yes, dear. We are all sadly aware of the fact."

Ellie bit her tongue, banking her first response and settling for something more genteel. "I'd rather not go out, Charlotte. If you don't mind, I will stay in."

Her sister scowled hard across the table, apparently trying to freeze her to stone. Finally she snapped, "Of course I mind. I went to great lengths for that invitation. Have you no idea how difficult it is to have a sister who adamantly insists on shaming us all, floating about the country like a gypsy, doing as she pleases? You are lucky to be invited anywhere with your scandalous reputation—" She stopped, catching her husband's grim expression just before he forked more kipper into his mouth.

"Surely I'll only embarrass you further by going out into Society," Ellie remarked, reaching for the butter. "You know how I am."

"What you need is a respectable husband." Charlotte lowered her voice. "And you won't find one unless you go out to respectable parties."

"Dear Charlotte, I know you mean well, but truly I don't want a husband. I'd rather get a little dog for companionship. Much easier to train. If he tries to wander off, I can simply scoop him up and keep him under my arm." After all her failed engagements, she expected her family to understand by now how unsuited her temperament was to the institution of marriage. But still they persisted in this idea that she could be tamed.

"It doesn't matter what you want. It's what you need."

What you all need for me, Ellie thought as she buttered her blackened toast and wondered why, wherever she stayed, her toast was always burnt to a cinder. Probably because the staff were busy gossiping about her. At times like these, she especially missed the duke, with whom she might have shared a good chuckle about the toast.

It seems Beelzebub had his way with the bread, Ellie, the duke might have remarked. *As he shall have it with me in time.*

"Papa insists that Amelia and I help you find a husband before this Season is over," Charlotte babbled onward under her breath, squeaking like a frantic mouse trapped in a biscuit jar. "He says at your age there's no excuse not to be married, and it's very awkward for him to explain to friends why you are not."

Ellie's stepfather worried about the embarrassment she caused him, but he never gave a thought to the trouble he made for her as she struggled to pay his bills every month, supplementing his stretched Navy pension with her winnings as the count. She wondered where the admiral thought the money came from. He never asked, probably preferring not to know. She'd hoped now that Charlotte and Amelia were married, their husbands might be able to contribute something to the admiral's upkeep, but subtle hints had so far gone unheard. Ostrichlike, her half sisters stuck their heads in sand, just as their father did. Charlotte practiced this denial so thoroughly that she'd become enviably skilled. So far that morning she had not asked a single question about Ellie's strange arrival on her doorstep in the small hours. Even roused from her bed while it was still dark out, Charlotte had kept her composure and her curiosity in check, shepherded her sister to a bedroom, and organized a fire as if this sort of thing happened every day. Ellie, knowing her sister must be bursting to ask who brought her to the house at such an uncivilized hour, had already prepared a gruesome tale of being kidnapped and manhandled by highway robbers. She was naturally disappointed not to have the chance to tell it.

"I suppose," she said with a hefty sigh that blew toast crumbs across the cloth, "what I need is a very rich husband, on his death bed, with no other relatives to lay claim to his fortune. A man capable of over-looking my aged state and many sins. A rarity, indeed, I think you must agree."

Charlotte's lips tightened in an angry line. Ellie smothered a snort, aware of her brother-in-law's stern, silent disapproval joining that of his wife's as he glowered at her while wiping his mouth on a napkin. He'd never said more than three words to Ellie in the entire span of their acquaintance, and she knew his wife must have nagged him into letting her stay. She was not the sort of houseguest in which an earl's son could take pride—even if he was only a younger son and had no title of his own. Ellie was a liability. Wherever she went, trouble frequently followed.

And not all of it was even her fault. Not that anyone ever believed her.

Charlotte put down her teacup. "If you do not soon find a husband, Sister, who will look after you as you get old? You must think of these things, for Herbert and I can do only so much, and we will soon have the expense of children to raise. Amelia and her husband have only that small house in Grosvenor Square for now, until his papa dies, and I'm quite sure they haven't room for you. Who else may provide for you in the winter of your years, when we cannot?" Her lips drooped with concern for the aging Ellie's predicament—but probably mostly for her own misfortune in having such a sister. "I think you do not try hard enough. You *can* look pretty with effort, and I daresay some men find dark coloring quite appealing." She patted her own blonde curls with more than a hint of smug satisfaction. "But hair like yours shows the gray much quicker. Time passes, Sister. Mark me, each year will add a half hour to the time spent at your mirror each morning. You must find a man now while you still have some hope, before your looks are utterly gone. If only you were less…less…" Waving her slender hand, she plucked at the air for a word. "Giddy!"

Ellie almost choked on her toast.

"You laugh too much," her sister continued in a fraught whisper, so as not to disturb her husband again. "You always did. It is most off-putting for a gentleman to be laughed at."

"I see." Ellie nodded solemnly. "I shall try not to laugh from now on."

"Be a little more serious, Sister, and for goodness sake, don't argue. Men hate to be argued with."

"I shall take your advice to heart, Charlotte. Thank you."

"Soften your tone of voice, and always let the gentleman know you're listening avidly to anything he says."

"I see now where I went wrong all these years." She could honestly say she rarely listened to any man for more than a minute. Frequently, far less time than that.

"And you will come tonight, for I called in a favor to get you invited, and if you cared at all about my comfort, you'd think of the inconvenience to me. Here I am with a child on the way." Charlotte looked proudly down at herself as if she already saw the swelling that would not appear yet for months. "Don't you think I would rather not be out in Society, either, in this delicate condition? But I put myself to the trouble for your sake."

Ellie winced. "Of course." She had only one more day until she escaped to precious peace and her aunt in Sydney Dovedale. She could put up with it until then, surely.

Her sister was content with her muttered reply, and breakfast resumed in utter silence but for the scraping of Ellie's knife across her brittle, charred toast. Every charcoal crumb rolling from her plate to the tablecloth was observed by the dour gaze of her reluctant host and probably counted as a mark against her. When she pressed a little too hard with her knife and the slice snapped into three pieces, one of which whirled recklessly across the table and landed in his lap, he finally got up and left the dining room without a word. The fierce scowl he gave his wife communicated sufficiently on his behalf.

"Oh...*Ellie!*"

Apologizing to her sister, she scrambled to retrieve the broken pieces of toast and, in the process, banged her head on the table, spilling the tea and letting out a curse that was surely heard in the kitchen below.

Chapter 4

JAMES ENTERED HIS CARRIAGE THAT EVENING IN A hurry and a bad mood. The last thing he expected or wanted to see was the small shape already perched there on his seat, feet dangling and eyes peering out from the shadow of a fur-lined, hooded cape. Behind him the groom waited, a lit faggot raised in one hand. When James moved aside, the dancing light from that breeze-blown flame skipped over a small, pale face staring back at him, fearless. Even, it might be said, pugnacious.

"I'm running away," the creature announced, "to Gretna's Greens."

James sat heavily and reached over with one hand, tugging her hood back to reveal a bright head of copper hair. "It's Green," he corrected. "Gretna Green. Not Gretna's Greens."

"Oh. Are you sure?"

"Positively."

She glowered at him as if he might lie to her deliberately.

"And you, Lady Mercy Danforthe, are going directly home to your brother."

"We could be married there at Gretna's Greens."

"If you were not young enough to be my daughter," he murmured wryly. "And more irritating than a nest of ants at a picnic. Now kindly remove yourself from my carriage, young lady."

"But it's dark out. How will I get home?"

"The same way you came."

She swung her booted feet, knocking her toes on the side panel of his carriage. "I sent my maid home already. I told her she needn't stay."

If he wasn't mistaken, she had cake crumbs in her hair and strawberry jam smeared on her cheek. She'd at least had the sense to bring refreshments on her otherwise ill-conceived adventure. Opening his door again, he called for Grieves, who was on his way back to the house. The valet swiveled around on his heel and returned to the carriage. "See to it that Lady Mercy is safely delivered to the Earl of Everscham immediately. And tell him we would be grateful if he kept a closer eye on his little sister in the future. Failing that, manacles."

"Mr. James Hartley, you're being most unreasonable," the obstinate chit exclaimed.

"Yes, I know. I'm good at it."

She widened her eyes and squeezed out a tear that gleamed in the light of the groom's torch. "And terribly cruel."

"See? I can't imagine why you'd want to waste your time with a man like me. Off you go." He scooped her up under the arms and swung her carefully down the carriage step. As her boots touched the cobbles, Grieves solemnly took her by the scruff of the neck, held her at arm's length, and steered her toward the house.

James tapped on the roof of the carriage, and it jerked forward at once. He sat back, grimly considering his misfortune in attracting the notice of that copper-headed imp. No wonder her brother, the earl, called her The Bad Penny. Perhaps he kept sending her off, hoping she wouldn't come back. Inheriting his title at a young age, being only just one and twenty himself, Carver Danforthe was far more interested in his own entertainments than he was in keeping watch over his troublesome sibling.

James was certain that if she were *his* little sister, she wouldn't be running about the streets of London at night and writing love letters with excessive use of hearts instead of dots above the letter "i." Neither would she throw herself at disreputable rakes like him. Someone should warn her about men like James Hartley. Indeed, he thought sternly, once he had daughters, they wouldn't be allowed out of the house until they were twenty, and then only in his company. No one knew the dangers that lay in wait quite so well as he did, of course.

❧

James stood with his shoulder propped against the door frame and scanned the tightly packed drawing room, discarding faces with contemptuous haste, searching for only one in particular—the woman he knew to be the count de Bonneville's mistress. His link to the missing necklace.

Ah. There she was.

His relieved gaze settled on a dark head of carelessly tumbled curls. A warm blush of candlelight accentuated a high bosom and the arch of a slender neck. He'd know those curls anywhere, and that throaty, mischievous laugh he felt all the way to the soles of his feet. A laugh that was usually at his expense.

Mariella Vyne.

He thought he'd heard her laughter within minutes of his arrival. Lady Clegg-Foster's standards must have fallen, or else the old dear was desperate to enliven her usual dull party with a few stray fireworks. Then he recalled that both Ellie Vyne's half sisters had recently married very well—to a baronet and the younger son of an earl, if he remembered correctly—thereby raising their status. His grandmother had read the marriage announcements out to him over breakfast one morning during her last visit to his London house, and commented with scorn on the ambitious conniving of certain desperate women. *Half breeds* as she disdainfully referred to the daughters of Admiral Vyne and his—oh, the word itself caused her to tip sideways in her chair as if the room spun—*American* wife.

Tonight the scandalous eldest sister chatted amiably to a potted palm. James quirked a bemused eyebrow. The potted palm, of course, couldn't answer her back. That explained it. She'd probably chat away to him too, in that pleasant manner, if he had no means to reply. As it was, they could never have a conversation without a quarrel.

Mariella Vyne was left unguarded for too many years, got away with too much. Now she'd entangled herself with the count, a man to further ruin her reputation. If there was anything left for salvage. How many times had she been engaged, exactly? No matter. She'd taken none of her fiancés seriously. One might imagine she caused scandal with her behavior merely to put the men off and get out of marriage. These days her reputation for being difficult was well known, and despite those tempting curves, most sensible men kept their distance. After all, her provenance was distinctly foggy. Nothing was known of her real father, and her widowed mother, plucked from the waves of the Atlantic by Admiral Vyne, had come to England with little more than the clothes on her back. Ellie was born seven months later and adopted by the admiral when he married her mother. After such an uncertain beginning, it was perhaps only natural that her life since should be full of ups and downs as violent as the waves from which her mother was once rescued. Only the elderly, widowed Duke of Ardleigh had the bravery to take her on recently, and then look what happened. The poor fellow died of a heart attack. In bed.

Where else? James carefully eyed the woman in the deceptively innocent white gown, measuring every treacherous curve. *Nurse companion* indeed! Everyone knew what that meant.

Now James had caught her in the count's bed—witnessed her brazen, unapologetic behavior with his own two eyes.

Unequal standards indeed! There were rules in this world, and women must follow them. At her age, she ought to know that. Clearly she hadn't yet reached her maturing moment of clarity. The way he had.

He imagined his grandmother's voice in his ear:

Look at her! Lurking in wait behind those leaves, ready to leap out on some unsuspecting fellow. That girl is completely without direction or guidance. Mark my words, she'll come to a bad end.

His grandmother would urge him to stay well away, and he would do that too, if not for his diamonds. They were, he reassured himself, the only reason he planned to approach her tonight. What other reason could there be to seek her out?

Apparently her lover, the count, left her untended, but he couldn't be far away. No man meaning to keep Ellie Vyne to himself should let her out of his sight for long. One never knew what she might do next. This was a woman who, ten years ago, loudly convulsed with laughter in the presence of the Prince Regent when the royal backside abruptly lost contact with a saddle and tumbled to the grass in the midst of an impromptu horse race. Not even the prince's indignant fury and the incredulous glances of other onlookers had silenced her laughter, only increased it. The incident spelled the end of her chance of becoming a royal favorite and also closed many doors socially. Despite this, she was a woman who attacked life with a restless enthusiasm that, according to James's grandmother, should have been safely exhausted in the decoration of bonnets and the sewing of petticoats or embroidered screens.

"A young lady's fingers," his grandmother commented sharply whenever anyone mentioned Mariella Vyne and her sins, "even those of an American, could not make quite so much mischief were they better occupied with a needle."

Personally, James felt it was a mistake to give Ellie Vyne anything sharp.

Tonight most of the female guests snubbed her, and she looked as if she longed to be anywhere else. A few years ago she would have danced every dance, showing a grievous amount of ankle and bouncing about the room like an India rubber ball. But tonight she tried merging with the wallpaper. Why?

A few seats to her left, two frosty-faced matrons took no pains to hide their contempt as they critically examined her from head to toe quite openly. Meanwhile, she squeezed behind the potted palm, almost knocking it over. Another lady joined the two seated and began whispering behind her fan, but in such an obvious fashion that the only mystery remaining was the whereabouts of her manners. A light pink flush stained Miss Vyne's cheeks, although she kept a merry smile on her face, and her eyes turned away from the gossiping harpies as if she hadn't seen and couldn't hear them. James frowned.

Young Robert Clegg-Foster made an ambitious beeline toward her from across the room, halted only by his mama, who suddenly wanted his ear for some reason.

Uh, oh. Better take the plunge or miss his opportunity.

James straightened his shoulders and took a deep breath. Time to get his diamonds back.

And try not to think about her damned legs.

But with only three steps across the room he was intercepted. "James, darling!"

He could scarce believe that Ophelia Southwold

dared approach him this evening, but she was, it became quickly apparent, tipsy. He recognized the glazed eyes and heightened color.

"James, I hope you don't blame me about the necklace. I swear the count boldly removed it without my notice. I tried to see you this morning, but your stupid valet said you were indisposed."

His way blocked, he stopped and looked down at her. Although his first instinct was to take the woman by the arms, lift her aside, and ignore her, twenty years of flirting with pretty women, charming them out of their drawers with the finesse of a magician pulling doves out of his turban, was too deeply ingrained. Tonight he went through the motions again. A slow smile, a tilt of his head, a partial lowering of his eyelids as he gave her gown a careful, appreciative perusal. "Ophelia—dear—can we discuss this later? I'm in rather a hurry."

"But, James, darling—" she draped her hand over his sleeve—"what can be more important than me?"

There was only one way out. "I'm afraid I'm going to be sick. Too much punch."

At once she drew back. "Oh!" Success. Now she made no more attempt to waylay him, but sent him on his way with a poke of her fan in his back.

✺

Ellie was ten when she drew an elaborately curled ink moustache on a sleeping James Hartley's face. Seventeen years later, she knew he still remembered the incident, particularly the humiliation of walking around for a full day with no one mentioning his strange appearance. Such a crime, to a man of his sizeable vanity, was unforgivable. Even worse than that, she was a Vyne. Since her disreputable stepuncle once ran off with James's mother, for an adulterous affair that caused the scandal of the century, Hartleys did not speak to Vynes or even acknowledge their existence if it could be helped. And vice versa. The feud was fiercely adhered to on either side. Therefore, seventeen years ago, young Ellie, with her mischievous pen and ink, had upset her adoptive family just as much as his.

She'd been urged, many times, to stay away from James Hartley, and suspected he was warned the same about her. All good advice and possibly well intentioned. Now to be summarily dismissed. Again. They just couldn't seem to stay away from each other. She watched his approach in her peripheral vision.

Standing beside the potted palm, she'd just begun to get that chilling sensation again, of being followed and spied upon. It must be the effect of Hartley's blue gaze on her shoulders, she decided, and shrugged it off quickly.

He thrust his way through the crowd, bumped into her with one hard shoulder, expelled a tired breath, and grumbled in her general direction, "Are you dancing?"

Spilled wine stained her borrowed evening gloves and seeped through to her skin. She looked up and immediately felt the familiar shiver of annoyance. It was quite disgusting that one man should have so much in his favor—all of it wasted.

Ellie Vyne or Ellie Phant? She heard those mocking words again in her mind as if he'd just uttered them aloud. Even the laughter still echoed around her head as it did all those years ago.

"Do I look as if I'm dancing?" she snapped.

"Do you intend to?"

"I made no plans one way or the other."

He smiled thinly. "Perhaps you can decide now."

"Why do you want to know my plans?" She fluttered her lashes in feigned ignorance. "What interest can they be to you?"

A heavier sigh squeezed out between his lips. "You know very well, Vyne, that I am asking you to dance."

"With whom?"

"With me."

"Well, you might have said. It's quite simple, but you always have to complicate things. In your tiresome, arrogant English way I suppose you assumed I was waiting in absolute desperation for you to ask." Although she was born in England, Ellie considered that purely an accident. She liked to think of herself as an American, like her mother.

"I don't intend to stand here arguing with you for another five minutes, Vyne."

Not waiting for her reply, James swiftly removed the empty glass from her hand, gave it to a passing footman, and gestured with a stiff bow of his towering form, for her to exit the room and join the line of couples currently gathered in the hall, where lack of furniture made it more suitable for dancing.

"I can't," she said, feeling hot, anxiously watching the security of her empty glass moving away.

"What's the matter with you? What have you done now?"

"It's not me. It's the dress." Her sister's maid had done her best with the gown but, just a few moments ago, an entire seam of hasty stitches had snapped apart under her sleeve and down the side of her bosom. This required Ellie to keep her arm rigidly clasped to her side or else expose her chemise and corset to the room at large. Added to that, she'd accidentally sat in a dish of trifle half an hour ago, and that left a stain in a very unfortunate place. She was doing her best to hide and not move very much. Her sisters had disappeared, abandoning her soon after they all arrived at the party, but she'd been hoping one of them would come to find her so she could explain her predicament and leave.

Instead, James came along and suddenly, after all these years, wanted to dance with her.

His quizzical gaze now assessed the front of her gown.

With a low groan she lifted her arm to show the tear. His eyebrows arched high.

"And…" She turned, showing him the trifle stain that marked her sister's lovely, white muslin frock.

James considered her decrepit state with all due solemnity.

"So you see," she said, "I can't dance with you." For some reason she was close to weeping. It was most unlike her, and she had no excuse for it.

"I can assure you, Vyne, I've danced with women in far worse states. Is that the best you can do to get out of it? I always imagined you'd have far more intricate and nonsensical excuses at the ready to turn me down."

The idea that he might ever have considered asking

her to dance before could not have occurred to Ellie. Not in a thousand years.

He held out his arm. "I'm not going away, so you may as well dance with me. It'll be over with before you know it."

"That's what they say before they pull teeth." Still, she hesitated, feeling every eye upon her already— everyone waiting to scorn something about her. Sometimes she was able to overcome her self-conscious fears; sometimes, like tonight, when fate seemed determined to work against her, Ellie's courage failed.

"Do you really care what they think, Vyne? I thought you were braver than that."

"That's easy for you to say, Hartley. You haven't got trifle on your behind."

"Aha! But I have had an ink moustache, thanks to you." His eyes were very blue in the candlelight. "So this will make us even."

Even? Apparently he chose to forget the insults he'd once thrown her way so casually over his shoulder. They were a long way from even.

But he tempted her now with dancing, and Ellie loved to dance. So far—before the rip and the stain occurred—she had enjoyed only two partners that evening: a boy with pimples, a grievous squint, and two left feet; and an elderly, highly inebriated gentleman, who seemed to have a great deal more than the requisite two hands and whose breath entered a room half an hour before he did. Now she could relish the shallow, sinful pleasure of a hand-some partner—even if he was arrogant as the day was long—and enjoy the envious glances of those other women, for in their fevered minds, her stock rose the moment this rake noticed her.

Countless hordes of young, hopeful ladies crammed themselves into parties like this one, just to fling themselves at James. For many, his wicked reputation, while it should have been a warning, was merely incitement. Naïve girls thought they could take him in hand, make him change his ways. They saw James Hartley as a challenge. Ellie blamed it on romantic novels.

"Let them all look," he whispered. "Now they'll have something worthwhile to talk about for once." He gave Ellie a brief smile that further surprised her. "You might even start a new fashion."

She made up her mind to be bold. If James Hartley didn't care that her gown was torn and she had custard on her rear, why should she?

As they joined the other couples, there were no words immediately exchanged. She'd let him speak first. In Ellie's experience, there was never anything very enlightening to be learned from a gentleman's conversation while dancing. Subjects were limited to the weather, the state of the roads, or any other inane topic regarded as harmless, not likely to offend, but guaranteed to bore her stockings rigid. However, she had promised Charlotte to listen this time.

Speaking of her sisters…her gaze casually moved over the guests and settled on their astonished, anxious faces staring at her from the drawing-room doorway. Their ringlets twitched violently. She thought she just made out the words *Typical* and *Will she never learn?* formed by the peevish arch and snap of her sisters' lips. They even tried signaling to her with frantic little flips of a fan, gestures more appropriate for an errant child or a naughty puppy. They wanted her to put James Hartley down, stop playing with him at once, and come to heel. As if she'd just dug him up out of the garden and dragged him inside.

She smiled at them. It was their idea to make her attend this party, when all she'd wanted was to stay in and watch her "middle-aged" bosom continue to expand.

But then her gaze wandered away from her sisters and tripped clumsily over another familiar face in the crush of dancing couples.

Oh, Lord! There was Walter Winthorne, who had the dubious honor of being her very first fiancé. Now wedded to another, he usually avoided Ellie, with a sympathetic, condescending manner that suggested it was for her own health. She sometimes wondered if he feared she might attempt bodily harm to herself with an oyster fork simply because he switched his affections to another woman nine years ago. Tonight, when he saw her dancing with James Hartley, a glimmer of surprise then irritation passed quickly over his broad, flat face. Ellie never considered herself a spiteful creature, but that falter in his self-satisfied countenance was rather gratifying. She was only human, after all.

Further sneaky and gleeful inspection revealed that Winthorne had grown quite fat, and not in the pleasing, jolly way of a man settled and enjoying life. He carried it very ill. There was a definite sagging of the jowls, produced no doubt by the wear and tear of married life. His shoulders were dreadfully hunched.

Oops, now she'd missed her steps.

Her partner winced when she stepped hard on his

toes. At last, his somber perusal of the other guests interrupted, James addressed her again. "Your lover has disappeared from London, it seems. Have you done away with him out of jealousy, because of his flirtation with Lady Southwold?"

Her dark sense of humor was piqued. So that was why he was being nice to her. He meant to pry for information about the count and get his diamonds back. "How did I dispose of my lover? What is your theory? Do tell."

"Knowing you, it's more than likely you turned him into a toad."

She knew he would have her arrested in an instant if he discovered the truth—that she'd masqueraded as a man, lied her way into gaming clubs in Brighton and Bath, as well as here in London, and cheated with sleight of hand she learned when she was only six from her stepuncle, Lieutenant Graedon Vyne, who always said she had a natural talent for it.

"Where has he gone, Vyne? You may as well tell me where the thief hides with his loot."

"Thief?" she exclaimed. "Did the count remove those diamonds from your mistress with his own hands?"

James gave no reply.

She watched his jaw grinding. "Are you certain this isn't just about Lady Southwold?"

He lifted one shoulder in a lazy shrug. "Lady Southwold was a pleasant diversion for a short while. Women come and go. I've learned better than to expect honesty or faithfulness from any."

Ellie was astounded by his candor. Although his tone was casual, his eyes were cooled by sadness. "Yet you gave her those diamonds?"

He grimaced. "I was in a generous mood."

"You mean you were pickled." She curbed her smile, catching again the wistful shadow in his blue eyes.

James Hartley was looking at her like a dejected pup in need of a home. Is this how he drew women into his web? She carefully studied his waistcoat rather than look into his eyes again. Other women might be fooled into sympathizing with the wretched man, but she knew better. With all his advantages in life, he didn't need her empathy. He tried playing her for a fool, as he did all those other dizzy-brained hussies who chased after him. Well, they might not know what he was about, but she knew. She was no—

Uh, oh.

His strong fingers were now holding hers too tightly. He didn't appear to be drunk again, but he was certainly gripping on to her as if she was a life raft on a stormy sea.

Yet, it was strangely comfortable dancing with the enemy, even with a torn frock and custard on her posterior. The sad state of her gown no longer mattered now that the handsomest rake in the room had given his seal of approval, and Ellie was vexed to find herself depressingly shallow, after all. As a woman whose only passable looks were late in blooming, she should have had more sense.

For the next few bars of music, they were separated as they joined with another couple in the dance. She was aware again of her sisters watching. Oh, dear. She made her eyes wide, imploring their sympathy, raising her shoulders in a hapless gesture. *What choice did I have?* she would say later. *He forced me into it.* When he snatched her drink away, what else did she have to do with herself? To refuse at that point would be churlish and cause an even bigger scene.

His hand gripped hers again, and they were reunited.

"Stop distracting me, Vyne," he growled. "The count. Tell me where he is."

Wondering what she'd done to be accused of "distracting" him, Ellie answered pertly and for once, truthfully. "I keep him in a hat box."

He sighed. "If I don't get those diamonds back from him, I'll extract their value from you."

"Just how do you propose to do that?"

"I have a few ideas."

"I'm intrigued!"

"You should be." His index finger moved, curled under her palm, and then straightened again.

Was he *flirting* with her? It seemed too incredible to believe. Ellie decided to ignore the artful caress of his finger and instead raised her defenses. "You have more than one idea? Do be careful, Hartley. A gentleman's brain must be treated gently and never overburdened. It gets so little exercise. We don't want it strained."

There was another pause while they merged with a neighboring couple, and then as he returned within her hearing, he snapped out, "I suppose the count fed you that pretty line about escaping *Madame Guillotine* as a babe and drifting all the way to Dover in a barrel. Or was it his nurse's trunk? I'm surprised that you, of all people, fell for that story. The Brothers Grimm could tell a more convincing tale."

She cocked her head and smiled coyly up at him for the sake of all those who watched and could not hear their conversation. "If I cared at all for your opinion, Hartley, I daresay I'd ask for it. But since I did not, I suggest you save your breath. You never know when you might need it to say something actually worthwhile and meaningful. It could happen. Even to a Hartley."

The dance was coming to an end, but a set contained two dances, and he was not yet done with her. Horrified, she realized the next dance was a daring waltz. James clutched her gloved fingers again in his viselike grip and laid his other hand firmly against her waist, giving her no choice but to place her left hand on his right shoulder. There was nothing between them but an indecently few inches of air. Somewhere behind her she heard her sisters' muffled cries of alarm and agitation. They wanted her to find a husband, but James Hartley was not suitable marriage material. In their eyes, she wasted valuable time dancing with that rake. She might, after all, sprout her first gray hair in the next few hours. The inevitable crow's-feet could almost be heard, creaking across her face.

But here she was, dancing with the enemy.

Lost in thought, she studied his familiar, despicably handsome features. How did he get that bruise around his eye? What had he been up to? He could get himself hurt worse than he had been already. He ought to leave London Society for a while. Breathe some fresh air for a change. Not that it should matter to her. He never welcomed her advice, any more than she welcomed his. In so many ways, they were too alike.

"What now?" he demanded as he glared down at her. "I can almost hear the cogwheels of your mind turning, Vyne. What do you have up your sleeve for me next? What more degradation must I suffer at your hands?"

Ellie quickly lowered her gaze. Even if he had rescued her from a wallflower's fate this evening, his rudderless misadventures should really be of no interest to her at all. She studied his waistcoat again and composed her thoughts and, more importantly, her fast-beating heart.

A shrill woman's voice abruptly intruded. "James! Feeling better, I see."

There was no mistaking the tone of anger, the sharp, cutting edge of barely concealed claws. Ellie daren't turn her head, for she knew the voice. Only the night before, she'd taken an ugly necklace from that woman in a game of cards. If Ophelia Southwold should recognize her, the ruse would be over.

"Thank you," she heard James reply. "Much better. Now."

"So I see!"

Even as they spun around in the waltz, Ellie kept her head turned. He must have noticed her pushing to keep her back to the other woman. "Is there something wrong with your neck, Vyne?"

"Just a slight crick," she murmured.

Had she known those diamonds were his, she would never have accepted them from Lady Southwold, no matter how big the hole in her stepfather's roof. She should have returned the necklace to James when he followed her to that inn, but her pride got in the way, combined with a considerable helping of mischief. She could almost hear Charlotte's voice again: *Oh, Ellie!*

As usual, when anxious and annoyed with herself, she sought someone else to blame. "I hope this incident with the diamonds has taught you a lesson, Hartley. Treat the family jewels with greater care, and stop loaning them to women who will do you absolutely no good whatsoever."

"And how do *you* know what's good for me and my *family jewels*?"

"I'm afraid we've become too familiar with each other." She stole a timid glance upward.

"Hmm." A curiously uncertain smile played over his lips. "Like a bad habit we can't quite give up."

She made the mistake of looking all the way up into his eyes again and instantly regretted it. Although she'd never before been the target of his patented charm, she'd seen him in action many times, watched him make women melt in a puddle, which he then stepped over as soon as their company no longer amused him. She knew all the stages of his well-honed flirtation, although it felt different being the mark this time instead of a detached observer. She was very glad their dance must soon be over.

But then he went and said, "Wretched woman, you really ought to marry me. Better the devil we know."

Chapter 5

SHE RESPONDED AS IF HE'D JUST PINCHED HER BEHIND. "Don't be ridiculous. What a perfectly atrocious idea."

"Somebody ought to make an honest woman of you."

"Have you gnawed through your restraints, Hartley? I heard the wardens at the asylum are searching for a lost inmate."

"My grandmother assures me it's time I married. As for you, Vyne—you're getting on in years and clearly in need of discipline that only a husband can give you."

"And how would a husband do that?"

He cleared his throat but not far enough. His next words came out in a low growl. "Deliver a damn good spanking."

He thought about her legs again and how the warm curve of her satiny bottom might feel against the palm of his hand while the soft curls of her womanhood pressed against his hard, tense thigh muscle as he held her down in his lap for a long-overdue spanking. That would shock the smug look off her face. He liked the idea of shocking Ellie Vyne. He sensed that she was not often shocked, and she should be. Frequently, if he had his way.

"So I'm the best choice you could come up with?" she exclaimed. "Are you that desperate?"

"For your information, Vyne, I receive proposals often."

"Of marriage? Or for you to go and boil your head?"

"Just this very evening, I had a very determined young lady attempt to stow away in my carriage, intent on forcing me to Gretna Green, where she doubtless had very sinister things in mind for me."

She laughed, a sultry sound that shook him all the way to his toes again. He ought to be used to it by now, but somehow he was never ready for the effect it had on him. Each time he heard it was like the first. "You missed your chance with her, then. I wouldn't go to Gretna Green with you. Not for all the tea in China."

"But your younger sisters are both married before you," he persisted. "Surely you're anxious to wed before it's too late."

Her eyes sparkled with a sudden blaze of wildfire. "Too late for what? I'm younger than you, Hartley. Ten years younger. Too late, indeed!" If he wasn't very much mistaken, his words had hit a soft spot. Interesting.

"Men can wait," he said. "Women have a limited number of years before they lose their bloom. Not saying you ever had any. On a bad day, when in one of your abysmal sulks, you look like the very devil."

She scowled, instantly proving him right about both his statement and his previous guess.

"And with your scandalous behavior, who else

would have you?" he added, firm-lipped, struggling not to laugh at her expression. "I, of course, am accustomed to the sharp cuts of your tongue. There is no part of me you've yet to wound. That makes me immune."

"*Me* wound *you*?"

"Of course. Do you deny—?"

"I don't want to marry," she snapped. "I like my life the way it is, unfettered. I can't imagine making room for a man now."

"What about the count? Do you make no room for him?"

A quick little swallow fluttered in her slender neck. "He is free to come and go as he pleases. As am I. A husband is a permanent inconvenience. I'd much rather see a man occasionally, when he's in a good mood. Then, if he's sick with a cold and miserable, I can send him home again with a friendly word of caution to stay away from drafts, and he is no longer my responsibility."

She had a sharply satirical eye, and if he wasn't very much mistaken, that was a wry curve pulling on the left corner of her mouth. She kept winding it back again, determined to be cross with him, but the half smile was equally determined to unwind, darkly entertained at his expense. He'd meant only to tease her with his abrupt proposal of marriage, knowing how she had an aversion to longer attachments—that string of brief engagements, entered into and abandoned with equal haste, was evidence enough. But now that he'd begun to discuss the thought aloud with her, it actually began to seem…feasible.

Perhaps it was the heat of the room, the

headiness of her perfume, the mischief in her funny half smile.

Hmmm. Her smile. He'd seen it many times over the term of their unfortunate acquaintance, but there was something about it tonight. Something that poked an insistent finger at his memory.

She had very nice lips. They were the sort of lips that kept a man looking at them, wondering how they tasted.

"There are at least half-a-dozen women here tonight far more suitable than me," those naughty lips assured him firmly.

"Oh?"

"Lady Southwold. Was that not she just now?"

"Yes, it was she, and no, I'm not going to marry her."

"Why not?"

"You said yourself that she's a faithless hussy. Making overtures to your lover. Is that not what you told me?"

Her lashes lifted, and he basked in the warmth of her gaze again. "Yes."

"Then she's not right for me." He let his hand slide a half inch lower down her spine. If she noticed, she kept it to herself. He spread his fingers over the butter-soft muslin, already feeling a sense of possessiveness. In all the years of their acquaintance, he didn't recall her eyes being that color. Where had she kept those eyes all these years? Had she stashed them away deliberately?

Eventually she tore their beauty away and surveyed the room over his shoulder. "That woman, over there by the punch bowl. Miss Clarke, I believe is her name. Have you met her?"

"No." He hadn't even looked, too busy trying to think, searching his memory. What were those lips and eyes trying to tell him that she was not saying?

"I hear she's a very good sort and would never give you any trouble."

He finally followed her gaze. "Too tall and thin. And nervous."

"Nervous? If you've never met her, how can you possibly—?"

"She plucks her eyebrows almost out of existence, and her clavicle is so evident I can only assume that if she eats at all, food never has a chance to cling to her bones."

She sighed. "And there is the very pretty Miss Wilson, talking to her mama. There, by the plinth with the large Grecian urn."

"Grecian urn? Is that what it is? I thought it was some sort of coffeepot."

"Pay attention, Hartley! The young lady beside it…"

"*Plinth*," he muttered. "Isn't that a splendid word? Plinth."

"James Hartley, we are talking about Miss Jane Wilson."

He swept her around in a tight turn. "Her feet are too big. And she lisps."

"Well then, what about Lady Clegg-Foster's daughter? I can't recall her name, but she's a dainty thing and sings like a lark, so I'm told."

He'd make Ellie Vyne's lips sing too, he thought, given half a chance. "The young lady's name is Rosalind. She chews her fingers."

"You mean her fingernails."

"No. She chews her fingers. I've seen the scars.

God only knows what she'd do to a husband once she runs out of digits." He grinned.

She was still determined not to give him a full smile, it seemed. "Lady Aynsbury's niece in the yellow dress?"

"Doesn't like dogs or horses."

"Miss Walters, with the feathers in her hair?"

"Eats with her mouth open."

"Miss Gordon. Now what can you possibly find amiss with that sweet little thing?"

"She's too little. And too sweet."

She gasped irritably. "And you're too fussy!"

"I'm not surprised you've had so many broken engagements, Vyne, if you choose your men with the same carelessness as you expect me to find a wife."

Of course he knew she had questionable taste. A bolt of anger struck him viciously, even in the midst of their lively conversation. He couldn't imagine what drew her to that rogue Bonneville, but then the man's appeal was, in general, lost on him. He'd seen the fellow only from a distance and noted a prettily attired coxcomb with too many frills on his shirt, a small nose, and inadequate chin. The count had garnered quite a following in Bath last year, and in London, with admirers from both sexes. Since Beau Brummell fled to Calais, escaping his debts, the brainless sheep needed someone new to follow. But the Vyne woman, who possessed more than a sixpenny's worth of wit, had always struck James as the sort to be unimpressed by a satin-clad milksop.

That gown showed far too much bosom.

It kept interrupting his damned thoughts. Those sweet handfuls, heaving gently with every inhale, lured his imagination through a dangerous realm. He supposed it was deliberate, so she could then feign affront and reprimand him for looking. Women were devious that way. Men were mere pawns in their machinations, Grieves would remind him.

"There are fifteen," she said suddenly.

Dazed, he moved his eyes back to her face. "Hmmm?"

"There are fifteen miniature silk-ribbon rosebuds sewn around my décolletage, Hartley. I see you are interested in their number, as you've studied them pointedly for the past few minutes. You really are intent on creating a scandal tonight."

Of course, they caused a goodly amount of consternation just by dancing together—the Duke of Ardleigh's former mistress, an outspoken woman with a reputation for insulting royalty and countless broken engagements, and the man who was rumored to keep a different bedmate every night of the week. They were, in the eyes of the world, two notorious characters with little hope of redemption.

They were also two people who didn't have to pretend for each other. She knew all his worst traits, and he knew all hers. Their badinage had become routine over the years. Like toast soldiers for his boiled egg.

"There should be sixteen rosebuds," she added pensively, "but one tumbled off in my sister's carriage on the way here. My fault, because I'd been toying with a loose thread for want of anything else to do with my fingers."

Hmmm. Something to bear in mind. Keep her fingers occupied.

"It was too dark to see where it landed when it fell off, and I had no needle to sew it back on with in any case. I'm sure you noticed the hanging thread, Hartley."

He had not actually noticed a missing rosebud, but now she mentioned it, he had to look and count them again. His gaze lingered over her full curves. And the enticing way they rose and fell.

"I don't know how other ladies manage to keep their gowns so well preserved," she muttered. "By the end of the evening, I am often fortunate to have all my hooks still in place, and there is always, without a doubt, more than one stain."

James gravely shook his head. "Someone, Vyne, ought to watch over you."

"I daresay. But who could possibly handle the task?"

He surreptitiously moved her closer, taking even firmer possession of her waist. "Me."

"You, Hartley?" He felt the laughter trembling through her body. "It would be quite a shock to see you devoting your energies and time to something worthwhile for a change, I suppose."

"Meaning?"

"It appears you have an excess of free hours in your day and evening, which, although to be expected for a gentleman of your class, only leads to trouble. After a certain number of years passing in the same fashion, it must become altogether wearisome for a person with most of their senses and four solid limbs in their possession. I've always paused with admiration and wondered how you manage to do it—nothing all day, that is."

She was unaware, naturally, of his strive to change. Tempting as it was to set her straight, he chose not to. The new, improved James Hartley was still a work in progress. He was not ready yet for this sharp-tongued hussy to step in and judge. He leaned closer and took a deep breath of her soft perfume. Lilac and...was that almonds?

"Stop doing that," she muttered.

He was making her nervous. Good. "Worried the count might object if he sees us together? Perhaps he'll come out of hiding and challenge me to a duel. If he cares about you at all, of course. You're probably just another conquest to him."

"As any woman is to you."

"Don't believe everything you hear. And don't believe everything the villainous, so-called count tells you. I suppose he's seduced you with flattery to pamper your vanity, and now you imagine you know him well."

"Oh, but I do! He and I have a very close connection. We are almost inseparable."

His mood darkened again. It took him a moment before he could speak. He'd unhappily been witness to many of her relationships with men. They were always casual, short-lived. What made this one so different? "Then where is he tonight?" he managed finally.

"I cannot tell you that. I will never betray him."

Deep violet eyes perused his face. There was a twinkle—good or bad, he could not ascertain. Was she laughing at him again or simply smug about her love affair? A lash of jealousy tore into him like a cat-o'-nine-tails.

He twirled her faster around the hall. "Then I'll keep you for ransom, Vyne," he growled, watching a stray dark curl untwist beside her cheek. "If the count continues to hide from me, I'll take compensation for those diamonds from you." *Keep her dizzy; keep her moving along in my arms, and then she can't escape. She can't leave until I've remembered whatever it is she's trying to hide from me.*

"I thought you said they were priceless. What could I give you to compensate?"

"I'm sure you and I can come to some…arrangement." They were moving too fast, dancing too closely. He didn't care.

Laughing softly, she looked up at him again, and the small pearls in her ears gleamed like tiny moons amid all that rich mahogany hair. "When will you find the time? Surely your week is fully booked with similar *arrangements*."

Naturally she believed all the lies, every bad thing ever uttered about him. She'd do that superior thing in a minute with her lips.

He stared at her earring and then at her mouth again. For a moment, it felt as if they'd stopped dancing and the room moved around them, spinning by at a breathless pace. As if he was drunk.

Brighton.

But how could it be…?

He stared. Her lips still moved as she mocked him with her usual flair, but he couldn't hear a word, because his heart was beating too loudly in his ears.

Perhaps it wasn't her. He clutched at this faint hope, but then she raised her lashes again, and the secretive gleam in her eyes was all too familiar. Touching his soul, stirring his blood.

Found you!

Wretched woman! How dare she do this to him? That it should be her—his nemesis—of all people.

With massive effort he made his voice calm, steady. "I don't suppose you'd believe me if I told you I mean to reform my old ways."

Her eyes sparkled with more merriment. She was enjoying their scandalous dance, obviously, although she would never admit it.

"You are amused, Vyne, by the idea of my reformation?"

"Should a reformed rake manhandle a woman in this fashion and dance obscenely close?"

"With one woman, he might. The one woman for whom he is willing to give up all the others."

She looked away at the passing dancers. "Well, I suppose pleasing so many ladies at once must become tiring at your age, Hartley. But I have faith in you"—she patted his shoulder—"not to let them down."

It seemed hopeless. She never listened. Therefore he'd simply have to show her. "I've decided to concentrate all my efforts on just one, Vyne." Her eyebrow curved upward, and her lips parted, but before she could speak again, he added, "You'll do."

Her mouth snapped shut, but the peace was brief, and when she opened it again, prickles shot out to wound him. "Do you think me any less tiring? You'd best stick with your arrangements, and I'll stick with the count."

Another hot spark quickened to life somewhere deep inside James Hartley, this one a very wanton flame of rebellion long since repressed. Now it was freed and running wild. She'd poked a hole in his carefully erected barriers, somehow, with one of those naughty fingers that, according to his grandmother, needed more ladylike occupations to keep them busy. Fingers that she'd just readily confessed brought her trouble when idle.

Aware they were the focus of almost every eye in the room, he leaned forward and whispered in her ear, "Tell me where the count is tonight, or I'll lure him out with any means at my disposal." She pulled back. He held her tighter. She'd have to cause a scene by struggling harder, if she wanted escape.

But her gloves were too large, and it made her hand slippery, difficult to keep.

"For once take me at my word, Hartley," she exclaimed, breathless. "You'll never find the count, and you'll never flush him out by using me—pretending to flirt with me."

"Well, if you haven't done away with the Frenchie, I can guarantee he won't have gone far."

"What makes you say that?" Her eyes darkened as he leaned over her.

"Because I wouldn't leave you unguarded, madam."

Light danced and spun along the delicate shape of her cheek, reflected by the small pearls hanging from her ears. Overcome with the need to taste her, he lowered his lips until they almost touched the tip of her nose. "And I wouldn't stand by and watch another man do this."

In full view of the other guests, he made up his mind to kiss the enemy, another man's mistress, directly on her quarrelsome lips.

This too, like a spanking, was long overdue.

He could almost taste her lips already. In that moment he completely forgot where he was and the presence of other people. But she, apparently, did not. Pulling her trembling hand from his, she swept away into the crowd, leaving him holding her empty glove. He shouldn't have let her know his intentions, he realized, slightly dazed. One should never give a woman like her any warning.

Chapter 6

SHE STUMBLED THROUGH A CLUSTER OF OPEN-MOUTHED, wide-eyed guests—some pretending very badly that they'd seen nothing untoward—and along a candlelit corridor, until she found a book-lined library. There she took sanctuary and, forgetting about the custard on her gown, dropped to a couch beside the low-burning fire. At once she felt the cold, wet creeping through her clothing and even her drawers. Cursing under her breath, she looked around the room for something to clean up the mess she'd made. There were several cushions, but she was certain the Clegg-Fosters would not take any kindlier to having those stained with trifle than they would to finding their leather couch soiled.

Alas, now she'd better just sit here and not move, because she'd only get herself deeper into trouble. Hopefully her sisters must come looking for her, and she could send one of them for her coat. In the meantime, she waited for her pulse to settle and lamented that lost glove. Charlotte would not be pleased. Those gloves belonged to her, and she'd lent them under strict guidelines only. Like the gown.

An icy-cold draft grasped her by the ankles. A coal dropped in the hearth, and Ellie's pulse skipped a beat. Keeping her head very still, she swung her gaze sideways to a particularly dark corner. She could have sworn there was a movement. A billowing curtain perhaps? Her fingers curled around the fan in her lap. Someone was there, breathing, watching. She'd been followed again.

Ellie couldn't move. Her limbs were frozen, heart stalled.

Something creaked behind her. She closed her eyes tightly and held her breath. Perhaps this spy, whoever he was, knew the double life she'd been leading. Now they'd caught her. The truth would come out. When she was exposed, those who had lost money to the "count" would come braying for blood. She had sunk herself forever and harmed the family she sought to help. *This is what happens when one leads two lives*, she thought in anguish. Sooner or later, those two worlds collided. If she'd only given up the masquerade sooner, quit while she was ahead. But instead, there was always another game, another irresistible mark. It had become a sickness in her, she realized. And as the count, she could get away with a great deal, far more than she ever could as plain—

"Mariella…Miss Vyne…there you are!"

Her eyes flew open, and she exhaled in a rush. It was Walter Winthorne—Captain Winthorne as he was now, she remembered hastily. He came into the dimly lit room, stubbing his feet on furniture but apparently intent on spoiling her solitary reverie without the slightest encouragement.

In the dark corner across the room, all was still. Had she imagined that other presence? Perhaps the curtain had moved in a draft. Yes, that was all. A draft. How stupid she was!

"I am glad to see you looking so well, Miss Vyne," Captain Winthorne blustered as he moved around the couch and into her sight. She supposed he expected her to be pining away on a chaise lounge somewhere, consumptive and incapable of controlling her sobs because he threw her over nine years ago for another woman. Clara Shackleford, of all people. A creature with the density, wit, and conversation of a suet pudding. A very rich suet pudding.

"Captain Winthorne—always a pleasure."

He glanced at the couch beside her, but she did not invite him to sit. Instead, she opened her fan and used it violently, exclaiming at the heat of the party.

"You misplaced your glove."

She looked down as if she'd only just noticed.

"I saw you dancing with Hartley." With one hand, he stroked his coat buttons. They winked in the firelight as they strained to control his flourishing girth.

Dancing? Is that all he saw? What could she be thinking to let James Hartley flirt with her? And what could *he* be thinking to try and kiss her on a crowded dance floor?

Alas, there was Brighton. She couldn't forget it—an impulsive kiss taken from a man who didn't recognize her. The scent of gardenias, a hot summer evening under a velvet, starry sky, and James in the guise of a highwayman. A stolen encounter that had troubled her all these months. She knew kissing him had been a terrible mistake. How could she have done it? What did she hope to gain from it?

Sadly, she knew the answer to that. She'd hoped, in some silly part of her being, that it would be vengeance. That he'd suddenly open his eyes and notice her without instantly seeing whatever was most at fault about her in that moment. Then he'd be sorry he ever ignored her, ever slighted her.

Why, Miss Vyne, you are beautiful! How wrong I was. Can you ever forgive me?

Ha!

She must have been suffering some temporary madness that night in Brighton, because she knew it was impossible to make him feel anything like regret. He was too damned vain, arrogant and, supposedly, still in love with the woman who'd twice jilted him—Ellie's good friend Sophie Valentine.

For at least seventeen years he'd been in love with Sophie. He played with others, sowed his wild oats, but his heart was always held in reserve for that one. The one who ultimately left him for another man, which was exactly what Ellie could have told him would happen, had he ever asked her opinion. As for Ellie, he'd never properly looked at her, never considered her as anything other than a nuisance.

Now he proposed marriage. It was incredible. No doubt he thought it was all very amusing. As indeed it was. Her stomach hurt from laughing.

Still…one day, she supposed, the fool must marry. It was inevitable. He needed an heir. Then, once he had a wife, they could never argue with each other again. Ellie could never again call him a great blithering ass, and he could not remind her that she was the world's most impertinent, flighty, contrary woman.

Nothing would be quite the same without Hartley grumbling at her, she realized. And without her insults to keep his head from becoming too big, his future seemed destined for ever-expanding hats. He would marry a wooden-pated creature too in awe of him to put him in his place. Just as Walter Winthorne did.

Oh yes, Walter...

"I feel it incumbent upon me, in light of our previous association, to remind you, Mariella, that James Hartley is an utter rogue."

She lowered her fan. "In light of our previous association?"

There was no blush of shame, just a wobbling of new-grown jowls, a subtle flaring of nostrils as he drew himself up, hands behind his back. She feared one of his shiny buttons might soon give up under the strain, spring free, and take her eye out. "I still feel some responsibility toward you and hate to see you make a terrible mistake."

Another terrible mistake, she mused. Something along the lines of letting a man make love to her before he changed his mind and chose to marry another woman—a sixteen-year-old heiress with no discernible brain?

"Never fear, Captain. Any mistake will be my own to make. They always are. I am not the sort to blame anyone else, whatever happens."

He stared at her, fat lower lip jutting out. "Why dance with Hartley? You know how he treats women.

He never has a pleasant thing to say about you. The man's an out-and-out bounder!"

Pot meet kettle.

"I have known you many years, Mariella, and just because I married another does not mean I will stand by and see you ill used." Once, years ago, his eyes were clear and gray; they were now dull, the whites jaundiced, peppered with a pattern of miniature red darts. In youth, he was lively, always active, full of good humor and wit. That was what attracted her to him. Now he moved sluggishly, his neck stiff, his breathing too heavy. "I am surprised at your sisters, allowing you to dance with a rake like Hartley. They are surely anxious to save your reputation before it is irretrievably lost."

"Oops, too late."

"Don't be flippant, Mariella."

Looking up at Captain Winthorne's bloated face while he grumbled about women led astray and the stringent measures required to set them straight again, she felt sick with anger. This was the hypocrite who took her virginity one afternoon in her stepfather's rose garden. He had the audacity then to think it was his for the taking since they were engaged. But within a few weeks, he'd switched his attentions to another woman.

She felt the sharp urge to kick him in the shins and sink her teeth into his kneecaps.

Even better was the second idea. She smiled with anticipation. "But I'm going to marry James Hartley. Did you not know?"

She thought he might explode. His face became very pink and puffy. "Marry? *Him?* Hartley?"

"Oh yes."

"You cannot possibly be in love with him, and he has no regard for you. He's in love with another woman—has been for years. I hear he holds a torch for Sophia Valentine still, even now she has a husband."

This fact thrown in her face was the last straw. "Ah, but there are other important, practical matters to consider in marriage." She stood quickly, fan clasped in both hands. "As you once told me, Walter, one cannot always marry where one loves. One must consider the future and one's financial situation and not be distracted by love."

Nine years ago he recited those words to her, when, having discovered the true state of her step-father's finances, he ended their engagement. Now she tossed them back again. Captain Winthorne didn't know where to look. But he was angry. Veins visibly pulsed in his shiny brow.

Excellent. This previously dull party, where the only being worth conversing with was a potted palm, had turned out to be quite inspirational.

A sudden shout interrupted their conversation. "Vyne! Are you in here?" James Hartley appeared in the library doorway, waving her glove, bellowing her name as if he summoned a hound to heel. "Vyne!"

"*Jim,*" she exclaimed. "You found my glove!" Never had she been so pleased to see that wretched man, and her feelings were in such disarray she hadn't time to hide the sheer relief.

A flicker of uncertainty crossed his face when he saw her eager expression and heard that unlikely tone of welcome. Then as his eyes adjusted to the weak light given out by the smoldering fire in the hob grate, he must have seen Winthorne standing beside her. He was across the room in the next beat of her heart.

"Do you know Captain Winthorne?"

"Of course." He thrust the errant glove at her. "Winthorne. They let you in, did they? Standards *have* dropped it seems."

The captain drew himself up, inflated again with pompous hot air. "What are you up to with this lady?"

"A great many things," James replied. "All extremely scandalous. None of them your business."

Ellie swallowed a chuckle and pressed her lips together. James was a curious mix of naughty little boy and grumpy, pontificating old man, but when his mischievous sense of humor broke its way through the superior starchiness, he was almost tolerable company. For a Hartley. She supposed that playfulness was a part of James that had once drawn her dear friend Sophie to his company. Ellie, being a very insignificant, unworthy person in his eyes, was seldom allowed to witness that side of his nature. Instead, she usually got the disapproving side, the side coached by generations of supercilious Hartleys to look down on anyone less fortunate.

"She tells me she plans to marry you," snapped Winthorne. "It cannot be true."

She? The Cat's Aunt, presumably.

James turned his steady gaze to her. The Cat's Aunt managed a taut smile.

"I fear it is," he muttered thoughtfully. "It seems Miss Vyne…has accepted me."

She was busy winding her recovered glove into a sweaty knot and couldn't quite meet his eye.

"You cannot possibly have Miss Vyne's best interests at heart. It is obvious you have no serious intentions toward her."

"Is it?"

"Don't think to toy with her as you do other women. Despite a wayward temperament and a lack of fatherly supervision, she is not friendless."

Ellie choked on another gulp of laughter and quickly opened her fan again to flutter it wildly before her lips.

Hands behind his back, James tipped forward. "I wonder why you dally here with my fiancée, Winthorne, when your wife seeks you out there. Quite loudly seeks you, in fact. I declare she has shaken all the wax loose in my ears."

Buttons ready to pop, his cheeks crimson, lips trembling, Walter took one last look at Ellie and then stormed out. Heavy footsteps faded away down the corridor.

Now the room was quiet again but for the gentle crackle and spit among the coals in the hearth. James watched her warily, hands still behind his back, clearly waiting for her to speak first.

"He and I were once engaged," she muttered.

"Yes. I know. Another of your mistakes."

"He broke it off when he came to his senses and realized how much trouble I'd be. Much the same discovery as my friend Sophie made before she threw you over."

His left eyebrow—always a somewhat restless creature—lifted high. Ellie looked away again and quietly cursed herself for mentioning that. Oh, why

was her first instinct always to lash out at him? She
didn't mean to cause hurt, and it was deeply regretted
the moment it was done. But she couldn't stop herself
with him. She felt as if she had to attack before he
could do the same to her.

She exhaled wearily, and her shoulders sagged.
"Look at us. We make quite a pair. You with your
black eye and me with trifle on my behind."

"Yes. I suppose I'd better marry you before you
get yourself in another pickle. Or another trifle."
Flickering firelight revealed a sudden, brief grin. She
would have missed it had she not returned her wary
gaze to his face at the exact second it happened. He
winced and touched the bruise under his eye as if it
hurt to smile.

"Don't worry, Hartley. I hereby release you from
the obligation." Surely he hadn't taken it seriously.

"But you just called me *Jim*. No one gets away with
that unscathed."

She began turning away, and then, as she remembered her stained gown, decided to back away instead,
just to save a little of her tattered pride. "I'm returning
to the party."

He took a step after her. "You're not wriggling
out of *this* engagement, Vyne. Not like you did all
the others."

"For pity's sake, I lied about marrying you only
for Winthorne's benefit, and you must know that.
Or has brandy deadened your brain to the point of
utter insensibility?"

"If you go back on your word, I'll sue for breach
of promise."

"I don't know what you can sue me for—sixpence, three sulky hens, and a confused goat is about all my portion can provide."

Before she could back away any farther, he grabbed her bare arm.

"Are you mad, Hartley? Unhand me at once!"

He cupped both her elbows in his hands and drew her against his chest. She stepped on his foot again, but he didn't seem to notice. He did have very large feet and was probably accustomed to having them stepped upon. Ellie was still pondering the outrageous assumptions of James Hartley when his hard lips closed upon hers, and all protests fell away like icicles melting from a roof on a sunny day.

He moved his hands from her arms to her waist and settled her against his body. The heat and strength of his powerful frame was completely overwhelming. His mouth devoured her leisurely. His tongue slipped over hers, winding around it, caressing it. A shudder of excitement vibrated all the way to her toes.

They were alone in the semidark. What did it matter if she let him kiss her? No one was there to see. Tonight he gave her his full attention, and she didn't even have to draw on his face to get it.

Her hands rested on his shoulders and traced the muscles moving under his fine evening clothes. It was brute strength contained by the façade of civilization. At once she withdrew her hands as if they were burned. But then realized there was nowhere else to put them. Nowhere that wouldn't get her into worse trouble. So she returned them to his wide shoulders and tried not to notice the strength flexing under her palms. He moved her closer, her hip pressed against his groin. A pang of reckless desire blossomed within her, opening like a rose, spreading its dewy petals. Her breasts began to ache and swell under her corset. His hands were tight around her waist, his fingers spread, gripping her again as if he feared she might pull away. Instead, she stroked his leg with her own. Between her thighs, in a very warm, vulnerable place, she felt the enormity of this danger with which she flirted, but she couldn't prevent herself. It was the perfect moment. One could get away with all sorts of things in the dark. Just as she could while wearing a mask or a disguise.

Her bare fingertips strayed upward, along his shoulder to his collar, his cravat, and then tentatively touched his jaw. It was smooth-shaven tonight, not like the last time they kissed.

Had she drunk too much wine tonight? No. She'd spilled her only glass when James knocked into her. In Brighton she'd blamed her naughtiness on moonlight and punch. Tonight she could not do the same.

Slowly he relinquished her lips, leaving them warm but suddenly frail, uncertain.

"Well, I must say, that was quite horrid," she snapped. "Don't do it again."

◈

Somewhere inside his skull a herald fanfare rang out. He'd found her! That kiss confirmed it. All these months he'd spent searching for his mystery woman—future wife and mother of his children. And here she was, right under his nose.

Damn her! How could she do that to him and keep running away?

Oh, she was walking this time, but it was very nearly a run, her slippers tripping along in haste to stay ahead of him down the passage. Before they fully emerged into the bright light thrown by Lady Clegg-Foster's crystal chandelier, he reached out, capturing her arm again. She turned to rebuke him. A faint flush colored her cheeks now, and her bosom too. Her lips looked swollen, darker than before, and her lashes drooped as if her eyelids were heavy. There was a definite strain to her breathing, her breasts pushing frantically at the white rosebuds trimming her bodice.

Even if that was a smile forming on her lips, there was no assurance that he caused it. Most likely it was the result of someone across the room slipping on a dropped piece of fruit from the punch bowl.

James didn't need to look down at himself to know that a return to the party just then was out of the question. He felt the urge to ride at once to the boxing club and work out some of his frustrations with anyone willing to spar. Because if he didn't, the brute inside him might take over completely. This was not good. Not good at all.

He'd found his future wife, and she was the rotten enemy. This was the worse trick she'd ever played on him. Worse even than the ink moustache. And she'd pay for it.

"What's the matter?" she exclaimed when he moved her back against the paneled wall, tucking her away behind one of Lady Clegg-Foster's ugly statues.

"A moment," he muttered. "I need a moment."

She batted her long lashes over those sinister violet eyes. "Have you hurt yourself? Anything I can do?"

James stared at her lips, and the memory of Brighton tore through his mind like spring shoots through newly warmed and softened earth. He fought the urge to kiss her again. "Were you in Brighton this summer, Vyne?"

"No." The answer was out before he'd barely finished the question, as if it was anticipated. "Never been there in my life."

Not that she'd ever tell him a fib.

He knew it was her. He knew the taste of that kiss. It was branded on his memory that moonlit night six months ago. No other kiss had ever affected him so deeply. Why hadn't he recognized her voice? Why hadn't she known his?

Perhaps because they didn't want to know the truth. It was much easier to talk to her when they were both pretending to be someone else. To talk without the usual shields and the banter.

"Are you still staying with your sister in Willard Street?" he demanded, breathless from that kiss and chasing her down the passage.

"Yes. Why?"

"I will call on you tomorrow. At noon."

"What for?"

"We're getting married, woman. Obviously."

She flapped her fan so rapidly he felt the breeze beneath his own chin. "Over my cold, dead bones. You know I find you quite despicable—an utter wastrel."

"Yes, I think there's a club somewhere for people who hate me. Aren't you a founding member?" He was feeling several ounces lighter, his pulse too fast. "Don't think this pleases me any more than it does you. But there it is."

Her stunning violet eyes were inquisitive, merciless as they scoured his face. "You've really knotted your noodle this time, Hartley." She shook her head and disturbed those dark curls until a few dripped lazily to her shoulders.

"Knotted my *what*?"

She reached up and tapped his forehead with her knuckles.

"I thought you were referring to something lower down, Vyne."

"Don't be crude."

"Listen, Vyne, I need a wife. If I don't find my own very soon, my grandmother will continue to present me with well-bred, timid young ladies who haven't an ounce of steel in their backbone, until I grow so tired of it that I rebel and marry a large-footed, loud-voiced, matronly woman who will make me drink sweet sherry and hunt foxes remorselessly with her overbearing father." He placed a finger under her chin and lifted it. "And you're a woman of twenty-seven, with a reputation for being difficult, too many engagements already broken, who knows how many scandalous affairs…and custard on her behind."

She knocked his hand away with her closed fan. "Thank you for reminding me." Any moment now she'd run off again as if she was a dainty, ladylike maiden. Which he knew to be untrue. She turned her face away. "What do you think you're doing, Hartley?"

"Making you an offer. Can't have you picking

a husband just because he is the first man to walk through the arch in a hedge."

Her restive gaze darted about the room. "That kiss was a mistake."

"Which one? Two minutes ago or six months ago?"

"The one in the library just now," she replied, terse. "There was no other. I can't imagine what you think—I told you I wasn't in Brighton. That kiss in the library was a mistake."

"You make a lot of mistakes."

"Yes."

So have I, he thought. "Too late for regret now. All we can do is make up for lost time." She tried to get by him again, but he held her arms firmly. "I'm making you a very good offer, Vyne. It may well be your last." He studied her eyelashes and the skilled downward sway as carefully evasive as the wielding of a lady's fan to hide her expression. "Think of the money and gifts I could give you if you marry me. How is Lark Hollow, by the way? I hear it's falling down around the admiral's ears."

"You're suggesting I marry you for your money?"

"Why not? Any woman who marries me will do so for that reason. I'm not foolish enough to expect anything more, Vyne. You're perfect, of course, because we have no illusions about each other. We neither of us expect anything but the worst. We can't possibly be disappointed."

"Marriage to you sounds so appetizing, Hartley. I wonder how I can resist."

"You'll be a rich woman married to me. What else matters?"

Her eyes were puzzled, the light dimmed. "Do you think me that mercenary?"

"You're a woman, aren't you? And a Vyne. This will purely be a marriage of convenience. For us both."

"If you can be content with a marriage of convenience, any of these other women will do."

"'No. They'll have expectations, romantic ideals. You, at least, haven't any of those." He kept his face solemn. "They don't know me as you do. I don't want to be blamed for breaking anyone's delicate heart, but I know there's no danger of that with you. I can't possibly sink any lower in your estimation. Who knows—I might even rise up." She said nothing to that, but fidgeted with her glove. "And I know you're desperate, don't I?" he added dryly.

Her eyes narrowed, and she drew a quick breath.

Was she considering? Hard to tell when her expression was that calm. The woman was probably a damn good card player.

Finally she spoke again. "And what requirements can *you* possibly expect to find fulfilled by me as a wife, Hartley? Escape from your most avid pursuers? Vengeance on your grandmother?"

"Exactly. What else would I want you for?"

She slipped away around the statue. "Good-bye, Hartley. Good luck in your search for a *convenient* bride. I pity the girl in advance, but I am not yet that destitute."

Before she disappeared completely, he recaptured her still-bare hand and lifted it to his mouth. "Think about my proposition, Vyne. I know your stepfather is in danger of losing his house to debt. I also know that your family is hounding you to marry. You told me that in Brighton."

"For pity's sake! That wasn't me! I wasn't in—"

He grazed his teeth over the tips of her fingers, reacquainting his taste buds with her sweet skin. The heaviness of desire pooled in the most sensitive parts of his body and then overflowed, raw masculinity released as if it was something she knocked over and spilled inside him.

"Stop that!" She belatedly retrieved her fingers from his lips and pulled on her wine-stained glove. "To marry a man I can't abide just because my family needs money? It would be wicked to marry purely for those reasons."

He was amused. "Beggars can't be choosers. And since when have you balked at wicked, Vyne?"

"James Hartley, I would rather live happily and free with meager resources than unhappily and fettered with unlimited riches."

"Oh, spare me, woman! You'd sooner be reduced to rags and never buy another mauve silk ribbon, just because you might have to marry to afford it?" He knew about her fondness for purple in all its shades.

"I'd better go," she muttered. "Mustn't be observed lurking in a dark corner with you. I think we've caused enough scandal for one night already."

"Will the count come out of hiding and challenge me to a duel when he hears of our engagement?"

She shot him a sultry-eyed glance. Light from a nearby wall sconce caught playfully under her lashes. "Hartley, you can stop this tomfoolery. There is no engagement. You know that."

He blinked slowly. "Know what?" Suddenly enthralled by the wall paneling, he studied it closely as he listened to her impatient sighs.

"There. Is. No. Engagement."

He tapped the wall with his knuckles. "I wonder if Lady Clegg-Foster has a problem with woodworm. I understand it's quite prevalent in these older houses."

Ellie folded her arms—a typically unladylike, stubborn gesture. "I expect to see the count tomorrow, and then I will ask him to return your diamonds. I believe you've learned your lesson and will guard your valuables with greater care in the future."

"Oh? The two of you were teaching me a lesson? There I was thinking him just a common thief, seducer of women who should know better, and you simply a rotten little troublemaker."

With one final exasperated gasp, she scurried off, tripping over her hem again as if she hadn't learned how to use those long legs properly yet. Like a young doe stumbling about.

James carefully felt his bruised eye with the fingers of one hand. What did one do about a woman like Ellie Vyne? Marry her, of course, and save the rest of the male species from her unique brand of trouble. All part of his reform effort. He was becoming quite the philanthropist.

Chapter 7

ELLIE HAD NO INTENTION OF WAITING UNTIL THE NEXT day for a visit from James Hartley. A woman simply couldn't take that rake seriously. Therefore, her first order of business the following morning was to return the diamond necklace with a messenger and a hasty note. That should absolve the man of any further need to flirt with her in public. Let him play those games with other women. There were surely plenty standing in readiness to oblige.

She paused with her pen in the inkwell, remembering his teasing.

You're a woman of twenty-seven, with a reputation for being difficult, too many engagements already broken, and who knows how many scandalous affairs.

Of course, his own affairs were not mentioned. The man needed a severe set down. Everything in life came too easily for him. Except love, because he chose entirely the wrong women. Now he thought he could bypass love completely and find a wife desperate enough to put up with his sins, just because he rescued her from spinsterhood.

She stopped again, tapping her quill in the inkwell.

It would serve the fool right if she did accept his proposal and held him to it. Then what would he do? He'd done it to tease her, of course. He must have known her answer in advance. Had it been anything other than what it was, it would have wiped the charming smile from his ridiculously handsome face.

With one glance over her shoulder to be sure she was alone, she slid open the top drawer of the bureau. There, nestled in a silk scarf, sat the five plump, gleaming diamonds that were causing James Hartley—and her—so much trouble. If only she'd never accepted them from Lady Southwold's hands. But how could she know the trouble they'd lead her into?

He'd very probably forgotten all about the woman he encountered in Brighton until last night, when she made the dreadful error of letting him kiss her. Truth be told, she had been curious to know if it would feel as wonderful as it did the first time.

Now she knew.

Ellie caught her reflection in the small mirror.

Women have a limited number of years before they lose their bloom. Not saying you ever had any. On a bad day, when in one of your abysmal sulks, you look like the very devil.

Perhaps she ought to wear a little of Pear's Bloom of Roses to color her cheeks, or use lampblack and burnt cork to darken her brows. Her sisters had recommended it, but she'd only laughed at the idea of painting her face. It seemed foolish, for the false color had to come off sometime. Then it must be a dreadful shock for the poor fellow drawn in by the deception. Well, she supposed some men deserved to be shocked.

Abruptly she stuck out her tongue at the mirror and returned to her letter. Only to be distracted again, almost immediately, by the naughty wink of light bouncing off the cut facets of those diamonds in the open drawer. She simply could not concentrate today.

Last night he'd danced with her for the very first time. It had rather turned things upside down for Ellie, got her in a muddle, made her forget all the things she'd promised herself never to do—never to let herself feel. Last night she'd acted like the very sort of woman she'd always observed with scorn.

She set down her quill and examined the diamond necklace. Each diamond was attached by little clips, allowing any number to be removed as the wearer desired. Trust the gaudy Ophelia Southwold to wear all five at once, when one made far greater impact. One diamond alone was eloquence itself and often the only jewel a woman required to make her point. She could, of course, take the necklace to a pawnbroker as originally planned. Then her stepfather's leaking roof could be fixed. But it didn't seem right now she knew the necklace belonged to James, and he'd offered her another way to help the admiral out of debt.

Ellie had always assumed she would grow old and poor with as little elegance as she'd been young and poor. She pictured herself wearing the cap of a spinster and lurking in dimly lit corners at parties—to which she was invited by her sisters only out of a sense of duty. There she'd sip too much wine, tell ribald tales of scant truth, and eye up the footmen. She planned on being a very difficult old lady who need not hold her tongue or her true thoughts, because everyone assumed she was losing her faculties and nobody dare tell her.

Should she now throw aside her plans and resort to practical, mercenary measures?

The last time Ellie conferred with her father's solicitor, he'd suggested she try persuading the admiral to sell his house and move to smaller, cheaper accommodations. All Ellie could do was laugh at the idea. Her stepfather firmly refused to be "exiled" from Lark Hollow, the crumbling country manor house he'd purchased at the height of his once-lucrative Naval career. He'd fallen in love with its picturesque beauty at first viewing, and the seller's agent had managed, with very little cunning, to hide all its faults. Admiral Vyne made his offer at once, consulting with no one else—not even his young wife—convinced another buyer might come along and steal the house away from him. It was the first of many impulsive financial choices.

Lark Hollow was a beautiful wreck of a house. A flourishing tangle of ivy and wisteria clawed up the walls, and when the sun dropped behind the crooked chimneys, the house was gilded as if by angel's paintbrushes. Anyone approaching along the gravel drive sighed in awe. That was enough for her stepfather. What did he care for practical matters such as how much it cost to maintain that splendid prospect?

Since retiring from the Navy, and after a string of unwise investments, Admiral Vyne continued his discovery of expensive tastes on an insufficient budget. Whenever Ellie tried to sit him down and discuss the state of the family finances, he feigned one of his sudden and dramatic illnesses, all the result, so he claimed, of a hard life at sea and never quite getting his "land legs" back. He assured Ellie that women knew nothing about money or decision making. She was supposed to look pretty, shut her mouth, and marry well. That was all he asked of her.

"And even at that," he'd reminded her once, "you failed, Mariella."

She could stop funding his excesses, but with her mother gone and her half sisters too preoccupied with themselves, someone had to look after the admiral. She'd promised her mother to always take care of the man who had saved both their lives—hers before she was even born. He was very old now, almost eighty. It was far too late to expect him to change.

Now, thanks to Hartley's proposition, she had the opportunity to fulfill that promise to her mother without having to disguise herself as the count any longer.

James Hartley needed a wife to save himself from the pushiness of Society matrons with marriageable daughters. Ellie Vyne needed freedom from her family's expectations and the financial burdens she'd taken upon herself. As he'd said, beggars couldn't be choosers.

Better the devil we know.

There was one thing James could give her. One thing she'd already acknowledged to be impossible without a husband. Thus, in an impulsive moment of madness, she put her pen to paper and wrote a very different note to the one she'd intended when she first sat down.

❧

James critically perused his reflection in the long mirror. "That damned tailor will have to go. Look at this!" He raised his arms straight out in front, showing how the shirt pulled, stretching the stitches at his shoulders.

"I am sorry, sir." The valet cast a timid eye over his master's breeches, which were also snug.

Seeing his expression, James exclaimed, "Quite, Grieves. I should like to be left with a little dignity at the end of the day." He took the new coat from the valet's arms and tried to shrug his way into it, pausing as he felt the warning tightness and heard stitches break. He turned, still hunched, arms curved. Grieves hastened to his aid.

"Let me help you out, sir."

"Bring me my gun, Grieves, and I'll shoot the fellow."

"It just requires a few adjustments, to be sure."

"My gun, Grieves!"

With an almighty heave, James extracted his wide shoulders from the coat, and Grieves reached up to smooth down his shirtsleeves. "I shall speak to the tailor, sir."

"Quicker to shoot him."

"Yet not quite so practical. He is, after all, the very best tailor in London, so they say."

"Humph." Turning this way and that, James examined his reflection. "I've never seen such shoddy workmanship. The fellow's eyesight must be fading if he cannot get a simple measurement correct."

Grieves politely suggested his master might have

gained an inch or two about the waist and chest since his measurements were last taken.

James pulled the new shirt off and flung a scowl over his shoulder. "It is evident, Grieves, that you are in league with this new tailor. I daresay he slipped you a few coins to recommend his services to me. You always were a conniving fellow."

"Indeed not, sir!"

"In any case, it's all muscle," James added, one hand laid to his stomach, fingers splayed to feel the ridges and reassure himself. "Thanks to the boxing club. Solid as a rock."

"A mountain of manliness, if I might be so bold, sir."

"If bold also means facetious, no you may not." He knew Grieves thought the boxing club was another example of James desperately clinging onto his youth, but it was, in fact, all part of his efforts for self-improvement. It gave him an outlet for his anger and frustrations, kept him physically fit and his mind focused.

The offending shirt back in its box, Grieves looked over at the silver tray loaded with the morning's post. "I see there are several invitations today, sir. Would you like me to…?"

Naked but for the tight breeches, James stormed over to the tray, and within a few seconds, his firm, quick fingers sorted through the pile of cards, consigning each one to his fire after a very brief glance.

With every passing day as the Season approached, the horrors of London Society mounted. Members of the *ton* returned to Town in drips and dregs, opening up their houses, preparing to see and be seen. In the

New Year, a parade of wide-eyed debutantes—mamas in tow—would descend on London like locusts to devour a crop of wheat. Before he knew it, he could be accused of ruining someone's reputation again.

One invitation, amid the drift of gilt-edged cards, caught his eye, and he paused to scratch his disheveled hair. "Archie Playter getting married *again*? Good Lord, I thought he was dead. The last time I saw him at the club, he certainly appeared to be stuffed and mounted."

The valet shook his head somberly. "It is indeed a curious match, sir. His valet informs me that the woman is a trifle shrill and has a curious taste in gowns. She is from Essex."

"That explains it then."

"Lord Playter has been unlucky with ladies," Grieves observed somberly. "One cannot help feeling a trifle sorry for him, sir."

"Sorry? For that arrogant, pompous fool? Archibald Playter thinks he's always in the right." He pretended not to notice the ironic smile briefly passing over Grieves's lips. "The man is riffraff, Grieves, without a doubt. He deserves what he gets." Even as he spoke, he knew this was something his grandmother would say. Some habits were harder to break, and she'd been a stern influence over much of his life, rubbing off on him in more ways than he cared to count.

"But he could be in love this time, sir. They do say that love changes everything."

James was still sorting through the post and managed only a very distant grunt.

"I am sorry, sir. Forgive me."

"What for, Grieves?"

"I mentioned *that* word again, sir. The one you did not want to hear ever again." The valet paused. "*Love*, sir."

James tossed the empty silver tray onto a nearby chair. Today that word barely bothered him at all. Strange. He strode to his window and looked out at the walled garden and its solitary pear tree, the branches bare now, waiting for an ermine cloak of snow.

Love. He'd let that word make a fool of him in the past. He'd believed in it because of Sophia Valentine. And look where that got him. It made him a laughingstock for months.

He finally became aware of Grieves holding out an older shirt, like a peace offering. As James tugged it over his head and shoulders, he sought some conversation to keep his mind on practical matters, to stop it spinning about and bumping into things. It wasn't good for his Hartley pride to be so excitable. His grandmother would advise an ice bath and a poultice, but he had no time for either this morning. He hadn't even taken a moment to shave, too anxious to get to Willard Street and collect his bride before she had a chance to run off again.

Glancing down at his tight breeches again, he exclaimed, "What happened to the previous tailor? He managed to make my clothes fit for the last twenty years at least."

"Mr. Chadworth has left us, sir," Grieves declared sorrowfully. "I did apprise you of it when it happened."

"Left us? How can this be permitted?"

"I doubt it was intentional, sir. The gentleman is dead."

"Dead? How damned thoughtless of the fellow."

"An attack of the heart, I believe. He was very elderly."

James stormed about the room, shaking his head at the sheer inconvenience. "Now that I think of it, he was a dreadful fellow, with breath that could strip fur from a badger. I daresay we're better off without him. But this new tailor? Are you certain he can fill Chadworth's shoes?"

"I am assured he is the very best. He is newly arrived from France, and he—" Grieves clammed up, grabbed a waistcoat from the edge of the bed, and slid it over his master's arms.

The slip, however, had not gone unnoticed. James exploded, "A *Frenchman*, of all things!"

"I am sorry, sir, but he—"

"Grieves, have you forgotten that scoundrel Napoleon?"

"But Napoleon is dead, sir."

"Just because the man is dead, Grieves, doesn't mean he's changed for the better. And he was French."

Nothing further to be said on the matter of the French, the valet took out a small brush and worked it briskly over the back and shoulders of his master's waist-coat. "Are you going out this morning, sir? So early?"

"Hmmm."

The events of the previous evening waltzed through his mind again. A pair of stunning violet eyes, a warm hand slipping out of his grip, lips trying not to laugh at him. Extraordinary lips he silenced with a kiss.

Ellie Vyne hadn't let him sleep a wink last night, and he swore that tonight he would repay the favor.

"What time is it, Grieves?"

"It is half past eleven, sir."

"Good. Order the carriage brought around, will you?" He whistled a light tune as he shrugged his shoulders into his coat.

"Is everything all right, sir?"

Grabbing the elderly valet by his ears, James planted a kiss on his furrowed brow. "Grieves, if I thought you wouldn't fritter it away, I'd give you an increase in pay at once."

"Good heavens, sir…that would have been very nice."

"I'm in an excellent mood today and shortly to regain the treasure stolen from me by that Frenchman."

"What a relief, sir." Clutching the little brush in both hands, Grieves edged cautiously around his master. "The treasure in question is the Hartley Diamonds, sir?"

"No, no! The Vyne woman. Do follow along, Grieves."

The valet swayed backward on his heels. "Miss Vyne, sir? The one you do not wish on your worst enemy?"

"The very same."

"Miss Vyne of the stubborn demeanor and quarrel-some streak? Little Miss Vyne of the ink moustache?"

"Not so little anymore." His gaze went foggy as he thought again of her long legs and the rosebuds framing her bosom. "But quite grown-up."

"I never met the infamous lady, sir."

"Think yourself lucky. She's naught but trouble, and I can't imagine what has possessed me. But there it is. Someone should take her in hand. It may as well be me, since I'm a reformed man, shouldering the responsibilities no one else wants."

"Hartleys are speaking to Vynes this year then, sir?"

"Indeed we are, Grieves." James swept out of the room and down the stairs, completely forgetting his boots, obliging Grieves to run after and stop him before he could walk out into the street barefoot.

The footman heard them coming and leapt into action to swiftly open the front door. A chill morning breeze blew into the hall, bringing with it several dry leaves that scratched across the black-and-white hall tiles and spun in a rapid circle. The footman, still holding the door and looking out into the street, froze in surprise.

Another man stood there, hand raised to pull on the bell at the exact same moment the door opened.

James, still barefoot and with Grieves following close behind, came to an abrupt halt. The man on the doorstep wore an old-fashioned white wig and a very self-satisfied expression on his face.

"Good morning. Mr. Hartley, is it not?" A pair of sinister dark eyes roved upward from James's bare feet to his face and then beyond, into the hall, scanning the place, circling, following the route of those dead leaves. "I believe you've been expecting me."

James straightened up. "I have?"

"Indeed, Mr. Hartley. I am the count de Bonneville."

෨ඏ

He took the visitor into his library and signaled for Grieves to leave them alone. The count was right, of course; he had expected this meeting sooner or later, in light of what happened at the party the night before. News traveled fast in Town. Scandal even faster.

The count, without all his evening finery, frills, and face powder, was rough about the edges, coarse in manners and appearance. He was older than James expected, his face much more weathered and worn, yet there was a handsomeness to his hard features. Most surprising of all, he had no French accent. Today, it seemed, he did not bother with his act. Seating himself—without being asked—in a chair before James's desk, he sprawled in a languid fashion, his boots leaving clumps of mud on the carpet. He brought the chill of the day inside with him, and there was a crisp rustle each time he moved, for his clothes had yet to thaw out. He was a fidget, fingers never still, eyes constantly surveying his surroundings.

His lips slid into a crooked smile. "I saw you cavorting about with my girl last night."

James stiffened.

"Surely, I says to myself, a gentleman like Mr. Hartley wouldn't think of stealing my girl away on the sly. He'd want it done proper." At first James thought the man was suggesting a duel, but then he added, "A gentleman's agreement."

James said nothing, just looked at the man's dirty heels now lifted from the carpet to mark his polished desk.

"If you want her, Hartley," the so-called count added jovially, "you'll pay my price, eh?"

"Pay your *price*?" James strode around his desk and sat, falling heavily into the chair.

"I can't just give her away, can I?" The other man smiled. "She's a very special girl, is my Mariella. From what I saw last night, you agree."

"You were there?"

"Oh yesss." The sound lingered, like the hiss of a snake. "I am always there. She doesn't go anywhere without me these days." His grin broadened. "We're a team, me and her."

James felt nauseous. "Is that so?" Anger rose quickly over the bile. So she was up to her neck in trouble with her lover, as he'd suspected the moment he saw her in the man's bed. What game were they playing last night at Lady Clegg-Foster's? What game did they play now?

"I have to be compensated, don't I? For my loss, if you take her away from me." The count swung his feet down from the desk and leaned forward. "I hear you're thinking of marrying my girl."

He'd thought it wouldn't take long for Walter Winthorne to spread that little gem. Silent, James eyed his unwelcome visitor, waiting for the next strike of the serpent's tongue. It was Ellie Vyne who'd started the engagement rumor, of course. Last night he'd assumed it was by accident, but now he wondered. Knowing her love of tricks and pranks all too well, he suspected it might have been deliberate.

"Like I said, if you're interested in my girl, you'll have to pay up. Otherwise I'll let the word out about a few things. Won't go down too well with Lady Hartley, once she hears all about your fiancée's crimes. Will certainly be the end for the lovely Mariella, won't it, if I tell what she's been up to?"

He faced the man steadily across his desk, heat rising under his collar. "What she's been up to?"

"Thieving from your fancy friends. Cheating at cards. Lifting a few jewels, emptying a few unguarded pockets. How else do you think she pays the admiral's bills?"

It felt as if the ground fell away beneath his chair and he was hurtling through the darkness. If she needed money, why had she not come to him? Instead, she'd let herself be dragged into criminal behavior, consorting with this crook.

He imagined his grandmother's scornful laughter as she derided him for foolishly imagining, even for the briefest of moments, that the Vyne woman cherished a tiny spot of fondness for him—enough to make her blush when he kissed her, enough to let him nibble playfully on her naked fingertips.

It had all been an act. A clever one that drew him in like a baited hook.

He reached for the letter opener on his desk and tapped it against his open palm. She'd tricked him into an engagement while slyly pretending all the time that she didn't mean to do it, and he fell for it, drawn in by her secretive, seductive eyes and elusive lips. She'd made a fool of him last night, running off and leaving him on the dance floor with her glove, knowing he'd follow her after she tempted him.

Disgust burned bitter in his throat. Then came jealousy, a hot fist that punched harder than any sparring partner.

He and I have a very close connection. We are almost inseparable.

He'd stabbed the letter opener into his hand. Not enough to draw blood, but it caused a sharp pain that brought him quickly back to the present. He spread his fingers over the desk blotter and waited for his vision to clear.

"I saw the way you looked at her last night, Hartley." The crook chuckled. "Surely you can't object to a little exchange. If you want my Mariella, want me to keep silent about our connection and her…shall we say…light-fingered tendencies."

"How much do you expect to get from me, Bonneville?"

"Shall we say a thousand pounds?"

He'd anticipated far more. Perhaps this fellow didn't know how much he was worth. But Ellie did, surely. "I suppose you plan to keep the Hartley Diamonds."

"Diamonds? What bleedin' diamonds?" His accent wavered between cockney, an Irish lilt, and something else, a drawl of indeterminate origin.

James wanted to reach across the desk, grab the man by the throat, and wring the laughter—and the last breath—out of him. How could she have given herself to this graceless oaf? Had the villain somehow bribed her into it? No. If that was the case, she would not defend him and conceal his whereabouts. She was no weak-headed female. She was in this with Bonneville, right up to her slender neck. He knew she'd come to this one day. His grandmother had always said the Vyne woman was a criminal in training.

"The necklace of diamonds you took from Ophelia Southwold."

"I don't know about that, Hartley. I'm here for my girl, Mariella, not some other woman. Now, do you want her or not?"

The man's behavior was not adding up. His manners—or lack thereof—and the strangely shifting accent were not what James had expected. But his thoughts were too focused on Ellie Vyne just then. He stared, and his fingers curled into claws against his desk. "Oh, I want her."

"Well, then." The other man stood, clearly too restless to remain still for long. Thumbs in his waistcoat pockets, he paced before the desk. "You'd better pay me for the pleasure. Fair and square. All I want is my due. What I'm owed for giving her up. And remember, Hartley, if I go down, I take her with me."

James knew he shouldn't care, after the lies she'd told him, the tricks and games she'd played.

But he did care. He couldn't help himself. He had no choice but to pay the man and get her away from him.

❧

When he finally left the house, his mood dark, Grieves met him halfway across the hall.

"This came for you this morning, sir." The valet produced a small box wrapped in muslin, a sealed note tied on with ribbon. "A messenger boy brought it."

James opened the box. One brilliant diamond winked up at him.

"Goodness gracious, sir, is that not one of the Hartley Diamonds?"

James closed the box and studied the messy, hurried writing on the attached note.

Catch me if you can. EV.

So she had his diamonds all along, and now she made a game of it. He thrust the small box inside his jacket pocket and realized he was grinding his jaw. With one hand he rubbed it, soothing his anger likewise until it was merely a dull ache.

James was not sure why she would return one of the diamonds, but it suited his temper at that moment to believe she was in this blackmail up to her neck. Then he could make her pay for her part in it. She now owed him for saving her from the count's clutches. As far as he was concerned, she'd spend the rest of her life paying him back. James Hartley was done with being a gentlemanly loser in romance. In fact, in the case of Ellie Vyne, he was done with being a gentleman altogether.

After this, the only games she'd play would be by his rules. In his bed.

Chapter 8

WHILE SHE PACKED HER TRUNK LATER THAT MORNING, her sisters took turns advising and lecturing. They both had presents for Aunt Lizzie and forced them into her trunk until there was barely room for anything of hers to be neatly packed. Instead, she resorted to jamming her clothes in wherever they fit, knowing they would be horrendously wrinkled by the time she arrived.

"Do give her our love," exclaimed Charlotte, sounding harried as always, a woman frantically busy at all times while achieving very little to show for it. "If only I had nothing to do, like you, and could get away for a pleasant, idle few weeks, but now I am a married woman and soon to face confinement…"

Charlotte had been married five months, and her child was not due for another six, but she talked of the impending confinement constantly, already taking pleasure in the attention in brought her, all the special needs she was now at liberty to claim. Their sister Amelia, married six months, was yet to announce a visit from the stork, which had caused some souring between the two women. Ellie hoped, for all their sakes, that both sisters might soon be so overburdened with sticky-fingered offspring they'd no longer have the time to meddle in her life.

Amelia produced string to help secure the bursting luggage. "Do not talk to strangers on the journey, Ellie. There will be all manner and class of folk. When you stop at the Barley Mow, keep a close eye on your trunk. I wish my husband had agreed to let you use our private chaise, but it could not be spared."

"Nor could ours, although I would have lent it to you in an instant," Charlotte exclaimed as if someone had accused her of deliberately sending her carriage out on errands rather than let it be used for their sister.

Ellie shrugged. "I daresay my fellow passengers in the mail coach should be warned about me as much as I should be about them."

"Oh, Ellie, do be serious. Papa will be very cross, you know, to hear that you are traveling with the post."

"But unless he can produce a set of wings for me to fly by, I must make do."

"Papa wanted you to stay the Season here with us," Amelia fretted as her fingers adjusted the golden ringlets that peeked out of her lace cap. "He said it was time you found a husband and settled down."

She hastily reminded them, "But Aunt Lizzie has not been well, and one of us must go to look after her. As married women, you both have far busier lives than mine, and it is only sensible that I go. I'm no use anywhere else, as you know." Then she found her winning ace and cast it down with a flourish. "Besides, look what happened last night when I went out husband-hunting."

Charlotte sank to the bed, clutching herself as if she felt contractions already. Both sisters left her alone to finish securing her trunk lid.

"You are quite sure it is only a rumor?" Amelia ventured, one hand to her throat, the other curled tightly around the bedpost. "There is no engagement between you and Mr. Hartley? Captain Winthorne sounded quite convinced of it."

"Of course there isn't any truth to that rumor," Charlotte admonished her. "Why on earth should James Hartley want to marry Ellie when he cannot stand the very sight of her face? It was quite evidently a heinous lie put about deliberately to embarrass us."

"But she did dance with the rogue, and he almost kissed her in the middle of the dance. Lord Clegg-Foster was so distracted he dropped sherbet down his wife's bosom."

Ellie straightened up, praying those hasty rope knots would hold for the long journey into the country and along bumpy roads. "I had no choice but to dance with the rake." She turned away before her sisters could observe the guilt-hued color on her face. "How was I—an innocent spinster—to defend myself from his vile clutches?"

It was only a little white lie, she reasoned, quite harmless by her standards, and neither sister noticed her failure to address the question of an engagement. Pulling her favorite bonnet quickly over her hair, she tied the lilac ribbons under her chin.

She wondered if he had received the diamond yet. No. James Hartley was very probably still in bed. Gentlemen didn't gain a reputation like his by being up and sensate before noon. "Materially he is very well secure," Amelia ventured. "I suppose she could do much worse than catch Mr. Hartley's eye."

"How could you suggest such a thing?" Charlotte reproached her. "Must I remind you James Hartley's adulteress mother caused our poor uncle to be ostracized from Society because she lured him into an affair? Our family has suffered ever since. Uncle Grae was chased out of the country, ruined. Now we have no idea where he lives or how he survives in some dreadful wilderness—"

"He lives in Spanish Town, Jamaica, Charlotte," Ellie interrupted pragmatically, "and keeps a tavern, the last I heard. Quite successfully."

"Even so, Jamaica is a dreadful, hot, sticky place, full of poisonous snakes, and a great distance away. I'm certain he would much rather be here."

"Where it rains all the time?"

"It does not rain *all* the time."

Ellie gave a deep sigh. "No. It just feels that way."

"In any case, James Hartley is a rake and a scoundrel. He has never had a good word to say about you. And although you are by no means so very plain," Charlotte added cheerily, laying a dainty hand of comfort on Ellie's shoulder, "you should not aim so far out of your…range."

Ellie opened her eyes wide. "My *range*?"

"What you need, Sister, is a quiet, respectable husband, not too attractive, but of adequate means. Someone safe, dependable, and settled. A solid, sensible member of Parliament. Someone my husband would not be ashamed to invite for dinner."

"Charlotte, can you truly see me happily married to a member of Parliament?"

Even Amelia chortled at that idea, and Charlotte put on her wounded face. Watching their reflections in the mirror, Ellie supposed it was, after all, very sweet of them both to worry about her. She could be in a good, forgiving mood now she was escaping into the country.

"My dear sisters"—she spun away from the mirror and smiled warmly at the two fussing women—"there is absolutely nothing for you to worry about. Now come, kiss me good-bye. It could be your last chance, in case I am mugged and left for dead on the road. Or I decide to run off to Gretna Green with some lecherous, unsuitable young man. I shall understand, of course, that my scandalous marriage will require you to cut me off. Should I need to resort to highway robbery, just to keep a crust on the table and buy shoes for my little ones, I trust you will remember your once-beloved older sister and stand witness at my hanging."

Her sisters looked at her as if she was absolutely capable of such an end.

❧

The frowning maid at Twenty-One Willard Street folded her plump arms and wedged herself in the door frame. "Miss Vyne has gone out."

He might have known. For a marriage of convenience, this was already damned inconvenient. Not to mention costly.

Another chilling thought occurred—had she run

off with the count *and* his thousand pounds? Perhaps she sent him that single diamond as some sort of jest. It would be just like her, naturally, to think all this most amusing. Yet again she got away with her mischief—or so she imagined.

One of her sisters appeared in the shadows of the hall, evidently come to see what the noise was about. She peered over the maid's enormous shoulder and blinked a pair of wide brown eyes. "Sakes, Mr. Hartley. Have you come for Ellie?"

"I have, madam," he replied, spitting his words out in anger. "I am told she has gone. Is this true?"

"My sister left on the mail coach to stay with our aunt in the country, Mr. Hartley. She did not expect you, surely," her sister exclaimed, still hiding behind the maid. "She said nothing to us about—"

Not waiting to hear what she hadn't said, or what lies she had told, James turned on his booted heel, leapt down the steps and into his carriage.

෴

At last the busy crowds of London were left behind. The ceaseless clatter of hooves, wheels, and wooden pattens across paved roads gave way to the softer thud of hardened dirt under the post horses. Streets emptied of rumbling wagons, and the shouts of tradesmen faded as the coach turned into narrow, rutted lanes bordered with bare trees that sometimes scraped brittle limbs along the sides of the vehicle.

Ellie, pressed into a corner, tried to ignore the cramp already burning in her left hip and kept her gaze on the view through the small window. She carefully avoided eye contact with her fellow travelers and clung to happy thoughts of her destination.

Tomorrow evening she would be with her aunt in Sydney Dovedale, a quiet little village where she'd spent several blissfully unfettered summers as a young girl. Whenever her stepfather had felt his patience pushed to the limit by three growing daughters, he sent them to their aunt Lizzie, his only sister and closest female relative. Since Lizzie had no children of her own, he considered her little cottage in the country a perfect place to send his motherless girls, out of harm's way for long periods while he was away at sea.

Sadly, in Ellie's case, "out of harm's way" had only put her into mischief's way. A girl with a vivid imagination and a penchant for trouble had so much more scope for both in the country, out of her stepfather's sight.

During one such summer she saw James Hartley for the first time. Then a young man of twenty, he rode at reckless speed down the country lanes in a jaunty curricle. He was always very tidy, too elegantly attired for the country, and that just made young Ellie Vyne—who couldn't be tidy if she wanted to—feel the intense desire to make him dirty. It was surely her responsibility to do so, because no young man should be so concerned with his clothes. He was obviously vain and conceited. Three times that summer he'd ridden by her in his curricle and muddied her pinafore by racing through a puddle, not seeing the little girl there on the verge.

James had begun courting her friend Sophia

Valentine at that time, for she was five years older than Ellie. Everyone said his grandmother was against the match because the Valentines had fallen on hard times, and Ellie rather thought this was why Hartley ran after Sophia in the first place. She knew something about defiance. Even at a young age she was already an observer of other people and their habits. She educated herself with books she was forbidden to read and eavesdropped on a great many conversations she should never have heard.

Aunt Lizzie warned her to stay well away from the young man, reminding her that Vynes and Hartleys had absolutely nothing to do with one another. That was, of course, the very worst thing anyone could have said, for no child of ten should be warned not to do something, because then she is most certainly obliged to do that very thing.

When she found James Hartley, one lazy, sunny afternoon, napping under an oak tree, apparently having emptied a jug of cider and eaten the contents of a small picnic basket all by himself, what else could she do but draw on his face? She just happened to have her ink pot in hand. After she'd run back to her aunt's cottage to fetch it.

Oh the trouble that got her in! But it was worth it for the laughs. As she'd said to her aunt at the time, "If everyone was virtuous and always good, would not the value of being so rapidly decline?"

No one had any answer to that.

She caught herself smiling at her blurry reflection in the coach window. Better stop that at once, or the other passengers might think her a little odd. After all, there was nothing worth smiling at in her reflection. Her stepfather once told her she had her mother's eyes, but that brought little comfort, since he also said his American wife was a nagging scold.

Ellie remembered her mother frequently chiding the admiral for his foolishness in buying Lark Hollow. A modest woman of simple tastes, always anxious to be seen as respectable and never to draw undue notice to herself, Ellie's mother longed for a smaller, more practical home, easier and cheaper to maintain. In the admiral's words she had "no vision."

According to him, it was her fault that he sired only daughters, when he wanted strong, seafaring sons to follow in his wake. That was possibly Catherine Vyne's most unforgivable sin. That, and dying nineteen years ago, leaving him alone to struggle with three mystifying little girls. But he did keep his wife's portrait in a small oval frame in his study, so he must have loved her a little.

Men, honestly! They were never able to admit the truth about themselves but preferred to keep up a silly front, either pretending they cared when they didn't or pretending they didn't care when they did. She, of course, would never do such a thing.

The path of her thoughts traced back to Hartley. Was he up yet? Probably not. He may not even be in his own bed. Who knew what the blackguard got up to after she left the party last night with her sisters?

Suddenly a very smart coach, drawn by four black horses, raced by her window, stones flinging up at the side of the lurching vessel as it almost hurled the mail coach over into the ditch. Passengers cried out in alarm as they plummeted from side to side for ten breathtaking seconds and hung on to hats and one another, disregarding propriety in that moment of near death.

Somehow the coach driver regained control. They bumped, rattled, and bounced over deep ruts, and then were back on the road, all groaning but mostly intact.

Ellie adjusted her aching seat as best she could in the narrow space she was allotted by the spreading thighs of the very large person beside her, and stared out again through the tiny, smeared window.

If she ever got to Sydney Dovedale in one piece, the first thing she wanted was a nice cup of tea and to warm her toes by the fire. *Yes, concentrate on that,* she thought, closing her eyes tight, drawing the pleasant, welcoming picture in her mind, shutting out the overly ripe body odor and the rough, damp feel of the worn upholstery that reeked of alcohol. She closed her mind to the jolts that rocked the carriage constantly and shut her ears to the angry scraping of branches against varnish and wheel spokes. She tried not to notice how the lane narrowed until it was a twisty deathtrap, overhung with hooked tree limbs that might as well be witches fingers poised to drag them all to their grisly end in a flooded ditch.

∽

James swung open the door, flung off his damp coat, and marched to the fire. The rowdy noise of the tavern below rumbled up through the floor joists and the soles of his boots. "Any sign, Grieves?" he bellowed at the valet, who was by the window, watching the inn's galleried yard.

"Not yet, sir. The mail coach is late. You made inquiries below?"

"Yes." He grabbed a tankard of ale that sat waiting for him by a tray of roast pheasant and baked potatoes. "No one here by the name of Vyne."

"We are certain she heads in this direction, sir?"

"Of course. The only aunt she has lives in Sydney Dovedale. Eliza Cawley is her stepfather's sister." He sipped his ale and glared at the fire. "She could, of course, be traveling incognito."

Grieves turned in surprise. "Why would she do that, sir?"

He growled into his ale, "To hide from me."

"Hide from you, sir? I understood the lady had agreed to marry you."

"Not exactly." *But I spent one thousand pounds on her already,* he thought churlishly. Not that he could tell Grieves about that. Explaining the blank space in his ledger beside the expenditure must wait until Mr. Dillworthy's next visit. "After what happened last night," James continued briskly, "she won't get away from me. That creature simply cannot continue blundering through her life, never listening to good advice. She's a woman prone to desperate impulses." He paused. "Why the face, Grieves?"

"Face, sir? I fear this is my usual one."

"No it isn't. You've something to say. Out with it."

The valet released a shallow sigh. "What exactly, if you don't mind my asking, sir, did happen last night at Lady Clegg-Foster's party? I heard several differing reports of it myself. Although I never listen to gossip, of course."

James paced before the fire, tankard clutched in his hand. "I asked her to marry me and explained the advantages to such an arrangement. She resisted naturally, being stubborn and contrary, but since she lured me into chasing her, I can only conclude she's come to her senses."

"One wonders, sir, why the lady did not remain in London to accept your proposal. Why she thought it preferable to have you chase her about the country in this dreadful weather."

"She's a woman, Grieves. They like to complicate matters. She does it better than anyone." She'd been complicating things for the last six months, since she kissed him in that maze and then ran off.

"I must say I am relieved, sir," Grieves ventured, "that you found your Marie-Antoinette from Brighton. Although I am not sure how Lady Hartley will take the news."

"Probably with a large dose of smelling salts."

"Aha," Grieves exclaimed, still looking through the window. "I see things are about to get even more tangled, sir."

"What is it?"

"Two things, sir. One—the mail coach has just arrived."

James strode across the room to watch over the other man's gray head. The bulky, dark vessel trundled into the yard, hooves clattering over the cobbles, boxes and people hanging on seemingly by willpower alone. Although the yard was lit by rush torches, it was still too dark to identify faces, and as heavy rain began to fall, even the torch flame dimmed until it was little more than a smoky, sullen flicker. The noise of disembarking passengers and shouting grooms now combined with the rattle of rain across the slate roof overhead and the general noise from below. James watched the passengers dashing about, rescuing their luggage from puddles.

"Why on earth travel in such company?"

Grieves remarked somberly that some people had no choice in the manner of their transport. "Most lives, sir, are decidedly less comfortable than your own. As I'm sure you've observed."

"If she'd waited for me this morning, I could have brought her in my carriage."

"Perhaps it did not occur to the lady, sir. Some folk learn to make do with the little they have."

"This is not another sly request for a raise in salary, is it by chance?"

"Indeed not, sir. I merely point out that some of us go about our business with little fuss. We just get on with it, sir. No matter how hard."

"Your life is so hard, Grieves?"

The other man's reflection in the crooked window-panes was slightly smug, masquerading as grave. "I do think, sir, that if you ever had the chance to walk a day in my shoes, you might be surprised."

"You don't think I could handle the life of a valet?"

Grieves stared out at the grim evening and changed the subject. "I daresay it will rain all night, sir. Abysmal weather."

James shook his head. Not at the weather, but at Ellie Vyne having disregard for her own safety. Anything could happen to a young woman traveling alone with the mail coach.

"Do you wish to know what the second thing is, sir? The second thing that has occurred to cause you trouble of a most inconvenient kind?"

He was almost afraid to ask. "What?"

"Lady Ophelia Southwold just exited a small equipage and entered the tavern below in some haste."

"Oh, good Lord, Grieves. You'll have to get rid of her somehow."

"Do we have a sack and some heavy stones, sir?"

"Unfortunately, no. Go down and waylay her. I don't care how you do it. Then see if Miss Vyne has arrived, Grieves. Ask discreetly. She won't know you, and I don't want her to see me yet."

"Very good, sir." Grieves disappeared at once on his mission, and James stood a while, watching the weary, bedraggled folk in the yard. He'd never traveled with the mail coach in his life, as the valet pointed out. The sole heir to a large export and import business begun by his great-grandfather, James had known only luxury from his earliest years. Because of the Hartley wealth, he was always treated with deference by others and accustomed to getting material things when he wanted them. Only true love was beyond his means. He was not the loveable type, it seemed. He vaguely remembered once trying to embrace his grandmother for a kiss as he left for boarding school at the end of a holiday.

"For pity's sake, James!" She'd pushed him away with cold, bony hands. "We're not on the opera house stage."

So he'd sought what he needed in the arms of a parade of pretty women. It was an empty sort of affection. They *loved* being seen on his arm and lavished with presents.

Icy drops spattered the old leaded window, and some of the torches below were extinguished altogether, but nothing dampened the new determination burning inside him. If anyone lived their life like an opera, it was Ellie Vyne. She liked drama and mischief. Teasing him, making him chase her.

This time, *he'd* play a prank on *her*.

Chapter 9

APPARENTLY THERE WAS ONLY ONE ROOM LEFT AT THE inn. The landlord handed her a lit candle in a small brass holder. "Up the stairs. Turn right. Door at the very end of the passage. I'll have my lad bring your trunk."

Ellie had no great hopes for it, considering this was the last empty chamber. She made her way up the narrow stairs, dripping rainwater and mud, so tired and aching from being squeezed into the overcrowded vehicle that her bones were almost unable to hold her upright. A thumping ache still vibrated in her temple just above her eyes, where it felt as if her head had hit the road that day as often as the hooves of the coach horses. Her mouth was dry, her stomach miserably clenched in a knot, and she could not get the stench of the mail coach out of her nostrils. It had taken hold of her airway and her lungs like invasive mold, but there was another day of it still to come. It was unthinkable, yet it must be faced, for she had no other form of transportation.

Expecting little more than a cupboard in which to wait out the night, she lifted the door latch and discovered instead, much to her pleasant surprise, a good-sized paneled room, with a cheery fire burning in the hearth and thick curtains drawn across the windows to keep out drafts. Ellie pinched herself, afraid she'd fallen asleep in the rocking mail coach and this was all a pleasant figment of her imagination.

No. It was real. She could smell the coal in the hearth and the mouth-watering aroma of roasted pheasant, tainted only by a slightly stale waft of beer that must soon cling to everything in her possession. A low rumble of laughter trembled up through the floor, and when she touched the wall, it was solid under her fingertips. Reassured, Ellie explored the room with a renewed burst of vitality, shaking off her weariness. Beside the door a fearsome suit of armor stood guard, proudly holding a medieval pikestaff. Something to add a sense of grandeur to the place, she mused, giving his hollow chest a friendly tap.

"Keep an eye on me, Sir Lancelot," she whispered. "You never know what I might do next."

Across the room a small, round table, lit with candles, held a supper fit for a queen. Or, at least, for one of the queen's ladies-in-waiting. The hungry creature in her belly reacted with a needy cheer, but she was temporarily distracted from that supper by the equally enticing sight of a large Tudor-style bed. Her head begged for sleep, and now a battle raged between that and her stomach.

Ellie had just set her candle down and begun warming her hands by the fire, when a tap at the door announced the arrival of her trunk. She rushed across the room to let the boy in. He was not alone;

a short, bright-eyed gentleman also waited there, smiling benevolently.

"Good evening, Miss Vyne. I hope you find the room satisfactory?"

"Yes, indeed. Thank you. Mr...?"

"I am Grieves, Miss Vyne." He bowed stiffly. "I am the gentleman who gave up the room for you. I trust you're comfortable and have everything you require?" He was an older man with a kindly face, his gestures polite, reserved, and somber.

She hadn't realized anyone made a sacrifice for her, and it took a moment to compose her countenance. Of course, she might have known this room was far too good for her.

"I am immensely thankful, sir," she managed finally, "but I'm afraid I cannot accept this generosity. It is not proper." Alarmed, she wondered where she could spend the night now, if all the other rooms were indeed taken.

"It is not a matter for debate, Miss Vyne," the gentleman replied.

"Oh but I—"

"Miss Vyne, you are in my custody until I hand you over to the proper authorities tomorrow. I'm afraid you have no choice in the matter."

"No choice?" She stared, nonplussed. "Proper authorities?"

He smiled again, sadly, almost apologetic. "You are under arrest, Miss Vyne. For theft of the Hartley Diamonds."

She opened her mouth and tried to push words out. None came.

"I have kept you from your sleep long enough, Miss Vyne. Good eve to you." Again he bent his head, revealing a small bald patch as he swept off his hat, backed out swiftly, and shut the door. Immediately, she heard a key turn in the lock.

Startled, she flung herself at the door and rattled the handle, but it was secured. She sank to her knees, peered through the keyhole, and found a gray eye blinking back at her.

"Sir," she exclaimed. "There has been some mistake. A very dreadful mistake. I insist you unlock this door at once."

"I'm sorry, Miss Vyne. It is more than my life's worth to let you out."

"But I can explain everything."

"Indeed, madam, and so you will. To the justice of the peace tomorrow in Morecroft." The eye disappeared.

Fuming, Ellie tossed her bonnet across the room. That damned rake Hartley had not bothered to come after her himself, but sent this man to apprehend her. He didn't know her so well as he imagined, if he thought she'd go meekly to a hanging. She ran to the window and tried the latch, only to find it thickly painted over, impossible to open. Returning to the door, hatpin in one hand, she knelt again and thrust the sharp end into the keyhole, intent on working the lock free.

She heard a low cough, and then Mr. Grieves's voice through the door again. "I do not advise it, madam. Evading justice will only make things worse. And you will find no horses free to take you anywhere tonight."

She sat back on her heels.

"I suggest you enjoy your supper, Miss Vyne," he added. "It may well be your last."

❧

"Did she fall for it, Grieves?"

The valet climbed up into the hayloft beside his master and sneezed hard. "I believe so, sir. Her comments as I left her locked in were quite strident, and her oaths fulsome."

James grinned, falling back on one elbow. "Good. And Ophelia Southwold?"

"She awaits you in the darkened recesses of a small buttery behind the kitchens. I explained to the lady that you are on a mission of the utmost secrecy and that you will be with her in due course."

"How long do you think that will keep her out of the way?"

"A considerable duration, sir." Grieves showed him a small key. "I took the liberty of locking her in also. The kitchen maid is a particular friend of mine."

"Really, Grieves? You are a dark horse."

"One tries one's best, sir. Pleasures should be taken where they can be found."

James chuckled. "Indeed."

Grieves rustled about in the hay, burrowing deeper. "'Twill be a bitter-cold night."

"Could be worse. At least it's not snowing."

The valet rubbed the end of his nose, where a drip of water had just landed after falling gracefully through the air from a hole in the roof above. "Forgive me, sir, but you did say this is a prank on Miss Vyne?"

"Yes."

"I see, sir. Yes. She must be greatly put out. In that large, warm, comfortable room. That should have been ours."

"I hear your tone, Grieves, and I remain unmoved by it."

"I am just too ill educated to understand the jest I suppose, not having the benefit of a Cambridge education."

James sighed and shook his head. "You keep my coat, Grieves. I'll manage without it." He was hot enough, thinking about the punishment soon to be carried out on the wayward Miss Vyne.

He gave her half an hour before he returned to the room, unlocked her door, and stepped inside. He expected to find her in a state of panic, ready to repent and plead for his help; instead he found the woman calmly seated, filling her face with his supper.

"There you are, Hartley. Now you can explain to that man, Grieves, that this is all a silly misunderstanding."

She took her arrest with a pinch of salt, he thought grimly. Probably been in similar situations before. The wretched liar looked quite at home in her imprisonment. She'd cost him a thousand pounds, he reminded himself yet again. She'd better be worth every penny. Every damn penny. It must be almost twenty years since he'd raced about the country after a woman.

Crossing the room toward her, he swept off his damp hat, aware of his unsteady hands. Twitches of anticipation moved through his body like dominos falling and tipping into one another. The bed in the room loomed large—as if it had grown since he was last there. He took a breath, reminding himself that he was in charge of this game. He was a Hartley, and Hartleys were always in control.

He managed a tight smile. "Misunderstanding?"

"That's right. I didn't steal those diamonds, and you know it." Brazen chit.

"Do I?"

Fork halfway to her mouth, she paused. "You know the count won them at cards."

"The count?"

"That's right," she replied, slowly and condescendingly, as if to a child.

He pulled up a chair to sit across the table from her. "I'm not certain I can convince my grandmother of your innocence, since you, and not he, possess the diamonds. She will blame you, naturally, for the theft." He licked his lips, tasting the rain. "I'm inclined to find you guilty myself. It goes against the grain to do otherwise with you."

"James Hartley!" She pushed back her chair and stood swiftly. "Those diamonds were never stolen, and you know it. They were acquired over a game of cards." She jabbed a finger at him. "Given to the count by *your* floozy Ophelia Southwold. Can you deny that you are as much at fault for losing them as he is for taking possession?"

Again he thought she'd missed her calling. Should have been on the stage.

Leaning back in his chair, James kept his face stern. "The diamond I received this morning came from you, madam. How did you get your hands on his loot?"

She had a ready answer. "I asked the count to give them to me."

"Perhaps you were in it together all along?" He needed to know how much she'd participated in knowingly. "Or is he out to get something more from me, by using you and my diamonds as bait?"

She shook her head, and agitated curls bounced around her face.

"I'll see what can be done to clear your name, but if the count can't be found…" He slowly crossed his legs and set his hat over his knee. "Save yourself and tell me where he is."

She began to pace, and her muddy hem swirled around her ankles. "You know he did not steal that necklace."

"Lady Southwold will swear he did steal it from her."

"She's lying, of course! She gave them to him, and she offered much more. Things I am too ladylike to speak about."

He laughed scornfully. "And I should believe you…why, exactly?"

"Don't then! I'm sure I don't care."

"Where is your lover now? Does he know you're here with me?"

She stopped with her back to him, her shoulders tense. "I don't know where he is."

Fibber. *He and I have a very close connection. We are almost inseparable.*

Spinning around, she suddenly ran over and knelt before him, fingers steepled under her chin. "I know you can save me, James. Please. I didn't mean any harm. Surely you can speak on my behalf to the justice of the peace in Morecroft." Her eyes were very big, shining.

"I'll do anything." She laid the side of her face on his
knee, and he almost leapt out of his chair. "Dear James."

"Well," he coughed. "I'll try my best." He shifted
uncomfortably on the chair, aroused by her closeness,
her sudden vulnerability—something he'd never seen
in her before. She kissed his knee and then, with her
shoulders, nudged his thighs apart, working her way
between them. Her soft hands slid up his chest, finally
reaching his neck, where she clasped them tightly
around his nape. Her face was close enough to kiss.

"I know you can save me, James," she whispered.

With her body pressed against his, he couldn't
speak. The ravenous stirring of desire held him down
in that chair, at her mercy.

"You will save me, won't you?"

She kissed his chin, then all the way along his jaw
to his ear.

"I can see now I've been a very bad girl." She
licked his earlobe. "Only you can amend my ways."

Aha! At last she saw it too. His hands went to her
bottom, gripping it tightly, holding her against him.
"Yes," he ground out, eyes closed, teeth grazing her
cheek. "Yes." He stroked her through her gown and
squeezed her rounded flesh, lurid ideas of how to
amend her ways filling his mind.

Hands to his shoulders, she pushed back to see his
face. "Is that what you wanted to hear?"

He stared as his pulse pounded in his temple.

"Let's not be foolish. We each have something the
other needs. You need a wife and, unfortunately, I
need money." She patted his cheek, hard enough to
shake raindrops from his stubble. "But I will not beg

you for your help, James. I've survived twenty-seven years on my own wits, and I daresay I can find another way to keep my family solvent. I've managed this long. So, if you want a weak woman dependent on you for everything, choose someone else." As she rose to her feet and brushed down her skirt, she added, "If you want a relatively painless marriage with a woman who won't ask questions, or expect your love and affection, or demand you spend time in her company and sulk when you don't"—she finally drew a sharp breath—"then you'll speak to this Grieves person, let him know it was a misunderstanding. Otherwise, I'll take my chance with the judge, and you can find another woman to marry you. Something you've evidently had no luck at, or you'd never consider me."

Point made, she returned to her seat and continued her meal. *His* meal!

James retrieved his hat from the floor and tapped it on his thigh. So that's how she wanted to play. She still protected the count—the man who used her for his own blackmail schemes. Perhaps she'd taken a share of that thousand already. It could have been her idea.

"Why did you drag me into the country like this, Vyne?" No doubt her excuses were colorful and entertaining.

"I had to get you away from London and all its dissolute distractions, because I want your sole attention."

"Why?"

She sipped her ale, those wide violet eyes watching him over the rim of her tankard. "I'll give you those diamonds back on one condition. Five conditions, actually."

He smiled stiffly, wishing his blood would cool, but her caress left him piping hot, rigid as marble. James didn't know what to do with himself. As, no doubt, the temptress was aware. "Hmmm?"

"I want your stud services for five nights. While we're in the country together."

Incapable of speech, he watched her pour ale with a steady hand, her expression unreadable. God in heaven she was a menace, he thought, more dangerous than he gave her credit for in the past.

"Five nights for five diamonds," she added as if he might not understand the significance of the number. "You see, I've been thinking about your marriage proposal. The truth is, I would like a child."

The surprises continued falling around him like ripened walnuts.

Then she added, "But what if you can't give me one?"

"I can't say the possibility had occurred to me."

"Of course not. To save us both unnecessary trouble, I'll give you five nights to perform your duty. We should make certain everything works. Is that agreeable to you?"

Words would not form.

"I don't mind if the five nights are consecutive, Hartley. Whatever is convenient. If I become pregnant, then we'll marry to make my child legitimate. If I do not conceive a child, then we'll both be free to go our separate ways. No harm done."

One thing was for sure, he realized, she would never cry on his shoulder with her problems. She didn't want to be saved by him, or comforted.

She wanted to be serviced.

"You've been thinking this through, obviously."

"Of course. To embark on any arrangement with a man like you is a mistake, unless one considers everything."

"Everything?" He was incredulous, although that was perhaps not a strong enough word.

"You may not be up to it, and I should hate to agree to this *convenient* marriage arrangement and then one day wake up and find I'm too old to have children." She shot him a glance that could be described as unladylike at best, blatantly lusty at worst. "Why shouldn't I give you a chance to provide me with the child I want?" Her eyelids looked heavy again. The tip of her tongue swept her upper lip, wiping off a little froth from the ale. "With your looks and my brains... Don't look so peevish, Hartley." She chuckled. "Bedding me won't put you out too much. I'll be very good, I promise, and oblige your every desire."

Her bold, teasing words made him restless, and his shaft stretched uncomfortably another inch, trying the material of his already too-tight breeches.

"Five nights for five diamonds, Hartley. You do want them all back, don't you?" Picking up her fork, she finished the last few bites on her plate, making the most of his hospitality. And his mute confusion. "There is only one other thing," she added.

Of course, there must be something more.

"For those five nights there'd better be no other women."

James choked out a response. "And no other men."

She nodded. "Good. I shall have your sole attention then for five nights. In the country."

He bowed his head. "And I shall have yours."

The fire in the hearth fizzled and spat as rain came down the chimney and tried to put it out. He knew the feeling. Nothing had put his flames out either. She'd lit them by crawling between his thighs and pressing her body to his. Now she'd left them to burn, deliberately.

"Unless, of course," he added quietly, "you don't want to give me up in five nights."

The impertinent vixen had the gall to laugh. "I'll take that gamble."

James said nothing. His fingers tapped his hat, and his gaze fixed on her lips as she swallowed the last morsel.

"And this is *not* an engagement, Hartley. It is an agreement to marry if—and only if—there is a child. I've had little fortune with engagements, so I prefer not to call it that."

"Whatever you wish."

Several moments passed while he gathered his thoughts, which she'd massacred into little pieces with the long sword of her tongue. Just when he thought he was in control of this situation, she'd snatched it away again. He did not like this. Not at all.

"Perhaps you'd like some ale?" she inquired. "You look rather apoplectic."

"No. Thank you." He could see he'd need his wits about him tonight.

He stood, walked to the door. When he swung around to face her again, she was licking her fingers and humming carelessly.

She paused and looked surprised he was still there.

"We'll begin now then," he said, turning the key with a loud click.

"Now?"

"You said at my convenience. Madam." He didn't trust a curl on her head, and she wasn't running away from him again. Never again.

Chapter 10

SHE GLANCED AT THE REMAINS LITTERED ACROSS THE table and realized there was nothing left to eat. No excuse to put this off.

He was pulling his shirt over his head. "Haste, Vyne."

Her body stirred, and her pulse beat fast enough to whip egg whites into meringue. "Could you look in my trunk for a Brussels lace bed robe?"

His knuckles rested on his hips as he glared at her.

"I'd like to change behind the screen," she explained.

Still he hesitated, already half-naked himself. From his expression, she worried he might not only refuse to get her robe but would rip the clothes off her with his teeth. Firelight swept over the ridges of his fine torso as he stretched his arms overhead, delaying.

"You do know what Brussels lace looks like?" she asked politely and with a deliberate smile. "I'm sure you've seen plenty. Or are you usually too inebriated to notice?"

Finally he stalked to her trunk, kicked the broken lid open, and crouched to rummage inside. He withdrew the flimsy garment and tossed it at her. She scuttled gratefully behind the dressing screen in one corner of the chamber, where she took a few moments to prepare and compose herself. Peeking between the panels of the screen, she watched him undress. He kicked off his boots and then stripped his breeches and smallclothes. His every gesture was sharp, concise, angry. She'd had no idea that demanding a stud service would infuriate him to this degree. But this affair had to be on her terms. She couldn't let him make the rules. She risked enough to be with him as it was.

He leapt onto the bed and sprawled there, waiting for her. Of course, he thought her experienced, but Ellie's practical knowledge was based on her one encounter with Walter Winthorne's small equipment and a few, merely exploratory misadventures with her father's groom when she was young and curious. She knew what happened next, but there were variants— mysterious things she'd only heard about. She eyed his muscular length and felt the warm heaviness between her thighs. James Hartley, her wicked plaything for five nights.

"Haste, Vyne," he bellowed again, hands behind his head, half-propped up on pillows.

His manner was cool, even detached. Ellie tried not to notice. After all, she knew what she was getting into when she suggested this arrangement. She had no one to blame but herself.

She tied the silk belt around her waist and stepped out into the firelight. His eyes narrowed. He went very still, reminding her of a panther at the zoo, waiting for the keeper to lower a lump of raw meat into its cage.

"About time," he said.

She couldn't agree more. He beckoned with one finger. Moving closer to the bed, she boldly placed her hand on his thigh. He was warm when she touched him, and the hairs on his body were soft, the muscle beneath hard as steel. Lying stark naked there before her, blue eyes afire and hair warmed by soft candlelight, he looked like a debauched archangel.

"You must have had many propositions like this one," she teased, "with all this male beauty fallen to your lot."

His thigh flexed under her stroking palm. "Have you *made* many such propositions before?"

"Countless. Haven't you heard the rumors about me?"

He exhaled softly. "What exactly did you have planned for me, Vyne?" Now there was a hint of amusement in his tone.

Her gaze traveled upward to his face, not skipping an inch, and her breath quickened. "Whatever you desire."

James hitched onto his hip and patted the mattress beside him. "Then we'd best get started."

Ellie felt her pulse flutter wildly. Candlelight danced over his hair, catching on the hint of gold and polishing it. One by one, she took stock of his features again: the slender nose, artfully sculpted lips that were always so quick to sneer at her, high cheekbones, and eyes of a brilliant, tropical hue tonight. The bruise around his right eye lent an air of danger, brought his proudly angelic features down to earth and within reach of a naughty little devil like her.

"If I must be used as a breeding device, Vyne, I'd like to get on with it."

Clearly he was ready. There was no hiding his arousal.

Dear God, what was she doing? She shook her head and laughed gently. God had no answer for her, but the devil might.

❧

As she fussed over the knotted belt of her lacy bed robe, he recognized her intent to delay again. James grabbed her around the waist, pulling her onto the bed and securing her quickly beneath his body. When she first stepped out from behind that screen, the firelight behind her, he saw she still wore her corset and chemise beneath the robe, but these items didn't keep him from admiring the shape of her legs or from seeing she wore no drawers.

His reaction was instant, and when she touched his thigh, he'd almost erupted on the spot. Now he ground his arousal against those flimsy fripperies she insisted on wearing to bed. She blew curls out of her mouth, her cheeks pink, eyes shining up at him, her warm sumptuousness separated from his hard, naked body by an almost transparent linen chemise, a bit of lace, and a corset. His heart thumped away, shuddering through his body.

Having approached him warily, like a wild animal cautious of a trap, she now laughed at him again as if he was there solely for her damned amusement. Each gasping breath made the swell of her breasts push upward into his chest. Her skin was fine, smooth. Not as pale as fashion decreed for a lady, but glowing in the warm, pulsing light.

"Are you ready for your first servicing?" He parted

her legs with his broad thighs, his hands firm around her wrists, holding them to the pillow on either side of her tousled head. "I'm not of a mind to delay."

She strained forward and reached for his lips, but he didn't give them just yet. She arched, and he moved his hips, ensuring she felt every inch of his desire for her. For the last few nights he'd endured this state of agitation and had no opportunity to soothe the pangs with a good release. It was all her fault, because he hadn't been able to look at another woman since the night he found her in the count's bed. Now he finally had this notorious temptress beneath him, restless, throbbing with barely restrained energy. Wanting him to give her a child. She spoke as if the child would be hers to raise—not theirs. She did not expect him to be around much or take any interest in fatherhood. As if he could donate his seed and not care. That was how little she thought of him.

James no longer felt the cold damp of that dreary day; his aches and pains swiftly dissolved. He was less than an inch from impaling her, his sac tight, blood filling his cock, his seed rushing. He stared down at her face amid the mess of dark curls. Desire flooded her eyes. She didn't try to stop it. Unashamed. Incorrigible. Downright impertinent. And beautiful.

Beautiful trouble. He'd always known it, always tried to look the other way and avoid temptation. Stood aside and watched other men dance with her, laugh with her, whisper in her ear.

No more.

Here was the woman so long forbidden to him, and now he would take what he wanted.

Those long legs stroked his thighs, his hips, and his flanks. The urgency between them both was about to overflow.

Finally he released her wrists and kissed her, his hands in her hair, binding it around his long fingers. He thrust his tongue and his hips at the same time, and he could have possessed her there and then, if not for her chemise—that thin barrier still in his way. All that wriggling had gathered the silk up to her thighs, and there it bunched, moistened by their mutual heat. It teased the head of his cock, caressing it. He wanted to rip the material aside and plow forward to claim her.

Somehow he reined it in. He had told her he was in no mood to delay, but having waited this long, perhaps he could wait a little longer. He'd make her wait too.

When he slid down the bed, the impertinent miss demanded to know where he went. Her hands clutched for him as he slipped from her grasp.

His palms flat to her inner thighs, he pressed them wide apart and then settled his shoulders between her knees. "Woman, you are altogether too impatient, too wanton. Please show a little restraint."

As he rolled her chemise up over her hips and out of his way, she tried closing her legs, but he had her trapped, spread now for *his* teasing. He pressed a gentle kiss to her sex, barely touching. Was that a purr he heard that rumbled softly down her body? If not, there was a kitten somewhere, hiding under the bed. He licked her just once, very quickly. The divine, creamy sweetness burst upon his tongue, and he wanted more, but he made her wait until she lifted off the mattress in frustration. Then he kissed her intimately again, lingering this time, letting her tender flesh bloom wet and hot under his lips.

"James," she groaned as her fingers scrabbled for his hair, "what are you doing?"

"This is one of five nights, woman. I'm not going to rush it."

He wanted Ellie Vyne completely at his mercy, because he was very nearly at hers.

Slowly he lapped at her sweetness, relishing the wickedness of teasing her, enjoying his treat. Her breathing changed, quickened. Shattered gasps broke over his head. James swirled his tongue against her soft, hot flesh and slipped inside. He closed his eyes. The need swelled within his loins, clamoring to be satisfied. His erect, throbbing shaft rubbed against the mattress.

She was trembling. Laid out for him. Breathless. Her fingers tugged on his hair, almost pulling it out by the root.

Close to giving in and letting her peak, somehow he held back again, delayed just to torment her. He drew a breath and then another as she squirmed before him, straining to close her thighs, wanting more, demanding he let her finish. She was a hair's breadth from implosion. Finally he touched his tongue to her sex again.

❧

She closed her eyes as the tremor shook her violently. Lord, what had he done to her? Was that sound her own exhale, broken into a low, throaty moan of a most uncivilized nature? Her fingers were bunched tight in the sheet, and yet she was flying, soaring.

This is one of five nights, woman. I'm not going to rush it.

True to his word, he took his time. She certainly could not complain. Finally reassembling her wits, she opened her eyes and found him leaning over her again, watching her face. Even through shadows and dim, flickering light, she felt the searching blue intensity in his eyes. She read his thoughts. He was well aware of the trouble they were getting into and couldn't prevent it any more than she could. They were hopeless cases. This forbidden desire had built in them both, and there was only one way to vanquish it.

"Turn over then," he whispered huskily.

"What?"

She felt the vibrations of his low chuckles. "Corset. Laces. Off."

"Oh. Yes." Ellie rolled over so he could tackle the job. "Hurry," she urged.

His lips moved wetly across the nape of her neck, and she felt his teeth nibbling her skin gently. "If you want to be mounted properly by this stallion, you must have patience, my naughty filly."

But Ellie found she had little left of that commodity. The sad remains were fast dripping through her fingers. "I wonder what your grandmother would say if she saw you now."

He tugged on her corset laces with far more strength than required, in the manner of an extremely surly, and incompetent, lady's maid. "I'm sure her words would be plentiful, whatever they were."

Ellie laughed. He did not.

As he knelt astride her legs, she jumped at the sensation of his naked manhood touching her bottom. The heat almost melted the thin material of her chemise. "I find it hard to believe you've never unlaced a woman's corset before, Hartley," she complained and gripped the pillow with both arms.

"I've never unlaced *your* corset before," he replied. "For some reason, I'm all thumbs in your case."

Startled by his candid confession, she lay still, her complaints sunk into the pillow, her body attuned to the touch of his fingertips, willing them to go faster, willing them to have sudden dexterity. The anticipation might kill her slowly, but she was certain he could revive her from death itself. The way he kissed her was unlike anything she'd ever known. The senseless delight that skipped through her at his every steamy, blue-eyed glance was likely to cause her injury if she didn't soon do something about it.

He pressed his lips to her shoulder, while his fingers continued pulling her laces free. His breathing was haphazard, each branding kiss to her flesh pressed a little harder, left a little longer, following the last much more swiftly. As he loosened the corset, he pulled down on her chemise, exposing her spine to his lips, one vertebrae at a time, one shiver per breath.

The last lace was almost free, and his kisses had reached the hollow at the base of her spine, when it suddenly occurred to Ellie that the intrusive thumping sound was neither her heart nor large hailstones falling against the roof. Someone was at the door, pounding on it with their fist.

❧

James swung open the door, breeches and shirt pulled on in haste, his mind boiling, hands ready to crush the windpipe of whoever had disturbed his night.

It was Grieves.

"I'm sorry, sir," the valet murmured, "but something has arisen of a most unfortunate nature."

Behind him he heard the sounds of Ellie scrambling off the bed, rushing behind the dressing screen. Frustration bubbled in his veins and uncomfortably heated certain parts of his anatomy.

"What is it?" he hissed. "Has the other one got out?"

"No, sir." Grieves lowered his voice to a whisper. "That item is still safely secured and sleeping like a pup, having imbibed a jug of cider."

"Thank Christ! Then what on earth—?"

"I had the idea of staying drier in the carriage, sir, but upon entering, I made a sudden, alarming discovery."

James realized his valet had a bundle of something at his side. In the shadowy light of the passage, it took a few moments for his eyes to adjust, and then the bundle looked up at him and exclaimed, "I told you I was running away. Men never listen."

He cursed under his breath.

"Indeed, sir," Grieves remarked. "A substantial snoring noise alerted me to the young lady's presence, and when I lifted the seat, there she was, inside the luggage compartment, tightly curled in the manner of a prodded woodlice."

Lady Mercy Danforthe yawned while both men looked down at her, one in bemusement, the other in despair.

"I can't have this, for pity's sake," James muttered. He had enough trouble trying to keep an eye on the Vyne woman, who may or may not be part of some dastardly blackmail plot, using her body, her lips, and her eyes to beguile him completely. His hands were full already, and the last thing he needed was this troubled little creature hanging onto his boot heels. He clawed a hand through his hair. His heated blood still hadn't yet returned to normal, and the beast of reckless desire still had some control of his voice. "What are we supposed to do with her?" he croaked.

"I can send her back to London, sir, with an escort. If someone trustworthy can be found. Perhaps—the item stowed in the buttery might be of some use."

"Good God, no!" Ophelia Southwold was the last woman he'd entrust with the care of a child.

"Or I'll take her myself, sir."

But James wasn't having that either. Things tended to go awry for him when his valet wasn't around to help, and it was a long way to send her back. He didn't want the blame falling upon his shoulders if anything happened to the wretched girl. "No, no. Let her brother come and get her. It's time he took the responsibility upon himself."

The short young lady regarded James with huge, cowlike eyes but said nothing.

"Very good, sir, I shall send a messenger to the Earl of Everscham and let him know his sister is safe and well."

"And in need of a ride home. He can surely abandon his pleasures in Town long enough to fetch her."

Grieves bowed. "Sorry to disrupt your evening, sir,

but I did not know where else to put the young lady. She could not very well remain in the luggage compartment."

"I don't see why not."

"Because it was very cramped," the child exclaimed. "I'm sure it has quite ruined my best sprigged muslin, and the fur trim on my coat is all crushed."

Suddenly, a soft voice emerged from behind the screen. "That's quite all right, Grieves, we were done in any case. The young lady can come in and have some supper."

Grieves, who seldom changed color, could now pass for a boiled lobster.

James began tucking his shirt into his breeches, and annoyance ripped through him. She thought they were done, did she? *Au contraire!* He grabbed the stowaway by a fistful of cloak and drew her into the room. "Lady Mercy, do meet my fiancée, Miss Mariella Vyne."

The girl glared at the dressing screen. "Fiancée? *Fiancée?*"

Victory! The chit was no longer gazing up at him with limp-eyed adoration.

"Very pleased to meet you, Lady Mercy." Ellie stuck her hand out around the side of the screen.

There was a moment of silence.

Then the small, angry creature opened her mouth, closed her eyes, and let out an ear-splitting shriek of horror. Fearing it could bring every soul in the inn to their chamber door, James attempted to cover her mouth with his hand. The result was a bite so hard that he swung his hand away and almost hit Grieves, who had the presence of mind to step back but, in so doing, knocked over the decorative suit of armor. James was cursing, doubled over and nursing his hand, when the armor fell upon him, followed by the pikestaff, sending him to the floor with a bang.

The last thing he remembered before someone blew out all his candles and thick darkness descended was the taste of dust, the clamorous cries of Lady Mercy, and the rapid approach of Ellie's slippers.

❦

"Is he dead?" Lady Mercy squealed as she fell to her knees. "Oh, my beloved James! I've killed you!"

Grieves helped Ellie lift the pieces of dented armor from the prostrate man. She couldn't believe it was heavy enough to fell him like that, for he was no small weight himself, but the pikestaff had hit the back of his head quite hard. Alarmed, she saw blood on his forehead where it had smacked into the floor. He was pale, his eyes closed, no movement.

"We need a physician at once," she exclaimed.

"I shall be hanged for a murder of passion," sobbed Lady Mercy, tears streaking her face. Ellie had no idea who the child belonged to or why she was following James, but it was nothing shocking to find women of all shapes and sizes trailing along in his wake. Half of them, she was sure, never knew why they did it either.

She reached out to reassure the child, but Lady Mercy shrank away as if she had leprosy. "Dreadful person. He was supposed to marry me."

"Let's not worry about that now. We ought to take care of James, don't you think?"

The girl sniffed, and a tear wobbled from her chin. "Poor, dear James."

With Mr. Grieves's help and Lady Mercy's hindrance, Ellie was able to get him onto the bed. She washed the blood away, using one of her own kerchiefs and some water from the ewer behind the dressing screen. Lady Mercy stood at the foot of the bed, wringing her hands with remorse. As soon as Grieves hurried off to find a physician, the patient opened his eyes.

"Oops. My head hurts," he groaned.

"I'm not surprised." Now she'd cleaned off the blood, there was only a miniscule bump on his forehead and a little scratch, nothing monstrous. Men always made more than necessary of a tiny wound. "Lie still."

"Thank you, my lady," he muttered, and his eyelashes flickered shut again. "I think I will, if it's all the same to you, my lady."

Ellie squinted down at him. *My lady?*

His voice drifted sleepily. "I won't be any trouble."

"Poor, darling James!" Lady Mercy rushed around the bed and seized his hand in both her much-smaller ones. He certainly had a knack for rousing female sympathy.

"I must get back to work," James mumbled, managing a weak smile.

Work? Now Ellie began to doubt that was such a small knock to his head after all. The damage could be worse than it looked.

"Can't lie about all day," he added. "Things to be done."

"I'm sure they can wait," she replied warily.

"But I've got…services…to perform. Stud services."

Ellie's face grew hot.

The wounded man murmured in a strange, soft voice. "I'm sorry, my lady. Shouldn't have mentioned it. Shhh." He pressed a finger to his lips. "Secret. Not to tell."

"Could you stir up the fire, Lady Mercy?" Ellie cried, her voice high and thin. "It feels a little cold in here." At first it seemed the girl would refuse. Only when Ellie pointed out that James might feel chilled was the request obeyed.

While the girl turned her back, apparently absorbed in prodding the coals, his lips popped open to expel a soft moan. "Mustn't forget the soldiers. There should always be soldiers. But she's got a lovely, lovely pair of bubbies."

Ellie looked over at Lady Mercy. Now violently and gleefully assaulting the fire with an iron poker, the girl had temporarily forgotten her concern for "poor, darling James." His piteous groans were too subtle to be heard at that distance.

"Stop it," Ellie whispered frantically. "Just be quiet. Don't talk."

"Someone ought to give that wench a spanking." He chuckled, low.

"James! Hush."

He gripped the pleats of her bed robe as she leaned over him. "A thousand pounds you owe me. I paid for your company. I'll take that back and with interest, madam. We are not done. You owe me five nights."

Carefully she pried his hand from the material, but then his fingers clung to hers with the same determination.

"Tell Mr. Grieves I'll be back to work as soon as the sun comes up, madam. A valet's work is never done. If you could walk a day in my shoes, you'd know."

≈

The physician was a rotund fellow with a wig that sat slightly askew on his head, waistcoat buttons that were all—apart from one—in the wrong holes, very bright eyes, and a merry disposition, clearly increased by drink. As he stumbled around the bed, examining James in a slapdash fashion that Ellie could only hope had some purpose unapparent to the layperson, he hummed under his breath and occasionally let out a raucous laugh. He swayed, clutching for the bedpost and missing by several inches.

"I'm sure 'tis naught but a little concussion, madam," he announced. "A good night's rest will help. Keep the feet elevated so blood returns to the brain. I do not advise the application of brandy or any other believed restorative. I don't hold with it." He punctuated this with a loud, rumbling burp, which, had she held a flame to it, would have set fire to the bed drapes.

She frowned. "But he seems not to know who he is or where he is. He thinks he's a valet."

"That, madam, is the nature of concussion," he slurred. "'Tis a sorry business, but there we are. Accidents do happen. The brain will right itself."

No sooner had he given her this straw of hope, than he snatched it away again.

"Or it may not, of course. There's nothing one can do but wait."

Ellie hated feeling helpless. The more she studied the man stretched out on the bed, the more wounded he looked. Much of his sorry appearance was due to the preexisting bruise around his eye, but when combined with the blood on his forehead, it was more than she could bear. "Surely there is something we can—"

"No. No." The physician snapped his bag swiftly shut. "In fact, madam, the least one does, the better. He must have no shocks. Let him come slowly around to reality. The brain is much better left to heal itself."

Grieves held out the physician's mud-spattered greatcoat. "You say we should let him believe whatever he has in his mind and not try to make him remember who he is?" There was a detectable note of glee in the valet's tone.

"Precisely. Forcing the memory does no good whatsoever and might only cause harm."

Shaking her head, Ellie walked to the window and looked out on the dark, rain-soaked yard of the inn. How on earth were they going to manage James now and get him safely to his grandmother in this state?

When the physician left, Grieves tried to comfort her. "We'll take him directly on to Morecroft and let his own physician examine him on the morrow, madam. Do not fret."

"But how can we let his grandmother see him like this? She'll think it's my fault, no doubt."

"Quite." Grieves gave her an odd smile, as if he tried to withhold it but gave in. "Perhaps her ladyship is better off not knowing. For now." He straightened his lips and attempted a solemn face. "The lady need not be worried unduly, and I'm certain he will soon improve. It is, after all, far from the first time something heavy has been struck about his head."

It was decided that Lady Mercy should stay with them in the room that night, and Grieves returned to the stables. The rain had eased off, and he assured her he was quite happy to sleep there. The valet seemed in a very good mood for a man whose master lay confused and helpless, but his blithely confident demeanor made Ellie feel a little better.

She ordered another supper for Lady Mercy and watched her eat. Continually she checked that James was still breathing, and then, satisfied that he was, returned to her seat at the table.

"Tell me how you came to be hiding in Mr. Hartley's carriage, Lady Mercy."

"I ran away, of course. To be with *him*." Her small face darkened in a fierce frown. "Now you're here. It's most unfair."

"Life very often is."

"But I am in love with James Hartley!" Lady Mercy's impassioned declaration sent the candle flames into a wild dance. "He saved my life, you know." Thus Ellie heard all about a rescue on horseback several weeks ago. "No one else came to my aid. My brother was not watching. I was quite alone. I could have died had James not ridden after me."

"That was very gallant of him."

"I remember it vividly. I was wearing a pink satin spencer topped with a rose-and-white striped scarf. And I had my lime-green gloves. Oh, and some extremely lush plumes in my hat that made Cecelia Montague blatantly emerald with envy. Although she denied it feverishly."

"I see."

"Has poor, darling James ever saved your life?"

She laughed. "No. I save my own." She'd always been her own savior.

"I know you don't love him like I do. You can't possibly. Do you?" the girl demanded.

Ellie hesitated. "It doesn't really matter whom we love, because the other person is sometimes incapable of loving in return. If you do not have those expectations, you won't be hurt or disappointed. A person is much better off independent, relying on no one else, keeping their heart to themselves."

Lady Mercy regarded her with that peculiarly precocious hauteur. "Are you his harlot?"

"I beg your pardon?"

"A woman of the night? A loose woman? A demirep?"

"Good gracious, no. Whatever—?"

"But your clothes were almost all off, and you were in bed with him."

Uh, oh. "I was merely changing my clothes. They were wet from the rain. Mr. Hartley was…helping me."

"I heard him say he paid for you. Something about five nights."

Ellie replied curtly, "He has a concussion. He does not know what he's saying."

"My brother prefers to spend his money on harlots than on proper young ladies, because they don't make things complicated. So he says."

"Does he indeed?"

"He says he's never going to get married."

"Probably a wise choice," she replied wryly. "For the sake of women everywhere." Reaching across the cluttered table, she took the ale jug from the girl's hands. "You should have lemonade."

The arrogant little madam wrinkled her nose. "I can have ale. This is very weak. My brother lets me drink wine at home. I even tried brandy once. He dared me to finish a whole glass of it for a shilling."

"Your brother sounds quite a character. I assume he's your only guardian?"

The girl nodded. "He lets me do whatever I like, since I got rid of Nanny."

Ellie smiled. "If life is so fine at home, why are you running away?"

Lady Mercy's green eyes widened just enough to show a sudden fearful glimmer. Ellie remembered what she'd said about the incident on the horse.

"Perhaps being with James makes you feel safer?"

Again the girl didn't answer. She yawned heartily instead, rubbing her eyes, shoulders slumped. Apparently no one cared much about her posture either.

Ellie made up a cot at the foot of the bed for Lady Mercy but resigned herself to a wakeful night in the chair by the fire. The child was quick to point out the impropriety of unmarried people sharing the same room all night. Ellie reminded her that James needed a nurse to watch over him. Under those circumstances, she said, the rules could be bent.

"And you will be our chaperone, Lady Mercy," she added.

"Yes. I shall keep watch! There will be none of *that* going on, while I'm here."

Indeed, she thought with a sigh, there could not be.

James opened his eyes a half inch. He'd lost his memory only for the first few moments after wakening from the blow. Then, once his senses returned full force, he took advantage of the accident. He was going to have a little fun with Miss Vyne, and if she came out of her five nights unscathed, it wouldn't be for lack of trying on his part. He'd get his thousand pounds' worth and then some. Stud services indeed!

Very cautiously he slid out of bed, taking a blanket from the many she'd laid over him, and carried it to where she slept in the chair. Lady Mercy snored away contentedly on the cot at the foot of the bed. He laid the blanket over Ellie, tucking it around her, trying not to think too hard about that luscious body he was prevented from enjoying fully tonight. She stirred slightly. Her eyes flickered open but did not quite focus on his face as he leaned over her.

"Sleep, my lady," he whispered. His lips brushed her twitching eyelids. "You'll need it before our next encounter."

"Hmmm."

He allowed his fingers to drift gently down the side of her cheek, then her graceful neck. As much as her steadily heaving breaths tempted, he couldn't let his hand stray any farther. Not tonight, alas.

Chapter 11

SHE WOKE WITH A START, SURPRISED SHE'D EVER FALLEN asleep. Her neck was stiff from sleeping in that chair. Lady Mercy, already cloaked and booted, a fur muff hanging around her neck, stood beside her, prodding her steadily with one finger.

"Wake up, Vyne woman. He said to wake you and tell you to go down."

"What? Who?" She leapt up and wiped drool from her mouth with one hand.

The bed was empty, last night's supper things all removed, and the room tidied, even the pieces of armor back in their place, guarding the door.

"He still thinks he's a servant," the girl added, singsong. "It's all your fault, because if you hadn't used your dreadful feminine wiles to seduce him, he would have waited for me. He would never be here with you, a strumpet bereft of virtue, and I would never have screamed."

How quickly the girl found a culprit to lessen her part in last night's accident. It reminded Ellie of herself.

She caught the girl's coat sleeve between thumb

and forefinger. "Lady Mercy, you must promise not to speak a word to anyone about what you saw last night."

"Why should I promise you anything?"

"Because until Mr. Hartley is fit and well,"—*and able to defend himself,* she thought miserably—"it is best not to mention it." The last thing he needed, in his current state, was his grandmother finding out through rumor that James had spent the night with Ellie Vyne at the Barley Mow. "For his sake," she added, knowing where this girl's loyalties lie.

The truculent child stuck out her lower lip.

Ellie sighed deeply. "I will owe you a favor."

Finally the girl agreed to do her best. "Although I can't promise," she chirped. "I am terrible at keeping secrets." With that crumb of comfort thrown out, she stuck her freckled nose in the air and flounced away.

Somewhere after midnight it must have rained hard again. Fat, rippling puddles dotted the inn yard, and the air was thick with damp. Misty clouds were emitted with every breath as the passengers waited for loading onto the mail coach. Several faces turned her way in envy when James carried her battered trunk on his shoulder and cleared a path through the bedraggled crowd, leading her to a private carriage. It was the same sleek black vessel that almost forced the mail coach off the road yesterday.

Mr. Grieves held the door for her and pointed out the heated brick for her feet, luring her inside with the promise of that luxury.

As she stepped up behind Lady Mercy, she heard

James cursing, struggling with her unwieldy trunk.
The catch had broken open again. The newly tied
rope knots were too loose, and several items fell to the
wet cobbles. She wanted to help him, but Mr. Grieves
advised her against it.

"Let the valet secure your trunk, Miss Vyne. Don't
trouble yourself."

"But I know the peculiar way it has to be—"

"Really, Miss Vyne, he will manage." Mr. Grieves
patted her hand and smiled broadly. "He's stronger
than he looks and very keen." Then he turned his
head and bellowed through the window, "Put some
wind in your sails, Smallwick, or I'll be forced to take
a horsewhip to your bony backside. You're keeping
Miss Vyne waiting."

Ellie flinched. "Surely that's not necessary,"
she whispered.

"Remember, he thinks he's a servant, Miss Vyne,
and the physician did say we should go along with it
until he recovers. We must not challenge his brain
with ideas so far unfamiliar to him."

"But...*Smallwick*?"

The valet gave a sheepish grin. "I thought the
name suited him, madam, and he has taken to it
without complaint."

"Mr. Grieves, that is quite evil of you."

"In life there are few pleasures to be had, madam.
One must take them where one can. Needs must."

A follower of that philosophy herself, she really
could not quarrel with it.

He raised his voice to shout through the carriage
window, "And one must talk to these fellows in the

language they understand, Miss Vyne. Smallwick must learn."

Another stifled curse preceded her trunk falling to the ground with a bang. Unconcerned by James's plight, Mr. Grieves filled the next few moments by loudly asking Lady Mercy if she slept well and how she liked her supper.

"Mr. Grieves, I do think we ought to help—"

"No, no, he has it. There. See."

Ellie gripped the window frame and peered out just in time to see his firm calves leaping up onto the back of the carriage. James was tall, which would make it doubly difficult to hang on to his precarious perch. Her mind traveled ahead to the narrow lanes, overhung with low branches. The poor man could be scratched to pieces. Looking around the relatively warm interior of Mr. Grieves's carriage, she suggested there was room for "Smallwick" inside, pointing out that rain must make his outside seat slippery. But her new traveling companion refused to entertain the thought.

She glanced out once more and saw a handsome woman waving her bonnet from the entrance of the tavern.

"James! Oh, James! Stop! James!"

Horrified, she shrank back in her seat, away from the window. Ophelia Southwold. What the devil was she doing at the Barley Mow? James, of course, having lost his memory, did not answer to the name.

The carriage jolted forward and splashed through puddles, picking up speed with no caution for anyone else in the yard. Ellie hung onto the leather strap beside her head and looked at Grieves, who was smiling merrily. He took mischievous pleasure in his master's predicament, and for the first half an hour, every bump they lurched over was accompanied by his snort of laughter and a misty-eyed grin.

Ellie tried not to worry about the unfortunate "Smallwick." But each thump of the poor man's knees against the back of the carriage made her teeth grind.

"Smallwick has quite a litany of curses," she observed finally.

"He does indeed, madam. I shall be obliged to thrash him for that language when we get to Morecroft."

Again they heard a shower of lurid curses from the man clinging to the outside of the carriage. Ellie was glad Lady Mercy wore her fur-lined bonnet pulled low over her ears to keep them warm. The girl had apparently come well prepared for winter weather. Since she'd confessed to getting rid of her nanny, it was evident she looked after herself to a surprising degree for such a small person. Some grown women of Ellie's acquaintance were not so capable of looking after themselves.

Needs must, thought Ellie, glancing again at the self-contained little girl beside her.

As they sped along, the vessel heaved from side to side, and James's knees knocked against the back of the carriage like bell clappers.

Mr. Grieves leaned across the small space to reassure her with a whisper. "It will do him good, you know, madam, to see how the other half lives."

"I suppose so." If he should remember any of it later.

The carriage bounced over a rut so violently they were almost tossed out of their seats. A loud, ominous crack followed immediately, and the barouche tilted at an angle before bumping to an abrupt, bone-wrenching halt.

"I believe we lost Smallwick," she muttered. "I heard something heavy fall."

Mr. Grieves scrambled to the door and leapt out, directly into an ankle-deep trench of rainwater. She heard the shouting but remained in her seat. She daren't look, fearing her trunk was in the mud and all her articles of intimate clothing strewn about. How typical of James to hire a driver whose main interest was speed, not the comfort of his passengers.

Lady Mercy hung out through the open window and reported on the situation with suitable tragic emphasis. "The wheel broke. Looks like we're stuck. And it's raining again. The lane will soon be flooded. We'll be swept away and most likely drowned. I'm glad I wore my best lace underthings, for I should hate for my corpse to be found in only linen."

They had to climb out before the carriage could be righted. Having helped Lady Mercy out first, Ellie took her turn and stepped backward, looking down to ensure she missed the puddle. But while her left boot was still suspended in the air, searching for a dry spot, she was seized by two strong arms and lifted bodily from the carriage.

James carried her easily, his expression earnest, his gaze directly ahead.

"It was quite all right," she said. "I could manage."

"I must take care of you, madam. It is my job to take care of you."

"Oh, dear. I must be heavy, Smallwick."

"Light as a feather, madam," he grunted.

She could feel how wet and cold he was, even through her own layers. He limped, yet gallantly carried her onward with only a few straining gasps.

Ellie ventured to lighten the mood. "I shouldn't have eaten all that supper last night. If I'd have known you'd have to carry me today, I would have starved."

He was very solemn, his gaze focused on their destination—the drier patch of road. "Would it have made a great difference, madam? One supper?"

"Yes," she replied crossly.

"What a pity it is then, madam, you had that extra pudding last night."

She glared at him. "And how do you know I had an extra pudding last night?"

He blinked innocently. "I guessed madam. It seems inevitable. Most women have so little willpower."

"If I was on my own two good feet, Smallwick, I could admonish you severely for that remark."

"Then I had better not set you down again, madam."

"Won't you get dreadfully tired?"

"Keeping you in my arms, madam? Where you can't do any harm to me, but I can do anything I please to you?" His lips twitched. "I don't believe tired is the word for it. Rather something completely opposite. Even now I feel the blood surging with vitality into certain organs."

Ellie was amused and outraged in equal measure. "Smallwick, whoever was responsible for your training, I cannot help thinking they were a trifle lax."

"You find me inefficient, madam?"

"No." She studied the slope of his fine aquiline

nose. "But your manner lacks a certain...for want of a better word...decorum."

The sound of horses approaching at a steady pace made them all turn and look. A grand coach-and-four pulled alongside their stricken vessel. A face looked out.

James did not set her down, despite her whispered urging. He kept her in his arms, holding her firmly to his chest.

"Miss Vyne! Is that you, my dear? Goodness gracious, it has been many years. What has happened here? Are you harmed?"

From her lounging pose in James's sturdy arms, she replied, "Lord Shale. How pleasant to see you," trying to sound normal. "It is just a little accident. No one was badly hurt."

Lord Shale was a portly, affable gentleman, one of her father's closest friends and a frequent visitor to Lark Hollow when she was young.

"My son, Trenton, is with me—you will remember Trenton." A thin-faced young man looked out over his shoulder and managed a slight nod in her direction, before immediately retreating to the warmth of the carriage.

Oh yes, she remembered Trenton Shale—a spoiled, sly, whining boy who once ate all the eggs she'd collected at the Easter hunt, stealing them out of her basket when her back was turned. Having eaten them all, he then promptly vomited on her gown, an incident for which he was never punished. He was a wretched, awful child, and although younger than Ellie, she was forced to "entertain" him whenever he came to the house with his father. Somehow her sisters escaped the onerous task. As, just like their father, they avoided anything unpleasant that must be done.

"Please do say you will join us," Lord Shale continued. "We can see you safely delivered to your destination."

The rain fell heavily, but there was more still to come, for the clouds above sagged like the hammocks of particularly corpulent sailors. The temperature had dropped rapidly. James was drenched, his hat lost, his hair flat to his brow, but he now plowed onward, sloshing through the deep puddle. When he finally reached dry ground, he set her down at last, his hands lingering only a little longer than necessary. No one noticed but her.

Grieves trotted over and whispered in her ear. "Take him with you, madam. I'll see to the carriage and fetch Dr. Salt as soon as we get to Morecroft."

Turning to Lord Shale, she smiled brightly. "If you have room for Smallwick and my young charge, Lady Mercy Danforthe, I should indeed accept your offer, sir."

Lord Shale's lidded gaze swept warily over the tall form of the man beside her. "Smallwick?"

She decided it was best to pretend he belonged to her, which, in a way, he did. For five nights. "He has a service to protect my luggage."

"But my man will see to that, Miss Vyne."

"No, no, sir. Smallwick is the only one I can trust with anything of mine."

Lord Shale's grooms looked at James with sheer envy. He smiled back menacingly, a leashed tiger guarding his property.

"I'm getting wet, and I don't like it." Lady Mercy marched to the Shales' carriage with no further ado and yanked the door open. The offer could not very well be withdrawn now, even if it had been meant only for Ellie.

Grieves helped Smallwick secure her broken trunk and Lady Mercy's much neater luggage to the Shales' carriage. Ellie stepped up, holding the door with one hand.

"Move over, Trenton," Lord Shale exclaimed. "Make room for dear Miss Vyne."

"Come up, Smallwick," she called out, "you must sit by me."

Behind her, the Shales mildly protested, but she was adamant that the servant join them inside where it was dry. James had gone through enough, and she didn't want him hurt again. "But, madam, I should—"

She raised her voice to a haughty pitch. "Smallwick, I insist. Don't make me angry. Inside the carriage."

He licked his lips, eyes wickedly amused. "I wouldn't want you angry, madam."

"I'm quite sure you do not."

James climbed in, bent double to fit through the door, and then squeezed his large frame into the narrow space beside Ellie. "Thank you, madam."

She was now wedged firmly between James and the spindly body of Trenton Shale. Across the carriage, Lord Shale fought for space with Lady Mercy, who insisted on riding with her box of "necessities" on the seat between them.

"Don't crush my gown," she warned the elderly gentleman. "It is best branched velvet, so mind you don't sit on it. You're so fat you'd likely crush the pile right out of it." She looked around the interior, her small nose in the air. "This is a very small carriage."

"It doesn't generally have so many people in it," Lord Shale replied, shooting James another wary glance.

"And it smells like sawdust and tobacco," the girl added. "How unfortunate that my lavender sachet is in my other trunk." She glowered at Trenton from beneath heavy copper ringlets that remained unflattened by a solid night's sleep. "Someone has stepped in something. If I did not have a strong constitution, I should be sick."

Being so close to James, his thigh pressed to hers, his hand almost touching her leg, Ellie had allowed her mind to wander. Now she drew it back again, although it was a tortuous effort. "We are going only so far as my aunt in Sydney Dovedale, Lord Shale. We shall not trouble you for long."

"My dear young lady, it is no trouble. It was most fortuitous that we should be passing and see you. It was Trenton whose sharp eyes recognized you, my dear, and he insisted we stop at once. Did you not, Trenton?"

His son sighed out a disinterested, "Yes, Father."

Trenton Shale hadn't changed much, she noted. He was just taller and thinner, as if someone had stretched him out on a rack. *If only,* she mused dryly, her mind gleefully composing the image of her own hands turning the wheel.

"Doesn't Miss Vyne's beauty quite brighten the dismal weather, Trenton?" his father prompted, tapping his cane on the floor of the carriage. "I daresay you've seldom seen such prettiness. In winter it is a blessed sight. Like spring bloom at last. A snowdrop peeking through the slurry."

"Yes. Quite," came the begrudging reply.

Ellie somehow kept a disciplined countenance at the idea of herself as a delicate snowdrop, but maintaining a straight face was made even more trying in the next moment.

"I don't consider her pretty at all," Lady Mercy grumbled, swinging her feet. "Faces like hers are two a penny on any high street. In fact, I think she is quite plain. Her lips are uneven, and there is nothing distinctive about her nose whatsoever. She is all legs and bosom."

A brutal assessment, but an honest one. Ellie could hardly disagree with a word of it. Her nose had indeed been a dreadful letdown ever since she first realized the importance of owning a good one. She felt James shaking with stifled laughter beside her. Mr. Grieves was right, she thought with a huff; his manservant needed a good thrashing to improve his behavior.

"Smallwick," she whispered, "I do hope you're not perspiring on my gown."

"I shall cease all sweating at once, madam."

Ignoring the interruption, Lord Shale continued, "But what could have prompted you to travel in winter weather, Miss Vyne? No emergency, I hope?"

"Not at all, sir. I simply decided to visit my aunt in the country for the Christmas season. London has grown very dull."

"Without you gracing the streets of the town, Miss Vyne, I daresay it is even less lively. Now we know you shall not be there, Trenton will certainly be in no hurry to return. He will very probably urge me to stay in the country as long as possible in the hopes of your pretty face cheering his day again."

She raised her brows at this awkwardly excessive flattery. Lord Shale kept looking at his son expectantly, but Trenton did not play along. Arms folded, he glowered through the window. On her other side, James fidgeted, trying to stretch out his legs in the cramped space.

"How very odd, Miss Vyne," said Lord Shale, "that you should have a manservant. Most unwed young ladies—"

"It was quite by accident that he came into my hands, and now I should be quite lost without him."

James stilled, his fingers spread over one muddied knee, their tips touching her damp coat.

"I heartily recommend a male servant to all my lady friends," she added.

After a moment's pause, Lord Shale forced a vexed laugh and shook his finger at her. "You always were a joker, Miss Vyne. Now I see you look to shock me, young lady. Tsk, tsk! Someone, Miss Vyne, ought to look out for you. Indeed they should." He must have hit his son's foot with the end of his cane, for Trenton shifted sideways and became very red. Young Master Shale was pretty rather than handsome, but his unpleasant attitude made him appear sallow faced and pinch lipped most of the time.

On her other side, Smallwick growled low, "*I* look after Miss Vyne."

He was pressed so close to her that she felt the words rumble through his body and into hers. It started the heavy, wanton heat again, stirring it up inside her.

Lord Shale glowered at James, clearly annoyed and perturbed that a servant should speak without being spoken to.

She felt James's thigh shift, and the hard muscle reminded her of what happened last night—before the accident. Afraid of blushing, she quickly shook off the pleasant memory. "In truth, I have always looked after myself," she said, directing her words at Lord Shale as if the man beside her had never spoken.

"Yes." The elderly gentleman shook his head sorrowfully. "And see how that has turned out."

Tension in the carriage was palpable, thick enough to bite, and with her handsome manservant beside her, it was increasingly difficult to say or do anything very sensible that might lessen the strain. Continued breathing was challenge enough.

"Never mind that now," Lord Shale added eventually, brightening up, resting both hands on the silver head of his cane. "We shall put you to rights. Shall we not, Trenton?"

His son looked terrified at the prospect.

She wondered vaguely why all these men thought she needed putting to rights. But she liked James Hartley's method of tackling the job far better than any other. Hopefully he would resume, once he got his memory back. It was not right at all, taking advantage of a servant. Even if he was being deliciously noble and delightfully saucy. And holding his breath each time she moved her leg against his.

Ellie Vyne, she admonished herself severely, *you are an irredeemable hussy.*

She'd known this sad fact for a long time, but

never had it been so evident as it was in the presence of the very confused, terribly naughty, insubordinate manservant. If only she had a Smallwick completely at her disposal on a permanent basis. She wondered idly how much it might cost to keep one.

Chapter 12

THE SHALES' CARRIAGE ROLLED AROUND THE VILLAGE common and drew to a smooth halt beside her aunt's garden gate. Ellie looked out with intense relief. Throughout their journey she'd feared Lady Mercy Danforthe might give James's identity away. A parade of coy glances had warned Ellie that the child expected something in return for her silence.

Now, at last, their painful journey was over.

Ellie leapt out of the carriage, not waiting for assistance to lower the step. "Thank you for the ride, and please, do not get out, your lordship. It is wretched cold."

Lady Mercy skipped down after her, looking around with superior interest, while James once again struggled with their trunks.

"We ride on to the Red Lion Inn in Morecroft, Miss Vyne," Lord Shale told her through the window. "I shall hope to see you again while we are in the county."

She agreed, falsely, that she hoped the same.

James tugged her broken trunk from the back of

the carriage and let it fall loudly to the path, apparently having had enough of that bulky, unpredictable weight.

As the carriage wheels crunched slowly away, she turned to find the door opening a crack, her aunt peering out cautiously through small, round spectacles.

"Ellie! Can it be? My dear girl—to travel in this weather!"

"I came to look after you, Aunt Lizzie!" She beamed and embraced the lady with such enthusiasm that she almost knocked the lace cap off her head. Delighted to find her aunt looking quite rosy cheeked and not at all as ill as she'd expected, Ellie gave her a warm hug and lifted her off her small feet in the process.

"But this is most…unexpected." Back on her own feet, her aunt looked at the tattered traveling trunk on the path behind Ellie. "You should have warned…I mean to say, you should have *told* me you were coming. I had not…" Moving upward, her poor eyesight must finally have discovered the tall, crumpled, wet fellow with muddied knees. Her jaw fell slack. She pointed one shaky finger. "Is that—?"

"Aunt Lizzie, this is Smallwick. A manservant."

James bowed politely from the waist, hands hanging at his sides.

Still her aunt stared, and her pale lips worked loosely. *"Smallwick?"*

His breeches were very tight, leaving little to a lady's imagination. It seemed Ellie's proximity in Lord Shale's carriage had caused James a most unfortunate reaction, which, had his breeches been slightly looser fitting, would not have been so apparent. Smallwick by name, she mused, not by nature.

"He is on loan to me," she explained quickly, "for my safety. We were all traveling in the same carriage, you see, and there was an accident. His master, a gentleman by the name of Mr. Grieves, thought I should have an escort for the rest of my journey, and he will come later to retrieve Smallwick."

"Saints preserve us," her aunt gasped, "it is most strange that he should look so much like—"

"Aunt Lizzie, your front door is wide open and letting in all the cold air!"

At once her aunt was all apologies for keeping them out on the path. "You had better come in and get warm. What am I thinking to keep you all standing out here?"

Smallwick grabbed the broken handle of her trunk and dragged it over the doorstep, while her aunt held the door open, fretting now about the terrible weather and Ellie's idea to travel in it. Finally Lady Mercy was noticed. She stood on the path, hands in her muff and shoulders huddled against the cold, looking rather woebegone. Like lost luggage.

"This is Lady Mercy," Ellie explained. "She is also being collected in a day or so. I'm sorry to burden you, Aunt Lizzie, but I couldn't very well leave her behind at the scene of the accident."

"What sort of place is this?" the young lady demanded. "Don't you have a footman to open the door?"

"Goodness no, my lady," Aunt Lizzie replied. "Only me. I'm afraid I must suffice."

Surrounded at once by the familiar and the beloved, Ellie looked around the narrow hall. Nothing ever seemed to change about her aunt's house. "I thought to surprise you!" she exclaimed, flinging her arms around the lady for yet another joyous embrace. She knew she should have written, but as was often the case with Ellie, there was barely time from decision to application of the deed, and in all likelihood she would have arrived before her letter. "Is it not wonderful that I can stay for Christmas this year?"

"My dear girl…of course…quite wonderful, as you say. Goodness, yes indeed. What a shock you have given me. I mean to say—*surprise*! Surprise—yes—that is the proper word, so it is. Coming all this way by yourself…and not a word…but I daresay I shall recover."

Ellie removed her coat and bonnet and hooked them up by the door. She pushed by James and hurried into the parlor to greet her aunt's parakeet, making sure everything there was exactly as it should be, unchanged for the last twenty-seven years. Lady Mercy followed her, perusing the cottage as if it was an exhibit at a museum and inquiring if there was anything to eat.

"The stink in that old man's carriage was positively wretched. I shall be surprised if I can eat very much, because it has rendered me nauseated. But I should try to eat, or else I might faint. My head is feverish sore."

Aunt Lizzie assured her that food would be prepared immediately.

"Where is the rest of your house?" Lady Mercy asked in the same brusque tone. "Did it burn down? Is there more beyond?"

"I'm afraid this is all there is, my lady."

"But it's all so small and confined. Why, I could

walk from one end to the other in less than a minute. There is nowhere to hide."

"It's quite enough for me to keep up. 'Tis all a widow like me can need."

"Of course it's enough," Ellie agreed warmly.

"And there's not much call for me to hide. Not at my age, my lady."

On the outside, her aunt's cottage was somewhat shabby: the roof dipped in the middle, and the old casement windows were in need of fresh paint on the trim. The interior leaned toward practical rather than elegant, but it was as comfortable and as beloved to Ellie as a dear old friend. She took a glad breath of the familiar smoky odor, for her aunt's chimney was stubbornly reluctant to let smoke outside, preferring to blow it back into the house. Underfoot was the same crooked flagstone floor, and above her head the upper storey of the house still tilted west at a steep angle, requiring the inhabitants to find their bed with a somewhat drunken lurch every evening.

Everything was as it should be. Few things in her life were this reliable.

She hugged her arms and crouched by the parlor fire to let the heat tickle her face, and listened to the muffled thumps of James dragging her trunk up the stairs to the guest room. He must be taming his curses on her aunt's behalf. Now what was she going to do with him until Grieves arrived with Dr. Salt?

"I had better make some tea." Her aunt was tidying the parlor with quick, fidgety hands, folding sewing away, closing a newspaper, and reorganizing pillows on the sofa.

"I'm very disagreeable if I'm not fed on time," Lady Mercy exclaimed before catching sight of the parakeet and dashing over to study it. "Does he speak?"

"Quite frequently," Aunt Lizzie replied. "And always when I don't want him to do so. The things he picks up…oh dear!"

"He is beautiful," the young lady exclaimed. "I should like to buy him. How much, my good woman, will it cost me?"

"Cost…oh dear…he is not for sale, my lady. I could not part with him. He belonged to my deceased husband, Captain—"

"Of course he is for sale. Everything is. For the right price."

"*Lady Mercy*," Ellie admonished her, "indeed, everything is not for sale! Mind your manners. And your coin."

The girl pouted ferociously, her lion's mane of copper curls seeming to stand out from her head, bristling with anger.

Ellie ignored her and silently greeted the familiar objects along her aunt's mantel. The old clock and its steady, galloping click-clack reminded her of quiet afternoons by this fire with her sisters, whenever the summer rain kept them indoors. Her sisters played with their dolls and quarreled with each other, while she played solitaire or wrote in her diary—elaborate, adventurous stories, seldom with a shred of truth. She looked farther along the mantel, at the little china ornaments, and then the framed pictures above the spinet in the corner.

"I won't be any trouble this time, Aunt Lizzie. I

promise." It was something she'd uttered many times, standing in this room. Now it came mechanically from her lips.

The scuffing, groaning cacophony of James as he labored with her trunk across the floor above made all three women roll their eyes to the ceiling to follow his bumpy progress. First to glance downward again, Ellie saw the anxious frown pleating her aunt's brow.

"I assure you, Aunt Lizzie, I am quite beyond all mischief now and content to be good. At my age, what else can I be?"

The ancient parakeet let out a slow, tremulous squawk that sounded very much like an "uh, oh" from his large cage by the window.

She threw the bird a quick frown, and her aunt scurried off to make tea.

As she perused the mantel again and rubbed her arms, Ellie's gaze came to rest on a clay pipe beside the clock. Her eyes had only skimmed it before, taking it for one of her uncle's possessions kept by her aunt out of fondness. She picked it up and sniffed the bowl. There was a strong odor of fresh tobacco smoke, and if her fingertips did not deceive her, the pipe was still warm, as if it had not long been put out.

Carefully she set it back where she found it. She assumed her aunt must have taken up the pipe in tribute to the dead captain.

She realized suddenly that the lady went to make the tea herself, when she would usually call for her housemaid, so Ellie hurried down the passage and into the kitchen. She entered just as the back door closed. Her aunt turned, almost dropping the teacups she was setting on the tray.

"My dear girl, stay by the fire in the parlor and get warm. You must not catch cold."

"Was that Mary Wills just gone out?"

It seemed her aunt's hearing had also deteriorated, for she didn't answer, causing Ellie to repeat her question in a louder voice.

"Goodness, no," came the rattled reply eventually. "I have not had Mary here these last two winters. She went to look after her sister in Thrapstead, you know, and it was well she did, for I could scarce afford her any longer. I have little Molly Robbins only a few times a week now to help around the house. She's hoping to secure a post as a housemaid in a year or two, in Morecroft, and the experience is good for her."

"Perhaps Smallwick can give her some advice." Smiling, Ellie stole a shortbread biscuit from the tea tray.

Her aunt set the teapot down with a bang. "That is James Hartley, is it not? My eyesight is poor, but not that bad, Ellie! What can you be up to now?"

"Aunt Lizzie, it is nothing to—"

An ominous crash stole the sentence from her. The two women hurried out into the hall just as James tumbled down the narrow stairs and landed at their feet.

He lay there in an ungainly sprawl, blinking up at them. "I banged my head on the ceiling and tripped. Who built this damned cottage? An elf?"

Poor James. He wasn't used to small houses with narrow stairs and treacherous, threadbare carpets. As Aunt Lizzie helped him upright, that entitled, peevish expression vanished from his face again, replaced by a blank look. One more befitting the "injured" subservient valet.

But for those few seconds in which he let down his mask, startled by the abrupt fall, the old arrogant James was there again.

Ellie saw, and now she knew for certain what she had previously begun to suspect.

The lying hound!

She was unable to restrain her laughter. It burst out of her in a gale and swept her double.

"Well, really, Ellie!" her aunt cried. "This is no time for hilarity."

James, rubbing his doubly abused head and clambering unsteadily to his feet, quite agreed. How typical of the woman to find humor in his pain. She was laughing so hard she almost choked. If his head fell off, she might expire with amusement.

Lady Mercy immediately wandered out into the passage to see what all the fuss was about, and with her talent for observing fault, pointed out that he'd split his breeches.

Eliza Cawley took charge. She shooed him down the passage into the kitchen, trying to cover his behind with her apron. James ducked his head to pass into the small, warm kitchen.

"Now you take those off, Mr. Hartley, and I'll have them sewn up for you in no time."

He glowered down at the little woman. "The name, madam, is Smallwick. You confuse me with someone else."

She squinted through her round spectacles, lips drawn together in a small "o."

"I assure you, madam," he added firmly, "the name is Smallwick."

The little woman knew otherwise, and he feared she might turn him out of her house, but instead, her misty-eyed gaze perused the bump on his brow and the black eye. Her expression softened. "I can see you've been in the wars, young man. Trailing after my niece has brought you little good fortune, no doubt."

Her kindly tone surprised him. She must have been put out to suddenly receive three guests all at once in her tiny house—especially with one of them being a Hartley—yet she took time now to fuss over him, and he was grateful for it. His back ached from hauling that woman's trunk around all day. His clothes were uncomfortably damp, and he was quite certain he had a broken ankle.

"Take off your breeches," she repeated, "and I'll have Molly Robbins mend them. She's a bony wisp of a girl, whom a good gust of wind could blow clear across the common, and she's in possession of a fright-fully melancholic disposition, but she has a very neat stitch. Worry not a bit, young man, I've seen it all before. Drop your breeches. At my age, precious little is a shock anymore."

He'd never been treated like this in his life. Servants were helpful but detached, and they did not chatter or pat his cheek as if he was a little boy up to no good. But it was quite pleasant.

Although she'd been widowed more than twenty years, Eliza Cawley produced another pair of breeches for his temporary use. They were too wide around the waist and too short in the leg, but "any port in a storm" as she remarked merrily—attributing the saying to her dear departed husband, Captain Cawley, as if he was the first person ever to use the phrase.

When Ellie saw him in the borrowed breeches, she exhaled another guffaw that continued, off and on, for half an hour, before they all thought she finally had it tamed.

"Poor Smallwick," she remarked as they sat down to tea in the parlor, "what a day you have had."

Her aunt was silent for a while as she periodically stared at James, then at her niece. Ellie eventually found a subject to distract her aunt from any potentially difficult questions. "Tell me what news of the village. There must be so much that has happened since I was last here."

"Well!" The little woman got comfortable in her chair. "You will remember I wrote to you that Henry Valentine was selling his land?"

"Yes."

"He and that dreadful wife of his have moved to Norwich."

"Ah. Good."

"And Miss Sarah Dawkins married Obediah Shook over in Sydney Marshes, only to find that she did not like him very much after all and fled—to Bury St. Edmunds, of all places, with his gardener. That was a dreadful scandal. Then her sister...you will remember Amy Dawkins? Not to be outdone, she eloped with a brush salesman. Can you imagine? He simply came to their door one day to sell brushes, and before anyone knew anything about it, she up and left with him. Now, I understand, she goes by the name of Mrs.

Arthur Hopper, although whether or not there has been a proper marriage to warrant the name is a matter for dispute." The little woman gave an emphatic shrug. "Poor Jane Osborne remains unwed. She no longer comes to visit me as I have only the one parlor, and she thinks herself suddenly too good now to visit anyone with less than two."

"Really?"

"It all began when she went to Bath for a Season this year. Her father paid a vast sum for an entirely new wardrobe and arranged for her to stay with a good family there. He had hoped, you see, to broaden her horizons. I suppose he thought she would return with a husband, or at least a beau. Alas, she returned only with a very fashionable but ugly parade of new bonnets, and a swelled head upon which to wear them. Now no one can get a word out of her about anything except her visit to Bath and her many dances there at the upper rooms. And that was very nearly twelve months ago."

Ellie looked enthralled by this gossip. She nodded, encouraging her aunt.

"However, I do believe there was one gentleman—a distinguished, titled, older man. She talked of him quite a lot when she first returned to Sydney Dovedale, and her father thought there might be a connection, but the fellow never wrote, and it has all come to nothing. As these things often do." Every other word or so, Eliza Cawley threw James a quick glance and then looked at her niece.

By the by, he wanted to say out loud, *I bought your niece for a thousand pounds, and she's agreed to spend five nights with me.* Now that was news.

"You came to Sydney Dovedale just in time, dear Ellie," her aunt continued, "for the Kanes are holding a Christmas party tomorrow evening up at the farm. The entire village is invited, although I daresay some will not attend. Old Mr. Carstairs has the gout and does not go out for fear of someone knocking into his foot. And Mrs. Winstanley is in mourning for her youngest son, who was killed most tragically near Oxford when his carriage overturned, so she will not venture out for the party. But Sophie will be so delighted to see you again. She asks me, each time I see her, how you are doing and if I have had a letter from you lately. Even though I know she has letters from you at least as often as I."

James looked down at his hands where they rested on his thighs. Sophia. He hadn't seen her for two years. Oddly enough, while following his quarry into the country, he had not given any thought to what else he might find in Sydney Dovedale. His thoughts had been filled with Ellie Vyne and only her.

He looked up. Their gazes locked. He saw the doubt, the question in her eyes. Quickly he looked down again, wondering why she cared whether he still had feelings for Sophia. She wanted only his money. And a stud service.

"A party! That sounds wonderful, Aunt Lizzie," she said.

"I want to go to the party," Lady Mercy announced through a large bite of sponge cake.

"You may not still be here by then," Ellie told her. "Your brother comes to take you home."

The girl fell into a sulk, lifted only when Eliza

Cawley offered her more cake. "Considering you keep no cook, this is really rather good. Quite edible," the girl announced, watching another slice descend to her plate. "Of course, since these people have neglected to feed me today, I could eat anything. I would not know if it tasted vile. No one gave a thought to me once on our journey, although my stomach has rumbled like a lion all morning. They were both too busy looking at each other and touching—"

"Your nausea has passed, Lady Mercy?" James interrupted swiftly.

"Oh…yes." She bit daintily into her slice of cake. "I am, fortunately, of a strong constitution. I am seldom ill for long."

"More tea, Smallwick?" Ellie asked.

"No thank you, madam." He'd never liked tea and really drank it only when forced.

"Yes, I daresay you'd prefer something stronger."

Eyes narrowed hastily, he looked at her across the table, but her expression betrayed nothing. He was quite sure he still had her fooled into believing his amnesia.

"You ought to let me go to that party," chirped Lady Mercy, glaring hard at Ellie. "You owe me a favor. *Remember?*"

Ellie sipped her tea. "I remember."

"Besides, my brother won't be in any hurry to come and get me. Carver hates leaving London and hasn't been to the countryside since Papa's funeral. He doesn't even visit the estate because he says it's too boring there. You'll see. He won't come for ages. Whether you like it or not, you're stuck with me, so there! You'd better entertain me, or I shall be very sour, I daresay."

Eliza Cawley made a small whimper of distress as she watched the diminutive tornado work its destruction upon the food she'd provided. James felt a sharp twinge of guilt for leaving the child to this poor woman's care, but he could not take her to Hartley House, for it would expose his own presence in the county, and he didn't want his grandmother knowing he was there yet. She would instantly try to involve him in a storm of social activities, forcing various titled young ladies down his throat. All he wanted was to spend time with the villainous, lying baggage for whom he'd paid a thousand pounds.

She had a little speck of sugar on her lip. He itched to wipe it for her, but their eyes met again just as she found it with the tip of her tongue and swept it clean. Her lips toyed with a smile. "Are you sure there's nothing more you want, Smallwick?"

James stared.

"You look as if you want to ask for something," she pressed.

Miss Vyne was in the mood to flirt with her manservant, apparently.

"Nothing…at the moment, madam."

He thought about that narrow bed upstairs in the spare chamber. It was barely big enough for one careful sleeper, let alone two clandestine lovers. If she meant to seduce the hapless Smallwick, how was she going to manage this? For once the problem was someone else's, not his. Inwardly, he smiled. There were advantages to being a servant, it seemed. Tonight's arrangements were her problem, if she wanted her nightly servicing. From the smokiness of her eyes, she wasn't about to let his memory loss stop her. Why would it? The woman was a stranger to scruples.

When Grieves failed to arrive with Dr. Salt and night began to close in with the brutal swiftness of winter, Mrs. Cawley told James he might sleep on the parlor sofa. It could be made quite comfortable with pillows and blankets. Lady Mercy was to sleep with Ellie in the small spare bedchamber above.

"What will people think?" the old lady muttered. "A single man spending the night in the house of a respectable widow! Had Merryweather's Tavern any rooms free, I could send you there, young man."

"Thank you for the hospitality, madam. I am grateful, for until my master arrives, I have nowhere else and would be forced to spend the night on a park bench were it not for your kindness."

She turned to leave, taking a candle from the mantel with her.

"Good night, madam," he said as he plumped his borrowed pillows. "And thank you again for the breeches. It was a lucky thing you should have some here, in this house of a respectable widow."

She looked over her shoulder, and a flush stained her cheeks. "Yes. I...I kept some of the captain's things when he died."

James smiled. He remembered Captain Cawley as a lofty, spare fellow. The breeches she'd lent him belonged to someone as broad as they were tall. While dragging Ellie's trunk into the spare room earlier, he'd chanced to look out of a window just in time to see such a rotund figure departing the back gate of the cottage in the manner of someone who preferred not to be seen. Eliza Cawley apparently had a gentleman friend.

❧

Ellie had some memory of which stair creaked loudest, but it seemed as if that changed depending on the old house's mood. Consequently, she was caught out before she reached the bottom, when one wretched groan shattered the peace of the darkened hallway. Closing her eyes tight, she waited, foot poised to meet the floor of the hall, her hand clasped around the acorn-shaped newel post. There was no sound from above, not even the restless heave of a body turning over in bed. Slowly and carefully, she stepped that last distance and turned in the narrow passage, heading for the parlor.

A blur of white moved in the corner of her eye. The door to the kitchen stood open, and a spectral shape moved about in the shadows. She padded bare-foot down the flagged passage and then stopped. The ghostly vision raised a hand and silently unbolted the back door.

As her eyes adjusted, she recognized the small shape with the long gray braid hanging down her back. *"Aunt Lizzie?"*

The little woman jumped and spun around. "My goodness, Ellie! You startled me so."

"Where are you going at this time of night?" *And in your nightgown and slippers,* she might have added.

Segments of moonlight slid through the arched

window above the door and shone pale over her aunt's anxious face. "I just came down to…make certain the back door was bolted. Why are you out of bed?"

"Me? Oh, I just wanted something." She looked around, finally remembering she was in the kitchen. "A glass of water. It's become a habit of mine to have a glass of water by the bed. I forgot to take one up with me."

Aunt Lizzie bustled her back down the hall toward the stairs. "You go on up to bed, and I'll bring it for you."

"No, no. I can get it. You go back to bed and get warm."

The two women blocked each other's paths for a moment, both clearly on missions other than those to which they'd confessed. Ellie had seen that her aunt left the bolt open. In a village like Sydney Dovedale, there was really no cause to lock a door, but her aunt was usually the cautious sort and did so anyway. Tonight, having locked that rear door earlier in full view of her niece, she came down in the dark to open it again.

"I'll go and get my water, Aunt Lizzie. Good night." At the foot of the stairs, she kissed the lady's soft cheek. "Do go back to bed."

"Yes…very well. Good night, my dear. You will go directly to bed yourself?"

"Of course."

"Good. Good." Her aunt tapped the newel post with her fingers. Ellie smiled with all the innocence she could muster and then hurried down the hall, back to the kitchen.

She listened for the creaks as her aunt mounted the

stairs, followed by a slight pause and then a gentle thud as she closed her bedchamber door.

Once a safe number of minutes had passed, she crept to the back door and rebolted it. Poor Aunt Lizzie must be getting senile. She shook her head, thinking what a good thing it was that she had come to take care of the old dear. When the doctor arrived to examine James, she'd ask him to look at her aunt too.

Chapter 13

HE LAY STARING UP AT THE LOW BEAMS AND CRACKED ceiling plaster. After the tiring day he'd had, James expected to fall asleep quickly, but instead he was wide awake. The parlor fire smoldered low, a wire screen placed before it. The captain's bird was quiet, his cage covered by an embroidered throw.

James looked around at the memorabilia of Eliza Cawley's life, some humble objects that meant nothing to anyone but her. This was not a house filled with fine art and grand oil paintings, collected solely to impress visitors. It was a home filled with happy memories. Very different from the places in which he was raised.

There were five miniature portraits in little frames on the wall above the small spinet in one corner of the room. Eliza Cawley had a keen eye for portraiture, and they were very good likenesses. He'd studied them earlier and knew they were of his hostess, her deceased husband, Captain Cawley, and her two brothers— Admiral Vyne and the disreputable Lieutenant Graedon Vyne. The last portrait was of Catherine Vyne, Ellie's mother. They must have been painted twenty years ago at least. It was a handsome family grouping. James had never met Ellie's mother in person, but he saw now that she bore a great resemblance to the lady. That was clearly where she came by her incredible eyes. A man could lose his soul in eyes like those.

Admiral Vyne, in the oval beside Catherine's image, looked quite mediocre and considerably aged in comparison to his pretty wife. Then there was Lieutenant Graedon Vyne, his flirtatious charm recorded for posterity in a frame that hung slightly askew. James had studied that picture almost as long as he reviewed Catherine's. He was sixteen when his mother ran away with the reckless young lieutenant. After that, James's father could not bear to look at him because he said his son reminded him too much of his faithless hussy of a wife. So whenever he was not at school, James was sent off to live with his grandmother. There he was kept in her stranglehold for years, never allowed to consort with other boys his age in case they were bad influences. Not permitted to indulge in any fun pursuits until he finally became bold enough to escape her house. Yes, Lieutenant Graedon Vyne had a lot to answer for.

He smiled sadly, thinking his grandmother would have a convulsion if she saw what became of him and his clothes over the last day, since he transformed into "Smallwick." Grieves had made that name up for him, aware, of course, that James couldn't argue, or else he would have to admit he hadn't lost his memory at all. Grieves was a shrewd old bugger.

The door creaked. His gaze lowered to the twisting latch.

Ellie peeped around the door and then, seeing him awake, came in.

He sat up, assuming his valet act. "Madam. You should not be down here."

"I wanted to be sure you had everything you need, Smallwick." She crossed the room, barefoot, on tiptoe.

I do now, he thought. Funny how her presence lightened his mood. Looking at her in that nightgown, all primly buttoned up, he was amused, surprised the notorious Ellie Vyne had such a chaste garment in her possession. How did one sleep in that thing? He'd always slept nude himself, although most folk would be scandalized by that. In his grandmother's opinion, nudity was appropriate for nothing, not even death.

"Your ankle improves?" she asked.

"I'm keeping it elevated. Madam."

"You must not walk around too much tomorrow."

He was thirty-seven, had known a great many women, but never wanted one as much as he wanted her tonight. In that cozy parlor. In her white, nun-like nightgown, with her hair down, loose and wild. "I'll do whatever you say, madam." He would never say that to another woman on earth.

"Good." She looked over at the fire. "Shall I put another shovel of coals on for you?"

"I'm quite warm enough. Thank you." He paused and then said again, "You should not be down here. Alone with me. Madam."

"Fortunately for you, Smallwick, I set little store by shoulds and should nots. If everyone was virtuous and good all the time, would not the value of being so rapidly decline?"

Not much he could say to that.

❧

Although "Smallwick" kept the blanket around his waist like a shield for his honor, Ellie still had a very pleasing view of his sculpted torso, which rippled in the low firelight. Every muscle was well defined. His arms, holding him up from the sofa, swelled with potent masculinity, a power that went beyond mere physical strength to reach inside, tear the sheer need out of her, and hold it up to her face, where she could no longer deny it.

Saying nothing, he watched her walk around his sofa, and she let her fingers trail along the back edge.

"I could work the aches out for you. I know how. I have some experience." Oops, she should not have said that, for his eyes darkened, his jaw hardened. "An elderly gentleman I worked for—as his nurse companion," she explained, "often had knots in his neck and shoulders, so I learned how to relieve them. It was quite innocent."

His skeptical expression annoyed her.

"It is quite true, Smallwick. I learned how to rub liniment on the Duke of Ardleigh's shoulders. He needed it because, in the last months of his life when his legs gave out, he walked with two canes. It made his arms and shoulders sore."

He leaned against the arm of the sofa. "I did not know the duke had trouble with his legs."

"He tried to hide it. His health was much worse than he liked people to know."

James was studying her face. She looked back

boldly, knowing he must have thought as others did, that she was Ardleigh's mistress.

"Let me see if I believe you," he said. "Show me your abilities."

"I haven't any liniment," she warned.

"Do your best then." Finally he remembered his act. "Madam."

༄

"There. Isn't that better, Smallwick?"

"Yes, madam," he mumbled into his arms, eyes closed, while she rubbed the sore muscles of his back. She had lovely, flexible hands, but he'd never fully appreciated them until now. How could he?

"You were very tense."

"Hmmm."

She moved onto the couch beside him. His eyes fluttered open.

"Lie still, Smallwick." Her hands pressed down on his back, skilled fingers working out the myriad of tiny knots. He felt the lace of her robe rubbing against the side of his naked torso. She went to a great deal of trouble for a man who thought he was her manservant.

He opened his eyes again and glared at the arm of the couch. She was up to something.

Steadily, her hands moved down his back, working cleverly together, taking his aches and pains away. Occasionally she moved beside him, and her robe slithered sensuously against his skin.

Just a minute. Where were her hands going now, pray tell? They slid under the blanket and under his waist, moving downward with shocking confidence.

"Madam," he muttered, his tongue thick.

"Yes, Smallwick." She touched her goal.

Overheated blood pumped through his ears. "Do you…need help, madam?"

A soft chuckle blew against his ear. "I think I can manage, Smallwick."

The blanket slipped down his body as he lifted his groin slightly off the couch and let her caress his cock. Her lacy sleeves and the long, loose curls of her hair brushed the exposed skin of his back, buttocks, and thighs. She took her time over it. Teasing almost beyond endurance. He wanted to turn over and grab her, wrestle her beneath him and quickly take possession. His mouth watered at the prospect of what she might do next. Here it came. She straddled his hips, and when she leaned forward to rub his shoulders again, her breasts kissed his bare back, the nipples tantalizing through a thin layer of material. Her firm inner thighs moved against his hips, and her nightgown—a mere whisper of linen—touched the back of his legs. She wore no stockings and, he suspected, no drawers. He certainly hadn't seen any through her nightgown when she stood before the fire.

"Well, this is a first for me," he sighed into the pillow, blissfully relaxed but for his rigid manhood which, now that he'd lowered himself again, pressed so hard into the couch it was almost painful.

"A first?"

"A fine lady like yourself, Miss Vyne, touching me intimately…"

It came without warning, just a very slight parting of the tense air.

She spanked him across his bare buttocks.

The sting reverberated upward and outward, and the snapping sound echoed around the parlor. Before he could even respond, she leaned down, her lips close to his ear, and chuckled, a low, sultry sound. "There, Hartley. I beat you to it, didn't I? Always knew what you needed. *A damn good spanking.*"

A shocked breath had stalled in his lungs, and now it rushed out in a groan. His pulse thumped through his veins like a marching band of drummers. He flipped over onto his back and grabbed her around the waist before she could escape.

∾

She sat astride his hips and laughed softly, a finger to her lips. "Remember my aunt is only upstairs. As is the sleeping Lady Mercy."

His eyes narrowed. "When did you know?"

"About what?"

"That I hadn't lost my memory."

"Almost immediately."

"Liar."

Smothering a giggle, she placed her hands on his bare chest and let her fingers wander over the firm ridges. He was in splendid form. "Why did you pretend?"

His hands tightened around her waist. "I wanted to play a trick on *you* for a change." He shifted his hips beneath her, and she felt his manhood rearing up. "Can we finish where we left off last night, Miss Vyne?" His eyes had gone very hot, very wicked. He seemed to have trouble breathing.

"How is your back now?" she asked as she ran her fingertips across his nipples.

He inhaled sharply. "Wonderful, suddenly. Now kiss me, madam."

"Smallwick, you are awfully naughty."

"Isn't that why you hired me, madam, for this stud service?"

"Ummm." She leaned forward and let her lips touch his very lightly. His hands left her waist and cupped her bottom through her nightgown. As she sat up again, he arched forward, trying to reach her lips fully. When she denied him as he had first done to her the night before, his nostrils flared, and his eyes darkened, holding her mouth in a blistering, covetous gaze. The lines of his face seemed harder, rougher.

Ellie felt his potent desire, could even taste it in the air between them.

They shouldn't be doing this in her aunt's quiet, cozy, innocent parlor. Yet, the heaviness of imprudent want gathered in her loins, an even hotter flame of desire sparking to life *because* they shouldn't. Because it was her aunt's genteel parlor, where she held Book Society meetings and sipped tea with the vicar once a week when he visited with his wife.

Making a quick, reckless decision, she pulled the nightgown over her head and heard James expel a low growl of approval. It was wrong, absolutely. What if her aunt woke and came downstairs for any reason?

But she was stark naked now. No changing her mind. She wanted this man who lay under her, the light in his eyes purely carnal, his body poised to claim hers. Clearly his desire was just as tempestuous and demanding as her own, and his needs outweighed any sense of propriety. They'd left that far behind.

～⁂～

Arms wrapped around her, he rolled over and pulled her under him on the couch. He wanted the dominant role this time. She could play all she wanted next, but this first one would be the way he wanted, with him in control of her—the scheming, unprincipled prankster and possible accomplice to blackmail.

He kissed her deeply, grinding his mouth to hers. The waiting since last night had wound him tight, and now he was released, spinning madly in a vortex of raging lust that would pull her down with him, suck her in, take them both to hell or to heaven. Perhaps to both. It was bewitchment possibly, this intemperate desire for her.

He paused, needful breath scorching in his throat.

Her eyes were half-closed, her lips parted in a breath of excitement.

He reached between their bodies and touched her intimately, pressing down with slow, deliberate strokes of his fingertips. Her lashes fluttered and then raised to show eyes shimmering with tiny stars that burst apart and joined, making new patterns, new shapes in the satiny dark.

James wanted to claim her with all the raw, pitiless intensity he'd felt back in June when she kissed him and left him wanting. He was wild, perhaps even a little mad.

She raised her hips slightly off the couch, reacting to his caress, wanting more.

"Do you like that, madam?" he purred as he stroked her slowly. "Does your servant please you?"

"Oh yes, Smallwick."

"Shall I continue?"

She nodded and bit her lip.

"Say you want more, Miss Vyne. I can't take what you don't permit."

Her eyes widened, flared like the tail of a comet. "I want more, Smallwick. Much more."

"But what if someone should come in, madam, and see us being wicked together?"

"They won't," she gasped.

"Why? Because you will it so?" Just like her, he mused, to think she could dictate even that.

"Yes," she confirmed cheekily.

He lowered his head to the full mound of her right breast. Her breathing deepened, and soft, needy whimpers dampened her parted lips as she writhed beneath him. James slid his trembling fingers inside her warm haven.

Her fingers scraped through his hair. Her left leg climbed up his back.

He took her peaking nipple in his mouth and sucked gently.

She moaned his name and made a demand he wasn't certain he'd heard correctly. Lifting his mouth, he observed her flushed face for a moment and slid his fingers out of her.

"What was that, madam? Surely you don't want me to…?"

She writhed impatiently, and her hand reached for his cock.

"Is that what you want, madam?"

There was no mistaking that expression, but just in case he might doubt, she hissed at him in a low, heated whisper, "Get on with it, damn you. You don't want to lose your post, do you, Smallwick? Why do you think I hired you?"

A throaty chuckle ripped out of him. "Very well, madam. Here I come."

Her beautiful, nimble body yielded to his hard, forcefully driving muscles. Her curves undulated beneath him, so incredibly soft and warm, sheathing him, clinging tight, possessive, demanding.

They melted together in a licentious heat, until they became liquid and swirled around each other. At last.

As the first climax built in shuddering leaps through his body and sweat broke across his back, he thought of the next time. And the next.

James closed his eyes, head back, mind spinning like a child's top. Aware of her hands on his arms, gripping tight, her body holding him likewise, pulsing around him, slick and hot, he knew she reached her peak at that same moment. It was too soon, and he'd meant to relish this moment, but there was nothing he could do to delay his release. Theirs was a cataclysmic joining, a sensation very like falling from a great height. When he hit ground, she was a featherbed beneath him, molded to his shape, absorbing the fall.

❧

Four more nights after this one. It should be enough, she reasoned as she finally felt the real world closing around her again. James Hartley probably never wanted the same woman two nights in a row, let alone five.

Ellie, choked with her own emotions, wondered if he thought now of Sophia—or of some other woman, and compared her to them. He hitched onto his side and removed his heavy, solid weight from her body. The couch was not very wide, a tight fit for two bodies. But her aunt's furniture was not made for debauchery. It was made for delicate posteriors to perch upon while their owners sipped tea and nibbled crumpets, strawberry jam, and scones. Tonight she was the crumpet James nibbled upon. She ought to be ashamed of herself. Ought.

"Was that satisfactory, Miss Vyne?" he whispered as his fingers stroked her thigh.

"Indeed, Smallwick. Most satisfactory." No point being coy. She wanted to say it was terrible and he needed to try harder, but even she couldn't lie this time. "I should go back to bed, before—" She caught her breath and shivered as his palm cupped her breast. Her nipple reacted instantly, and his lips rediscovered that sensitive spot at the side of her neck.

"I'm not done with you yet, my lady notorious."

"Oh?"

He had a vast amount of stamina and energy. Shocking in a man of seven and thirty.

"If a job's worth doing, madam, it's worth doing well. Let me know when you're ready for me again."

As it happened, she was ready half an hour later, by which time he'd administered tiny kisses to every part of her body.

"I must have the most devoted manservant in England," she muttered.

"I have the most irresistible mistress."

She found she rather liked the sound of that word, whispered on his lips just before he planted yet another kiss to her navel.

Even Ellie Vyne had never been able to deny that he was handsome. Yet tonight, caught in the soft light of the dying parlor fire, looming forth out of the flickering shadows, his beauty took on a new edge. She imagined Vikings once looked like this—the fair coloring, height, and broad shoulders. Especially the savage intensity burning through those blue eyes. This man took no prisoners; he was merciless.

She gently touched her fingertips to the discolored skin around his eye. "What happened?"

"A boxing match."

As her fingers drifted down his cheek, he turned his face and kissed her palm. "Boxing?" she exclaimed, shocked.

"It's very good exercise. Helps me"—he lowered his mouth to her wrist and kissed that too—"burn off"—his tongue traveled down her arm—"certain"—and he licked the inner curve of her elbow, making her squirm and giggle—"vital energies."

So that explained his stamina. *How many rounds could he go?* she wondered wickedly.

He bent his head again and trailed the tip of his tongue between her breasts. Wildfire streaked through her body, just from that one damp touch. She was alive as she'd never been. Each tiny pore on her body had been made love to this evening, and now they were all insatiable, spoiled, clamoring for more. Even the soft brush of hair on his strong thighs, tickling her

legs as he slid them apart, threw more coal on her fire.
The feel of him, the weight and the scent as well as the
sound of his harsh breath, filled her senses, awakened
her as nothing ever had. She almost screamed with
relief when he finally filled her again, slowly this time,
inch by blessed inch. He smothered her muted cries
with another kiss, surely bruising her lips with his
hunger. James Hartley, gentleman rake, was quite a
savage beast when roused.

She tried not to think how he'd honed his skills
in bedchambers all over London. Instead, Ellie gave
herself up to greedy passion. Her body arched to meet
his, and her hands clawed at the muscles of his back
as he sweated above her, moaning her name. She
wrapped her legs around him and forced James over
onto his back. This time she rode him as hard as he
rode her.

He pressed his hips upward, and she joined the
frenzied motion, quickly falling over the precipice
and into blissful oblivion. He pounded the breath out
of her, and here it came again—*la petite mort*, as the
French called it.

Dropping forward, wilting, she buried her face in
his red-hot shoulder and let the tremors flow from her
body to his.

James, however, had not yet spent again. This time
he delayed, holding back to torment her further. Still
tingling inside, her core even more sensitive than it
was earlier, she felt another quake building. Dear Lord,
surely not more! She never knew she had it in her.

Through it all, she was conscious of that door—
unlocked—only a few feet from the couch. At any

moment they might have been discovered. There would never be enough time to hide what they were up to.

She didn't care. Tonight she was every bit the wicked creature false rumor painted her.

Her lover licked her breasts, smothering the nipples with playful kisses, sucking and tickling, giving each globe within reach of his hungry mouth an equal share of attention. How obliging. Then he slid his hands over the curve of her bottom, holding her down while he increased his thrusting.

Ellie groaned and spun over the edge. Sweat poured off her.

Her heart was galloping, reckless and happy as a horse let out to play. This climax was quicker, rougher, stronger than the first two. She was hazily aware of her fingernails digging a little too hard into his shoulders, but she had to cling on to something or she might never survive. She'd be washed away on a tidal wave. Even that image struck her as funny, made her want to laugh out loud.

When she glanced downward, his eyes were full of oceanic swirls, tropical shades of blue one never saw on the English coast. He gave two achingly slow thrusts that made her jaw grind, her sheath tighten again around his shaft. When he came for the second time that night, it was hard, wild.

He fell back onto the couch. The thin sheen of sweat coating his body glistened in the firelight. "Is my head still attached?" he rasped.

"Yes." She collapsed over him, and he wrapped his arms around her. "But still empty inside, I fear,

Smallwick. You know this was most unwise, here in
my dear aunt's parlor."

She felt the chuckle bubbling through his warm
chest. "I assumed that was part of the pleasure for you,
madam." He tapped her bottom in a light, playful
spank, much gentler than the one she'd given him
earlier. "The danger excites you." He paused, and
then his lips brushed the top of her head, kissing her
hair. "Isn't that why you're here with me? The man
you're not supposed to have?"

How well he knew all her faults.

While she drifted into sleep, James slid carefully off
the sofa and shrugged into his overcoat. He was thirsty
but didn't want to disturb her. She looked delectable
with her lashes fluttering against her flushed cheeks,
dark curls tumbled over her naked shoulders, her softly
curved arms and long legs sprawled across the tapestry
sofa with graceful abandon. He'd begun to realize that
she had no idea how beautiful she was. He remembered the first time he saw her all grown up, when she
was sixteen and out at her first ball—what a shock it
had been to his nerves, and how stupidly he'd reacted.

Suddenly he couldn't resist waking her after all. He
planted a quick kiss on her nose, and she wrinkled it.
"I'll be back momentarily," he whispered.

"I must return to bed."

"Not yet. Stay. Don't you dare move."

"Smallwick, are you giving your mistress orders?"

"I am. If she defies me, she'll be punished."

Ellie smiled drowsily, and he chose to take that as a

sign of acquiescence. James tucked the blanket around her, lit a candle from the fireplace, and then crept out to the kitchen at the end of the hall where a brief search revealed the presence of an ale barrel in the larder. For a while he was distracted, too busy thinking about the indecent things he'd just allowed to happen in that cozy parlor. He kept picking up mugs and setting them down, and his gaze wandered stupidly over the shelves of pickle jars and their labels as if they might hold some key into the heart of a certain mystifying wench. Better get back to her. Not wise to leave her unguarded too long, or she might slip away.

But no sooner had he poured two mugs of ale and walked back into the kitchen, than he heard a scratching sound. Mice? He set the full mugs on the kitchen table beside his candle and grabbed a saucepan from a hook on the wall. The scratching stopped and turned into a rattling. It came from the back door.

Frowning, James put the saucepan down, took up his candle, and strode to the door. The iron bolt was shaking. Someone on the other side tried to jostle the handle enough to work it loose. He slid the bolt back and opened the door.

"Yes?" he demanded, candle raised.

A short, square figure stood on the path, a milk churn by his feet, hat in hand. "Oh! I expected Mrs. Cawley."

James recognized the same portly fellow he'd seen disappearing through this door when they first arrived. "In the middle of the night. sir?"

"It is early morning in actual fact." The man smiled genially.

Ah, how time flew when one was enjoying oneself.

"Osborne's the name. I came to deliver Mrs. Cawley's milk."

Searching his memory, James recalled the earlier conversation over tea. Osborne must be that local farmer Eliza Cawley had mentioned—a widower with a difficult daughter, sent off to Bath in hopes of getting her married. "You deliver Mrs. Cawley's milk in person?"

The gentleman's smile broadened, and plump fingers fidgeted with his hat. "She is a very dear and valued customer."

"I see. Then you'd better bring it in." He stepped aside, gesturing with his candle, and the farmer carried his churn into the kitchen to set it carefully on the stone floor.

"You look familiar to me, but I cannot quite place—"

"Smallwick is the name. A servant on loan to Miss Vyne."

"Ah yes. I heard that Miss Vyne had come to visit her aunt. Unexpectedly. Smallwick, you say? Indeed?" The elderly fellow screwed up his face. "I thought I'd seen you before, but I—" Those small, bright, wandering eyes quickly surveyed the kitchen table and landed on the two mugs of ale.

"I'll tell Mrs. Cawley you delivered her milk, sir." James had thought he heard the parlor door click open. Now he feared Ellie might come out to see where he'd got to. Farmer Osborne could, any moment, be a witness to their late-night tryst.

"Ah." The little man looked again at the two mugs of ale, then at James's bare legs beneath his coat. "Very good, Smallwick. Do give Mrs. Cawley my regards."

James glanced out into the hall. "I shall, sir. Good evening."

"Good *morning*!"

"Yes, that too."

"You must be a thirsty fellow, Smallwick."

"What?"

"Two mugs of ale?"

The men eyed each other in the flickering light of the candle. "Yes," James replied. "I like my ale at night as much as Mrs. Cawley enjoys her milk."

Pause.

"You say you're on loan to Miss Vyne, Smallwick. Do you mean to stay long in the country?"

"That, sir, is up to Miss Vyne. But I shan't disturb your...*deliveries*, Farmer Osborne. I'm generally a sound sleeper. As long as I have my ale to enjoy."

Finally he got the man out and shut the door. Hmmm. Interesting. He looked at the churn and laughed softly, almost extinguishing his candle flame. Eliza Cawley must drink an awful lot of milk to be such a valued customer that the farmer delivered her order personally. And as far as James was concerned, whatever Farmer Osborne said, it *was* the middle of the night. People up at this hour of the night were generally up to no good. Himself included.

Smirking, he carried the churn into the cold larder.

Chapter 14

ELLIE ROSE GRUMPILY FOR THE SECOND DAY IN A ROW, having achieved no more than a few hours sleep and even those very disturbed. How she wished she could have stayed with James on the sofa! Even when they were cramped for space, his companionship was preferable to that of Lady Mercy who, while a sound sleeper, was active in her dreams, kicking and twisting, wrapping herself in the quilted coverlet and laying diagonally across the narrow bed, taking up maximum space. Come the gray dawn, the girl was snoring into her pillow, stretched out and blissfully sunk into her dreams, while Ellie had lost all hope of the same.

Molly Robbins came up to the room as soon as she heard Ellie moving about, and offered to help unpack her trunk.

"I'm hoping to be a lady's maid one day, Miss Vyne," the girl whispered, anxious not to wake Lady Mercy—indeed, they were all glad of the peace for now. "As soon as I've sewn up that gentleman's breeches, I can iron all your things for you, mend holes, and scrub out any stains."

She remembered Molly as a shy little girl who usually ran behind the other village children, always hiding, afraid of her own shadow. But she'd grown up a few inches into a calm, steady girl. Her long, mousy-brown hair was tied back in a ribbon, and her small face was very grave for one so young. The Robbins family had little in the way of money, and Molly was the youngest of twelve children. She'd been sent out to find work as soon as she was deemed capable by her harried parents. Ellie supposed that would make anyone rather somber.

"Good luck to you then," she replied, yawning. "You'll have your hands full tending my clothes."

The Robbins girl immediately set about unpacking for her, while Ellie finished dressing. It occurred to her as she watched the busy young girl and the one slumbering in the bed, that they were about the same age yet lived very different lives.

"Perhaps today you can show Lady Mercy around the village, Molly," she suggested. "Otherwise she'll be under my aunt's feet all day until her brother comes."

Molly raised her head, and her dark eyes timidly assessed the unconscious lump on the bed. "But what can I show her, Miss Vyne? I'm sure she's used to much grander things than we have here in Sydney Dovedale."

"That is the point entirely, Molly. It is important to discover new things."

Molly looked doubtful. "I'll try, Miss Vyne. She's got awful fancy clothes though, for walking in the country." She gestured at the smart boots, neatly set by the foot of the bed, toes aligned perfectly, and her lace petticoats laid over the nearby chair, folded neatly.

Lady Mercy was well prepared and well shod for a runaway. She'd packed some very fashionable attire for her adventure. "There aren't many clean places around the village."

"I daresay a little dirt will do her good." She'd always thought that about James too.

Ellie stood at the bedchamber window as she combed her hair and looked out on a depressed, leaden sky that hung over her aunt's cottage as if it might drop to earth at any moment. She felt oddly askew this morning. Her insides danced about like sparks from a bonfire, while on the outside, she tried hard to contain it all and be sensible. She was no longer a silly girl with an easily turned head—*if,* she thought dourly, she ever had been—and she ought to be able to conduct this affair without making a fool of herself. So what if James, her delectably wicked lover, was just below this floor, and she would see him again shortly? Surely they could make eye contact without her melting into complete mush this morning. But she delayed going down, just to make certain she had control of herself.

The village was quiet, very few souls out and about on such a grim day. Across the common, two little girls played with hoops, running them through puddles. A gaggle of geese flew overhead and shattered the peace with their gargled chorus.

Suddenly there was James, in those borrowed, ill-fitting breeches, leaving her aunt's cottage and walking up the lane. Ellie paused, hairbrush tangled in a particularly stubborn curl.

Where the devil was he going now? She'd warned

him to rest his ankle today. He couldn't possibly walk all the way to Morecroft, and there was no one in Sydney Dovedale he would want to visit.

Except Sophie.

The thought crashed in, like Farmer Osborne's old bull that chased her one summer all the way across a field and pushed its horns through a wooden fence, trying to reach her. She'd climbed a tree to escape and waited there for an hour before anyone came to her rescue. Now she felt that same fear of being gored on sharp horns, and then the utter helplessness of being stranded. She couldn't very well run after him like a child, demanding to know where he went. For all her mother was an American, she wouldn't go running down the lane after a man.

Her heart ached from beating too rapidly, too hard. Had last night meant so little to him that his first thought this morning was of Sophie, his old flame?

"Ooh, Miss Vyne, this is a lovely gown."

She looked over her shoulder. Molly knelt beside the battered trunk, lifting out an old ball gown. "That thing? I haven't worn it for years, and it's quite out of fashion now." She wondered why she still carried the garment around with her. As far as she remembered, it had a large soup stain on the skirt, the hem was ripped, and many beads were missing around the high waist because she'd caught her sash on a door latch while running away from an overenthusiastic beau.

Molly held the gown up to the soft morning light. "But the muslin is still in good condition, Miss Vyne."

"If you can make use of it, you may take it."

"Are you sure, madam?"

She nodded. "You may as well put it to some good. And if there are any other garments you'd like, just take them."

"I couldn't, madam."

"Nonsense. I'm sure there are several too irretrievably damaged to be worn again." Her sisters always said she was as hard on her gowns as she was on the men who courted her.

As she looked out through the window once more, she spied a tall, angular shape, recognizable at once as her aunt's indomitable, busybody friend, Mrs. Flick, emerging from her own front door on the corner and heading along the lane in considerable haste. No doubt Mrs. Flick had heard of Ellie's arrival. Any minute now she would rap her knuckles on the cottage door.

Making a hasty decision, Ellie ran down the stairs, shouted a quick "good morning" to her aunt, who was lighting a fire in the parlor, grabbed her boots and coat, and slipped out through the back door in the kitchen. Although it was still early, she would visit her friend Sophie. Only because the last thing she needed this morning was to face Mrs. Flick's prying—nothing to do with James or caring where he went. Nothing at all.

The cool breeze was brisk and refreshing, a wonderful change after the mostly unpleasant reek of London air. Taking a few great gulps of it, Ellie walked quickly away from the village and up the muddied, narrow lane to the farm where Sophie lived. There was no sight of James, but he was a fast walker with a long stride. Perhaps he was so eager to see his old love that he ran. That thought made her laugh in hysteria, until she had to stop and catch her breath.

Drops of rain spat upon her bonnet, but not enough to make her turn back despite the considerable distance she had yet to walk. She preferred a drenching than facing Mrs. Flick's interrogation over breakfast.

Dead, dampened leaves blew across her path, some sticking to her hem. A faint smokiness, carried on the air from a smoldering bonfire out in the fields, ticked her nostrils and made her smile, made her remember seasonal traditions from her youth—bobbing for apples on All Hallow's Eve, burning her tongue on hot roasted chestnuts, collecting colorful leaves when they fell to the damp grass.

Ellie passed the old stile where she'd once tied one of her younger sisters by her apron strings, pretending the girl was her horse, and forgotten about her for an hour or two. Here, under an oak tree, she once paused to ink a moustache on a sleeping young man's face. She patted the thick bark as she walked by, greeting the tree like an old friend. For the first time since leaving London, she no longer felt as if she was followed. That slightly threatening sensation, which had hovered over her in varying degrees of intensity for some time, was today lifted from her shoulders. She walked with a lighter step, her arms swinging.

How many times, she pondered, had she run along this well-worn lane to call on Sophie Valentine? Although Ellie was five years younger, the two girls became close thanks to their mischievous curiosity and shared enjoyment of observing people. In many ways, Ellie felt closer to Sophie than to either of her younger sisters, and her summertime stays with Aunt Lizzie were greatly enhanced by Sophie's company. Until, of course, James Hartley came along and monopolized the other girl's attention.

There he was. As she turned a bend, his tall figure came into view, his appearance comical in those borrowed breeches, the legs barely long enough to tuck into his riding boots. No sign of his bad ankle this morning, she noted. Probably because he thought he was alone.

Suddenly he turned and glanced back down the lane. Ellie ducked out of sight behind a tree. A moment later, she peeped out and saw him walking onward. Once more she followed, chiding herself for the impulse that made her hide. She quickened her steps. What did she care if he heard her? But when he stopped again and swung around, she took a dive over the nearest hedge and landed with a muffled squawk. This time she lost her bonnet and had to retrieve it from a muddy ditch, under some brambles. By the time she recovered, back on her feet, he'd vanished around another bend. Now extremely disheveled, she hurried along the lane and plucked thorny sticks from her bonnet.

The Kanes' farm was eventually in view, the flint stone wall and ornate, black iron gates gleaming wet with rain. Forgetting the sense of pride that had made her shy of being seen, she ran up just as he pushed open the rusty old latch.

"You might have told me you were coming to see her," she gasped, breathless, rain blurring her vision.

He looked puzzled. "You've got mud in your hair."

Only a rake like him, she thought, fury popping like gunpowder, considered nothing amiss with making love to one woman and then, the next morning, rushing off to visit another. Without a solitary explanation. Not that he could have given her one she'd accept. "I suppose you did not want me to know you where you went."

"I owe you no explanation. Why does it matter to you? I'm just your stud."

"Exactly! Make a fool of yourself again over her, but I won't stand around to watch this time."

"And what *will* you do? Run back to your lover, the count?"

"It's none of your business where I'd go."

Towering over her, he suddenly lost his previous composure. "It is very much my business."

"You question me, but I cannot do the same to you?"

"Damn you, woman!" Of course, whenever he was losing an argument, he resorted to insults.

"I'm supposed to have your undivided attention for these nights. That was our agreement, Hartley."

"So you shall."

But in Sophie's presence, she would be insignificant again. That was always the way of it. Ellie tasted the bitter resentment already and was ashamed. She didn't want to be the sort of female whose tender heart flinched at every threat of a wound.

The farmhouse door opened, and a young boy dashed out to tear across the yard, an excited, rust-colored spaniel leaping and flopping around his feet.

A woman's voice called out, "Rafe, you will not go out there in the rain. Bring that dog back inside. You'll both be covered in mud in no time, and I have no intention of—" Sophie appeared in the open doorway, still scolding the boy. When she looked up and saw them both by the gate, she almost dropped the bowl of batter in her arms.

"Ellie! James? What on earth…?"

The boy stopped out of curiosity and grabbed his dog by the collar.

Ellie was struck instantly by the familiar features of the boy's face but couldn't think where she'd seen them before. He couldn't possibly be Sophie's child, for she'd been married only two years, and the boy was at least ten, possibly a few years older than that. As far as she knew, the man Sophie married had no previous children, although the boy's thick black hair was very like his.

"Come inside out of the rain," Sophie exclaimed. "I wish I had known you were coming. Why did you not write?"

"I did not think of it, I confess. The idea of a Christmas visit to Sydney Dovedale came upon me suddenly, and before I knew it, I was halfway here." Muddy curls dripped down the back of her neck as her bonnet leaked raindrops. Oddly enough, in that moment of so much greater discomfort, her mind focused on that one sensation.

"Oh, Ellie! You never change." This was uttered with a gusty sigh as if, perhaps, it was time she did change.

Ellie glanced at James. His expression was guarded, as was Sophie's.

"Hello, James. You look very well." Her friend hid her amusement about the breeches much better than Ellie could. Sophie was always better at hiding things—like her thoughts and her feelings.

"And you," said James. "Your family is in good health?"

"Oh yes. Very."

Ellie wanted to scream. They were being so very formal, speaking lines like characters in a novel. As if there had never been anything between them.

"Do, please, come in."

The boy and his dog followed them into the farmhouse, where the warm, delicious scent of baking teased Ellie's stomach, reminding her that she came out without breakfast. That fact was soon remedied. Sophie, familiar with Ellie's appetite, insisted she sit at the table by the window, while she made tea and laid out a plate of warm mince pies. Ellie removed her dampened bonnet and slipped off her gloves to eat. She watched her friend potter about the house with a contented efficiency. Marriage, she mused, comparing Sophie to Walter Winthorne, suited some folk better than others. Sophie, of course, was always a beauty. *She* would never be caught rolling about in a ditch, trying to hide.

James was very quiet. Anger rolled off him in waves, and all of it directed at her. She should never have followed him. Hiding behind trees, for pity's sake! What was she thinking to confront him like that? It was fortunate Sophie had not heard.

A baby cooed gently in a crib by the hearth, above which a line of freshly laundered men's shirts hung to dry. On the mantel, nestled between bunches of mistletoe and holly, rested three sketches undoubtedly drawn by Sophie; one of her husband, one of the boy, and one of the plump baby, soon introduced as Petruchio.

"Petruchio?"

"It was that or Romeo." Sophie sighed. "My husband has just begun to read Shakespeare, I'm afraid." Ellie knew Sophie had been teaching her husband to read. Apparently the lessons progressed well. "At least this way we can call him Peter," she added with a smile. "There is not much to be done with a Romeo."

Throughout this conversation, James remained silent and watched the black-haired boy who sneakily fed pastry crusts to his dog under the table. Sophie, naturally, was too polite to ask how she and James, once enemies, came to be traveling together.

"I heard you say this is Rafe?" Ellie prompted.

For some reason, her friend had offered no introduction to the boy. Now Sophie fussed with her apron strings as she joined them at the table. It struck Ellie that there was a vast deal of nervous fidgeting in her presence ever since she arrived in Sydney Dovedale. First her aunt and now Sophie. That village never used to have so many anxious people who couldn't look her in the eye.

"Yes," her friend said finally. "Rafe is my husband's nephew."

"Who are you then?" the boy wanted to know.

"Ellie Vyne." She held out her hand. "Pleased to make your acquaintance, young man."

The boy looked at her hand then her face again.

He wiped his grubby palm on his breeches and shook her hand warily. Again she clutched at a spark of recognition, but it was gone, evaporated before she could make sense of it. "You live here with your aunt and uncle?" she asked him, since Sophie volunteered no further information.

"'Course I do," the boy sputtered, spraying sugar and pastry crumbs. Then he stopped, dropped his pie, and glared at her. "What are you doing here? Strangers don't come here much. You haven't come to take me away, have you?"

"Rafe," Sophie exclaimed, "don't be silly. This is my friend Ellie, and she and Mr. Hartley have come all the way from London to visit. Why on earth should she want to take you away?"

The boy rounded his shoulders, still glowering at Ellie from beneath a thick fringe of ebony hair. "Just makin' sure. She looks like trouble."

James spoke finally. "Perceptive child."

Rafe flicked his hair back. "What's that, mister?"

"You have Miss Vyne pegged already."

The boy wiped his mouth on his sleeve and looked at Ellie. "Why are you trouble then?"

She shrugged, unable to reply because James had just put his hand over hers where it rested on the table. She didn't know what to do about it. Did it mean she was forgiven? "I'm not really," she replied. "It's just rumor and gossip. Mostly unfair and unfounded."

Beside her, James gave a small snort of derision, which she pointedly ignored.

"They say that about me too," the boy blurted. "That I'm trouble."

Sophie passed him a kerchief and urged that he wipe his mouth on that instead of his sleeve, and then she reprimanded him for not washing his hands before he came to the table. Reluctantly, the boy slouched off into the scullery to complete that task. The dog galloped after him.

"Aunt Lizzie told me that your brother sold his property."

"Yes, to a very grand fellow by the name of Sir William Milford, a bachelor, who is not often in residence—thwarting the hopes of every single lady within twenty miles. Although one cannot blame the fellow for declining to live in that drafty fortress. There are rumors of extensive plans to improve it." Sophie shrugged. "One wonders what can be done with such a place and what madness he suffers for shouldering the burden. But his tenants and workers say he is kindly and just." She gave a wry smile. "Aunt Finn says that is merely because he is so seldom here."

"Your aunt is out?" Ellie asked, disappointed not to see the lady in her usual rocking chair by the fire. Finnola Valentine was a lively character with a good share of scandal in her own past. She could always be counted on to say or do something shocking. Ellie had a great fondness for her and vice versa.

"Aunt Finn spends a few weeks in Norwich with an old friend," Sophie replied with another quick smile. "As far as I know, the town still stands. We expect her back for Christmas, but if she enjoys herself, I daresay she'll be in no hurry to return."

"Yes, I'm sure."

"You plan to stay for the New Year, Ellie?" Sophie asked, her voice fragile suddenly.

"I desired a pleasant change, and London is so—"

"We're engaged," said James.

Breath snagged in her throat. "We most certainly are *not* engaged!"

His fingers tightened over hers. "We most certainly *are*, woman!"

"Not yet we are not." She felt her cheeks getting warm. She was embarrassed in front of her friend, who must think she'd gone mad. Engagements scared her to death these days. She'd never had any luck with them before. In her experience, men quickly settled into taking her for granted once they were engaged. "I believe I told you quite clearly that there is no engagement. Just an arrangement. Of sorts."

Poor Sophie was gazing at them both, completely befuddled.

"It's merely an agreement to consider marriage," Ellie explained further. "If the conditions are favorable."

"Call it what you will," James snapped, taking his hand away.

The boy returned from the scullery, dropped into his chair, and this time addressed James. "You live in Lunnen, mister?"

James irritably scratched the side of his nose. "I do. Presently."

The interrogation returned to Ellie. "Where do you live, missus?"

"All over the place."

"All over?"

James muttered, "Like a gypsy."

She tried to explain. "Sometimes I stay with my sisters in London. Sometimes I visit my father, or I go to Brighton or Bath and stay with friends." She forced each word out, although her mind was preoccupied.

"Really? Brighton?" James laughed harshly. "I thought you said you'd never been there in your life."

Rather than answer, she took a large bite of mince pie.

Having considered what she'd said, Rafe exclaimed, "You move around a lot. Like a crook what don't want to be caught."

"Rafe!"

James smiled. "Once again, a perfect understanding of Miss Vyne already. She doesn't wish to be caught."

The boy grinned. "I moved around a lot too. Before I done come 'ere."

"*Came here*," Sophie corrected, looking frazzled.

"Done came here," the boy repeated. He pointed at Ellie. "You've got brambles in your hair."

Ellie realized then that there was something familiar around his mouth. She tried picturing the boy with lighter coloring.

James muttered, "Miss Vyne lurks under hedgerows to spy upon people."

There was a short silence until Sophie found another subject, chattering about all the renovations her husband made to the farmhouse. Ellie tried to pay attention, but her mind would not behave, and she saw that James, equally inattentive to the conversation, was fascinated by the boy. He stared across the table until Sophie's husband came in from the stables.

The greeting between James and Mr. Kane was cool and less comfortable than an Indian fakir's mattress of knives, but passed without incident. Since his wife forgot to mention it, Mr. Kane extended an invitation to them both for the party that evening.

Before they left, Sophie took Ellie into the pantry

to give her some preserves for her aunt. With the door partially closed behind them, the women surveyed the shelves full of preserves, until Sophie suddenly reached for her hand and whispered, "My dear friend, there are things you don't know about James."

"Really? I've always thought I knew everything about everything."

"Do be serious for once! James is a man with…a past."

"And I am a woman with the same."

"But there is—"

The door opened, and Rafe stuck his head in. "What are you whisperin' about? Are you whisperin' about me? You are, ain't yer? You've got a guilty face."

"No we are not, for pity's sake," Sophie snapped, rather more angrily than necessary it seemed to Ellie. "Why would we have anything to whisper about you?"

But it was enough interruption to dissuade Sophie from whatever warning she'd meant to give. She'd seemed torn as to whether she should speak or not and, with only very slight discouragement, gave up.

Ellie didn't push for more. In truth, she didn't want to hear any bad things about James. Part of her took umbrage at her friend suggesting there might be anything about James of which she was unaware. She'd known the man and all his faults for seventeen years, for pity's sake.

Yet something had troubled her friend for the entire visit and so deeply that, until Sophie's husband raised the matter, she forgot to mention the party altogether. Under normal circumstances, a party would be the first thing either woman mentioned to the other. Today, however, they were both too distracted.

Ellie had seen Sophie glance at James with fearful, hollowed eyes. Whenever she dared look at him at all. Something was very wrong. Ellie's doubts and fears needed little nurturing to flourish like weeds through her mind.

Had her friend's strange, stilted manner stemmed from knowing how Ellie and James were always at odds? Did she wonder how they could overcome the infamous feud? Or was it simply the differences in their background?

James Hartley was filthy rich, the son and grandson of knighted merchants. His grandmother was the daughter of a marquis, niece of a duke, and the most important person in Morecroft. It was said that she kept a servant just for holding her smelling salts. Invitations to her social events were almost as sought after by the county elite as invitations to Court. James, her only grandson, had known nothing but the best schools, the finest tailors, the most sought-after chefs. The most beautiful women.

She, on the other hand, was a wayward, stray stepdaughter of an impoverished, eccentric admiral. Her mother had been a pretty nobody—even worse, a foreigner. Slandered wherever she went, Ellie knew the world saw her as a clumsy, irreverent creature of little beauty, scant charm, no fashion sense, and just enough wit to keep the gates of debtor's prison at bay.

What on earth was James Hartley doing with her?

Chapter 15

So that was over with. James had worried about seeing Sophia again, wondered how it might feel after two years, feared the return of those familiar pangs he'd carried for so long. But he'd merely experienced a pleasure such as he knew at seeing any old friend after a period of absence. Even his old animosity toward her husband was muted.

Ellie walked ahead, leaping over puddles—frequently landing in them—while he circled each one and maintained a safe distance.

This was the very lane along which he'd traveled the first time he laid eyes on Ellie Vyne. On his way to visit Sophia as he trotted along in his new curricle, he'd mistaken the girl for a gypsy. She wandered along the verge untended, her dress muddied, her dark hair loose down her back and ornamented with a wilted daisy chain. He'd turned his head to look at her as he passed, just as his wheels splashed through a deep puddle and coated her from head to foot. He would have stopped, but when she cursed at him in some very foul language, he felt no guilt and continued on his way.

If anyone had told him back then that he would consider one day marrying the girl, he could only have laughed at the absurdity. *Ellie Vyne? But she's feral,* he would have said. Of course, he was never very tactful back then.

Now he was intensely sorry for many things he'd uttered in the past while trying to be amusing.

"Why did you tell her we're engaged?" She looked over her shoulder.

"People must know sooner or later." It had been his sole purpose in seeing Sophia that day. He felt it only right that she should know. In a sense, he wanted her approval, and if Ellie had not followed him there, he would have asked Sophie's advice too.

"But it really isn't true. It's not an engagement."

"This again?" He stopped walking; so she did too. Sometimes he wondered if she truly planned to go through with marriage to him. She seemed fearful of the commitment, always avoiding any serious conversation on the subject. There was also her history of broken engagements, a pattern of disastrous, ill-advised romances. Would he be just another casualty of her restless attention, another fool bewitched and cast aside when he'd outlived his usefulness and his entertainment value?

"Did you say it to wound Sophie?" she demanded.

"Why would I want to do that, pray?"

She exhaled heavily and pushed a stray curl back under the limp brim of her rain-soaked bonnet. "You were in love with her, and she threw you over for another man."

James looked at her small, troublemaking fingers.

They were turning a bluish pallor, because she'd lost her gloves again. "Was I in love with her?"

"Everyone says so."

"Then it must be true. Will you take my gloves? You're cold."

"No. Thank you." Her expression was vexed. "And I don't care for the word *engagement*. It's never brought me much good fortune, only more scandal."

He looked at her stubborn, bossy mouth. He wanted her hand, but it was never still. "What about the word *marriage*, Miss Vyne? Does that word trouble you too?"

"We will marry only *if* these five nights prove fruitful."

She looked particularly beautiful in her windswept state. Very tempting.

"That was the agreement, James." She began backing up; something about his expression apparently caused her anxiety.

"Smallwick," he corrected with a smile and walked toward her.

To his relief, a little twitch turned up the corner of her willful lips, and she stopped at the verge, her back to a stout oak. "May I keep Smallwick a while longer then?"

"Yes." He raised a hand to her face and curved it slowly toward her cold cheek, letting his gloved fingertips drift slowly downward. "If he's making good use of himself."

"Oh, he is." She smiled.

"Then he's yours."

He bent his head, but just as he expected to claim a kiss, she dodged around him and walked on. Sighing heavily, he straightened up and followed. "Until

Grieves comes with Dr. Salt," she said. "What can be taking them so long?"

James winced. "No doubt Grieves enjoys his freedom from my service and is kicking up his heels in Morecroft." He wouldn't put it past his valet to have gone off on another holiday somewhere. Grieves was a shrewd fellow and probably knew this was a ruse.

At steps running after them down the lane, they both turned. The boy, Rafe, flew toward them, waving worn leather gloves.

"You left these behind, missus!"

"How many gloves have you lost?" he muttered to the woman at his side. *How many men have returned them to you?* he might have added. If seeking another quarrel.

"My sisters say I should have them attached to me on strings as I did when I was a child."

The boy tumbled into them, red faced. James was struck with a memory of another similarly raven-haired creature once looking up at him and smiling. *Oh, sir, you forgot your hat, sir.* A pretty young housemaid running after him as he left a party. It was the first time he'd noticed her, and after that they'd enjoyed a brief affair. It lasted no more than a week perhaps. He was a lusty young man, and she was eager, available, most obliging. A lovely girl with very dark eyes and a soft voice. She was the housemaid he'd known more than ten years ago—the young woman who sent for him too late and died. Supposedly, along with her child.

His child.

This boy's eyes were blue, startling, an unusual combination with the ebony hair.

At the farmhouse, he had been too caught up

in relaying the news that was burning a hole in his tongue. What Sophie said about the boy hadn't fully sunk in. Now it did. Rafe was Russ Kane's nephew, so she'd said. Two years ago, when she accused James of letting a woman and child die, she'd hinted that the dead woman was Kane's sister. Which is how she knew about it. If the housemaid was Kane's sister, and this boy was Kane's nephew…

He struggled to remember his conversation with Sophie two years ago, the night she ran away from him to marry Kane. She'd definitely told him the housemaid—Rebecca—had died. What did she say about the child? The memory was shrouded in fog, and he'd been half cut on brandy at the time, but he was sure she'd told him the child died too. If she had told him otherwise, he would have asked about the child, wanted to see him, paid for his education.

Ellie took her gloves, thanked the boy, and with a thoughtful, pensive expression, watched him run back to the farmhouse gates.

James, too, followed the boy's retreat with his narrowed gaze.

His son? Was it possible that Rebecca's child had lived? The boy was surely the right age to be his. He swallowed hard and stared down the lane until his sight began to mist over. A crushing weight settled over his chest. In the distance, the farmhouse gate clanged shut.

Perhaps it was a coincidence. After all, he knew very little about Kane's background, and he could have many siblings, many nephews.

He closed his eyes.

Breathe.

He had a son. Dear God. He had a son? If Rafe was his, Sophia had kept the truth from him for two years. Unforgiveable.

"Look," Ellie said.

He opened his eyes. She was pointing at the heavy sky.

"I can almost taste the snow already. Won't that be lovely if it snows for Christmas?"

He looked down the lane again toward the farm-house surrounded by that flint stone wall. The boy's face haunted him, would not let him rest.

His son. *His son?*

The more he thought of it, the more convinced he became.

"I do hope Molly Robbins has mended your breeches," Ellie exclaimed. "You look quite ridiculous in those you borrowed from my aunt." She giggled and then covered her mouth, pretending to be sorry.

He straightened his shoulders and lifted his chin. "I can't help it if your aunt's lover happens to be short and wide."

"My aunt's *what*?"

Glad to see her amusement snapped off at last, he relayed his suspicions about her aunt's early morning, personal milk delivery.

"How dare you suggest such a thing? James Hartley, that is positively untrue."

"I saw Farmer Osborne with my own two good eyes, sneaking out of the cottage yesterday after we arrived. And last night he was trying to get in through the back door, clearly surprised to find it bolted."

"My aunt is a very proper lady, and she's devoted to the captain's memory!"

"I'm telling you, woman, I know what I saw." He gestured at his breeches. "And how else do you explain these?"

Reminded of them, she broke into another chuckle, putting both hands up to her lips this time but unable to hide the wicked gleam in her eyes.

"It seems to me," he added, "that Farmer Osborne had more than one reason to send his daughter off to Bath and get her out of the way."

"James! Not my aunt and Farmer Osborne. Two more respectable people you could never meet."

Head up, James walked on, lengthening his stride and leaving her to walk behind.

"Your ankle must be much improved, Smallwick," she called out wryly.

So he faltered, limping belatedly. Laughter rolled out of her yet again.

How could one person have so much laughter inside, waiting to come out on the slightest provocation?

"Apparently everyone in this damnable village is keeping a secret," he muttered, thinking not only of Eliza Cawley and her clandestine visitor, but of Sophia and that cheeky-faced, crow-headed boy.

❧

Ellie caught her reflection in the hall mirror as they walked through the front door. She noted, in some distress, her reddened cheeks and dampened, wind-blown curls. No wonder James kept looking at her oddly. She must be the most unkempt woman with whom he'd ever been observed in company. Thinking to run upstairs and tidy herself, she was prevented by her aunt, who greeted them in the hall, agitated again.

"Ellie, thank goodness." She lowered her voice. "Lord Shale is here with his son. I am unaccustomed to grand visitors and could not think how to entertain them." Perhaps seeing her intention to run out again, her aunt quickly seized her coat and clutched it in her arms. "You cannot leave them in my parlor. Go!" She began herding her niece along the hall and away from the door. "Go in. They are here for you, not me, and Lady Mercy has already sung several songs on the spinet."

"Good. Let Lady Mercy entertain the Shales."

"But, my dear Ellie, her songs are not very ladylike. Someone has taught her the wrong lyrics out of mischief. I dare not say anything, but Lord Shale has gone quite puce in color. Besides, although the young lady has much to say for herself and could never be described as a shrinking violet, I fear she is much too young to be 'out.' She tells me she is only ten, Ellie. Yet she insisted on sitting down at the spinet, and nothing dissuaded her."

"No. I can imagine."

"But surely she is not 'out' so young."

"I believe her upbringing has been rather unusual, Aunt Lizzie. She has very little supervision."

"Why don't you take charge of her then," James interrupted. "You like being in charge, Miss Vyne. Ordering people about."

"Indeed I do not."

"I've never known anyone so fond of laying down rules, madam. You do it so well." Then he strode onward into the kitchen to look for his mended breeches.

Feet heavy, she entered the parlor. Lord Shale stood to greet her, and his son eventually followed suit. To Ellie's horror, Mrs. Flick was still there, having extended her morning visit beyond the usual half hour, very probably to glean as much gossip as she could. The arrival of the Shales was an added bonus. Her small eyes bore into Ellie from across the parlor.

"So there you are at last. Your aunt said you'd gone out walking. In this weather. And all alone. Really, you young girls are so careless of your health. I am an advocate of *indoor* exercise. Outdoors, one is inclined to exert oneself overmuch. Indoors, one is in no danger of choking on insects or catching too much sunlight."

"I believe fresh air improves the health, madam," Ellie replied. "I take in as much of it as I can in the country."

Although she smiled at Mrs. Flick, the gesture was not returned. Even the woman's clothes bore a grudge—tightly buttoned and sparsely decorated.

"The benefits are plain, Miss Vyne. You are the picture of good health," Lord Shale assured her. "A brisk walk can be very beneficial, I always say. Trenton loves to walk. Do you not, Trenton?"

His son, having already slumped back onto the couch, was examining his pocket watch. No one ever looked less like a person inclined to walking.

"And what brings you to Sydney Dovedale so suddenly?" Mrs. Flick demanded, shouting to be heard above Lady Mercy's heavy-handed playing.

"A visit to my aunt for Christmas," Ellie replied and crossed to the spinet. "I heard she'd been under the weather. I hoped to cheer her spirits."

Mrs. Flick made a huffing sound, as if the idea of Ellie's presence cheering anyone's spirits was patently ridiculous. "It was a little cold, and she is well recovered now. Thanks to my remedy. I daresay she could have been very ill had she not listened to me about the goose grease and calf's foot. There was no occasion for *you* to come charging across the country, I'm sure."

As Ellie's aunt entered the parlor behind her, Mrs. Flick raised her voice another decibel. "Isn't that right, Eliza? My remedy was all you required."

"Oh yes, yes, indeed."

Ellie leaned over the spinet and closed the music Lady Mercy was following. "I believe Molly Robbins wanted to take you on a tour of the village, my lady. The rain has stopped now, and you should take advantage of it."

"She's sewing in the kitchen."

"But I'm sure she's done now. Run along."

"I don't want to. She's a dull, plain girl."

Ellie gritted her teeth in another smile. "But you do want to go to the party tonight?"

Blackmail the child understood. She climbed down from the stool, curtseyed to the guests, and allowed Ellie to shuffle her out of the parlor.

"And what is this I hear about a *manservant*?" Mrs. Flick exclaimed, her small mouth hemmed with deep lines engraved by a lifetime of disappointment in the behavior of others. When she closed her mouth, it was as if the strings of a miser's purse were pulled tight.

Everyone looked at Ellie as she sat beside her aunt. "Oh, it is quite the new thing to be had among young ladies in Town, madam."

Mrs. Flick's eyes shrank to wary slits.

"They are very useful for carrying boxes and lifting heavy items. Opening stuck doors and bottles. That sort of thing. Very good for a woman who lacks a husband." Ellie was getting into her story. "I hear the Princess Sophia keeps one. A Male Peculiar is the correct term."

All eyes were on her still. Mrs. Flick's gaze widened only very slightly. "A Male Peculiar? I never heard of such a thing."

"I can assure you, madam, they are all the rage. In Town."

There was a pause. Aunt Lizzie blew her nose soundly into her lace kerchief, and Lord Shale tapped his cane against his shoe. In his cage, the captain's parakeet let out a low cackle. "Ooh...Smallwick! Small...*wick*!"

Ellie looked down at her skirt, hiding a smile.

"How are you getting along without Mary Wills?" Mrs. Flick demanded as she turned her fiercely critical attention to Aunt Lizzie. "I do not know why you gave her up, and now you have guests, you will rue the day you let her go. Guests do make an awful mess, especially when they descend upon a house without warning and bring small people in tow."

Aunt Lizzie swallowed fearfully, her fingers pulling at the pleats in her skirt.

"If Mary ate too much," the other woman continued, "you could have got a girl of less appe-tite and considerably less heft from the orphanage. A younger girl, grateful for the roof over her head and who takes up only a little air. Mary Wills had a tendency to fill spaces, and this is only a small house with narrow rooms."

"But I am managing quite well without a maid," Aunt Lizzie ventured. "Especially now I have Ellie here to help."

Mrs. Flick drew back with a sharp jerk of her head. "How much help she'll be to you, I can't imagine. Dashing hither and thither in all weathers. Like most young girls, never about when she is needed."

Lord Shale cleared his throat. "If the rain has stopped, Miss Vyne, and you are not too tired from your walk, I'm sure Trenton would very much enjoy a stroll about your aunt's garden."

It was the lesser of two evils. At least she'd be in the fresh air. So she forced a brighter smile and let the unpleasant young man escort her out through the French doors into the small, walled garden behind the cottage.

Mrs. Flick, she knew, kept an eye on them through the gothic arched panels of the door. No doubt she'd already begun preparing her next round of gossip to share later with the good folk of the village. It was lucky James had not joined them in the parlor, because Mrs. Flick would have recognized him immediately, and she was not the sort to play along with a masquerade.

James found his breeches mended so skillfully he couldn't see the stitches at all. The Robbins girl plainly had a great deal of patience and a steady hand.

"I let them out a little for you, sir," she said, blushing faintly, eyes averted. "So they should be more comfortable."

"Yes, I see." He cleared his throat. "Thank you." She'd done a better job of it than his fancy French tailor, he mused darkly.

Lady Mercy Danforthe stormed into the kitchen, face like a freckled thundercloud. "She says you're to take me around this stupid little village, Robbins. I'm forbidden to play on the spinet or talk to the adults. I'm supposed to be content with your dreary company."

"But I was just in the middle of all the mending, Lady Mercy."

"I don't care. You're to take me out at once. It was her idea, not mine." She glowered at James. "I hate her—that bossy woman."

"Yes," said James, "she is an acquired taste."

The Robbins girl jabbed her needle into the cushioned lid of Eliza Cawley's little sewing cabinet. "Very good, my lady. I'll just get my coat."

"Well, make haste."

James looked down at the imperious creature. Lady Mercy had been without a father for the last few years, and her brother, clearly, was not up to the task of her guidance. Since James planned to take on fatherhood himself, perhaps now was a good time to practice. After all, becoming a good father required a great deal more than simply donating the seed, whatever Miss Vyne thought. He knew that much from his own experience as a son.

When the Robbins girl had dashed out into the narrow hall, James leaned down to the petulant Lady Mercy and whispered in her ear. "That little girl is your age and has eleven siblings. Her family are so poor that they had to send her out to work. I daresay she has many other things she would rather do with her time than escort you about. The least you could do is be polite to her." He paused. She finally looked up at him, biting her lip hard. "I see your brother hasn't taught you any manners, but nobody, Lady Mercy, is ever going to like you without any. People you may one day want to befriend will look for excuses to rid themselves of your company, and then you'll regret many things that you've said in the past. I suggest you add some kind words to your vocabulary. Words like please and thank you will be a start. Are we clear?"

She was silent, mulish.

"Are we clear?" he repeated.

"Oh...very well."

"Good. I don't want to hear you being rude to her again. Now go. Be a child for once and play with children your own age. Make friends. Don't be in so much haste to grow up."

෴

Her aunt's garden was a patchwork of neat flowerbeds divided by narrow grass strips and a gravel walkway that led under a willow-branch arbor. Ellie marched along at some speed to get it over with, but Trenton dragged his feet, slowing to a complete stop as they turned with the path, and stood behind the tall yew hedge that screened the cottage from view.

"Miss Vyne," he said abruptly, "I would like to make you an offer of marriage."

Stunned, she almost toppled sideways into the knotted frame of the arbor. "I beg your pardon?"

"For some years now you must know I have cherished—"

"Trenton Shale, did your father put you up to this?"

He faltered. His thin cheeks paled. "He is most eager for the match."

"But I don't have—"

"I must save you, he says, from the scandals you get yourself into." When the young man began to fall to his knee in the gravel, she grabbed his sleeves and forced him upright.

"Pull yourself together, Trenton. You don't want to marry me. Why did you not tell your father that?"

He looked as if he might argue, but when she folded her arms and tapped her foot, he saw she was not to be trifled with. Sighing heavily, he replaced his hat and assessed the hedge with gloomy eyes. "He has discussed the matter with your stepfather, Miss Vyne. The admiral has given his permission—indeed, his encouragement."

She stared.

"Admiral Vyne has not written to tell you?" he asked plaintively.

"No, he has not." Her stepfather had not written to her in a good many years, except to ask for her help with a creditor. *Well, I never know where you'll be from one day to the next, Mariella,* was always his excuse for the lack of correspondence, although his messages had no trouble finding her when he required an outstanding bill paid.

The admiral was always somewhat absentminded. Still, it was difficult to believe he'd forget to tell her this charming nugget. So he'd given up waiting for her to find a husband and got one for her himself.

"May I ask when Lord Shale met with my stepfather?"

"Just last month, Miss Vyne. After I left Cambridge. Papa decided it was time I married."

She'd heard that his father took him out of university because he'd fallen in with some bad influences. Lord Shale was very protective of Trenton, his only son and heir.

"He thought Admiral Vyne may be desperate enough to let you marry me," the young man continued. "He was right, as it turned out. The admiral is of the opinion that you will not get many more offers at your age, and my chances of marriage are slim. I'm not one for girls, Miss Vyne. I never have been."

For the first time in their acquaintance, she felt sorry for Trenton Shale. She could almost forgive him for stealing all her Easter eggs at the hunt. Almost.

She studied the twisted branches of willow arbor and tried to let her thoughts settle from the surprised dance into which they'd just spun. "I'm sorry, Trenton, but I can't marry you."

He bowed his head. "I didn't think for a moment that you would. But I had to ask. Father insisted."

Still amazed by all this, she exclaimed, "After all these years, I wonder how he fixed upon me as your bride."

"My father believes you might provide him with a strong, healthy grandson. A 'good breeder' was the term he used."

She had just snagged her skirt on the arbor and was tugging it free. It took a moment for the words to register. "A good…?" When she pulled herself loose of the willow, the force sent her tumbling into Trenton, and he steadied her with his hands on her arms.

"And the count de Bonneville told us you were coming into the country. We were following you on the road yesterday, you know. It was no coincidence. I told Father that he wasted his time, but he was adamant that I try."

"The count de Bonneville?" Surely he must mean someone else, she thought.

"Yes. I have become acquainted with the gentleman recently." Trenton shifted his feet uneasily on the gravel path.

"The count de Bonneville?" she said again.

"Indeed."

Ellie stared at the hedge, her mind struggling to make sense of that. "May I ask where you met the count?"

"In Bath last spring and in Brighton this summer. I lost rather a lot of money to him."

Who the blazes was out there pretending to be the count de Bonneville? And in the same places she traveled, on the same schedule. She thought of the shadow following her lately. Now she knew she was right all along to sense danger.

"Miss Vyne, you look very pale. Are you ill?"

She scraped fingertips over the nape of her neck where the tiny hairs had begun to tingle again, starting a chain of goose bumps down her spine. "Not at all, Trenton." Were her antics about to catch up with her, just when she hoped to put it all behind her?

"What shall I tell Father? I never can do anything to please him. As his only son, I'm a great disappointment."

Ah, approval. That was what everyone wanted

from the people they cared about. She used to think it didn't matter to her. She thought she could go through life pleasing only herself. But it wasn't true. She knew that now. The world was a cold place when one was always on the outside, never properly belonging anywhere. Just once she'd like to be warm, loved for who she really was, faults and all. To belong somewhere, in someone's arms.

Thinking hard, she stared again at the hedge over Trenton's shoulder then managed a tight smile. "Don't tell your father anything. We have just enjoyed a pleasant stroll together in the garden. There is no need for him to know anything more than that. He can hardly expect you to woo me with one conversation."

"I suppose not," he replied doubtfully.

She took his arm, and they walked on.

Someone was masquerading as her count for their own devious motives. Ellie did not know what to make of it, but the cold fingers of fear suddenly had a firm grip on her heart.

Chapter 16

WHEN THE SHALES LEFT, SHE WENT UP TO THE SPARE bedchamber and found James trying on his mended breeches. He stood in the light of the casement window and examined his reflection in the cheval mirror.

"That Robbins girl is a talented seamstress," he muttered.

"Yes, we poor country girls all have hidden talents."

He glanced at her. "Poor country girls?"

"That's what I am. Do not forget it."

He sank to the chair by the little crooked writing bureau. "Come here then, my country maid. I have a hankering for your hidden talents."

But she hesitated. "Smallwick," she began carefully, "you do know I haven't a penny for a dowry, don't you?" Most men married to increase their wealth and consequence, not decrease it. "The admiral cannot afford—"

"I have no intention of asking Admiral Vyne for anything. Except your hand, of course. I'm marrying you because you need *my* money. And because you are too hard-hearted to fall in love with me and make unnecessary scenes. I need a wife, and you need coin. It's a simple trade."

Yes, he had chosen her for purely convenient reasons. She should never read more into it.

"Now why this sudden reminder of your financial state?" A line gathered between his brows. "You're not trying to get out of paying my wages, are you, madam?"

"Wages? We never discussed wages."

He patted his broad, muscular thigh. "Come here, country maid."

Ellie advanced slowly until she stood between his knees. He put his hands around her waist. "Get astride me then, Miss Vyne, and I'll take the wages you owe me in kind."

"You're awfully bold for a servant, Smallwick."

"Ladies who employ me don't generally complain. Get astride me."

"Very well then. You have three more tries to win yourself this convenient wife you need."

Now he looked up, branding her with a very hot blue gaze. "Four."

Luckily for him, she wasn't inclined to dispute it just then. His presence brightened up that small, cramped chamber. The light outside was gray and drear, but where it slid through the window and fumbled over his gilded hair, it changed, became sunny, reminding her of kinder, gentler seasons.

"How long will it be before we know?" he asked.

She was confused, too busy watching the gold in his hair as it transformed the winter light to something merrier.

"If I have performed my duty?" he pressed.

"Duty?"

"Your menses? When should we expect them?"

It wasn't delicate to mention such things—or so her sisters would remind her. That James Hartley even took note of a woman's cycle was, frankly, shocking. "Two weeks or so," she mumbled.

"Good." He smiled up at her like a hungry leopard. "We needn't trouble ourselves with it yet then. Nothing to interrupt us."

"No." Dear Lord, she hoped she wasn't blushing like a grass-green maid.

"Where's your aunt?" he said as his hands slowly lifted her skirt.

"She went out to visit a friend."

"Her gentleman friend?"

She scowled, still refusing to believe her demure aunt capable of that. "Just out."

"And Lady Mercy?"

"Still with Molly Robbins, hopefully getting some of the sauce knocked out of her by the village children."

He eased her down astride his lap. "Grieves could be here soon. Any minute." He blinked, softened his mouth, licked his lips. "And we're all alone in the house."

She looked out over his head and surveyed the empty lane. A troop of swans ventured onto the common from behind the tavern, where a patch of flooded ground had, over the years, become grandly and optimistically referred to by the villagers as The Lake. Across the way, a row of chestnut trees, bare now of leaves, waited mournfully for spring again. In full summer, the Norman spire seemed to grow out of those trees, but in winter, the gray stone church was visible through the stark branches, and there was no illusion.

"What if my aunt comes back soon?" She reached down into his lap and felt the hard ridge already waiting. He was a wonderful playmate, these games with him a splendid way to take her mind off her fears.

"We'll keep an eye out through the window," he replied, his voice deepening.

He touched her between her thighs, not waiting for her agreement. "But someone might see," she gasped.

"The swans?"

"Be sensible."

"Can't. Sorry." His fingers slid through the slit in her linen drawers. "Ah. You're as eager as I am, madam," he purred, pressing his fingertips over her sensitive flesh, knowing exactly how much pressure to exert, where to touch her, and when to retreat. Leaving her breathless. "You've been yearning for your next servicing by the ever-diligent Smallwick, I see."

She shook her head, speechless, overflowing with desire.

"Well, I'm sure it wasn't young Trenton Shale who got you in this state, madam."

His manhood, she realized suddenly, was already free and standing to attention. When had he opened his clothing? The man had too much practice. "Now brace yourself, madam. Here I come." He lifted her and then lowered her again, grunting as he thrust upward through the slit in her drawers.

Ellie exhaled a small cry of wanton delight. As she clutched his hair, she brought his face to her bosom, and his warm lips sank into the full curves, his tongue lapping at her through the material. She shivered, head back, riding his lap slowly, trying to make it last, holding off the worries a while longer.

❧

He tugged her sleeves down, breaking a few hooks in his haste. The lacy straps of her chemise followed suit, and then her breasts popped free. While her eyes were closed and she was preoccupied with the first surge of climax, James surveyed her upper body greedily; a possessive flutter of delight traveled fast through his veins. Her curves fit against him so perfectly. It was a match unprecedented in his experience.

When he'd looked out on the garden earlier, he'd seen her with Trenton Shale—the lanky boy had held her arms, keeping her partially hidden from the parlor window by that high hedge. James, from the vantage point of a small window at the top of the stairs, saw all. At first, he was furious, wanted young Shale's head on a plate. Then he came to his senses. She owed him her time, and he would not let her renege on their agreement.

He thought again of the many times he'd watched her dance with other men, seen her laugh and chat so amiably with them when she could barely spare him a solitary word of conversation.

But this vexing woman should be his plaything and no one else's. His. He tightened his grip on her bottom and bounced her hard in his lap, up and down on his shaft, watching her breasts tremble, inches from his lips, the excitable peaks tightening under his fierce regard.

Finally, unable to resist, he opened his mouth and latched onto the nearest honey-sweet, rosy-pink treat.

❧

Ellie's eyes opened just enough to see Mrs. Flick walking across the green, her steps hurrying to escape the swans, which had a reputation for violent behavior when the mood took them. She remembered they'd never had much fondness for Mrs. Flick. Perhaps it was her sour face or the somber black taffeta she wore.

Oh Mrs. Flick, she mused, *if only you could see me now. Getting my exercise indoors with my Male Peculiar.*

She giggled, and was tempted to open the window and shout a greeting to the lady.

But there was a limit to the amount of scandal even she could survive.

❧

Laughing together, they ran down to the scullery. He held the washbasin while she pumped the water.

"Hurry before your aunt comes home, Miss Vyne." Cold water splashed over the rim to wet his arms and the flagged floor. "Look at the mess you're making."

"It might help, Smallwick, if you kept the basin still!"

Playful, they couldn't wait to touch each other again. With the washbasin swaying about in his arms, they hastened back upstairs, and there, in her room, they washed each other off. After, they made love again, this time on the bed under the low, crooked rafters.

There was no debate about the number of times they had left. Neither was counting anymore.

Chapter 17

THE KANES' FARMHOUSE WAS DECORATED INSIDE AND out with lush bowers of evergreen sprinkled with bright crimson holly berries. A profusion of candlelight glowed amber through all the windows, and a small band of musicians played beside the inglenook hearth. There were no more than five and twenty adult guests and half as many children present. In London Society, it would be termed an intimate gathering, but for Sydney Dovedale, it was a grand occasion.

A fat bunch of mistletoe, tied with ribbon, hung over the front door, and as they crossed the step, James captured his lady's arm, leaning down to steal a kiss. Ellie shrank away.

"Smallwick! Behave yourself. The festive season is no occasion to forget your place."

She enjoyed playing the role, it seemed, too much to abandon it. Most people at the party must recognize him as James Hartley, yet she insisted on treating him like her manservant, just to confuse everybody. Also probably to avoid remarks about The Feud, or any serious questions.

Since her aunt had no carriage or horses of her own, Farmer Osborne had offered them all a ride up the lane in his own cart. Ellie expressed a desire to walk, but James, reminding her it was dark, cold, and likely to snow, had persuaded her to ride in the cart.

It was plain to him, as he watched her aunt with the widowed dairy farmer, that they were indeed clandestine lovers; but Ellie, stubborn as usual, refused to see it.

"He is just a kind, helpful gentleman," she'd hissed in his ear when he threw her an *I-told-you-so* look. But as they'd rolled along, bumping and lurching from side to side in Farmer Osborne's cart, she must have watched the older couple sitting together and let those suspicions dwell longer in her mind. She muttered under her breath, "My aunt is in her fifties, for heaven's sake. Why go through all that again at her age?"

James had laughed. "You think people are ever too old for *all that*?"

"But she had it once already with Captain Cawley."

Looking down at her pert, determined face, he'd said, "And no one ever deserves a second chance at love?" A charge of smoldering hot desire swept through him when he gazed down at those lips.

His words had hung in the air between them with far more gravity than he was ever accustomed to causing with his statements. He'd always thought Ellie Vyne never really listened to anything he said. More often than not, she heard what she wanted to hear and laughed scornfully at the rest.

He'd never known a woman so afraid of attachments

of the heart. Except his own grandmother, who must have a beating heart somewhere under all the armor. But after his own disastrous affairs with females, he probably should be more skeptical of it himself. Before Brighton, he was ready to give up on finding anyone special. At least, that was what he'd told himself. Then along came this creature, thrusting her way back into his life, making him confused, making him look into her eyes when he'd resisted for so long. Sometimes James felt as if he was still struggling to find his way out of that maze.

When they entered the warm farmhouse, it was already crowded. He saw the boy, Rafe, complaining and squirming in a corner as Sophia Kane tried to smooth his wild black hair down with a wet cloth. He was dressed tonight in smarter, cleaner clothes, as if someone—no doubt Sophia—had really made an effort to make him look his best. Molly Robbins was complaining that he'd deliberately spilled eggnog on her dress, while Rafe protested that she'd tried to kiss him under the mistletoe. Sophia attempted to make peace. James looked for her husband and found him strolling around the party, carrying his baby son, showing off. Every inch the proud father.

Something that had been denied *him*. Again he felt a surge of anger toward these people who'd kept Rafe's survival a secret. He looked at the boy, certain now of the resemblance, both to the housemaid Rebecca and to himself. With nervous hands, he smoothed over his own hair and then his waistcoat. What could he say to his son? How did one introduce oneself to a son of twelve? For now it was delayed, in any case. Finally free of Sophia and her wet cloth, the boy ran off, closely followed by Molly Robbins, and they briefly disappeared among the other guests.

The lower floor of the house consisted of one large room with an adjoining pantry and a scullery. Tonight with all the furniture moved aside, the openness of the space was perfect for dancing. A group of young people had already formed a set for a wild jig.

Lady Mercy pushed her way between Ellie and James. For the party, she had dressed in a very fine spencer of maroon satin with a military-style trim and high collar, looking every bit the young lady of fashion. Hands dug into a matching muff, she coolly surveyed the house interior and proclaimed it, "humble and drafty, but rustic and picturesque in a country way." Then her eyes sought Molly Robbins. Apparently, during their afternoon together, the two young girls had formed a tentative friendship—or as close to one as might be achieved in so short a space of time and between two complete opposites. Lady Mercy, it turned out, liked "projects," and plain, meek Molly Robbins was her latest, whether she desired to be or not.

"There is that Robbins girl. I lent her my *coquelicot* flowers for her hair." Lady Mercy sounded surprised that the other girl had actually worn them. "She looks almost pretty tonight. The flowers lift her features. I told her so."

James suggested she talk to her new friend.

"But she's dancing with that horrid, common boy!" Lady Mercy shuddered and clutched her muff tighter. "I wouldn't talk to him if he was the last boy on earth." Evidently she and Rafe had met that afternoon, and it had not gone well.

That horrid, common boy is my son, he wanted to say. Best not, though. He had yet to inform Ellie, and she ought to be the first to know he had an illegitimate child. A rush of cold air suddenly chilled his ankles. James turned instinctively to see who had just entered the house, and saw Grieves with Dr. Salt.

Ellie saw them too. "I suppose you'll have to go now"—she smiled sadly—"Smallwick."

"Not yet." He didn't want to leave Smallwick behind just yet. "Perhaps you'll dance with me, madam." He winked and held out his hand. "It is Christmas, after all."

"Not quite," was the pert reply.

"Near enough."

Looking around, she drew his attention to a young woman standing alone by one of the stout wooden beams. "Dance with her," she urged him. "That's one of Molly Robbins's elder sisters, and I'm sure she would love to dance with you. It will make the carpenter's son jealous."

There was a time when James Hartley would have refused to dance with anyone he didn't know at a party. But there was also a time when he thought himself too grand for a country-village party like this one. So, to show he was a reformed man, James made his way through the crowd toward the mousy young woman and put on his most gallant manners.

❦

"My dear friend, it is so wonderful to have you here." Sophie embraced her warmly this evening, a little flushed already perhaps from too much eggnog.

"I must confess your news surprised me earlier, and after you'd gone, I realized I did not even properly congratulate you and James."

Ellie smiled uneasily. "You did seem preoccupied."

Sophie took her hands. "It was wrong of me to doubt your decision. It is none of my business, of course, and I'm sure you'll be very happy." She sighed pensively as her pretty green eyes wandered over Ellie's shoulder. "You'll certainly be very rich."

It seemed as if even her closest friend thought she was with James for the money.

"I worried only because...well..." Sophie looked down at their hands, her fingers entwined with Ellie's. "Because I know how you like to laugh, be silly, and pretend you don't care. And I wanted to be sure you'd really thought about this marriage."

"You mean, not like all my other engagements?" Ellie curbed her laughter, since her friend was so solemn.

"I want you *both* to find happiness, Ellie. You are both dear friends to me."

"And you think we'd do better finding that happiness with other people?"

Although Sophie's answer was firm, it was evasive. "I just want you *both* to be sure. I don't want either of you hurt. This is not another of your pranks, I hope."

Ellie understood that Sophie was worried mostly for James. He'd been unlucky with his previous choice, and his wounds were slow to heal. Sophie genuinely cared about him still and must be afraid he'd be hurt again, because Ellie never took anything seriously. At least, she never had until now. In the beginning, her plan seemed simple—give James the convenient marriage he required as long as she conceived the baby she wanted. But somewhere over the last few days, it all became so much more. It was no longer just a simple trade without risk, without deeper attachment.

"I promise you, Sophie, that I am finally growing up. At my age, I decided it was time to repent all my sins and be a good girl. And don't look at me that way. Have you been taking lessons from my sisters?"

Sophie smiled at last and embraced her again. "Then I shall say no more and leave you to it." When her smile gained strength, Ellie was relieved to see the old Sophie back again. The twinkle was just as she remembered, undiminished. "Now"—she curved her arm under Ellie's and drew her close to whisper—"let me fill you in on all the Sydney Dovedale news. The news I could not tell you while the men listened."

Although she'd heard much of it already from her aunt, she nodded eagerly and let her old friend talk, for Sophie always had more juicy details to add. Aunt Lizzie's news revolved around sickness, death, birth, marriage, and mourning, with not much happening otherwise. Sophie and Ellie knew that what occurred in between was often just as important and a vast deal more entertaining. Soon they were back to normal, giggling together over memories of other parties long gone, reminiscing about less complicated days. But they were both older now and wiser, both embarking on new chapters.

❧

James finally found Ellie again. "Now you must dance with me," he demanded. "I've earned it, madam."

"But it's a minuet. People will think we're in love, Smallwick."

"They know us better than that, madam." He grabbed her hand and tugged, leading her into the dance. "Dine with me in Morecroft tomorrow evening. I think it's time we broke the news to my grandmama."

When she looked up at James, her eyes seemed to reflect every candle flame in the room. He was dazzled for a moment. "But we don't know yet if there will be any marriage. Why tell her until you must? This could all be for nothing, you know."

"You doubt my stud abilities, madam?"

"Don't talk so loud, Smallwick. Do you want the entire village to know?"

James made no attempt to lower his voice. "I'm quite certain the job for which you hired me is done, madam. Very well done."

Her lips puckered, ready to purse and sulk, but then they wavered, almost laughing.

"By New Year you will be my wife, Vyne. Mine." He stroked his gloved thumb across her knuckles. "The child in your womb makes you mine already."

"Do you have magical powers that tell you my state already, Hartley?"

"Yes," was his concise reply. "It happened this afternoon. I felt it."

Her cheeks flamed, and her lashes fluttered downward. James was amused. She'd never been the timid, bashful sort. When had that started? He didn't want her to suddenly change too much. Accustomed to her wickedness, he had grown to expect it, enjoy it.

As the music came to an end, James followed her

wandering gaze and watched her aunt fill a glass cup with eggnog for Farmer Osborne. The older couple talked intimately, smiling and happy.

"Now I know why she was so anxious when I arrived." Ellie's shoulders drooped. "She was afraid I'd find out. My coming here got in the way, didn't it, Smallwick?"

"I fear it did, madam."

She sighed gently. "It is often so."

"What is?"

"Me. In the way."

James could sympathize with that. "When it comes to my family, I have frequently been in the way too." He was the irritation that had to be coped with, first by a mother who suffered in a loveless marriage and left him to the care of nannies, then by a deserted, humiliated father who could not stand his presence, since it reminded him of a failed marriage. Finally his grandmother had been left to cope with the burden of raising James. "Perhaps," he told Ellie, "we have more in common than we realized."

"I've been rather selfish," she said. "I've forgotten that other people have lives too. They can't always stop everything when I show up on their doorstep, demanding attention."

"Quite. What you need, madam, is a home. In one place." He smiled. "And then you can have that dog you wanted."

Surprise flickered through her eyes.

"You thought I wouldn't remember?"

"I didn't think you were listening that night, Smallwick. You were rather pickled."

But her words, uttered softy under the stars in Brighton, remained in the warm embrace of his memory. Along with her very pleasant kiss and the manner in which she'd betrayed, for once, her vulnerability.

"Come outside with me a moment, Miss Vyne." It was pleasant to talk with this woman and not fight. He wanted more time alone with her before he faced the confrontation with Sophie regarding his son. It was a matter that had to be discussed tonight, and then he could tell Ellie. But first, he needed one last uncomplicated moment. He had no idea how she would take the news that he had an illegitimate son, or how it might change things between them. Although he knew the real Ellie much better now, her moods were changeable, and she had, after all, quite recently cracked him over the head and shoulders with a china ewer.

"Smallwick, it's cold out."

"I'll keep you warm, madam."

She glanced hastily around the room to be sure no one watched, and eventually agreed, letting him tug her away from the dancers and outside into the crisp air.

He took an oil lamp from a hook over the door and led her out to the barn across the yard. Three horses, a donkey, and two goats looked up at the first creak of the wooden door, but they returned to the food in their mangers, none too impressed by the visitors. The warm scent of beast and hay filled his nostrils, reminding James of the summers when he used to come there to court Sophia, dragging her away from her chores. All of it a long time ago. He set the oil lamp on a high, safe ledge and led Ellie into an empty stall.

"What are we doing here, Smallwick?" she demanded.

"I wanted to be alone with you a while, madam. I find myself possessive of your company."

"Anyone could come out to check on the animals, especially if they see the lantern light."

"They're all busy dancing and carousing. Now kiss me, madam." With a flourish, he produced a small bunch of mistletoe nabbed from the farmhouse doorway. It was spontaneous, very un-Hartley-like, but tonight he was in the mood to play. She brought out the devil in him, he mused, amazed by the fact that he'd sought a wife as part of his efforts to reform, yet the very woman he needed to fulfill the role should have these rebellious effects upon him. Oddly enough, this woman he'd always criticized to anyone who would listen, turned out to be the perfect partner for him. Could life be any stranger—could it possibly hold any more surprises?

She moved back into the shadowy corner of the stall, and he followed, closing her in.

"I haven't had your lips on mine for several hours now," he said huskily as he held the mistletoe over her head.

"Smallwick, you are incorrigible."

"Yes, madam."

Unable to wait for her movement, he leaned in and kissed her on the lips, warming them for her. Ellie's hands quickly moved to his shoulders and then curled around his nape. Despite her feigned reluctance to enter the barn with him, she responded hungrily to his kiss. Very soon, one of her hands swept down his chest to his breeches.

"Smallwick, I never did ask you how you came by your name." Her fingers trailed over the mound that grew with speed. "It is not very appropriate."

"I believe it was one of Mr. Grieves's little jests, madam."

"Ah."

"He does like his little jests."

"Smallwick, these stud services don't have to be performed all at once. You can take a rest."

"I have no need of one, madam."

"So I see."

He paused. "Do *you*?"

Her eyes twinkled, and she bit her lower lip. A dimple appeared in her left cheek. "Good Lord, no, Smallwick. You'll have to work a lot harder than this to wear me out."

Lifting her until her legs wrapped around his waist, he murmured gratefully, "Excellent, madam, because I am of a mind to make every moment we have alone together count."

❧

The wooden slats at her back rattled and creaked. The plow horse in the next stall made a low whinny and shook his mane.

"Ouch, Smallwick," she muttered. "Have a care, or my hair will all come undone."

James entered her before she'd finished her sentence, bending his legs and thrusting upward with the full force of his lower body. He grunted, "Your hair won't be the only thing undone, madam."

It was a quick, savage mating. Very fitting for a stable, she mused.

She should have declined his offer of a rutting there and then, should never have crept away from the party with him, skulking around and being very naughty in the hay. But she couldn't keep her hands off him, and he appeared to suffer the same condition of beguilement. It was irrepressible. One might almost think he had some devil to exorcise tonight, something burning up inside him, needing release.

He shuddered and braced her against the wooden divider, his mouth on the side of her neck. His strong male scent mingled with the sweetness of the hay and the waxy oil lamp. She closed her eyes, drinking it in, relishing that moment, holding onto it with all her senses and trapping it within her memory forever. As if this was the last time. Her heart stalled at that thought, and her eyelids flew open.

Eventually he set her feet on the ground again and, like any diligent servant, straightened her clothing and her hair for her. He did not speak. She'd known him many years, and it was apparent to Ellie that he had something on his mind. Some trouble he pondered. She wanted to help, but since he did not share his problem with her, she did not know how. Like her, he was accustomed to keeping his troubled thoughts locked away, hidden behind a smile and a sharp-tongued comment.

❧

As they reentered the house, he tucked the mistletoe away inside his coat pocket.

"No one else must be tempted to kiss you," he said.

She seemed far away, not hearing. "I should talk to my aunt."

James pressed a warm kiss to her hand and watched her walk away through the merry mob. She had a little straw in her hair, but it was too late to call her back and remove it.

Now he had an important conversation to face himself. Turning sharply, he looked for Sophia. To his surprise, she was looking for him too. Their eyes met, and a silent signal passed between them. She knew he was going to ask about Rafe. Apparently, she was ready to explain.

Chapter 18

"ELLIE, MY DEAR, I DIDN'T WANT TO KEEP IT FROM you, but I did not know what you'd say." Her aunt looked down at her toes. "You must think that at my time of life it is quite absurd to marry again. But I've been a widow now for more than twenty years, and it does become very lonely."

"Aunt Lizzie, I am delighted that you found love again. There is nothing I could want more for you." She gently kissed her aunt's soft, warm cheek. "I wish you'd told me when I arrived. I thought you had some awful secret. My imagination has been hard at work on all manner of gruesome thoughts." Ellie paused as another realization slowly dawned. "That is why you let Mary Wills go!"

"It was one of the reasons, Ellie my dear. It is true that I could not really afford her any longer, but Mary was a terrible gossip, and she did like to pry."

"And then I came along!"

"You are always welcome." Her aunt patted her hand. "But whatever you do, say nothing to Mrs. Flick. I have not got up the courage yet to tell her."

They laughed together.

Quite suddenly, Ellie decided to be brave. "Now I have news for you too. Prepare yourself, dear aunt, for a monstrous shock. I have an understanding with James Hartley."

Her aunt took off her spectacles, wiped them on her lace kerchief, and put them back on. "I should hope so too. It's about time."

"Aunt Lizzie! You're not surprised?"

"Why would I be, dear girl? You've been in love with him since you were ten."

Ellie swallowed hard. A gale of embarrassing tears threatened to pour out of her, when she was never usually prone to fits of hysteria.

"Did you think me blind, Ellie? I've seen many love-struck glances back and forth across my parlor over the years. I've witnessed acknowledged love and thwarted love, anguish, passion, and denial. Oh yes. It all happens here in Sydney Dovedale." Her aunt reached up to extract a piece of straw from Ellie's hair. "Don't be fooled by the sleepy image."

Anxious to be busy, Ellie ladled herself a cup of eggnog. Aunt Lizzie was quite a romantic, she mused. In love with James all these years? Ha! Ridiculous. Their arrangement was one of mutual convenience, brought about by the shared enjoyment of a good argument. That was all.

However, if it pleased her aunt to think of it as love…well, she would not argue. Why spoil it for dear, sweet Aunt Lizzie?

She glanced slyly around the room and was relieved to find no eyes upon her at that moment, because she felt the Christmas spirit going to her head already. Confessing about James to her aunt had taken a load from her shoulders. An understanding. Yes, she could call it that without suffering the pangs of fear produced by any mention of an engagement. An engagement sounded too planned, too formal. An "understanding" suggested a meeting of minds and ideas.

But he had looked at her tonight with such warmth in his gaze that she could almost believe...

Oh, she was being a fool.

She used to think James was an uncomplicated fellow, that she had his character neatly pegged. But over the past few days, there seemed to be more Smallwick in him than there was Hartley. Ellie didn't like to think she'd been wrong all those years when she'd determinedly set about convincing herself and everyone else that she thoroughly despised him.

Her aunt was still talking. "My brother, for instance. He was so in love with Catherine—your mother. She swept him off his feet as no other woman ever did. And he knew many women. The first moment he laid eyes on her, it happened. I was there. I saw it then."

"Really? It is odd how the admiral never speaks of my mama very fondly. He says she was a scolding nag, and he should never have married her."

Her aunt turned, smiling, head tilted. "I don't mean your stepfather, my dear. I speak of my younger brother, Graedon. He was desperately in love with Catherine. Completely smitten. I believe she was the same for him. But there was nothing they could do about it, because she'd already married our elder brother."

The eggnog slipped too quickly down Ellie's throat. She coughed.

"When Grae went off with James Hartley's mother, I knew he was trying to forget Catherine. The Hartley woman was unhappy in her marriage, and she used Grae to escape it. That I saw too. Theirs was an affair of temporary convenience and passing lust, not of love. Unfortunately, it wounded so many innocent folk."

All this news sank in slowly. Ellie gazed across the room and saw James talking to Sophie. He looked very stiff, angry. Sophie looked…guilty. What were they talking about? Was she being a fool to think he could ever care for her as he once did for her friend? Her aunt was so right—all these secrets, all this jealousy.

She thought of her uncle Grae. Her childhood memories of him were mostly of a tall, lean, handsome fellow with a big, booming laugh, bouncing her on his lap as he taught her card tricks. He had often come to Lark Hollow, and she assumed, naturally, that he came to visit his brother, the admiral. She closed her eyes and pictured him, a commanding presence striding into their drawing room, filling it with his jokes and laughter. He always went immediately to the chair in which her mother sat, so he could kiss her hand before he greeted anyone else.

Ellie remembered his gallant manners, the way his eyelashes flickered upward even before the kiss on her mother's hand was complete. A look passing between the adults. A look she was too young then to understand.

"When Grae left England, I gave him a portrait I'd painted of Catherine. She wanted him to have it, and it was my way of telling him I knew, I understood. I forgave him for the Hartley scandal, but my elder brother never could. Then only two years after Grae left England, Catherine was dead, of course. Poor Grae. It must have broken his heart all over again that he could not even attend the funeral."

Would James marry her but always, secretly—or not so secretly—continue to be in love with Sophie? Once again she tried to pretend it didn't matter. But it did. It always would.

Was she in love with him? She'd tried not to be. Ever since she heard him spitefully mocking her when she was just sixteen and a trifle plump, dreadfully clumsy, and extremely self-conscious. She'd tried to hate him with every part of her being. But even a rock can be dented over time by a steady, insistent trickle of water. What hope did her heart have?

❧

Sophia had clearly prepared herself for this. As she led him into the scullery where they could talk alone, she kept her head up, hands clasped before her. Although her pose was calm, he saw the whirlpool of emotion in her green-and-gold-grained eyes.

"I shouldn't have kept him from you, James," she confessed, "but I tried assuring myself it was the best for everyone if you didn't know. You had your busy life in London. How could you raise a child? I feared you might send him to live with your grandmother." She shuddered. "I could raise him here, in his uncle's home, where he'd be loved and cared for. I thought it was best for my husband too, if he did not know.

So I…" She swallowed. "I never told him that you are Rafe's father. He never knew the name of the gentleman who abandoned his pregnant sister."

James felt his temper mounting. "I did not abandon Rebecca. It was a brief affair. She left the house, and I never knew why. By the time I received her letter asking for help, it was too late. I rode back to London as soon as I could, but she was gone."

She studied his face, cautious, fearful.

"For these last two years, Sophia, I believed the child was dead."

"I did not say that he died," she demurred.

"However, you let me assume it was so."

Sophia's hands came up to her face, and he saw that she clutched a kerchief. "He loves it here. He thrives here. Don't take him from us."

His throat burned with anger. "You mean don't take him away from you as you took him from me, his father?"

The first gleam of tears bubbled over her lashes. James took a deep breath and rubbed his brow with one hand, trying to smooth his scowl away.

"You are fond of him, I see," he managed tightly.

She nodded, lips clenched.

"I won't spoil Christmas for everyone," he snapped. "There is no need to pursue this subject tonight, but he is my son, and he should know who he is."

She blew her nose into the kerchief and murmured a soft assent.

"And it should be his choice where he lives," added James firmly. "I may not have seen eye to eye with your husband in the past, but I believe even he would agree with me on that score. We'll discuss what is to happen in the New Year."

"Yes."

He sighed, shaking his head. "He should be in school."

"He is." She took the kerchief away from her damp face long enough to exclaim, "He comes to my school every day, except during harvest, and he improves greatly."

James knew Sophia ran a small village school, but in his opinion, a boy of twelve needed a more thorough education. He didn't say that though, for it would hurt her feelings.

Oh, he realized, chagrinned, how much he'd changed in these last few years.

"You won't send him away to boarding school?" she demanded, her face pale.

"We will discuss this matter in the New Year. All of us, including Rafe."

She wiped her eyes again. James was disconcerted by the strength of her tears for a boy who was not her own child. It was a good thing they'd never married, for he wouldn't know how to handle this many tears.

"You should be proud of him, James," she sputtered just before her face crumpled and she descended into more sobs. "He's a good boy," she wailed. "He's ever so patient with the animals on the farm and takes all his duties seriously. He's a little mouthy sometimes, but he works so hard! You should have seen him in the harvest this year—"

James cringed as she covered her face with the kerchief and mewled into it, making a sound not unlike

cats fighting in a coal scuttle. He winced, reached out
one arm, and patted her shoulder awkwardly. "There,
there. Don't distress yourself. I'm sure it will all work
out in the end." Once again, a woman melted to sobs
in his presence. This time she was crying for him, it
seemed, not for herself. He truly was getting old if
even Sophia felt sad for him.

She moved two steps closer and laid her head on his
shoulder, still sobbing. "I'm sorry, James. I should not
have kept your son from you. Now that I see how my
husband loves our son, I know I was wrong. Can you
ever forgive me?"

"Of course, Sophia." What else could he do? Hold
a grudge? There had been enough of that. He knew
it was too late to worry now about what should have
been done. The good thing was that Rafe, his son, was
alive and healthy. They must look to the future and put
things right. It was something Sophia had once been
fond of saying. Finally he understood her meaning.

❦

The dancing was set aside to give the musicians a rest,
and the party guests were just about to play "bullet
pudding." Ellie had looked all over the house for
James and then saw the scullery door ajar, a thin light
within. She approached quietly and peered inside.
James held Sophie in his arms and comforted her.

The shocking sight caused Ellie to turn away so
rapidly she almost knocked a plate of gingerbread from
Farmer Osborne's hand.

"Are you all right, m'dear? You look as if you've
seen a ghost."

Yes, the ghost of an old romance. "I was just looking for…something…"

The kindly gentleman raised his eyebrows and offered her gingerbread. She declined, feeling wretched. She thought of running all the way back to her aunt's house. Then she thought of bursting in and confronting them both, but she controlled both urges. Slowly her pulse settled, her mind likewise.

There must be some perfectly reasonable explanation for the embrace. Sophie was an honest and true friend, content in her marriage, and could never deceive anyone. It was patently ridiculous to suspect Sophie of being complicit in anything of that nature.

But what secret did they share that caused such tenderness after all this time?

Suddenly she felt a chill. It traveled right through her clothing as if she wore her thinnest summer muslin with no heed to the season. She finished her eggnog in one unladylike gulp. Ah, better. That got a little warmth back.

What, in heaven's name, did it matter? She knew what she was getting into when she agreed to this arrangement. Ellie concluded that her aunt's tale of a tragic love triangle had wound its way inside her head like the serpent that tempted Eve with the apple. She had briefly allowed herself to ponder hopes that should never be let in.

An affair of temporary convenience and passing lust, not of love. Her aunt might as well have been describing this "understanding" she had with James. There was no reason to suddenly expect more from him. Unfortunately, while he was the obliging, fun-loving "Smallwick," it was too easy to forget the reality.

She glanced at her empty cup and shook her head. No more eggnog for her, or she might end up saying something embarrassing to James—something she would hate herself for admitting once sanity returned.

She pasted a cheery smile on her face and returned to the party. When the missing couple reappeared a short while later, James came immediately to her side, but she was still too unsettled to look at him. She was not angry. She kept telling herself that.

But it's a minuet. People will think we're in love.

Nonsense. They know us better than that, madam.

"What's this?" he asked as he watched Sophie's husband carry a tall mound of white flour to the table, set it down with care, and then balance a bullet on the very top.

Ellie forced herself to answer. The easiest way to mask any unusual quavering was with a cross tone. "It's a bullet pudding. Don't Hartleys play games at Christmas?"

"No, we—"

"I suppose you just sit around being very grand and despising other people."

"What ails, Miss Vyne?"

"Don't you *Miss Vyne* me," she snapped.

Since he could not possibly know what to say to that, she was not surprised when he remained silent.

"The object of the game," she explained, churlish, "is for each person to take a slice. If the bullet falls from the top, the person making the slice must, with their hands behind their back, retrieve the bullet from the flour."

"Without their hands?"

"Just with their mouths, of course."

"Won't the flour get everywhere?"

"That, Hartley, is the point. You're supposed to get all floury and look ridiculous. It's fun." She folded her arms. "Not that you, precious, pampered Prince James, can understand the concept."

The wine and eggnog had flowed liberally that evening, so there was great jollity even before the game began, but Ellie felt only confusion and sadness. She should have joined the frenzy, for that game was once one of her favorites, and she was usually the first to cover her face in flour. Tonight, however, her heart wasn't in it.

She gave herself a stern lecture. James had never professed to love her. He'd been quite frank about two things—his need for a wife just to stop his dictatorial grandmother forcing candidates upon him, and Ellie's suitability because she would not fall in love with him or have grandly romantic expectations about their marriage. It was wrong to want more, to suddenly change the rules after they'd both agreed upon the terms.

If she was in danger of feeling too much, being hurt, she had better withdraw a few steps and save herself. She had let him too close, evidently.

As she turned her face to the window, she saw it had begun to snow. Fat white flakes drifted slowly down, and in her sight they glistened like diamonds because of the tears trapped in her lashes.

When James soon had his mouth and nose covered in white flour, she pushed herself to laugh, and he seemed to believe it. After that, he spent much of the evening with Rafe Adamson, discussing the spaniel the boy had trained to hunt rabbits. She'd never seen him so talkative and friendly, unless it was to some woman he tried to charm. Tonight he put his efforts into winning over the boy instead.

By the time they rode home on Farmer Osborne's cart, two inches of snow had settled, framing the tree limbs with white and muffling the steady clop of the old shire horses' hooves. They huddled together under woolen blankets and fleece in the back of the cart. Lady Mercy was the only one with enough breath left to chatter—something she did almost without pause for most of the journey. It was fortunate for Molly Robbins that her new friend lent her the pair of fur earmuffs, or she would have taken the brunt of that boundless, ebullient, one-way conversation.

Her aunt tried to organize the singing of Christmas carols, but she was perhaps the only one who'd imbibed enough to think that was a good idea. Lady Mercy was willing but did not know the proper lyrics to any, so that plan soon fell by the wayside. Instead, they began a game of "*I pack my bag and in it I put…*" All the things put in the bag were very silly and impractical, such as aardvarks, brass buttons, and cucumber, of course.

Grieves and Dr. Salt rode behind in James's mended carriage. Ellie had expected Lady Mercy to prefer riding home in the more comfortable vessel, but she chose the open cart instead. When Aunt Lizzie asked her why, the child replied that she wanted everyone to be able to see her hat. But Ellie wondered if the girl was simply enjoying herself for once, going with the mood of the moment, experiencing life like everyone else.

James gave her waist a gentle squeeze. A plume of misty breath evaporated around his lips. "I'll miss you tonight, madam," he whispered.

But once back with his familiar luxuries, in that big, warm, soft bed at Hartley House, he wouldn't suffer overly much. She'd never seen his bed, of course, but she had a picture of it in her mind—a monstrosity passed down through generations, with four ugly posts and grim drapes that smelled musty and had probably witnessed the deflowering of many genteel, well-connected, perfectly behaved Hartley brides on their wedding night.

Back at the cottage, they said their good-byes very properly and civilly, as might be expected of a lady and her servant. Ellie watched the carriage taking him back to his world and felt a deep chill settle into her bones now that he was no longer there to keep her warm.

Yes, it was a good thing she had awoken to the dangers that evening. She had begun to get entirely too reckless and forget the terms of their bargain.

Just a few days ago, at Lady Clegg-Foster's party, he'd said, *I don't want to be blamed for breaking anyone's delicate heart, but I know there's no danger of that with you.*

That, after all, was why he chose her, and she would do well to remember it.

Chapter 19

"ENGAGED? *ENGAGED?* TO THAT TROLLOP!"

He couldn't even slip unseen by the drawing-room door. She lurked in her lair, waiting for him. His grandmother's shrill tones echoed around the elegant walls of Hartley House, shaking flakes of plaster loose in some of the older sections of the building.

"Come here at once and explain yourself! Lady Clegg-Foster informs me by letter that your scandalous engagement with that infamous hussy is widely known in London already. Yet I am oddly uninformed in the matter. What can be the meaning of this?"

He hadn't meant to spring it on her quite this soon, but there it was. Sprung already by Lady Clegg-Foster, who saved him the trouble. James took a deep breath, squared his shoulders, and strode forward into his grandmother's drawing room.

"Dear God," she exclaimed the moment his face felt the glow of her nearest candles. "What has she done to you?"

He'd almost forgotten about his blackened eye and the small cuts on his brow—one from the ewer she cracked over his head some nights ago and the other from the suit of armor falling upon him. "What has who done to me?"

"Mariella Vyne," she exclaimed, flourishing Lady Clegg-Foster's letter. "Once again, I am the last to know my grandson's intentions. And of all the women you might have chosen! But still...how many times has she been engaged already? No doubt it won't stick." She lay on her chaise in lonely splendor, her only company a little pug nestled tightly in her lap.

Tonight, after enjoying himself so thoroughly at the Kanes' farmhouse, the emptiness of this great drawing room with its marble Corinthian pillars and opulent carved cornices was more evident than ever. The elegant arrangement of soulless artifacts and alcoves of precisely placed Wedgewood ornaments must not be touched, merely admired from a distance. Guests at Hartley House were meant to feel awed, not comfortable.

James stooped to peck her cheek. "I thought you'd be pleased to see me, Grandmama." He was joking, of course. She hadn't been pleased to see him in years, not since he became too tall to be cowed by her and stopped taking her opinion as absolute fact.

"Do be careful, James. Don't lean all over me." Her little pug leapt up, baring its teeth in a low growl of surprising resonance for such a tiny creature. "Is that *flour* in your hair?"

"Yes, Grandmama. I've been to a party."

She drew back, nose wrinkled. "I smell the wine on your breath."

"At least I am still upright."

"Barely."

How would she take the news, he wondered, when he told her she had a twelve-year-old great-grandson? One shock at a time perhaps. "As to those rumors of an engagement, Grandmama, I'm afraid they are true."

She wilted against the arm of her chaise. "I suppose this is one of your foolish rebellions, James."

"Undoubtedly. I have invited her to dinner tomorrow. Then you can congratulate us as I'm sure you'll want to." He could only blame his carefree mood on the party.

"Here?" His grandmother's pug jumped from her lap and lunged at his boots. "You invited that gel here? A Vyne? Have you forgotten how her uncle ran off with your mama, causing a scandal from which we were fortunate to recover? Now you want to bring another one of them into my house? Let her sit on my furniture?"

Actually, it was his furniture, he could have pointed out. The house and contents had been left to him in his father's will twenty years ago. He let his grandmother live there and run it the way she wanted, because he was most often in London these days, and also because he preferred to manage a smaller house and fewer staff. He'd avoided responsibilities. For far too long.

"I promise Miss Vyne will behave herself, Grandmama." He tried to extract his foot from the pug's jaws. "We should be able to keep the damage to a minimum if we are vigilant."

"I forbid it!"

"Alas, the engagement cannot be undone, or she will doubtless complain to all and sundry, slandering the Hartley name yet again." He finally succeeded in bribing the pug with a sweetmeat from the dish on a nearby console.

His grandmother rang the little bell beside her chaise. "A Vyne. I never thought to see the day when another one of those people should walk into this house. Atrocious! You've parted from your proper mind, clearly. Now you are here again, I shall expect you to reunite with good sense."

When the housekeeper, Braithwaite, arrived in answer to the bell, Lady Hartley regained her wits enough to command that the house valuables be locked away out of sight before dinner the following evening.

James watched the comedy from a safe distance. Sometimes it was best to let the storm pass before making any attempt to fix the damage. He walked to the sash window and looked out on the finest street in Morecroft. Across the paved curve of road, lit by oil lamps, there was a pretty park bordered by black iron railings. As a child, whenever he visited his grandmother and long before he came to live there permanently, he stood at this same window, watching other boys run around the park, rattling the railings with sticks, chasing one another, and causing a ruckus. James was not allowed to join them, because he had to keep his clothes clean and tidy. It was a rule that prevented him from having many friends of his own age for years. Not until he became a young man did he find the courage to test a few of his grandmama's rules, and his romance with Sophia Valentine had been one such rebellion. Then, when he courted Sophia, he walked in that little park with her, strolling in circles, while his grandmother took her turn watching from

these windows, disapproval oozing from every pore. It
had been a small victory against her tyranny.

She was quick to assume now that Ellie Vyne was
another such strike against her.

"I might have known you'd do something like this,
James Julius Hartley! This is your idea of sport at my
expense, naturally. Well, you've had your fun. We
must end this mischief at once and nip this gossip in
the bud."

Mischief. Perhaps that was how it began, but Ellie's
acquisition of the Hartley necklace had finally landed
them both in trouble they couldn't get out of. He,
for one, didn't want to get out of it, although her
behavior when he left her side this evening had a
distinctly cooler air.

Behind him, his grandmother grumbled away. "If
you marry that bold, ill-bred creature, you will never
be welcomed in the finer drawing rooms of Society.
You know how she once insulted His Majesty. He
never forgets a slight. If you marry her, a knighthood
shall never be yours."

"A disappointment I'll struggle to bear," he muttered.

"Your grandfather strove hard to raise this family's
status. And his father before him. Now you will
endanger everything your ascendants worked to gain,
by choosing such a bride? What you need, James, is
a wife of high rank or great fortune. Or both. Miss
Vyne, it hardly need be said…"

"But it will anyway."

"…is neither."

James cleared his throat. "Unfortunately, I bought
her for a thousand pounds, and she can't be returned.

An impulsive purchase, I'll admit, and regrettable. But we must make do now."

His grandmother reached behind her for the arm of her chaise, apparently expecting to faint upon it. She did not, however, having stouter blood than she thought. "You *bought* her for a thousand pounds?"

"I did, Grandmama."

For the first time in his memory, she was silenced.

"By the by, I intend to begin taking greater interest in the family business," he added. "From now on, I shall take a more active role in the company. It was recently pointed out to me that I have most of my senses and four solid limbs in my possession. I ought to do something worthwhile with them. So it's time I got to work, don't you think?"

Her eyes became very round; so did her mouth.

"Excuse me. I must retire to bed and get some sleep. I had virtually none last night." With a smile, James walked out of the drawing room, leaving her to digest these stunning developments.

An ostentatious staircase led up to the second floor of the house, partnered by a carved banister with a swooping curve, perfect for sliding down. He'd often thought that, but never dared try it. He took the stairs three at a time—something he hadn't done in ten years—his hand caressing that smooth banister. At the top he paused and looked down. He itched to slide down it, but at his age he'd probably damage something irreparably, and he needed all that intact for Miss Vyne.

So…perhaps another time.

He gave the banister a fond pat and hurried onward

to his room in the east wing of the house, where he burst in through the door with such force that the candles were almost extinguished, and Grieves, busy organizing the closet, banged his head on a shelf. "Is someone on fire, sir?"

"Not yet, Grieves. Possibly on my wedding night." He smirked and glanced at his bed, a frisson of excitement leaping through his veins when he pictured Ellie Vyne lying in it.

The valet watched him with a circumspect eye. "Your head is quite back to rights then, sir."

"Oh yes." He waved a hand. "Dr. Salt found nothing amiss."

"And your memory is fully returned."

"Yes. Things are back to normal."

Grieves gave him an arch look. "Are they, sir?"

He laughed, dropping onto the bed. "Perhaps not completely. And where, pray tell, did you get to, Grieves?"

"I took a room at the Red Lion Inn, sir, here in Morecroft."

"Well, why the devil—?"

"I knew, sir, that you were quite in your usual mind, and I guessed your intentions with Miss Vyne."

James scowled and propped himself up on his elbows.

The valet added with a half-inch of smile. "I might occasionally forget toast soldiers for your boiled egg, but I am not completely worthless. I have seen the ups and downs of your various relationships with young ladies and taken note of all the signs."

"Fortunately for you, I was not seriously hurt, but—"

"And upon my arrival in Morecroft with the mended carriage, sir, I happened to see a face I recognized."

"Hmmm?" James was barely listening, as he was too busy thinking about his wedding-night plans.

"The bewigged gentleman, sir, who came to your London house the same morning we left in haste to follow Miss Vyne."

James sat fully upright. "The count? In Morecroft? Are you sure?"

"He has taken root at the Red Lion Inn, sir." Grieves finished folding the brocade dressing gown he'd drawn from the trunk, and laid it over the foot of the bed. "I took a room there, sir, last night, just to observe his movements. I did not wish to alarm you unduly, if his presence here was innocent. I'm sure you have much on your mind already."

"What is he doing here?"

"He has participated in a number of card games at the inn and at the club in Morecroft."

"They let him in?"

"It appears he gained entrance with Lord Shale and his son." He paused, bowed his gray head. "If I might say so, sir, I fear the count's presence here can have no good end for you or for Miss Vyne."

James thought about this. Was the man hoping to get more money out of him? He was a blackmailer, could be capable of anything. "Why are the Shales entangled with that fellow?"

"Young Master Shale has lost considerable sums of money to the count. I found this out when I made inquiries at the local of the Gentlemen's Gentleman's club. Lord Shale's valet is a member."

"I see. I was not aware your club had branches, even in Morecroft."

"Oh yes, sir. We are to be found all over, and our membership is very loyal. It is good to have connections, and few people know more secrets than a valet. Lord Shale's man is quite perturbed by the situation. And Lord Shale is not the only gentleman inconvenienced by the count de Bonneville."

James stood and walked across the room to rest his hands on the mantel above the fire.

"I should further warn you, sir, that Lady Ophelia Southwold has also arrived in Morecroft and also taken a room at the Red Lion."

"Good God."

"Quite. I had the misfortune to run into her there, and she demanded to know where you were. It seems she has followed you from London."

He groaned. "What did you tell her?"

"I informed her ladyship that I could not divulge your whereabouts, that you were on a mission of great importance and utter secrecy." Grieves chuckled. "She is now convinced that you are a spy for His Majesty and on the trail of that Frenchman, the count de Bonneville." The valet made his face somber again. "She came by this notion through no fault of my own. I told her very little, as you see, and her small mind has assumed the rest."

"But you did not dissuade her from it."

"Indeed not, sir. Surely to protest would only increase her certainty."

James was amused but had other things on his mind.

"Lady Hartley is in a fretful mood, sir," said Grieves. "I assume she has heard about your engagement."

As he stared down at the hob grate, James was distracted. "What? Yes. Oh yes." He was thinking of Ellie, how oddly she'd behaved that evening. He knew the way she laughed—he'd heard it at his expense enough times—and for the second half of the party, she was not laughing, only pretending.

Had she grown bored with him, as she had with past fiancés?

He swung around, one hand thrust toward Grieves. "Look at me. I'm a bundle of nerves. I must be sickening for something."

Observing that still hand carefully for a moment, the valet replied, "Should I send for Dr. Salt again, sir?"

James took a slow, deep breath. His eyes stopped darting about, looking for someone to scalp, and came to rest on a point just a few inches above Grieves's head. "I know she is absolutely the wrong woman for me. She is irritating in the extreme, argumentative, contrary—has a habit of showing her ankles off at every opportunity and then blaming me for admiring them. She's ensnared herself with a worthless crook and is very possibly in league with him still, working me for every penny. Her intention, quite calmly stated, is to use me like a stud horse, without so much as a thought for my feelings. And yet—" He couldn't finish the sentence. Words stalled on his tongue. Frustrated, he returned to the bed and sat, elbows on his thighs, fingers locked, head bowed. *Poor, country maid* indeed!

❧

When he called at the Red Lion Inn the next day, the count was no longer occupying a room. According to the landlady, the "charming French gentleman" had left early that morning.

When he returned to Hartley House, James found his grandmother—who had kept late to her bed that morning, complaining of an unspecific illness caused by him—was finally up and insisted he join her for tea in the drawing room. Expecting to find her alone and ready to chastise him again, instead he found her holding court on her chaise, her color returned, thanks to the liberal application of rouge and face powder. And the company of visitors.

He tripped to a halt.

Ophelia Southwold perched upon a small chair facing his grandmother, and beside her sat a shorter, rounder, older woman, currently waging discreet battle with the pug. Immediately, he thought about retreat, but Braithwaite blocked his route with a very ornate tea tray on wheels.

"James, do sit down and stop getting in the way," his grandmother exclaimed. "Come and entertain Lady Ophelia Southwold and her friend, Miss Bicknell. You know Lady Ophelia?"

"Yes," he muttered reluctantly, glancing at her briefly.

"James and I are old acquaintances," she purred.

Miss Bicknell said nothing. She was too busy fighting the pug, which had latched on to the hem of her gown and proceeded to shake it like a dead rabbit.

The tea tray forced him to reverse across the carpet until the back of his knees collided with a chair. He sat abruptly, and the thick scent of floral perfume stuck unpleasantly in his throat. "I did not know you were in the country, Lady Ophelia," he managed tightly, lying through his teeth.

"It was a trip made quite on the spur of the moment." She, too, lied, of course. Her lashes swept down and up again, the practiced smile never leaving her face. "London can be so gray and tiresome this time of year. I decided to visit Miss Bicknell, my former governess. Imagine my surprise when I came to call upon Lady Hartley this morning and heard that you, too, were in the country."

James knew her trip to Morecroft had nothing to do with Miss Bicknell, whose residency in the town merely served as a convenient excuse. He suspected Miss Bicknell knew this also, for the older woman threw her former charge a bemused sideways glance and then resumed her war with the ill-tempered pug.

The following silence was broken abruptly by his grandmother. "I've invited Lady Ophelia to dine with us this evening."

When James glowered at her, she coughed feebly into a lace handkerchief, and both ladies expressed lavish concern for her health.

"It is nothing," his grandmother gasped, dabbing at her lips with the handkerchief but never quite dislodging the blood-red color daubed upon them. "The surprise of my grandson's midnight arrival yesterday has quite shattered my nerves, that is all. I was not expecting him until the end of the month. At my age, surprises of *that* fashion can be most distressing. However, now you are here, Lady Ophelia, perhaps you can entertain my grandson for me, keep him out of trouble, and save me the task."

James said nothing. Lady Ophelia watched him with a smug, victorious expression on her face. The second heavy silence was interrupted only by the slow ripping of worsted as his grandmother's pug succeeded in tearing off a strip of Miss Bicknell's gown.

He could not think why he was ever entertained by women like Ophelia. James supposed he'd imagined he *ought* to enjoy her company. But it was never fulfilling and had left him with a sense of emptiness and frustration. He eyed the fondant delicacies carefully arranged on his grandmother's china cake stand and realized that Ophelia was very much like one of those confections. All decoration and no substance. Once he bit into it, he knew it would taste no more appealing than a mouthful of dry sawdust. The only treat he had a taste for now was Miss Ellie Vyne, and it was becoming more and more evident by the moment that waiting several hours without another nibble was quite out of the question.

After lunch, Ellie went with her aunt and Lady Mercy to find some last-minute Christmas gifts at the one shop in Sydney Dovedale—Hodson's—an emporium of delights that no one could ever simply pass by. As a child, Ellie spent hours there, perusing the many shelves and glass-fronted cupboards, her pocket money growing sweaty in her hand. The bow window looked onto the main thoroughfare of the village, and Mr. Hodson himself made certain no one walked by without exchanging a few words with him. He could be found at any time, sweeping his front step and polishing the brass doorknocker, looking over his shoulder at the first sound of a prospective customer approaching.

Today when he saw the three women advancing in his direction, he almost fell over his broom in haste to shepherd them inside. He had, Ellie learned, some experience of Lady Mercy and her spending habits already since her visit there the day before. While Lady Mercy kept Hodson busy unraveling all his ribbons for her consideration, Ellie and her aunt wandered farther into the shop. Here were a few other customers, but since Ellie had not taken a great deal of notice—her attention caught by a particularly splendid pair of very costly kidskin gloves—the sudden arrival of Jane Osborne at her shoulder was somewhat jolting.

"Miss Vyne, fancy seeing you here at this time of year," the young woman exclaimed through her ponderous bucked teeth.

"Miss Osborne," she replied, still admiring the gloves. "You were not at the Kanes' party last night."

"Good gracious, no! I don't consort with the likes of them."

"Oh?"

"I told my papa he should not go either. But he is never mindful of our status in society."

"The Kanes are very good people."

"But not our sort of people."

"What can you mean by that?"

"Come, Miss Vyne. Lazarus Kane is a common man with no pedigree. Sophia Valentine fell considerably in the world when she married him." Jane lowered her voice, but only slightly. "I daresay she often regrets it now, since it cut her off forever from all good society, but she has only herself to blame."

Ellie knew that Jane Osborne once wanted Sophie's

husband for herself. Jealousy was a terrible emotion and could make any woman into an ass. She, of all people, ought to know. "The Kanes seem very happy," she replied, her voice curt.

Since Miss Osborne had no interest in the happiness of anyone but herself, she quickly steered the subject in another direction. "I recently returned from Bath, did you know?"

"My aunt mentioned something about it."

"I plan to go back in the spring. The entertainments are superior there, of course, and the fashions far beyond anything here. People say Bath is no longer the attraction it once was, but I quite disagree. I suppose you go often to Bath, Miss Vyne."

"Not often."

"I was just talking to the count about Bath. You do know the count de Bonneville, Miss Vyne? You and he have some passing acquaintance, he informs me."

She almost dropped the gloves she was examining.

A man approached, gestured forward by Jane Osborne, who chatted excitedly about having met him while she was in Bath and then almost tripping over him in Morecroft yesterday. Ellie stared, and the man stared back with a pair of cunning dark eyes. He bowed stiffly from the waist. "Mademoiselle Vyne."

She couldn't think of a solitary word to say. The count de Bonneville—a character she knew to be pure invention—was standing before her in an old-fashioned white wig and a set of clothes that, despite his proud posture, had an unmistakable air of "better days" about them. There was a thread hanging loose on his coat, where a button must have come off. Jane

Osborne, never a very observant person, appeared not to notice the missing button. The woman was clearly in awe of her new aristocratic friend and eager to show him off, like a trophy won at the county fair for the best homemade jam.

"The count dines with Papa and me this evening. Perhaps you will join us, Miss Vyne?"

"Sorry…no. I dine in Morecroft with the Hartleys."

"A great shame," the "count" intoned gravely in a thick French accent. "I shall 'ope to see you again while I am in the country, Mademoiselle Vyne."

Her gaze drifted downward, to where Jane Osborne slid her hand through the man's arm. "Yes," Ellie murmured awkwardly. "I'm sure we shall meet again."

He smirked. "I doubt it not."

Fear gripped her heart and then shook her pulse until it started again. Whoever this man was, it could only be trouble. His eyes had not once blinked as they roved over her face. He seemed amused by her frozen state—almost to relish it.

She clawed for that infamous courage of hers, wrenching it back inside her skin, patching the tears rendered in her gumption by the sudden shock of coming face-to-face with a make-believe creation. A man who could expose her past exploits and ruin any chance she might have of putting it all behind her.

The odd couple soon left the shop, and her aunt whispered, "He must be old enough to be her father."

"How long has she known that man?"

"Since she was in Bath, it seems. Although, from all her papa tells me, it seems the fellow never maintained the connection. I suppose she met him again quite by accident in Morecroft, and then he could not escape further acquaintance." Aunt Lizzie sighed, shaking her head. "For a count, he has some very dirty footwear."

"I fear he is not the man he pretends to be."

"You know the count?"

Ellie watched through the bow window as they crossed the lane. "I know *a* count de Bonneville, but that is not the same person with whom I am well acquainted."

"Are you certain? My goodness. I hope he does not lead poor Jane along for some devious motive."

"I would advise Farmer Osborne to be wary of that gentleman, Aunt Lizzie." It was worrisome to hear that the imposter dined with the Osbornes that evening. Even if he had, as her aunt suggested, attempted to escape any further entanglement with Jane after meeting her in Bath, he was clearly ready to ingratiate himself now. Farmer Osborne lived very comfortably, Jane was his only child, and the generous fellow had not thought it necessary to entail his property for the good of any distant male relative. It was common knowledge that he spoiled Jane. The chance that this might make her a target for fortune hunters had always appeared minimal in light of her unpleasant, cross disposition that could turn the most brazen gallant to a block of ice, but also because of her own sense of superiority.

Now she had found someone who put up with her, and a man she deemed worthy. An unlikely combination to be sure.

"Oh dear! She is a very stubborn girl," said Aunt Lizzie. "Her father struggles so. I fear she will pay no heed to warnings."

Heavy footsteps creaked across the wooden boards of the shop, and Mrs. Flick's less-than-dulcet tones rang out loudly. "I thought the Osborne girl had found herself one of those Male Peculiars. But apparently he's a French count. I always knew her father was desperate to get rid of her, but a Frenchman of all things! And he has very coarse manners. Did not even hold the door for me. I could have sworn I smelled brandy on his breath. I am told he is acquainted with you, young lady." She gave Ellie a scathing, up-and-down assessment, "Sydney Dovedale will go to rack and ruin before the year is out. Folk coming here and spreading their strange ideas. Bringing their uncouth, foreign friends and *Male Peculiars*."

Naturally it was all Ellie's fault; her presence there stirred up trouble for that quiet village.

"I think you'll find, dear Mrs. Flick, that there were a great many strange things going on behind the curtains of Sydney Dovedale long before I came back."

The woman sniffed, and her starched shoulders crackled. "And behind curtains is where they should be kept. Not running up the lane for all to see."

She watched Mrs. Flick stride away down the shop. Perhaps that old curmudgeon was right—perhaps it was better to keep some things hidden and pretend they didn't exist. Exposing this "count" as an imposter risked exposing herself also. But doing nothing at all left Jane Osborne to the "count's" motives—which could not be good or amiable—and possibly cause great trouble to Farmer Osborne, thereby to Ellie's beloved aunt.

Mr. Hodson's sharp voice broke into her thoughts. "Do you mean to purchase the gloves, Miss Vyne?"

She hastily handed the beautiful gloves back, and he put them out of her reach in a glass cabinet where her unworthy hands could not fondle them with yearning any longer.

Chapter 20

UPON THEIR RETURN TO THE COTTAGE, TWO MESSAGES awaited. The first was for Lady Mercy, whose brother, the Earl of Everscham, had arrived in Morecroft, none too happy at being ripped away from his pleasures elsewhere. According to the note, he expected his sister at Hartley House that evening. He waited there for her. It was, of course, beneath him, to visit a small cottage in Sydney Dovedale and fetch his little sister. He preferred the grander environs of Hartley House.

Ellie had decided already that she didn't like Lady Mercy's brother very much. The rest of the village was of the same opinion, especially since Lady Mercy told everyone at the party last night that her elder brother spanked her with his shoe at every opportunity. This was not quite in order with what the young lady had said about her brother previously, but Ellie was now in the mood to imagine all men to blame for something. She refused to consider what had got her into this querulous, shifting temper. As usual, she turned her anger in all directions, seeking a culprit other than herself.

The second note was a message for her.

"What is it?" Lady Mercy wanted to know, bouncing on her toes, trying to read the single line scribbled on the paper.

Ellie hastily tucked it away in her pocket.

"But, Ellie, you cannot go out again," her aunt exclaimed, seeing her drop her packages and head for the door, still in her bonnet and coat. "It has just begun to snow."

"I won't be long, Aunt Lizzie. There is just one more thing I forgot."

She hurried across the common, dodging the swans and geese. Speckles of snow filled the air. Like goose feathers from a pillow fight, they took a long time to fall and were too light yet to make much of a layer on the ground. As she passed through the church lych-gate, a robin flew out from above her head, startling her. She was too jumpy. This would not do. No point facing this man, whoever he was, with fear upon her face. He was clearly up to no good, and she must take care in her approach, show no weakness.

Her fingers were icy cold. She'd left her gloves behind again, having removed them before she opened the notes. She walked faster, rounded the corner of the church, and saw him there, leaning on a headstone. The imposter.

"Ah, good. You came, m'dear. I feared you might ignore my note." No sign of a French accent now, but a cockney one, tainted with something else. A voice uniquely shadowed, capable of many identities. "I had the tavern keeper write it for me. Charged me a penny, bleedin' tight-purse."

"What do you want with me, sir?"

His lips cracked apart in a broad grin. "I tried to catch you alone now for some time, but always *someone* gets in the way."

Ellie blew out a quick breath, the frigid air cloudy around her mouth. "Again, sir—who are you, and what do you want from me?"

His tongue rasped over dry lips. "My name is Josiah Jankyn, my dear. And I rather thought it was time we became acquainted."

She couldn't breathe, as if her corset was suddenly too tight. Her head felt light, dizzy.

His words slipped out calmly, as if oblivious to the turmoil they caused. Or, at least, not caring.

"I'm your pa."

౧ఌ

James had left Morecroft before the snow began, and since his mind was on other matters, he gave no thought to the winter weather but drove his grand-mother's curricle along the lane as if it was a summer's day. Only when he passed a few farmer's carts and saw the drivers looking at him oddly, did he realize how unwise it was to choose an open vehicle for a jaunt along country lanes in December. By the time he reached Sydney Dovedale, his face was frozen, his feet and fingertips likewise.

Then the snow began to fall. The bare branches filled with pristine white, and a stillness settled over the countryside. The rhythmic clip of the horses' hooves became as soothing as a lullaby. In the distance, soft puffs of gray smoke billowed from cottage chimneys, and there was the church spire, snow clinging to the clock face. Almost there and in anticipation of seeing Ellie Vyne, he felt warmer already.

෴

Her first emotion was disbelief, naturally. "My father is dead, sir. He died before I was born."

"'Fraid not, m'dear. Here I am. As you see with your own two eyes. In the flesh. Still 'live and kickin'.'"

Fingers clasped tight in a vain effort to warm them, she stared at the man before her. He was in his fifties, tall, rugged, weathered by life. There were signs of a once-handsome face, but worn now and sagging about the mouth. His eyes were very dark, and his gaze probed deeply. Snow gathered on his wig until he took it off and shook it. His hair underneath was brown, lightly peppered with gray.

"It was you," she stammered. "You've been following me for months." A ghost. Surely that was what he was. An apparition.

"Oh yes." He sucked on his teeth, drawing out the "s" in a long hiss. "The minute I saw you, o' course, I recognized you were my Jenny's girl. Almost the very image of her you are. And then I saw you wearing those pearls she stole from me."

Snowflakes clung to the edge of her bonnet and the lavender ribbons under her chin. "I don't understand. Who is Jenny?"

He stepped closer over the whitened grass. "Jenny was my wife. My partner in crime. My pretty little pigeon." Then the smile snapped off his face. "Until she ran off and left me. Decided she could do better.

Took off with a box full of jewelry, got on a boat, and got herself shipwrecked." He paused, and when she said nothing, he added, "She was your mother, m'dear."

"My...my mother? But her name was Catherine. She was a widow—"

"Yes, I heard that fairy story. Poor widow woman, rescued from a storm at sea by Admiral Vyne, married and settled down like a proper lady. Has a few babies. Lives a life of lies, while her real husband thinks she's drowned." He snapped his thick, callused fingers inches from her face. "Gone. The ungrateful hussy. For years I thought she was dead." He turned and strolled around the gravestone, his hands behind his back. "Then, one day, there I am, in Jamaica, sitting in a tavern down by the docks, rifling my way through a few untended pockets, running a few cons to pass the time until my boat sails, and what do I see on the wall, right above all the bottles of rum covering a hole in the plaster?" He looked at her again over his snow-laden shoulder. "Guess, Mariella my girl. What did I see?"

She couldn't think. Her hands were numb with cold, and her mind rapidly followed suit.

"My Jenny. In a portrait. Large as life. Couldn't forget those eyes of hers, could I? And you've got them too, m'dear."

Ellie closed those eyes now to protect them from his pointing, accusatory finger. "So I ask the proprietor of the place—an exiled Englishman—and he tells me the tale of the lovely widow called Catherine. Rescued at sea and now his sister-in-law. Married to Admiral Vyne, no less, and kicking up her heels in the English countryside like the fine lady she ain't."

So he talked of the portrait her aunt gave Uncle Grae when he left England in disgrace.

"Then I knew she'd tricked me, didn't I? Decided to come and get the wench back, but when I got here, she was dead. Again." He gave a hollow laugh. "I went to see the grave this time to make certain."

She reopened her eyes and looked at him. Now she knew he was flesh and blood, not a ghost at all. The father she'd thought dead all these years was here before her.

Josiah stood straight, rough hands clasped around his coat lapels. "The parson's wife showed me the gravestone. 'What does it say then?' I asked her, and she told me." He raised his voice to a new pitch, high and haughty. "'Here lies Catherine Vanderlilly Vyne, devoted wife and mother.' Catherine, indeed. Nah! Jenny Jankyn lies here. Deceiving whore. That's what that stone should've said."

"Don't you say that about my mother!"

"It's what she was, m'dear. You may as well face the truth."

But whatever she was once, her mother had clearly tried to change her life, not only for herself but for the child she knew she carried. When she was shipwrecked, she must have seen the opportunity to reinvent herself and seized her chance for redemption. Ellie knew all about the desire for peace.

Her gaze tracked to the right and caught Mrs. Flick passing along on the other side of the churchyard wall. The old busybody couldn't hear their conversation, but she stared quite openly, probably taking note of every detail. Josiah Jankyn waved a greeting, and Mrs. Flick walked on in haste.

"Curious folks in Sydney Dovedale, eh?" He sniffed and wiped his nose on his sleeve. "That's the trouble with a village this size. They'll soon have something to talk about, won't they?"

"Will they?"

"When you announce the return of your long lost pa, just in the nick o' time"—he grinned—"to give you away at the church." A sudden wind blew a flurry of snow from the shivering branches of a nearby yew tree, and he was lost from her sight for a moment, smothered in white. But he was still there. "Unless, of course, you'd rather not. I can see how that might be, m'dear. An old crook like me for a pa...and the fact that your ma was a lyin', thievin' whore." He scratched his chin, his gaze fixed on her face. Then he added slowly, carefully, "That your ma was still wed to me when she took the admiral for a husband."

The flurry thinned, and she saw the finger placed to his thin lips.

"Now that doesn't quite seem lawful, does it, Mariella? Marryin' two men at once?"

She tried to swallow but found her tongue swollen, her throat dry.

"I believe they call that *bigamy*. Ain't that what they call it? That makes those fancy sisters of yours...oh, what's that word now? *Bastards*." He spat the word out, half-laughing. "Aye, that's right. Those pretentious, fancy sisters are about to find out that they're the bastard offspring of a lyin', thievin' little strumpet. Won't go down too well for them, will it? Tsk, tsk!"

Thus, slowly he peeled back the layers, revealing the damage he could do to the people she cared about and had looked after for so many years. All her hard work to get her half sisters well married would be for naught if this man brought it crashing down around them. She might survive the scandal—she might—but her stepfather and sisters never could. And James?

As if he read her thoughts, Josiah continued, "Well, m'dear, here you are, on the verge of marriage to that rich gent. What will he say, I wonder, to find the likes o' me as a father-in-law? Will his grandmama welcome me to Hartley House with open arms?" He laughed. "No. I suppose I'd better stay out o' sight. You'll be ashamed of your old pa."

Suddenly she saw again the faces of those women at Lady Clegg-Foster's party, sneering at her as she tried to hide behind a potted palm with trifle on her backside, and then of James, coming to her rescue. He couldn't save her this time.

"I hope those fine folk never hear about that trick you've been playing, m'dear. Running about in men's breeches, taking advantage of a few rich fellows who can't hold their drink. Cheating at cards, even gambling in clubs where ladies ain't permitted. You and the good old *count*." He rubbed his gloveless hands together. "Perhaps now that we're reunited, while I'm here in the country, you might find your way clear to helping your old pa out."

"I take it you mean financially, sir."

"Don't we talk fancy? I see that admiral fellow raised you up to be a lady. Fair brings a tear to my eye, Mariella. Aye, *financially*. And don't clench your lips at me, my girl. Would you rather I went to the workhouse? I'm only asking for a little help from a relative, my own dear daughter. Surely you can help your ol' pa out with coin for board and lodging in this bitter weather?"

"Where are you staying?"

He gestured with his hat. "Yonder tavern by the common. The room for rent is small and drafty, and the roof merely strains the rain, but it does. I've stayed in worse places."

There was nothing else for it but to help him. After all, she'd spent years helping her adopted family, and this man was her own flesh and blood. She dug her frozen fingers into the small reticule hanging from her wrist and passed him a few coins. "Here, this should be enough. I can't imagine Merryweather charges much for his room." She refused to give him more, in case he spent it on drink. The last thing she needed was a drunken "pa" spilling all her secrets tonight in the tavern.

He looked at the coins she'd dropped into his palm. "You're a good girl, Mariella."

"That's all I can give you," she warned. "I haven't much money of my own, and you surely know that since you've been following me."

Her father did not deny it. "Aye, and on the matter of finances, my girl, I hope you will allow me to guide you from now on, as is my fatherly duty."

"Your fatherly duty? Isn't it a little late—?"

"I wouldn't want you to put all your eggs in one basket, Mariella. What if your fine beau changes his mind? That old hag, Hartley, might put a stop to her grandson yet. Now that highborn hussy, Ophelia Southwold, has come chasing him across the country, I daresay he'll soon forget about you."

Ellie inhaled a quick, startled breath of frigid air.

"Folk like that always stick to their own kind in the end. Oh, he'll enjoy himself with you in the meantime, and you, my girl"—he shook a finger in her face—"must take what you can get from him while the pickings are still good. But when push comes to shove, he'll let you down in favor of riches and a wench with a title." He paused and squinted at her. "Don't take it to heart, girl. There's always another rich idiot around the corner. You'd do well to keep the Shales in your sights, and if I were you, I'd go for the older one, since he's not so long to live. Unlike your Mr. Hartley, they cannot afford to be choosy. It's always good to have a contingency plan."

She dug her trembling hands back into her pockets. "Thank you for the offer of *guidance*, but I'll manage my own life. I always have."

He sniffed and closed his fist over the coins. "So I see. You've done nicely on your wits alone, Daughter. Makes your old pa proud, it does. Chip off the old block. But it wouldn't do any harm to listen to your pa, now he's come all this way to find you."

Ellie wondered if he expected an invitation to tea. There did not seem to be any proper etiquette for dealing with a father returned from the dead.

While she was still pondering this strange situation, he said, "Your Mr. Hartley is rich as Croesus, so I hear. Must have plenty to spare."

Uh, oh. "Do not get any ideas on that score, sir."

"Just a thought, m'dear."

"I will not ask him for money," she replied, terse.

"P'raps you'd prefer it if I paid him a visit and asked

for the money meself? He's been having his way with my daughter. I ought to get something out of it. I ought to collect my due."

She was horrified. "Don't go near him."

"Tsk, tsk. Ashamed o' me, I suppose."

Ellie said nothing to that.

"Aye. 'Tis as I thought—you are ashamed. That you should find your father after all these years, and he is but a poor, friendless fellow who must scrape together a living."

"No. I am saddened, sir, that I should meet my father after all these years, and the first thing he asks me for is money."

He raised heavy eyelids, his expression mournful, the smiles hidden for now, although she suspected they were not gone far. "Without money, a man is reduced to poaching for his food and breaking into houses for a place to sleep warm. Would you want that for your pa?"

No she would not. She wanted that here in peaceful Sydney Dovedale even less.

He tipped his head back and sniffed at the snowfall. "I like this place. Might stay a while."

"Do as you wish."

He looked at her and laughed. "Since you're dining at Hartley House tonight, you'll have ample opportunity to ask your *gentleman* for a few pounds for a new frock or such like. He doesn't look as if he'd refuse you anything, m'dear. For now." He reached over and tapped her ice-cold cheek with two fingers. "To a fellow like that, a purse full o' coin is never missed. 'Tis a mere drop in the ocean. And a few lost trinkets around the house can always be blamed on the servants. They eat with silver knives and forks, no doubt, none of that Sheffield plate?"

"Sir, you are mistaken if you think I—"

"Now, now, Mariella." He chuckled and bounced on the balls of his feet. "Your ol' pa was only speculating. Enjoying a little jest. Don't frown so. Think of me tonight, getting by as best I can, while you dine at that elegant table with folks who have more than they know what to do with. More than they can possibly need."

"I thought you were invited to dine with the Osbornes."

"Ah yes." He shrugged. "The toothy young lady is heir to a considerable sum, so I hear. I did not know it when I first met her in Bath." Raising rough fingers to his chin, he scratched the stubble thoughtfully. "Luck was on my side when I ran into her again, eh?"

Ellie shook her head. "I would advise you not to pursue Miss Jane Osborne in hopes of getting your hands on her father's fortune. Farmer Osborne is in very good health, and in any case, it is likely he will marry again soon." There was no need to elaborate. Let him think the good farmer about to take a young bride and sire more heirs.

His face fell.

"Good afternoon, sir," she added hurriedly.

"A little kiss on the cheek for your old pa? Is that too much to ask?"

She hesitated. Wind and snow whipped around her feet and seemed to reach right inside her boots.

"You complained when I asked you for money,

and you turn up your nose at a kiss. Some daughter you are."

"Some father you are."

Rather than take offense as she expected, he looked bemused. "It seems we both need time to get accustomed to the idea."

Making her face as calm as could be, Ellie rose on tiptoe and kissed his rough cheek. "That's better." His eyes brightened. "Now I'll be here at nine in the morning, if you should want to see me, daughter dear, and bring me a bit o' breakfast."

"I'm sure Merryweather can provide you—"

"Aye, but that bread is stale, hard enough to break a man's tooth, and the stew his wife made last night is bad for the digestion. At my age, a man should cosset his insides."

She rolled her eyes. "Very well. I'll bring what I can."

"Good girl. Now you go and make yourself pretty for your fancy gentleman, and while you still hold his interest, you should find your way into his pockets—"

Ellie scowled.

"Just a jape, Mariella! How serious you are, just like your mama."

No one had ever called her too serious before. But Ellie had finally found herself in a situation that could not be improved by laughing.

❧

James stared through the snow. It fell faster now in fatter flakes. He was almost blinded by it. He wished he had been.

He'd drawn his horses to a halt the moment he

recognized the bright lavender ribbons of Ellie's bonnet. What was she doing, standing in the graveyard in this weather, talking to a man? The snowfall had muffled his horses' hooves, but he stopped far enough away that they wouldn't notice him anyway. As he watched her talking intimately with the count and then kissing the man on his cheek, he felt his happy mood rapidly disintegrate until it was merely dust.

≈≈

She ran home to her aunt's cottage, head bowed against the white fleece shroud, her tear-filled gaze on the ground as it flew beneath her boots.

Her father was alive.

Part of her heart wanted to celebrate the fact that she had a living blood relative. It seemed only natural that she should feel some joy. Yet what pleasure could she take in this turn of events? He had come to find her only when he thought he might use her to his advantage. For months he must have followed her, seen what she got up to as the count, and then decided he ought to have his share.

If James knew, he would be horrified and distance himself from her as soon as possible. Ellie did not know how she'd managed to capture his attention this long as it was, when he was used to the company of fine ladies with elegant manners—ladies who did not run after him down country lanes, making an exhibit of themselves, casting discretion and their pride to the four winds.

≈≈

The snowy lane rolled fast under his horses. He'd traveled all this way to surprise her, and he was the one surprised. He'd meant to ride with her back to Morecroft for dinner, but now he knew he needed time to get his temper under control. He'd send the carriage for her instead and wait for her on his own territory. Let her come to him this time.

Deceiver! Hussy! Was every word out of her lips a lie?

To think, he'd begun trust her, begun to imagine—

He saw the boy in the nick of time. The horses swerved, and his wheel went up on the snow-blanketed verge.

"Oy! Mister, look where yer goin'."

Rafe Adamson had run out across the lane, holding a dead goose partially hidden under his coat.

James swore. His hands were shaking. "You look where you're going, boy! I almost trampled you into the ground." He pulled the horses to a halt as his curricle bumped back down onto the lane. "Damn it all, boy! You could have been dead." Those words echoed through his aching head, tore further into his shattered nerves.

"Well, I ain't, am I?" the boy replied cheerily, peering up at him through a snowy fringe of hair. "Don't get your breeches in a twist." He proudly showed off the dead bird under his coat. "Look what I got, mister."

James swallowed, and his fury slowly fell away. The boy was right. He wasn't dead, was he? He was alive, blood pumping through his veins. James had given him that life.

"Did you poach that bird, Rafe Adamson?"

"Nah. 'Course not. It was give to me right and proper."

He didn't believe a word of it. "Going home?"

The boy nodded.

"I can take you as far as the farmhouse gates. Want a ride?"

The boy nodded again, more eagerly. His eyes shone with unguarded admiration for the curricle and the fine horses. James leaned down, offering his hand. The boy flung the dead bird up into James's lap before climbing up over the wheel and bouncing excitedly into the seat beside him.

"Can I drive, mister?"

"Well, I—"

"Go on!" The boy grinned broadly and altogether too charmingly. "Give a poor boy a bit o' fun. It won't cost yer nuffin'."

He shook his head wryly and passed the boy the reins. "Now be cautious and don't—"

They were off at speed, jolting and jerking down the snowy lane, and James was obliged to hang on for dear life. At least it gave him something to take his mind off Ellie Vyne and her previous lover.

The boy was laughing, head back, and his startling blue eyes reflected pure, uncomplicated delight. His cheeks were red with the cold wind, but he was careless.

Just the way James was once, traveling down these very same lanes.

Rafe's laughter was infectious, and soon James too was laughing, even as he shouted his words of caution to the reckless driver.

Fate had given him a second chance with this boy;

perhaps he could give Ellie the same. He should not have run off like that without giving her a chance to explain herself, he realized. But he would see her tonight at dinner. He would not be angry and churlish. No indeed. He would be civil and quite calm. Let the mischievous, ungrateful wench make up her excuses then. If she could.

❧

The valet brought him a glass of brandy, striding across the carpet with his usual stalwart grace, balancing the small silver tray in one hand.

"I thought you would be in need, sir. The weather is frightful out."

"Yes, thank you, Grieves." He took the glass as he slumped into a chair beside the fire, still wearing his coat. His nerves had certainly had a bit of a shock—first from the sight of that blackguard Bonneville with Ellie, and then from the death-defying curricle ride with his son.

"You left in some haste this afternoon, sir. I do hope it was not an unpleasant mission."

This was Grieves's way of asking where he'd been, of course, while maintaining the polite distance expected. James winced. "I went to Sydney Dovedale."

"I see, sir. Quite an undertaking in a curricle. In the snow."

"Hmmm."

"Something most important must have driven you to it."

James coughed as he swallowed his brandy a little too fast.

It was her fault, he decided briskly. Ellie Vyne had

got him so tied up in her silky corset ribbons that he was hard pressed to make a solitary practical decision. Thus he went racing to see her without a thought for his warmth and comfort.

Grieves tucked the silver salver under his arm, but rather than walk away, he remained standing by James's chair.

"You hover, Grieves. Is there something you wish to say?"

The valet cleared his throat. "Yes, sir. If I may."

Wearily, James waved a hand. "Proceed." May as well get it over with, he mused. Probably some lecture about risking his health by riding out in the snow. For a damnable woman.

But Grieves said suddenly, "When I worked for my previous employer, the Earl of Leighton, the countess gave all the indoor servants a day off and a trip to the sea in celebration of our victory at the battle of Waterloo. It was a very overcast day and I, having been warned against sand in my shoes, stayed on the promenade."

James was barely listening, feeling too sorry for himself. "Hmmm."

"There was a young chambermaid by the name of Hetty. I was very fond of her. Sadly, nothing could come of it. The countess was most adamantly set against romance below stairs, and quite rightly so, of course."

He watched a wisp of white hair on the valet's head, standing upright, caught on a draft.

"Dearest Hetty," Grieves warbled. "She had the prettiest pair of blue eyes. She wore a bonnet of blue flowers that day by the sea, and I…" he paused, cheeks flushed. "I pinched a flower from it to keep it pressed between the pages of my Bible."

"I find it hard to believe you capable of such villainy, Grieves."

"I was young then, sir, and impulsive. And terribly fond of the color blue."

"I sincerely hope we advance to the point, Grieves. If there is one. Or have I just wasted more precious seconds of my life?"

"The point, sir, is that Hetty walked down on the sands, and I was too afraid to follow, having been warned against the inconvenience of sand in one's shoes. Soon after that trip, Hetty left us to nurse a sick aunt in Northampton. Scarlet fever, I believe it was."

"And what became of the erstwhile Hetty and her blue eyes?"

"She died, sir. Taken by the same fever as her aunt."

"Oh." He cringed. "I'm…sorry."

"You see, sir, I suppose my point is that I should have seized the moment, taken a chance, and walked on the sand. We never know how long we have, do we?" The valet raised a hand to pat down that rebellious sprig of hair. "I still have the flower I took from Hetty's bonnet, but it is brittle now. The once vibrant color has faded. Time takes everything away from us, sooner or later. But I never felt again for any other woman what I felt that day for Hetty. It was most extraordinary. As if I knew that she was meant for me, as if I recognized a soul mate. Love is a very odd and challenging thing, sir. I was too cowardly to accept it for what it was."

James glowered down at his brandy. Love? Was he

in love with that wretched, deceiving woman? He'd thought himself in love before, with Sophia, and look how that turned out! Yet he wanted to please Ellie and protect her. He wanted to make her happy. It seemed such a simple thing, but no one had done it before, evidently. For someone who laughed often, she was sad inside. He'd noted it when he sat beside her on that little bench in Brighton and they pretended to be other people. Or, perhaps, *not* pretending to be other people, for once.

"Of course, sir. I did not mean to suggest you capable of any such feeling as love," Grieves continued as he turned away again. "The countess used to say that love was a weakness of the lower classes. I daresay she was as right about that as she was about all things, even those in which she had no experience."

James tapped his fingers against the pleasing curve of his brandy glass and found himself thinking of other pleasing curves.

Of all the creatures to fall in love with. Just his luck that she should be wicked, wild, and extremely wary of capture.

Chapter 21

ELLIE WAS TOO ANXIOUS TO SIT LONG WITH HER AUNT that afternoon and went upstairs to dress early. She flirted with the idea of falling ill to escape the dinner party at Hartley House, but then she made up her mind to be brave. Someone had to return Lady Mercy to her brother, and she must face James bravely and unashamed, give him his diamonds back, tell him it was over. It was not the sort of thing one could say in a letter. At least, *she* could not. At the best of times, her writing was full of blots and misspelled words. She couldn't risk any misunderstanding. The connection must be severed now. It had been a fun game while it lasted. Yes, that was it. With merry laughter, she would tell him how entertaining it had been.

No use wavering, she admonished her reflection sternly in the cheval mirror. James wouldn't want her with Josiah attached. For as long as the story behind her birth was an intriguing mystery, she could get away with things. No one really knew where she belonged, and so she moved about freely between the classes. Who could object? She'd made her story whatever she chose it to be, whatever her imagination could create. But now that Josiah Jankyn had appeared in her life, there could be no more fantasy.

Molly Robbins had done an excellent job with Ellie's best sarcenet frock, sewn up the fallen hem and mended a tear at the shoulder. Despite this, Ellie feared it was still not nearly grand enough for Hartley House. Her transient lifestyle and lack of funds for herself had made it difficult to stay abreast of fashion. Her nicest clothes were all things the duke had bought her two years ago. It was lucky she didn't go tonight to seek Lady Hartley's approval, she mused sadly.

"You look lovely, Miss Vyne," Molly exclaimed, standing behind her, just tall enough already at thirteen to peep over Ellie's shoulder.

"Thank you, Molly." But she was ready early. Now what? She'd simply pace up and down, getting more and more nervous, perspiring indelicately. All while convincing herself that she was not ashamed of her own father, not regretting that he came back to find her.

Aha! The Hartley Diamonds. Mustn't forget them. She wanted nothing more tying her to James, for his sake. She hurried to her trunk at the foot of the bed, opened the broken lid, and knelt to rummage inside. Now, where had she put those diamonds—the very objects that started all this? They began it, and now they would mark the ending of it. Here, surely this is where she put them, under the torn lining.

No. Not there.

She slid her hand back and forth through the tear, but the knotted silk scarf with its priceless cargo was gone.

Panicking, she searched her trunk. The diamonds were gone. She'd lost them. James would be livid. She could already hear him blaming her for the loss. Or accusing her again of being a thief.

She sat back on her heels, hands clasped around the edge of the trunk, and ran her mind over the possibilities. Now be sensible. They had to be here somewhere. When was the last time she saw them? Before she left her sister's house in London. She hadn't looked for them since. Yet her trunk had been tossed in the air, dropped, banged about, opened and closed many times over the past few days.

Molly Robbins had taken everything out of it just the morning before. She must have seen the diamonds. It was odd that she hadn't mentioned them. Had Molly taken the diamonds? No, it was not possible. Ellie had offered her anything she wanted from the trunk, but she meant clothes. The girl understood that surely. She was no simpleton.

"What is it, Miss Vyne?" Molly wandered over, seeing her in evident distress. It was most awkward. She'd have to ask the girl without making it seem as if she accused her of theft. She closed the lid. She could hear horses and creaking harness outside in the lane. The carriage had arrived for her.

Ellie's pulse didn't race. It flew like a hummingbird.

"Molly, when you went through my trunk yesterday morning, did you see a blush-pink silk handkerchief tied in a knot?"

"No, Miss Vyne."

"Are you quite sure, Molly? Think hard, for there was something very valuable in that handkerchief."

Molly looked frightened now, and her fingers twisted at the end of her long braid. "I...I don't know...no, I..."

"Molly?"

"Oh, Miss Vyne, I'm sorry. I took it out and opened it."

Thank goodness! At least now she knew where they were. But then the girl added, "I put them back where I found them. I looked at them only for a little while, Miss Vyne."

How quickly the relief was snatched away from her!

"Are you certain you put them back, Molly?"

"Yes, Miss Vyne."

"Then why are they not here?" Anxiety made her voice high and cross. She had to give those diamonds back to James tonight. There must be no further connection—no cause for him to follow her again when she left. "Did you take the diamonds? Tell me the truth, Molly Robbins."

Molly shrank away, looking as if she might cry. "I put them back in the trunk, right where I found them. I swear I did."

Downstairs, her aunt was calling for her and then for Lady Mercy.

Slowly she got to her feet. "I must go to dinner now." Greatly vexed, she took another look around the room, hands on her waist. She certainly wanted to believe Molly's protestations of innocence, but she couldn't think who else...

Or could she?

Now she joined in the shout for Mercy Danforthe. Fifteen minutes later, they were still shouting her name, because the little runaway was nowhere in the house.

❦

A search party was quickly arranged, but it was a frigid-cold night, the moon a mere slip of silver, and since it had snowed off and on for most of the day, a pristine white shroud had settled over her tracks. An hour of searching around the village with rush torches produced nothing. Even Rafe Adamson, who had taken an immediate dislike to the arrogant girl, brought his spaniel to aid in the search, although Ellie suspected he was merely eager to join in the activity and didn't particularly care if the bratty girl was found. He solemnly proclaimed to Molly Robbins that her fine new lady friend was probably dead in a ditch somewhere with fox cubs chewing on her fancy, superior bones.

"Her brother, the earl, ought to be told, Ellie," Aunt Lizzie exclaimed. "He should come here and help find his sister."

Ellie had hoped the girl could be found before the earl need know she ever went missing again, but she realized her aunt was right. Unwilling to postpone her own search, she sent Molly Robbins to Morecroft in James's carriage.

❦

"I told you, James, that Vyne girl is flighty. I knew she'd change her mind. She won't come. She dare not show her face in this house."

He checked the mantel clock again. It was almost

half past seven. The carriage should have returned with Ellie by now, especially at the rate Jasper drove. Something was wrong. He should have gone himself to fetch her. He shouldn't have ridden away in such a temper that afternoon, but he was stupefied, frozen with jealousy when he saw her standing with the count in the churchyard. He had not dealt with it very well. For those few, horrifying moments, he'd seen a woman being taken away from him, leaving him for another man again. Just as it happened with Sophia two years ago.

Now here he waited, fearing Ellie might not come. Perhaps his grandmother was right, and he couldn't be trusted to find his own woman. Or to keep her.

A moment later, they heard the bell, and his shoulders relaxed a half inch.

The Earl of Everscham stood, ready to admonish his naughty little sister for making him—as he'd put it earlier that evening—"traipse across the damnable, filthy countryside, looking for the wretched, ungrateful brat."

The footman showed the guests in. It was the Shales. James's heart slowed almost to a dead halt.

His grandmother looked victorious. "Did I mention I invited the Shales, James?"

"No, you did not."

"I wanted to make up numbers at the table, and we must have *some* people of quality to converse with the earl. Good thing the Shales were nearby."

Lord Shale had never met James in his true guise before, and upon their introduction, the first word on his lips was a startled, *"Smallwick?"*

James feigned no knowledge of this manservant

with the curious name, but neither the Shales nor his grandmother believed a word of it. Fortunately, there was no time to discuss the matter, because Ophelia Southwold and Miss Bicknell arrived at that moment.

Ophelia immediately swept across the drawing room to James, staking her claim in an obvious fashion. Lord Shale looked relieved.

"Darling James," she whispered, "I yearn to know everything."

"Everything?" He frowned down at her, perplexed.

Ophelia took a quick survey of the other guests and assured they were all occupied in other conversation, whispered, "About that dreadful crook, the count de Bonneville. Your man Grieves explained that you are on a mission to track him down. I was quite distressed at being locked in that little room at the Barley Mow, but now I know it was for my own safety. Your pursuit of that common Vyne woman is entirely forgivable, since it is all for the purpose of capturing the count. All for the good of King and Country."

He swigged his sherry and winced at the sweet taste.

"Your poor grandmother," she said with a giggle. "She actually believes the rumors of your engagement. It is cruel of you not to let her into your secret, but I understand the necessity."

James forced a smile.

"Now I am here to look after you. If only I could be of some service in your mission."

He could bear it no longer. The anxiety of waiting for Ellie had frayed his nerves until he lost his grip on them. "Ophelia, if you desire to be of some use, I suggest you go back to London."

That halted her giggles. Thin eyebrows bent high, her surprise too sudden to be hidden under the usual mask of cultivated carelessness.

"For your own good," he added hastily, not wanting a fight with her here and now.

His grandmother's voice rang out like a bell and cut through every other discussion. "My grandson arrived yesterday, unexpectedly and before he was wanted," she was explaining to Lord Shale. "He was not supposed to come until New Year's Eve, in time for my ball."

James used the excuse of joining her conversation just to escape Ophelia. "But I was impatient to see you, Grandmama."

"And I must heave myself off my sickbed to entertain, because you took a fancy to come early."

Lord Shale's subsequent, polite enquiry into her health was met with a stiff response.

"Well? Of course I haven't been well," the old lady snapped. "At my age, one is seldom *well*. A fact young people like my grandson fail to understand."

James watched the Shales closely and wondered about their acquaintance with the count. "Did you have any success at the races this year, Lord Shale?" he asked as soon as his grandmother paused for breath. "I thought I heard young Trenton suffered a few bad wagers at Newmarket."

Lord Shale replied, "My Trenton fell in with an unruly lot while at university. That is why I took him out, to keep a closer eye on him. You know how young men can be so foolish when they have nothing else to occupy their time. The devil makes work for idle hands. But hopefully he will soon be out of trouble. A married man with other things to think about."

"A married man?" Lady Hartley inquired with a slow drawl.

Lord Shale beamed. "It is time he found a suitable wife and produced my first grandson. I cannot wait forever, as I told Trenton yesterday. Get the job done with as little fuss as possible. It is the only thing expected of him, after all."

Trenton looked as if he might be sick, and James heard Lady Ophelia's teeth click against her sherry glass as she hid a spiteful laugh.

When the front bell rang again, at least two men in that room were vastly relieved. James straightened his cuffs and prepared to face this woman who had better have a damn good explanation for being late.

All this trouble she'd put him in—making him fall in love with her.

But again he was disappointed. The footmen showed in a thin, bedraggled creature in a patched cape. A sense of foreboding quickly returned tenfold.

"Molly! What on earth has happened?"

His grandmother sat up, lorgnette raised to one beady eye. Her pug began to bark.

"You're not the brat," Carver Danforthe muttered redundantly, and fixed the poor girl in a merciless beam of his steel grays. "Unless no one's fed her since she ran off. Where is she? What have you done with my little sister?"

Molly surveyed the drawing room, apparently rendered temporarily mute by the cavernous space and grandiose decorations. James took her bony arm and drew her to the warmth of the hearth, while his grandmother demanded to know, three times in quick succession, who she was. Her voice rose indignantly with every word, because no one answered her.

"Tell him," Molly whispered, nodding in the earl's direction, "his sister's gone missing, sir."

❦

"When I catch the brat, I'll tan her hide," Carver Danforthe muttered, glaring out at the dark.

"You shouldn't do that, sir."

Startled, James looked down at the girl beside him. She hadn't dared speak a word in anything above a whisper, until now.

"I'm not surprised she ran away. From the things she tells me, you are a cruel, horrid man. I'm glad you're not my brother."

Danforthe snorted unpleasantly. "I see she's told everyone I beat her with my shoe again has she?"

No reply. After that burst of courage, Molly Robbins held her tongue.

"My sister tells monstrous fibs purely for attention," the earl continued. "I'm quite accustomed to being the villain in my sister's stories. But I certainly need not explain myself to you. Or to anyone. You believe what you like and think however ill of me you choose, little country ragamuffin."

James saw the girl flinch, but she did not rise to the bait when he called her that. In fact, she was remarkably composed physically, sitting very straight, hands in her lap, lips tight. Yet haughty disapproval was written so plainly on her face it was almost comical.

"She'll turn up again, just like the proverbial bad penny." Danforthe yawned and stretched. "She always does."

"One of these days she might not," said James. "You should keep a closer eye on your sister."

"You haven't any sisters, have you, Hartley?"

"No."

Danforthe sprawled in the seat, long legs spread wide, an arrogant sneer on his lips. "Then I think I know more about the matter than you. I'll reserve the right to handle her anyway I choose."

"And as she gets older, she'll grow even more troublesome." James might not have any experience with sisters, but he knew about difficult women.

"By then she'll be someone else's problem, won't she?"

Danforthe was evidently looking to be rid of his sister as soon as legally possible. He had no time for her. His days and nights were spent in pursuit of pleasure. James knew the young earl kept a tight group of similarly entitled friends—young blades with names like Skip Skiffingham and Sinjun Rothespur. The sort of men he was once himself, before past regret caught up with him and he realized reckless youth couldn't last forever.

"Once my sister's safely married and out of the way, she won't come back again. Good riddance."

James heard the Robbins girl exhale in disgust. Danforthe must have heard, too, for his gray eyes narrowed, focused across the carriage, and fixed on her face. She slowly and grandly turned her head to watch the ink-black sky through the window of the carriage. Impressed, James hid a little smile behind his gloved hand and feigned a yawn.

"People who don't know all the circumstances and have not heard them from unbiased lips," added Danforthe, "shouldn't be so quick to judge others."

Another breath—this one a sharp huff—disturbed the cool air around Molly's mouth, but she kept her gaze on the window.

James looked out on the other side and stared into the night. He hoped they would find Mercy Danforthe in one piece. She might be a plaguing creature, but he couldn't help feeling responsible for her being in the country in the first place. He hadn't done anything to encourage her, but it seemed as if she didn't need much encouragement.

When the carriage pulled up by the common, they saw a stream of torchlight reaching out across the fields. Danforthe climbed down and finally looked worried about his sister. He hadn't realized, he told James in a low, tense voice, how many folk were out searching for her.

James looked for Ellie, but she was nowhere in view. He saw Rafe with his dog and hurried over to join them.

"We'll find 'er, mister," the boy shouted. "I'm going up to the farm to fetch my uncle. He'll know what to do."

Affronted by the suggestion that Kane might know how to search better than he would, James puffed out his chest and strode after the boy.

"Don't want you to get your fine clothes dirty,

mister," the boy chirped over his shoulder when he heard James following.

He'd forgotten he was still in his evening clothes. His grandmother always dined very formally. "Have you seen Miss Vyne?" he called out, quickening his pace to keep up with the boy's dog as it trundled along, muzzle to the snow, head weaving from side to side, tail wagging violently.

"She went up the lane that way with Bob Robbins, up toward the churchyard. Best keep an eye on her, mister." Rafe winked and laughed. "She might go missing too."

James turned off to follow the direction the boy pointed. He could see light ahead—torches moving along by the gray shadow of the church wall and under the lych-gate. That must be her.

⤫

Despite the coat thrown on in haste over her best frock, Ellie was freezing. She bitterly regretted leaving the cottage without changing into her boots, but she couldn't run back and change now. She couldn't think of her own comfort until Mercy was found safe. The girl had been left in her charge, and she'd been negligent. Here she was, wanting a child of her own, and yet she couldn't look after one, for only a brief time, who wandered into her custody.

Bob Robbins was ahead of her by a few steps. He moved speedily through the gravestones, holding his torch high and bellowing the girl's name every few seconds. Ellie's head hurt. She slowed down with a stitch in her side. They ought to go more carefully, she thought. What if Mercy was hiding behind one of the headstones? If they made too much noise coming for her, she could run off again.

Or she could be lying injured somewhere. There were poachers' traps under hedges in some of the fields. There had been horrific accidents before. Oh, Lord.

Wait…was that her? Her eyes had made out a darker lump against one of the gray headstones, but when she picked her way through the churchyard toward it, the lump suddenly moved, stared at her with gleaming wild eyes, and then scuttled off on four legs. A fox or some other creature. Her heart skipped a beat, and she laughed nervously. Only a fox.

Bob Robbins and his torchlight had streaked onward without her, and Ellie suddenly realized how far she was from the other searchers.

The shouts were distant now, and a chill brushed the back of her neck under the collar of her coat. Tucking her hands under her armpits for added warmth, she walked bravely onward. Her eyes struggled to identify shapes through the thick folds of shadow. She chided herself for those fits of wild imagination that made the skin of her arms prickle. Really, she thought, at her age she should get that under control and not be such a fearful ninny. So she lengthened her stride, determined not to be afraid of the dark.

"Ellie." A hand clasped around her arm from behind, and her heart leapt into her throat.

"James!"

His face was a mere blur of shadow in the dark. "I came back with Molly and Carver Danforthe." He tugged her a few steps closer until she could see the gleam of his teeth and the trace of his nose and eyelashes where the snow fell. "I hope you realize the trouble you've put me in, Vyne."

"Trouble?" Her heart thumped against her ribs.

"Because I—" Whatever he planned to say, he changed it at the last moment and tripped over his own words. "Why is he here?"

Her pulse fluttered like damp linen hung up to dry on a breezy wash day. "Who?"

She watched his lips tighten, his eyes narrow. "The count," he spat. "I saw you with him today."

"It was not the count."

"I *know* who he is."

She stared up at his angry, stern face. "You know... you know who he is?"

"He paid me a visit before we left London."

Confusion knotted her nerves and her tongue.

"He wanted money from me."

Of course he did. Ellie knew all hope of a quiet life was gone now that her father had found her. She would simply have to face the truth of her provenance and make the best of it. He might not be the most impressive and loving of fathers, but he was hers. "Since you know who he is, James, you will understand why I cannot turn my back on him. I'm sorry if that makes me unsuitable now."

His eyes flamed, and his breath clouded around his mouth like the wild manes and tails of angry horses. "Cannot turn your back, or will not?" He spoke in a clipped manner, cold and formal. The old James back again. "He treats you as his lover still, I see. Perhaps I was a fool to believe I had your full attention."

"Lover?" For a moment she was utterly flummoxed. "He is my father, Hartley. I thought you knew…"

His lips parted to expel a crisp, gray breath. "Your father?" His tone overflowed with disbelief, even disdain. "I thought he was dead before you were born."

"Apparently, that is not the case." She was still adjusting to the idea herself, and the uncertainty made her voice quake.

Through narrowed eyes, James glared at her as snowflakes temporarily landed on his lashes and the tip of his fine nose. "You expect me to believe this? It has your usual flair for a well-embellished falsehood. One of those you use to get yourself out of trouble."

"I assure you he is my father. Unfortunate as it might seem to you." She gathered her courage to face him boldly, ready to defend herself again by going on the attack. James was not the only one back to his old self. "And he tells me that Lady Ophelia Southwold is in Morecroft."

His frown deepened. "What does that have to do with anything?"

"Have you seen her?"

"I see you try to change the subject, Vyne!"

It smarted that while he felt free to interrogate her about her own father, he avoided questions about both Ophelia's presence and his admiration for Sophie.

"You demand answers from me, yet I am not entitled to know anything when you rush off to see Sophie or keep company with *your* old lovers?"

She looked up, and it seemed as if ice formed around her vision, giving his shadowy form angry bristles.

"Uneven standards, James. There they are again."

If looks could kill, she'd be slain where she stood. "You needn't be associated with us. Don't fear, James. I have no intention of holding you to our agreement now."

"We will talk of this later," he growled, "when Lady Mercy is found."

The way he spoke, it was as if he blamed her for the girl being lost. Why not? Hartleys blamed Vynes for every ill that befell them, and Vynes did the same to Hartleys.

Chapter 22

It was Rafe who found the missing little girl hiding in the hayloft of his uncle's barn, sulking because she did not want to go home with her brother. She had, apparently, tried to buy Rafe's silence when he found her, by offering him a large diamond. Rafe took it but turned her in anyway, and then showed the diamond to James.

"You're the richest feller I know around here, so this must be yours," the boy said.

"Actually, I'm not the richest," James replied, impressed by the boy's honesty in returning the diamond instead of keeping it. "Her brother is the Earl of Everscham and far richer than me. Richer than almost everyone else in the country."

"I thought she made that up."

"No. That much is true."

Thus James got his diamonds back from the young lady, who said she'd taken them only to pay for her journey to Ireland. All the money she'd brought with her on her adventure had been spent at Hodson's, the village shop. She was, it seemed, something of an impulsive buyer.

"Ireland?" Rafe exclaimed. "Why do you want to go there, pea brain?"

"I want to go as far away as I can," she snapped. "And raise sheep. So there."

"Sheep?" The boy burst out laughing. "I pity the bloody sheep."

James knew he should reprimand his son for cursing, but while he still wondered how to go about it, the moment passed.

"You'll get a clip 'round the ear from your brother now," Rafe informed Lady Mercy. "He's none too happy at being dragged away from his warm fire to look for you this evening."

"He won't tell me off." She stuck her nose in the air. "He daren't, or I'll tell everyone all the bad things he does."

"Shut up, do," laughed Rafe. "You're the biggest fibber I ever met."

"And you're the rudest peasant I ever met," she replied tartly and shot him a scowl that would fell a lesser boy.

James watched Rafe stand his ground and tease her again. "Crikey, wench. If I was your brother, I'd spank you too. He has my greatest sympathy."

Mercy sauntered away across the cobblestones, muttering under her breath. "I'm going back only if he lets me bring Molly, so there."

Rafe fidgeted at James's side and then shouted after her, "I can come with you, if you like, and make sure he doesn't spank you too hard."

She looked over her shoulder and stuck out her tongue, but James sensed the boy had been in earnest.

As she disappeared inside the farmhouse to face her brother's wrath, Rafe sighed gustily, and a thick lock of dark hair fell over his forehead. "Some girls are awful hard to figure out. Worse even than letters and sums."

"I couldn't agree more." He laid a tentative hand on the boy's shoulder. "Good thing you don't have to worry about it for a few more years yet, young Rafe."

The boy looked up at him. "You're going to marry that Miss Vyne?"

"That was the plan," he muttered grimly.

"Sophie says if Miss Vyne marries you, she can stop wandering around, causing trouble."

"Yes. Quite."

"Will you take her back to Lunnen?"

"Possibly. I am undecided on that score."

The boy nodded eagerly. "I'll go to Lunnen one day and make my fortune."

James hunkered down beside Rafe. In a few more years it wouldn't be necessary to get down to his level. The boy was tall already for his age. "Perhaps you'd like to come and visit me in London, Rafe."

His son's eyes widened, gleaming in the light of the lantern he held. "Can I, mister?"

"Of course. I should like that very much. Whenever you want to come." On a sudden impulse, he hugged the boy as he himself had never been hugged. It was easy once he started, once he took that first brave move.

"Everything all right, mister?"

He released the startled boy and smiled. "It's going to be." But then he remembered Ellie's angry, pinched face and her lips forming those words he'd dreaded, *I have no intention of holding you to our agreement.* He might have known she'd seek some excuse to wriggle out of this, just as she had done with all her other engagements. His buoyant mood quickly sank.

❧

Ellie watched the Earl of Everscham chastising his little sister. Or trying to. The young man was apparently as lackluster at punishing his sister—whatever Lady Mercy had claimed—as he was at keeping an eye on her. He was all bark and no bite.

"Well…" He waved a hand over the girl's head. "See that you don't do it again." He glanced around uneasily and saw Ellie watching. He cleared his throat and tried to sound stern. "These people have been troubled enough." He fell into a chair by the hearth. "Now I need another damned brandy."

"I'll go back to London on one condition," his little sister announced.

The earl eyed her warily. "What?"

"Molly Robbins must come and be my maid."

"Molly who?"

"The girl who came to Morecroft to fetch you."

Ellie saw the earl's face tighten into a bleak scowl. His long fingers tapped the arm of the chair. "You can't just pluck a person away from their life and set them down elsewhere."

"Of course I can. She has nothing to hold her here."

He sneered. "No, I don't suppose she has."

"Her family will be glad of the wage she can send home to them," Lady Mercy exclaimed.

And Ellie knew that Lady Mercy would be glad of the friendship. Molly could be a steadying influence in the spoiled girl's life. They could be good for each other.

When James opened the farmhouse door, looking for her, she considered slipping away and hiding, as Lady Mercy had done. But then she gathered her courage and prepared to face him. He'd been outside talking to Rafe for quite some time, neither of them apparently feeling the cold. The boy ran inside, full of excitement about his plans to visit James in "Lunnen."

"You certainly charmed that boy," she murmured as she joined him outside. She closed the farmhouse door behind her and stood under the hanging lantern. "I hope it's more than a passing phase—that you don't forget about your promise once you get back to your social life in Town."

He frowned. "Once *we* get back."

There was a pause. "You know that's impossible, James. Especially now." She glanced over her shoulder to be sure they were alone. The fewer people who knew about her real father, the better. She wouldn't want her deceased mother publicly known as a bigamist, or her half sisters exposed as illegitimate. Thankfully, James had kept her secret, but it would not go unknown for long if Josiah followed them both back to London, where he could cause more trouble. It was evident her father had marked James as an easy purse to prey upon.

"We had an agreement, madam. Now you lecture me about keeping *my* promises to Rafe?" He laughed harshly, his breath visible in the crisp night air. "I haven't had my five nights with you."

After the appearance of her father and an evening

spent searching for Lady Mercy in the snow, she was exhausted, fragile. She hadn't the strength for a full-blown quarrel with James, and part of her feared she might be tempted to give in—make love to him again despite the fact that they had no future together. It was all too comfortable in his arms, too easy to stay and let him protect her. But she had never relied on anyone to fight her battles, and she would not start now. She couldn't pass all her troubles onto James. It wouldn't be fair, when he'd wanted a simple, uncomplicated, unemotional marriage.

"I paid for your company, madam," he added, curt.

"You have that ugly necklace back," she managed, her voice sounding thin, petulant, and silly. "I have nothing else of yours."

He towered over her, his eyes the color of an angry sea. "Yes you do." She didn't know his height, but he was surely much more than six foot in his stockinged feet. In comparison, she felt delicate and tiny for one of the few times in her life.

"Indeed I do not." What did he accuse her of stealing now?

"There is the small matter of one thousand pounds."

"One thousand—are you mad?"

"The money I paid before I left London to that man who calls himself your father. In exchange for which, he gave you to me."

Ellie felt the blood draining from her face, all the way down her body and out through her toes. Her father had sold her like a sow at market. Like a very costly sow. Then he came after her for more money.

"In a sense, I bought you from him."

She gasped, infuriated by both men—one who used her callously while pretending his interests were fatherly, and the other who thought she could be purchased, like furniture or a new hat.

Shame squeezed her heart until it could barely manage a low pulse.

"So you see, Miss Vyne, now you belong to me." His words were arrogant. His eyes sparked with anger. Melting snow hung trembling from his hair before it dripped to his shoulders. "I suppose I can overlook everything else you've done to me. But you can show me your gratitude later. When we're alone again, I'll take the rest of my thousand pounds worth."

James wanted her because he'd paid for her. How typical that he thought she could be bought. Like everything else in his life.

"Come with me now, and we shall forget this conversation."

Presumably he meant to forget the truth about her father too. He wanted her to turn away from her own flesh and blood because it was not good enough for him. So how could she ever be? Always the knowledge of her humble stock would be there between them. Chafing.

"Do you remember what you once called me?" she demanded.

He said nothing.

"Ellie Phant. A girl with neither beauty, grace, nor sense."

James blinked. She saw his pupils expand, making his eyes even darker, his gaze reaching deeper into hers. "That was a very long time ago. We've both changed since then."

"Have we?" She desperately fought her tears. The pain of those words still haunted her. She hadn't realized how much until she said them aloud.

"Is that why you did this? Vengeance because of some silly, careless comment I once made?"

"I was sixteen and terribly vulnerable."

"Good God." He scraped a hand back through his hair, scattering half-melted flakes of snow. "I knew women could hold bitter grudges, but I never realized for how long."

Her anger soared. "Will you apologize now?"

"If I did, would you put the incident out of your mind? Or will you dredge it up again every time we quarrel?"

"Every time we quarrel?" She laughed sharply. "You assume we'll have them on a regular schedule."

"Why not?" Now his voice rose again too, even through gritted teeth. "Why break with tradition? We do it so bloody well."

"Apologize to me!"

"Will you apologize for the ink moustache?"

"I was ten!"

"Aha! So it's different for you. I'm to make excuses for *your* immaturity."

"Ten is not twenty-six."

Of course he changed the subject then, because he knew he was losing the argument. "So I was right, and you were in this with *him* all along. Taking me for what you could get. Wanting your silly revenge."

"Silly?" She was trying very hard to hold onto the last shreds of her temper. "It is over, James. It was fun while it lasted." She squeezed out a breathless laugh. "Thank you for the laughs and the—"

"You, madam, have lost your gumption."

"I have not!"

"I wagered everything on you, and you fall at the first obstacle."

How typical that he compared her to a racehorse. "Then perhaps you shouldn't gamble, if you're not prepared to lose!"

He pulled her into a kiss just as enraged and wild as the storm she'd watched brewing in his gaze. Hands to his shoulders, she tried pushing away, but his fingers pressed into her arms firmly, his mouth closed over her lips, and he took from her forcefully. Just when she thought he meant to leave her with no breath at all, he let her go. She stumbled against the door, blinking, struggling for air.

"Don't ever do that again!"

"I want my money's worth."

Ellie was livid. All he worried about was his damned money? She slapped his face hard.

He didn't even flinch. His gaze bore into hers, hard as flint. "You *owe* me."

"Send me the bill, Hartley."

"With interest, Vyne." He spun away and disappeared into the night, leaving her with throbbing lips and a fierce, unremitting bellyache such as she hadn't experienced since she ate too much cake on her seventh birthday.

It was for the best, Ellie reminded herself.

He was a Hartley; she was a Vyne—well, a Jankyn, actually. It was trouble from the beginning, and they were as bad as each other when it came to indulgence in all the wrong things.

Chapter 23

HE'D LEARNED FROM RAFE THAT BONNEVILLE WAS staying in Sydney Dovedale at Merryweather's tavern. The villain had settled in there like a cuckoo—or perhaps more appropriately, like a giant spider waiting to catch flies in his web. James could not forgive the man for coming back into Ellie's life at the exact wrong moment. He saw the hopes that had begun to form in his heart dashed again by that sly creature in filthy, muddied boots. If Ellie could not put herself first for once, what could he do to keep her? She was too damned stubborn. Fury heated his blood until even his vision was clouded in a scarlet mist.

Something gave that crook, Bonneville, enough bravado to think he had the upper hand in this entire business, and when James entered the tavern that evening, full of rage, the count didn't even get out of his chair. In fact, he smiled over his cards and beckoned him to the corner table.

"There you are, Hartley. She told you, did she? I suppose you want to discuss what you can do for me."

James looked around at the faces watching—all

exceedingly curious, surprised to see a man like him in that place. He shouldn't be there, making a fool of himself. He should leave, go back to Morecroft, and abandon that stubborn woman to her own problems.

But he thought suddenly of Grieves leaving the blue-eyed Hetty to walk alone on the sands. Of chances forfeit and time lost. He thought of little Ellie, the wild-haired girl wandering along the verge, stopping to curse at him for muddying her gown. He thought of Ellie hiding behind a potted palm with custard on her lovely rear. Of her trembling hand placed tentatively in his as he danced with her for the very first time. Of the melting snow caught in her lashes tonight when she blinked up at him and tried to laugh carelessly.

It was not snow dripping to her cheek, of course. He knew that.

"Do for you?" he snapped at her father. "Should you not think of doing something for *her*?"

"Well, I have, haven't I?" Still seated, the other man puffed out his chest. "Came back to look after my girl. Make certain she's not taken advantage of."

James swept off his hat. "Stand up, Bonneville."

A few chairs scraped away across the flagged floor as the more sober observers sensed trouble. The count watched him without blinking. "I thought you'd want to discuss this in private, Hartley."

James shrugged off his coat next and set it over the back of an empty chair. "Not necessary. Stand up." He began rolling up his sleeves. He could still taste Ellie on his lips. She thought it was over? Not until he was dead and buried. This time he would not retreat wounded. "We'll settle this here and now." He hadn't sparred at the boxing club since the night he ran into Ellie at the inn, and James had plenty to get off his chest.

The other man still held his cards, and his brow wrinkled in a deep frown. "You're too rash, Hartley. Surely we can come to some arrangement. Something more permanent than the one you and I discussed in London. I was thinking a monthly stipend?"

"Bonneville, you will stand and fight. I won't hit a man while he's seated."

The count laughed, his face red with drink. "Then I'd better keep my arse in this here chair."

It was the laughter that did it. James had reached his snapping point when it came to being laughed at. He saw Ellie laughing at him that night, tossing back her head in that typical dramatic fashion, exclaiming that it had all been "fun." As if it had never been anything more than that.

Damn her!

"What ails, Hartley? It will not cost you so much. A mere drop in the ocean to you, I'm sure. You want to play this game, you must pay."

"Game? This is no game to me, Bonneville."

"Of course 'tis. What else could it be for a fine gent like you to dally with my little girl? I've heard about you, seen you in action. You're a rake. Perhaps you had her fooled for a moment. I daresay her eyes will be open soon enough. I'll set her straight."

James saw nothing now, heard nothing but the count's laughter echoing hers, tumbling through his mind, mocking and cruel.

He swung his fist, but his temper, like that thrown

punch, was too wild. The count ducked, and James missed. Instead, by sheer, unfortunate accident, he hit the man sitting at a table behind. A large, thick-necked fellow with bulging arms and fists like ham hocks. In the next breath, James was defending himself against an unexpected opponent—the village blacksmith.

The count, however, did not escape. Someone else, looking to join in the fight and having a bone to pick with the villain, shattered a chair across his back. Within seconds, the tavern erupted, fists, feet, and heads flying. There were, James discovered, more than a few hidden grudges waiting for a chance to be aired and exorcised in that idyllic little country village.

Bob Robbins, a tall, lanky lad, shot to his aid against the count, apparently choosing his side in the blink of an eye. But the carpenter's burly son, whose nose remained out of joint since James danced with his sweetheart at the Kanes' party just the night before, quickly took advantage of the general confusion and took a running leap at him from behind.

James winced at the slow, ripping sound. There went the stitches in his sleeve shoulder.

He imagined Grieves solemnly shaking his head as he perused the mistreated shirt in the morning. But Grieves would understand that sometimes a man had to sacrifice a little sartorial elegance for the woman he loved.

The woman he loved.

Yes, he was head over heels. At that moment, quite literally.

◦✠◦

When Ellie returned to her aunt's cottage later that evening, a bulky shape leapt out on her from the yew hedge in the dark and then crumpled at her feet, falling heavily against the front door.

"Daughter dear," a voice slurred, "help your ol' pa! I've been beaten to within an inch o' my life by that rotten bugger, Hartley."

Her aunt, hearing the bang against her door, opened it to find Ellie crouched over the bloodied face of Josiah Jankyn.

"Goodness gracious!"

Oh, thought Ellie, *that is not the half of it.* "Help me get him inside, Aunt Lizzie."

Together, the two women hauled him into the passage and shut the door.

"Why, it is Jane Osborne's friend," her aunt exclaimed, a candle raised to inspect the man sprawled untidily in her hall. "I heard there was a brawl at the tavern tonight. Such a noise, such madness. And with Christmas soon upon us. 'Tis shameful!"

Since they couldn't leave him on the flagged floor and he was too bloody for the parlor, they managed to move him into the kitchen and sit him at the wooden table. Ellie filled a basin with water and washed off his face, while her aunt warmed milk over the stove.

"Milk?" Josiah whined. "At this time o' night, I'd rather have something that lies less heavy in the stomach. Have you no brandy? Or sherry? Or a bit o' sweet wine?"

"You'll have what you're given," Ellie replied crisply.

"Ouch! Be gentle, m'dear. I'm fair bruised all over from that Hartley blackguard. To be sure, you'll have second thoughts about him now, after he did this to me."

"I suppose you did nothing to provoke it?"

"I was sitting there, minding my own business, and in he comes, ready to fight. I had no chance to defend meself. None at all. Clearly he has no respect for his elders. Now, thanks to your fancy man, they threw me out, even after I paid for the room fair and square. I can't think where I shall sleep tonight."

She rinsed out her rag and watched thin swirls of his blood in the water. "James Hartley told me he paid you a thousand pounds for me. Is this true?"

"'Tis a bold-faced lie," Josiah exclaimed.

Ellie knew whom she believed. James might be a rake, but he was not a good liar. Yet this man, whatever else he might be, was her father. What sort of daughter would she be to turn him out in the snow? "I suppose, if I send you off again, you'll go to Farmer Osborne's and cause trouble there."

"Me? Cause trouble?"

"He sounds like you," Aunt Lizzie muttered dryly.

Ellie wiped her hands on her apron. "If my aunt agrees, you can stay here in the kitchen and sleep by the range where it is warm. But it is up to her."

They both looked at Aunt Lizzie, who certainly did not want any difficulties caused for Farmer Osborne. When Ellie whispered that they had better keep him there rather than let him run about the village, creating havoc, Aunt Lizzie reluctantly agreed.

"I will explain everything," Ellie assured her.

"Oh, dear. I am almost afraid to hear it." But the lady hurried off to fetch blankets and pillows for the newcomer. "Another strange man staying the night in my cottage. Goodness knows what Mrs. Flick would have to say about it."

Once she was gone, Josiah stretched out his legs. "Ah, good girl. I knew you couldn't see me suffer."

"I shall see you suffer—and gladly—if you cause my aunt any trouble. Keep your fingers in your pockets while you're here, or you'll be out in that snow, fending for yourself."

"Tsk, tsk, Daughter. I steal only from those who can afford it. Think of me as Robin Hood."

She sniffed. "Except Robin Hood stole from the rich to give to the poor, not to fill his own purse." Even as she spoke, she was reminded of the justification she'd given for her own sleight of hand deeds in the past. Always she'd found some way to reassure her conscience that it was not wrong to take from those so much better off than herself. She was as her father had said earlier: *a "chip off the old block."*

"I'll have a bit o' that beef and a slice o' bread before I shut my eyes, Mariella m'dear."

"For a man so concerned about his digestion, you should know it is unwise to consume food this late at night."

"But if I don't eat, my poor, rumbling belly will keep me awake all night." He smacked his lips and looked about the kitchen. "Any horseradish to go with it?"

∽

The next morning, Mrs. Flick, always to be relied upon for the latest news, called in at breakfast, while

Ellie's father was fortunately still asleep in the kitchen and therefore out of sight. From her Ellie and Aunt Lizzie learned that James Hartley had indeed started the fight.

"They say the Earl of Everscham took him home to Morecroft. He was in a dreadful state. In drink, no doubt. James Hartley always was a no-good rogue."

Ellie and her aunt exchanged fearful glances.

"It all began over a game of cards. Jane Osborne's foreign gentleman was involved. Furniture was thrown. Really, I have never approved of that tavern, and this is the last straw. It is not safe. I have always said so, and now I am proven correct. A place like that encourages drunkenness and lewd behavior. This is a good, peaceful village where the residents conduct themselves with decorum. It is not a garrison. Merryweather's ought to be shuttered."

Later, when the old busybody was gone, Aunt Lizzie asked Ellie if she thought they should go to Morecroft. "He might be badly injured, my dear. I will ask Farmer Osborne to take us. Or we can hire the fly, if it is not being used today."

Ellie shook her head. "James Hartley is no longer mine to worry about. We ended our engagement yesterday." Now, finally, just when it was all too late, she could call it that. Why was it so hard before? "If I see him again, it will only prolong..." Unable to finish, she ran from the parlor and up the stairs to her room.

In truth, she yearned to see James and make sure he was not badly hurt, but trying to take care of everyone had got her into this predicament in the first place.

One look from his despicably blue eyes could melt her completely, and yet she was resolved to put an end to the affair, for all their sakes.

What began as mischief over that ugly diamond necklace had turned into something much worse, brought both her and James so much trouble. Now it had transformed the charming gentleman rake into a down-and-dirty tavern brawler. Lady Hartley must be having fits today. No doubt she laid the blame solely at Ellie's feet. As well she should.

◈

"James Julius Hartley, of all the things you've ever done to cause me an apoplexy, this one surely takes the prize! Brawling in a tavern. And in your evening clothes. They are quite ruined, you know. Braithwaite, who never overestimates these things and is not prone to dramatics, assures me that the silk cravat is to be despaired of, and the shoulder of your coat has been quite rendered asunder, the stitches no more than beggar's teeth."

He stared at the wallpaper above her head as she leaned over him, complaining and shrill. She said nothing about his injuries, being more concerned by the wounds to her pride and the Hartley name.

"Braithwaite should leave the care of my clothes to Grieves," he muttered, aware of the dislike between his valet and his grandmother's housekeeper. "It is not her business."

James had broken his ankle for good this time as he fell over the tavern step, and would be unable to move about unassisted for some time. His jaw was bruised, he knew, having seen his reflection when Grieves held up the small hand mirror for his perusal. He had another cut across his right eyebrow and a second black eye to match the one that was on its way to healing. He was lucky, so the valet had gravely intoned, not to lose a tooth.

Despite all these injuries, the worst pain was inside, out of view. That damned woman had dared to finish with him. Just like that. Apparently she'd expected no objection from him. As if what they'd had these past few days never mattered—had been nothing to her but an amusement.

"Scrapping like a demented stray cur in the street! What were you thinking? Now you must recuperate, James. Put that dreadful hussy out of your mind once and for all. Perhaps now you see the depths to which any association with her will cause you to plummet." Lady Hartley clasped her growling pug to her bosom. "I want you in top form for the ball. The sooner we get you safely married and away from this latest scandalous mess, the better. A good wedding always takes people's minds off less savory matters."

When his grandmother's face withdrew, another immediately loomed over him, hanging there like a scavenging bird above a trampled carcass.

"James! Darling! What a good thing I am still here to look after you."

He groaned deeply.

"I know, my darling," Ophelia cooed. "Such pain you must be in."

He closed his eyes, but when he opened them again, she remained, attempting to order Grieves about. "There is no need for a shave today. Take the razor away. I'm sure he can do without."

"But, madam—"

"Now you've spilled water on my skirt."

"And fancy, madam," he heard Grieves reply, "you have not melted."

"How dare you! I have not forgot how you shoved me in that horrid, dirty cupboard at the Barley Mow," Ophelia hissed at the valet, a few inches above James's head. "Don't think I shall ever forget that little indignity."

"It was done for your own safety, madam."

"So *you* tell me. I know what he was up to there with *her*. Well, it won't happen again. He's mine now. This incident will bring him to his senses at last. If you like to protect your master so much, you should know that I could quite easily tell his grandmama how he lost the Hartley Diamonds. They are hers, are they not? He's not supposed to have them until he marries, and then they will be passed to his wife. I can only imagine what she will have to say about that."

James quickly shut his eyes again.

"Forgive me, madam," Grieves answered smoothly, "but I believe it was you who lost the Hartley Diamonds."

The sheer force of her fury scorched the air above James's head like the flames of dragon's breath. "The count de Bonneville stole those diamonds from me. I never gave them away. A gift from my darling James? As if I could ever let them out of my sight!"

"I daresay the count would insist otherwise. Since he is in the county, perhaps we can set the matter straight once and for all."

"And that's another thing," Ophelia exclaimed. "That horrid man with the dirty boots, who strides about Morecroft as the count de Bonneville, is an imposter."

If his eyes were not so sore, James would have rolled them. "Really, Ophelia, it no longer matters to me how you came to give him those diamonds."

"I'm telling you, James, that man is *not* the count. Most definitely not. The crook who stole the Hartley Diamonds from me was far prettier, not so rough about the edges, and certainly not as tall or broad at the shoulder."

He looked at her thoughtfully. He supposed she ought to know, having come into close contact with the villain.

Interesting.

"He wore gloves the entire time, whereas this man here does not seem to possess a single pair. And the real count has the strangest color eyes. I could have sworn they were lilac. Quite mesmerizing. I do believe that's how he came to remove the diamonds from my neck. He put me in a trance of some sort."

Grieves snorted quietly, and she glowered at him.

"In any case, that man who stayed at the Red Lion is *not* the count I met."

"Ophelia," James muttered feebly, "I need my rest. Please."

He heard the gentle clink as Grieves set down the bowl of shaving water, and then the rustle of her skirt as she rose from her chair by his side. "I shall return very soon," she snapped, as much, he guessed, for the valet's benefit as his.

"I await the event with baited breath, madam," Grieves replied.

James lay very still and stared at the ceiling. He remembered the night he found Ellie in what he assumed to be the "count's" bed at the inn. All rumpled and tempting in a ruffled lace shirt and nothing else. He envisioned the solitary pair of boots by the bed. The bottle of brandy and the single glass.

You're fortunate, sir, that although I can seldom afford it, I'm partial to the taste of fine brandy.

In Brighton, she'd whispered those words to him just before she ran away, her kiss still stinging his lips.

Then the single diamond in the box. *Catch me if you can.*

"Is everything all right, sir?" Grieves inquired.

"Hmmm."

"I wondered, sir, because despite the severe lack of humor in your current situation, you appear to be smiling."

Was he? He touched his lips with tentative fingers, just to be sure. Indeed, he was smiling.

Because the notorious Ellie Vyne was caught.

Her father finished his third cup of tea and leaned across the table to spear another slice of bacon on the prongs of his fork. Today his first thought, yet again, was his belly's needs. Followed by his next potential route to riches.

"If I were you, Mariella, I'd fix on the Shales. If you can't bring yourself to think of the elder one, then settle for the son and heir." He chuckled gruffly. "At least you won't be troubled with wifely duties in the bedroom there. He won't be as much trouble as that Hartley bugger. You'll handle young Shale much easier, m'dear. Any more tea in the pot?"

She watched the grease running down his chin. "I have no intention of marrying anyone."

"Nonsense. You'll marry as soon as the right opportunity comes our way. I see the admiral never took the matter properly in hand all these years. He let you waste too many chances of a rich husband. With me at your side, you can go far in the world. Now your pa is here to set you straight."

Another man who thought to set her straight, she mused. "You had some hopes of matrimony yourself, sir, with Miss Osborne, if I am not mistaken."

"The horsey girl?" He wiped a hunk of bread around his plate. "Aye, her father is a prosperous gent to be sure."

Her aunt came in with a letter addressed to "The Count." She placed it gingerly beside his plate and backed away. Ellie had explained Josiah's true identity to Aunt Lizzie last night. The amount of scandalous trouble he was capable of causing the Vyne family was now evident to her too.

"What's the matter with you, woman?" he grunted, bemused. "I don't bite." Snatching the letter up, he opened it with his buttery knife, but then passed it across the table to Ellie. "Tell me what it says, m'dear."

According to Aunt Lizzie, it had been brought over from Merryweather's by the chimney sweep, who was charged with calling at every house until he located the missing fellow.

Ellie unfolded it slowly, and her gaze fell at once on the embossed crest she could not fail to recognize. Her heart thumped against her ribs. It was racing uncommonly fast today.

"Well, m'dear?"

Sir, your presence is requested at Hartley House today at three in the afternoon. We look forward to resolving this matter to the satisfaction of all parties.

He coughed until a piece of bread shot out of his throat and landed on the table. "Looks like they're willing to pay me what I'm due."

Ellie stared at the words on the paper until they danced about like butterflies. "I'm not certain you should go," she muttered. It was likely they did not want her father for the same reason he assumed they did.

But he was an optimist. "I'm not afraid of those grand folks in Morecroft. In fact"—he poked a finger into the tablecloth and left a grease mark—"I ought to sue Hartley for beating me like that—me, a defenseless old man, minding my own business—"

"Cheating him out of a thousand pounds."

Her father's eyes narrowed. "I told you that's a fib, Mariella." Reaching over, he snatched the letter from her hand and stared at it upside down. A slow smile oozed over his lips. "My word against his. Aye. We'll see what I can get from that old bat, Lady Hartley, when I accuse her blessed grandson of trying to murder me with his bare hands. He threw the first punch. I've got witnesses. I'm due something, to be sure. These rich buggers think they can treat a poor fellow badly and pay no recompense. We'll see about that."

"Since you've masqueraded as something you're not, I hardly think any magistrate will take your word against Mr. James Hartley's."

Josiah tucked the letter inside his waistcoat. "Speaking of masquerades, you'd do well to hold your tongue, m'dear, unless you want me to tell everyone about your little adventures in breeches."

There was nothing more she could do. He would not be persuaded against going to Hartley House to get his "due." Ellie feared no good could come of it, but he insisted this was a "matter for men to mind." She was powerless, therefore, to prevent him going off to board the mail coach that afternoon.

❦

James swung his crutches impatiently, finding it very difficult to pace effectively without two working legs.

Grieves observed with caution. "It will not heal any quicker, sir, if you put weight upon it so soon. You did hear Dr. Salt, did you not? Perhaps his advice escaped through the opposing ear to which it entered, with little solid matter to obstruct its progress."

"Yes, yes. But I can't stay cooped up in this damned house, Grieves." He almost toppled over while negotiating a turn with his crutches. "I must be able to ride again." Trapped in that house, he was forced to endure daily doses of Ophelia Southwold, which only made things worse.

"And so you shall ride again, sir, as soon as your ankle is healed."

James had just discovered that his carriage was on blocks. According to his grandmother, it was leaking from the roof, the springs were inadequate, and the wheel had not been mended sufficiently. It was now waiting for a superior wheelwright coming from Norwich—as soon as weather permitted. His curricle was likewise out of commission for a variety of small problems. Lady Hartley insisted that she could not allow her grandson to risk his safety and health by venturing out of the house again until he was completely healed and had passed Dr. Salt's rigid inspection. As well as her own.

"You seem to forget, James," she'd told him during her last visit to his chamber, "that you are our only hope for the future generation of Hartleys. I cannot allow any more accidents to befall you. Had you any brothers or cousins, I daresay it wouldn't matter quite so much if you chose to fling yourself willy-nilly into a vehicle that defies death each time it goes out onto the road."

A mild exaggeration, but he knew what she was up to, of course. His grandmother assumed that by separating him from Ellie for as long as possible, she could break the connection. In the past, it might have worked. His attention did have a tendency to wander and was easily caught by a pretty face. But that was the old James.

This afternoon as he practiced with his crutches, she rushed into his room without knocking, out of breath from having hurried up the stairs for possibly the first time in her life.

"Her *father*, James! That man who has been masquerading about as an exiled French nobleman is naught but a confidence trickster and Mariella Vyne's father."

He hobbled around to face her. "Yes. I am aware of the fact." Had he not been in quite so much pain from his various wounds, he might have been able to enjoy the expression on her face more than he did. "He has arrived in answer to my summons, I assume."

"You summoned him here? What on earth for?" She dropped into a nearby chair, her clawed fingers wrapped tight around a lace kerchief. "You cannot mean to continue this charade with the Vyne girl. Not if you know her father is a—"

"I thought you'd like to have a count in the family, Grandmama," he remarked wryly.

"But he is not—"

"What grounds do you have to doubt his veracity?"

"For pity's sake, James, one only has to speak with the fellow."

"And so I intend to. As I cannot descend the stairs, he'll have to come up here, won't he?"

Horror rendered her face frozen, but behind her cold eyes there was a flicker of anguish, as if she knew he had finally beaten her, grown up at last and shaken off her claws.

"Grandmama," he said slowly, "you will accept my decision in this matter."

She looked at him blankly. "What matter?"

"That little thing—my future happiness."

"There is no need to—"

"You will tell no one about that man's true identity. Or I'll sell this house and everything in it." He could do it, of course. It was all his, every stick of furniture, every plate. "And I'll move abroad."

"James, you wouldn't—"

"It is just the two of us left now. We Hartleys are a dying breed. If you want me to treat you with respect, you will do the same to me and honor my wishes."

"Very well then." Her lips turned down, and her eyes watered, but still she shed no tears. Had she sat on a pin, her expression would be the same. "Do as you see fit. But do not blame me for the wretched depths to which she will bring you with her lack of decorum and undesirable relatives."

"Thank you, Grandmama."

The threat of tears briskly thrust aside, she muttered angrily, "Now I cannot think what you will say to Lady Ophelia, who has devoted herself to your nursing."

James arched an eyebrow and looked around the room, which was noticeably free of Ophelia's presence. "She did? Probably went off to buy a new hat and forgot her nursing duties."

"At least, James, Ophelia Southwold is a wealthy widow, still young enough to bear children. She is also the daughter of an earl. She may not be a fresh-faced ingénue in her first Season, but she would have sufficed."

"Any port in a storm, Grandmama?"

"Scorn all you wish, my boy, but she is everything that Vyne girl is not."

How true, James thought, and vice versa.

"If I might interject, my lady." Grieves stepped forward. "Lady Southwold did appear a trifle untrustworthy. I fear her devotion is a thing freely given out with very little value to it."

That caused Lady Hartley to demand whether James always allowed his servants to speak up without being addressed, to which James replied, "Grieves is not just a servant, Grandmama. He is a friend."

He had never realized it before, but it was true. How clear life had become of late.

"Kindly send the count up to my chamber. He and I have much to discuss."

Chapter 24

JOSIAH JANKYN RETURNED FROM MORECROFT eventually, looking considerably smaller than he did when he left. Ellie, watching her aunt make pastry in the kitchen, was shocked to hear the door bang suddenly and see him scuffing along the hall toward them with the lugubrious demeanor of a sick spaniel.

"Well?" she demanded. "Did you get what you expected?"

His gaze lifted slowly from the tiled floor. "I got the promise of coin, if that is what you mean, Daughter."

"But you do not look very pleased about it."

He took a deep breath, and his chest heaved. "Bleedin' fellow's only gone and given me a job, hasn't he? Means to make an honest man of me."

Ellie stared. "A job?"

"That's right. A post in some office, if you please. *Sitting at a desk.*"

From the way he said those last four words, anyone might think he was sentenced to be hanged. Ellie put down the rolling pin she'd been swinging merrily in both hands before he entered the cottage. "But you cannot read or write."

"Aye, but I can count, as he says. Seemed to think that was funny. Fancy it! He means to put me to work, Daughter. "

"The gall of that gentleman," she muttered dryly.

Aunt Lizzie wiped her hands on her apron and exclaimed at his "good fortune" in finding a post with a steady wage. "There are many who would be grateful for such a chance," she added with a quick glance at her niece. "A chance to settle down and be responsible. I daresay it will give you an opportunity to pay back some of your creditors, once you have a steady income, Mr. Jankyn. And then you need not hide and dash about from place to place."

His usually swarthy face became the color of her pastry dough. "Aye," he replied distractedly. "So it will."

Ellie turned away and looked out of the window at the snow-laden sky. So James had not felt it necessary to pay her father off. Instead, he'd tried to help with a long-term solution, even offered to give the man a place in his company. She dare not try to think what it meant. Surely he could not accept a man like Josiah Jankyn as a father-in-law. Yet, if he felt shame in the connection, he could simply have paid the man to leave, and he did not. Well, perhaps, it was nothing more than a kindly gesture.

Behind her, Aunt Lizzie continued in a jolly voice, "You must think seriously of matrimony now, as a widowed fellow, working and settled. Jane Osborne will be ordering her bridal linens before we know it."

Josiah mumbled something under his breath.

"Do be careful not to burn your mouth," Aunt Lizzie added. "Those tarts over there have not long been—"

He did not pay heed, and a second later, Ellie heard her father cursing broadly through a spray of pastry crumbs. The strength and longevity of his curses, however, suggested he was troubled by far more than some hot jam.

Early the next morning, as she came downstairs, Ellie found her father already half out of the door. He laughed sheepishly when she asked him where he meant to go. Perhaps, she remarked jokingly, he went to propose to Miss Osborne.

He shook his head. "A permanent arrangement of that sort would put the shackles on me. I don't want a large property to manage. I'm better off when I can move about. Settling in one place for more than a few weeks is not good for my bones." He paused on his way out and looked at her over his shoulder. "You're like me, Mariella. I see that. We weren't made for being still. 'Tis the gypsy spirit in us Jankyns. It won't be long before your feet itch again. I told Hartley that, but he's not the sort to listen. A fellow in love is often blind to the truth."

"In love? With me?"

"Oh, aye." He sniffed. "Why else would he punch my guts out and then turn around and offer me a bleedin' job? Fellow can't know whether he's coming or going."

With that, he was gone, leaving her standing in the hall, listening to the faint drip of melting icicles from the eaves of her aunt's cottage, her heart squeezing tightly under her ribs.

Well, James had been in love before, of course. Or thought he was. No doubt the pain would pass, like indigestion. Besides, Ellie was certain she would soon feel the signs of her regular visitor signaling that there was no babe and therefore nothing to hold him to the plan of marriage. It was only a little late this month.

Jane Osborne complained loudly to anyone who listened that she'd been ill used by the "count." Her tears soon dried however, and before too long she was declaring herself happy to see the back of him, because he'd taken enough money from her as it was. Over the course of the next week, it was discovered that Ellie's father, in just the few days of his residency, was reputed to have taken money and valuables from half the widows in Morecroft and made quite a good start on those in Sydney Dovedale too. How he managed it in such a short period of time no one could say. Ellie felt certain it was a gross exaggeration, and she suspected that some ladies claimed themselves victims merely to have their share of attention.

Since Ellie was a known acquaintance of his, it was widely declared her fault that the deceiving scoundrel had ever set foot in the county. Ellie Vyne had always been trouble, was the general consensus.

And it soon became much worse. Jane Osborne, still smarting from the loss of yet another prospective husband and the humiliation of being tricked out of her coin, consoled herself by spreading another new rumor.

When Aunt Lizzie heard it, she went directly to Ellie.

"Lady Mercy Danforthe apparently told Miss Jane Osborne that James Hartley paid five thousand pounds for five nights in your company. What a mischievous, wicked child to start such gossip!"

Ellie made no reply. She knew that by refuting the rumor she would only make things worse. No one ever believed her, in any case, and Jane Osborne had witnesses to her tale. Lady Mercy had told her all this while in Hodson's shop and within the hearing of several village ladies.

Sophie came to visit. "Let them all talk," she advised. "They do love good gossip, but soon they will find something else to talk about. Nothing is new news for very long. We all have secrets."

To Ellie, however, the rumors were like stains that could not be removed. Always they would remain, even if they faded slightly over time.

"I only hope Rafe might be shielded from inevitable scandal a little while longer. I want James to tell him in person," Sophie continued. "My husband agrees that it should be up to James."

Ellie forced herself to lay aside her own worries and pay attention. "Rafe? Is something the matter with the boy?"

"Nothing that can be cured." Sophie gave a wry smile. "I don't believe there is a remedy for inheriting bossy traits from one's father."

At first, hearing the word "father," Ellie thought her friend was talking about Josiah, but then she remembered that Sophie knew nothing about her blood connection to the missing man. "Rafe...Rafe's father?"

Sophie's smile faded. "James hasn't told you? Oh

dear, I thought that night at the party when you and he went outside…"

The two friends sat in silence for several moments. Slowly the pieces fell into place. She realized she'd seen Rafe's resemblance to James almost at once, but the difference in their coloring had confused her. "No, he did not tell me."

Sophie wrung her hands in distress. "Now I've opened my big mouth! James will be furious with me. Again!"

So he had a child. A son of twelve years already. "He kept the boy a secret all these years? Why?"

"Oh no!" Sophie hastened to explain. "He did not know Rafe was alive, until he came back to Sydney Dovedale with you. The fault for the secret lies with me. When I discovered that my husband's nephew was James Hartley's illegitimate son, I feared James would leave the child to Lady Hartley's guardianship. My husband adores his nephew, has looked after him all these years. I didn't want anyone to part them. But then I realized how selfish, how wrong I'd been to take away James's right to know his own son, and Rafe's right to know his father. I am so ashamed."

Ellie's heart beat calm and steady. Surprisingly so under the circumstances.

There was no doubt in her mind that James kept this fact from her out of fear. They were both afraid of what the other would think—James for having an illegitimate son, and she for having a scapegrace father.

"I hope James has forgiven me," Sophie added in a forlorn voice. "I believe we made our peace that night at the party."

Ellie closed her eyes for a moment and listened to

her own breath. She saw her old friend and her new lover embracing in the pantry, and this time she read the gesture for what it was. What a fool she had been. Of course, she told herself at the time that she did not doubt Sophie, but, like the stain of a rumor, jealousy could not be vanquished completely. The heartache had lurked shamefully inside her for seventeen years, because she loved them both.

୧୫

Her aunt's quiet companionship was a great comfort during those dark days, although, perversely, she found herself missing Lady Mercy's chatter. The most excitement she could look forward to now was the odd game of cribbage.

On Christmas morning, there was a package delivered. A beautiful pair of soft kidskin gloves for Ellie, with a note attached.

Don't lose me.

Now what sort of message was that to send to a person who was trying to be good, sensible, and restrained for once? By then the entire village had heard about the money James Hartley once paid for her entertaining company.

"And not for her singing, to be sure," Mrs. Flick was heard to exclaim.

But Ellie wore her gloves to church that day. A girl could hold her head high amid a great deal of scandal if she wore the right accessories—in this case, lilac ribbons on her bonnet and lavender kid gloves, the like of which a plain, ungainly spinster should never enjoy. Although a notorious one might.

Soon after Christmas she received a letter from the admiral, who was in high spirits, as usual unaware of any struggles she might be going through and concerned only with his own ups and downs. A buyer had been found for Lark Hollow, he informed her. Although he had not planned to sell, apparently the price offered had been most persuasive, and as part of the bargain, he was allowed to remain in a wing of the house and pay a nominal rent. It was all very mysterious.

For once someone else was taking care of things, and Ellie did not know how to feel. If she had no one left to manage, what would she do with herself? Just a month before, she'd been looking forward to her "retirement," but she was already restless again. Perhaps her father was right, and she was not made for settling in one place.

Chapter 25

December 31, 1822

SHE WAS SITTING WITH HER AUNT IN THE PARLOR AND
had just read the same paragraph of her book four
times, when the bell rang. Aunt Lizzie was on the
verge of falling asleep, her legs tucked under a quilt,
her feet resting on a small stool before the fire.

Ellie set her book down. "I'll go." She tried not to
sound too excited at the prospect of visitors, especially
since she'd insisted this quiet life was exactly what she
wanted now. Alas, her book was so very dull that she'd
almost become desperate enough to begin work on
a needlepoint pillow. Thankfully, here came distraction. As she hurried down the hall, she checked her
appearance briefly in the mirror, threw up her hands
in despair, and then opened the door.

"Trenton Shale." The name fell from her lips with
a dull thud.

The lanky young man bowed his head. "May I
come in, Miss Vyne? I have a confession to make. And
an apology." He was alone today, it seemed.

She restrained a terse sigh and let him in. "Come through to the parlor."

He followed her down the hall and into the warm room. Aunt Lizzie instantly began clearing away her sewing, but Trenton stopped her. "Please don't trouble yourself, madam. I do not mean to stay long, but before I leave the county, I wanted to see Miss Vyne."

Ellie gestured that he should sit, but he remained standing for once, looking uncomfortable, as if his boots pinched. "Miss Vyne, after our walk in your aunt's garden when I was last here, my father assumed that I took the opportunity to propose—as he wanted me to—and I could not bring myself to tell him that you turned me down. For once he was not disappointed in me, and I had not the heart to tell him the truth."

"Trenton!"

"I broke the news to him today, and he was not best pleased. Thus I return to London at once. I thought I should call upon you and apologize."

Bemused, she shook her head. "It matters not. I thank you for the apology, but really it is not necessary. I'm sure your father will soon recover from his disappointment."

Trenton studied his boots for a moment and then cleared his throat. "I have done many childish, selfish things in my life, but it is never too late to change, so I have learned from Mr. Hartley's example."

She wished she had something to do with her hands other than squeeze them together and make the palms sticky. "Mr. Hartley's example?"

"He does not boast of it, but I have heard about his

charitable works. I'd never met him until that night at Hartley House, but I'd heard of him long before."

She frowned. "Charitable works? Are you sure you have the right Hartley?"

"Indeed. He has funded several homes in London for unwed mothers and contributed vast amounts to charitable institutions."

Ellie knew her aunt was staring at her in astonishment. She was certain her own countenance must be much the same.

"I hope you will not mention it to him, Miss Vyne. He is, I understand, a very private man when it comes to those matters."

"Yes. I see."

"Well, Miss Vyne"—he turned to her aunt and bowed—"Mrs. Cawley, I bid you good day. I have a long journey ahead of me, for I am escorting Lady Ophelia Southwold back to London. We must make a good start before it grows dark."

She saw him out, wished him well, and returned to her seat by the fire.

"Goodness," said her aunt.

Ellie smoothed down her skirt, picked up her book, and stared at the print.

"That was a very odd visit," her aunt observed, bent over her quilt again.

"Very." She turned the page, though still not focusing on a word.

"Almost as if he came here on some spurious excuse, solely to inform you of Mr. Hartley's good deeds."

James Hartley involved in charity work? It seemed unbelievable. Or did it? She had discovered the real

James to be a very different person than the one she'd seen out in Society. He had, she recalled, once claimed he was a reformed man. At the time, she'd taken it as part of his routine flirting. She thought she knew him all these years. Really, she hardly knew him at all. It seemed she'd underestimated James.

Trouble was, they were both so wary of each other. They circled and poked, prodded and snapped. Whenever they put aside their weapons and masks, they did not know what to do.

"Will you put some more coal upon the fire, Ellie dear? Stir it up a little. Don't let it die away."

Ellie closed her book again and reached for the coal shovel. The clock on the mantel ticked gently onward, marking time.

Oh, James. They had kept so many secrets from each other, afraid to be themselves. And she'd always considered herself strong and brave, yet she had been so fearful of the truth about herself that she'd ended their affair rather than share it with him. All this time, she'd scorned women who used artifice, but she was just as bad, hiding behind a false front, maintaining an act. Pretending not to care.

"And light another candle, Ellie," her aunt added. "It is awfully grim this afternoon and the dark not far off. I don't want you hurting your eyes to read."

Anxious for something to do, Ellie went out to the kitchen, made a pot of tea, and found the shortbread biscuits. They were usually her favorite, and she depended on them to lift her out of any gloomy mood. But not even shortbread could help her this afternoon.

"You are very fidgety, Ellie dear," her aunt

exclaimed. "Perhaps a walk would do you good. Or a game of cards?" The lady sipped tea and chatted to the captain's parakeet in her usual loving manner. "Let's see, what can we do to amuse our young guest? How can we entertain her today and lift her spirits?"

The bird talked back at her in breathy gasps, "Small…wick…ooh…Small…wick."

Her aunt pretended not to hear the name.

"Wicked," cackled the parakeet, bobbing up and down excitedly on his perch. "Naughty boy, Small… wick. Naughty boy."

∽⚬∾

She retired early to her room that afternoon with a headache, fearing her aunt's anxiety about reading in poor light was justified. Perhaps she would soon need spectacles. She had done a great deal of reading over the past few days. There was little else to do until the weather improved. Then she could help her aunt in the garden or go to visit Sophie.

The house was quiet this evening; even the creaky floorboards were unusually mute underfoot as she made her way to her bedroom. It made her heartbeat and her breath seem unnaturally loud.

She opened her door. The small fire had already been lit, and a wasteful preponderance of candles filled the mantel and her small dressing table. Beside the bed stood Molly Robbins and Lady Mercy Danforthe.

Ellie clutched her book to her chest. "What are you girls doing here? Lady Mercy, you are supposed to be in London by now!" Oh dear, had the girl run away again?

They giggled and confessed that her aunt—in on the fun—had left the back door unbolted for them. Clearly they were overcome with merriment over their game. Then she saw the gown laid across her bed.

"I made it for you, Miss Vyne," Molly said proudly, her cheeks pink in the warm light of all those candles. "I hope you like it. I used bits and pieces of your old dresses, but it looks very new."

"It's all her own design," Lady Mercy added. "And I have new slippers for you to wear, and silk stockings from London. And a very pretty idea for your hair. I cut it out of *La Belle Mode*."

The two girls tugged on her arms until she stood in front of the mirror, and before she knew what was happening, she was being disrobed.

"In case you haven't realized yet," said Lady Mercy, "we've decided you're going to the Hartley ball tonight."

"But I can't go. For pity's sake!" She tried to stop them, but they pecked at her with their fingers like hungry baby birds, and her layers of winter clothing fell away. "Lady Mercy, does your brother know you're here?"

"Of course," the little chit replied as if it was such a foolish question to ask. "He's waiting for you outside with the carriage. He's taking you as his guest. I made him do it, and in exchange, I promised not to run away anymore or tell anyone else that he beats me with his shoe. Now if you refuse to go tonight, he will be most annoyed, because I dragged him into the country again, and all for nothing. But Molly said I had to do something to make it up to you. Do step into the new gown, Miss Vyne."

"Make what up to me?" she muttered doubtfully.

"I told that woman with the big teeth about you and Mr. Hartley, when I was supposed to keep the secret."

"Yes, you did, young lady, and if you think you can ever make recom—"

The two young ladies had pulled the gown up and helped her arms into the sleeves. Abruptly her image in the mirror was transformed. The material was a soft violet muslin she vaguely remembered, although it looked very different in its current form and had been edged with a new beaded trim of a very similar color. Whenever she moved, the trim glistened and gleamed. It was simple and pretty, with the magical ability of restoring youth. The bodice was silk, perfectly fitted and cut low to show off her cleavage without being too bold about it. The neckline was also trimmed, with the same light-catching beadwork, as were the small puffed sleeves. Ellie stared at the elegant vision in the mirror, and she was tempted to pinch herself hard.

"Molly Robbins, you're a miracle worker. For once, I don't look like a stuffed goose."

"I'm sure you never did look like that, Miss Vyne," Molly exclaimed, busy with the hooks.

"My sisters would disagree." She laughed, and her eyes shone back at her from the mirror.

She was still admiring her reflection with a shameful amount of vanity when Lady Mercy advanced with a comb, a handful of seed-pearl hairpins, and a pot of lip rouge. "Now for the next stage of your transformation." Apparently Ellie had become Lady Mercy's new project, and like all such victims, she was helpless in the path of that young woman's determination.

❧

Grieves had already expressed his concern, several times, about James being up without his crutches, let alone attending his grandmother's New Year's Eve ball.

"You do know, sir, that Lady Hartley has invited a parade of eligible young ladies tonight. I fear a bloody battle will commence when she learns of your plans. Perhaps you should stay in your chamber. I could make some excuse to her ladyship."

James winced, determined to manage tonight without a sling for his arm. "No. Forward into the fray. I have survived a tavern brawl. I'm sure I can survive a herd of marriageable ladies and my grandmother's most determined attempt to ruin my life." He watched in the mirror as Grieves fastened a plain gold pin to his cravat. "I had planned to wear the diamond pin tonight."

"I'm afraid that's not possible, sir."

"Why?"

"It is not here, sir."

"Where is it?"

Grieves stepped back to inspect his master. "In Master Trenton Shale's possession, sir."

"What?"

"I gave the diamond pin to him, sir, in exchange for a small favor. Two small favors. I hope you don't mind."

"Not *mind*?"

"Lord Shale's valet assisted me in the exchange. It was for your benefit, sir." Grieves calmly proceeded to help him into an ivory waistcoat.

"*Mine?*"

"Sometimes, sir, things need a little nudge in the right direction. When two people find the path too narrow for them to walk side by side, it is necessary to trim the overgrown hedges and clear the way." He held out the black evening jacket. "All the other arrangements are made, sir. The trap is set. And I wish you the very best of luck."

"Thank you, Grieves. I think I'm going to need it."

ᴄ⳾ᴏ

Ellie had never been inside Hartley House, and she wondered whether the roof might cave in when she was admitted within its elegant walls that evening. Indeed, she thought she detected a tremor underfoot as she crossed the gleaming hall tiles on Carver Danforthe's arm. Looking about keenly, she took in the excess of cold marble, the grand portraits of past Hartleys, and the wide sweep of an ornate staircase, the mahogany banister gleaming with polish, just perfect for sliding down.

They were led into the ballroom by a somber footman with prominent knees and a stiff lurch. As their names were announced, she did her best to hide behind Danforthe. He was tall, excellent cover, but she had no doubt Lady Hartley would soon fly across the room and try to have her escorted out. If she dared. The good thing about Carver Danforthe—and there weren't many of those, for he was a surly young man with a proud, disdainful manner—was that he was extremely wealthy and powerful. Lady Hartley, always mindful of her place in Society, would not wish to upset him. It was quite a coup for her to have the Earl of Everscham at her ball, since he so rarely attended any, especially outside London.

Ellie scanned the crowd, looking for James. She

didn't really know what she was doing there. Two romantically inclined young girls had dressed her up like a pagan sacrifice, and now here she was, about to make a fool of herself again.

Suddenly, James's grandmama was approaching at a rapid march. *Uh, oh.* She backed up behind her partner and bumped into a footman holding a tray of punch in little glasses. Although the footman managed a swift, agile maneuver to one side, some punch still spilled, landing on her new mauve gown.

"So sorry, madam. Do come with me, and I'll fetch one of the maids to tend to you."

"Grieves!" He was already rushing her smoothly toward the doors of the ballroom.

"Make haste, madam. We don't want the stain to fasten irreparably." He led her up the sweeping staircase.

"Where are we going?" she demanded, flustered, already feeling her curls fighting their way free of Lady Mercy's seed-pearl hairpins.

"The maid is in here, madam. She will look after you." He opened a door and gestured for her to go in. As she stumbled over the threshold, he closed the door behind her, and Ellie found herself in a bedchamber.

With James.

❧

He smiled, unable to help it now that she was there before him again. "You look breathtaking." He meant it. Her dark curls were piled up on her head, dressed with tiny pearls that shone like stars, reminding him of that night in Brighton when she'd looked up at the sky and asked how many stars he thought there were.

For him, now, there was only one.

Ellie Vyne. He loved her with all his heart, body, and soul. Deep inside him, a small voice whispered, *About time too*. He had the strangest idea it was Sophia's voice.

"Grieves brought me up here to find a maid," she exclaimed and gestured angrily at her skirt. For a usually perceptive woman, she was being very obtuse.

"I'm afraid there is no maid here." He limped forward. "And I can't get down on one knee, so we'll have to make do."

Her eyes widened.

He was studying her face. "Why are your lips so red?"

"My...? Well, Lady Mercy thought I should wear lip rouge, and I... James Hartley, what on earth is going on?" He heard the door to the adjoining room open behind him and knew she'd seen Parson Bentley enter.

He reached over and rubbed the color off her lips with one sweep of his thumb. "I like you and your lips just the way they were made."

"James, we can't—"

"Vyne, I have let you get away too many times. Now I have you where I want you at last. I am sorry I ever insulted you when you were sixteen, but I was stupid and careless. There now, I made my apology." He reached inside his jacket and drew out the special license he'd obtained. "We can argue about it later, as I'm sure we will. But right now we're getting married, woman." He narrowed his gaze to her lips. "Unless, of course, you would prefer to be arrested for masquerading as the count de Bonneville and stealing the Hartley Diamonds."

She pouted, but only for a moment. Almost

immediately, her mouth opened with an argument. "Blackmail again? How typical of you, Hartley."

"May I remind you, Vyne, you set me a challenge last summer in Brighton when you abandoned me in that maze?"

To that, she merely sighed, as if it was all too tiresome to recall.

He slid an arm around her waist. "Caught you, Miss Vyne."

❧

He was mad. Must be.

"Hartley, there is a ballroom full of prospective, *suitable* brides down there, not to mention your grandmother, who has, no doubt, vetted them all very carefully."

"Yes. Imagine their joy when we go down and announce our ill-matched, most unlikely, and wretchedly unwise union."

"Joy?" She could think of another word for it.

He pulled her closer and kissed her. "I need you to hold me upright."

"So I see."

"Are you finally ready to be Mrs. Hartley?"

She sought desperately to make him see sense. "I'll make a terrible wife. I'm sure we'll never be able to agree on paint color."

"Or names for the children."

"I'll make you sorry you married me. You'll be miserable."

"Then you'll get your vengeance, won't you, wretched woman?"

Oh yes. So she would.

"I deserve it," he added softly. "Torture me every day for the rest of my life. Please."

In any case, from the look in his eye, he was not about to let her leave that room a single woman. A very purposeful, naughty smile eased across his mouth, in full view of the parson.

"James." She laid a hand to his shoulder. "A very strange thing happened recently. Someone bought Lark Hollow. Do you know anything about that, by chance?"

His eyes lightened. "I thought it might make a nice country retreat. It really is lovely—or it could be, if it had the right owner. The admiral can stay, and I'm making one of the rooms over just for you. With some books, a fire, and chairs with lots of cushions. And the dog, of course. All overlooking a walled garden."

She was amazed that he remembered all that. Heart pounding, she gave in. Ellie flung both her arms around him for another kiss. He was not content with that one, but wanted another and then another.

"Thank you for my gloves."

"Someone has to keep your hands warm."

She gazed up into his blue eyes and feared if they did not stop now, he might get his own wicked way with her there and then. The arrangement of her hair would be spoiled, her frock probably torn, and they would be late going down to his grandmother's ball. "You don't mind about my real father?"

"We cannot choose our relatives, Ellie. Why did you think it would matter to me?"

"Because you're a snob and a Hartley."

"And you leap to conclusions, like all women."

"I believe I had every reason to assume—"

"You abandoned me rather than give me a chance to prove you wrong."

"For pity's sake, what else could I do?"

"Oh, I don't know. Explain everything and let me help you? I suppose that's too simple."

"Help me? As well as you help yourself? Good Lord!"

"Kiss me, wench. I've missed our quarrels."

So she kissed him again, a gentle, lingering caress. "It seems my father chose to leave rather than take the post you offered."

"I thought he might."

"You're very clever. Much cleverer than you look."

"A compliment, Vyne?" She was surprised and charmed to witness a slight sunset flush color his cheek. "Are you feverish?" he exclaimed. "You know I'm the stupidest person you ever met. An utter wastrel."

Perhaps she had better not tell him she knew about his charitable work, just yet.

She chuckled. "Rafe must come and live with us. He'd love Lark Hollow. It's close enough to visit Sophie and his uncle as often as he likes."

James nodded slowly. "If you agree."

"Of course. He is your son." Ellie had very few judgmental bones in her body. How could she afford any? And she had a feeling—a very certain feeling—that Rafe would have a little brother or sister before another Christmas came. "James Hartley," she said, suddenly somber, "you found your purpose finally."

He raised an inquiring eyebrow.

"To make me happy. All the time."

"I can only try." He winked, a little twinkle in his eye. "You're ready then, Vyne, to marry this despicable rake?"

Now that the moment was upon her, it didn't seem nearly as terrifying as it had before. It wasn't a wedding with orange blossoms and thrown rice, but then nothing about their courtship had been usual. Feeling brave, she tucked her arm under his good one. "Lean on me." They'd get through it together. He couldn't do without her, poor fellow. It was a very good thing she was there to love him.

⤬

A short while later it was done.

"Well, my darling wife, are we ready to announce our wicked wedding to the world?"

She opened the door. "Ready when you are. We'll face the scandal together."

He looked down at her, and just before they stepped out into the hall, he whispered, "I can't think of any scandal I'd rather have. I love you, Mrs. Hartley."

The notorious Ellie Vyne Hartley beamed up at him. "I knew that, of course. I just had to make you see it, didn't I? Sooner or later you'd find your way and follow me out of that maze."

Music and perfume drifted upward on a swell of warm air from the ballroom below. For a breath they hovered on the threshold, and then, on the count of three, tearing their gazes finally away from each other, they stepped through the open door and into a new beginning for them both. Together.

Acknowledgments

I'd like to thank Aubrey Poole for her terrific editing and all the folks at Sourcebooks for believing in me as a writer.

About the Author

Jayne Fresina sprouted up in England, the youngest in a family of four daughters. Entertained by her father's colorful tales of growing up in the countryside, and surrounded by opinionated sisters—all with far more exciting lives than hers—she's always had inspiration for her beleaguered heroes and unstoppable heroines.